I0614055

Never Fear - The Tarot

Heather Graham   Tim Waggoner

Michael A. Stackpole   Matthew Costello

C. L. Wilson   Tori Eldridge

Lisa Mannetti   Jaime Rush   Rebecca Paisley

Patrick Freivald   Edward DeAngelis   Richard Devin
Lance Taubold   Jeff DePew   Lee Lawless   Hal Bodner
Jennifer St. Giles   Lori Avocato   Michael M. Hughes   Tara Nina
C.M.C. Dobbs   Linda J. Parisi   Jason Pozzessere   Crystal Perkins
Aidan Russell   Mathew Kaufman

All rights reserved.
This is a work of fiction. Any similarities between real life events and people, and the events within this product are purely coincidental.

13Thirty Books
Print and Digital Editions
Copyright 2016

Discover new and exciting works by 13Thirty Books at
www.13thirtybooks.com

Print and Digital Edition, License Notes

This print/ebook is licensed for your personal enjoyment only. This print/ebook may not be re-sold, bartered, borrowed or loaned to others. Thank you for respecting the work of this and all 13Thirty Books' authors.

Copyright © 2016 13Thirty Books, LLP Authors' Cooperative

All rights reserved.

ISBN: 0997791209
ISBN-13: 978-0997791204

DEDICATION

All who inspire.

CONTENTS

NOTE TO THE READER

13Thirty Books asked twenty-six authors to agree to write stories based on the Tarot, with the cards determining which stories the authors would write.

Over the course of several months we reached out to some of the best genre authors and proposed our idea.

Once we had our authors, we took a Tarot deck and a list of all twenty-six names. We read the author's name, shuffled the deck, and drew a card.

That tarot card and its traits were all the authors had to go on.

The card was removed, the deck was reshuffled, and the next name was read off.

This anthology contains twenty-six stories based on the twenty-two cards of the Major Arcana and the four cards of the Minor Arcana.

Award-winning and New York Times bestselling authors combine their talents to deal out twenty-six dark tales influenced by the Tarot.

0

THE FOOL

LANCE TAUBOLD

Upright: Folly, mania, extravagance, intoxication, delirium, frenzy, betrayal
Reversed: Negligence, absence, distribution, carelessness, apathy, vanity,
nullity

Mincey was no fool. Of course, his moniker was the King's
Fool. But Mincey was so much more. He knew so much more. Very
few even bothered, or knew, his real name, but it mattered little to
him. They were all merely tools for him. Players in his game.

The real fool was King Zendar, the ruler of Boldovia, this small,
inconsequential, uninfluential, kingdom in northeastern Europe—but
then there were so many such kingdoms spread throughout the
continent.

But Mincey had a plan. He wanted to be king of Boldovia, and
he had the means to do it. His mother—God rest her miserable
soul—had seen fit to ensconce him in the Royal Court.

When he was growing up, his mother had always told him he
was destined for great success, and that she would help him achieve
it. He was special.

Then she had gotten sick, ague. Then it got worse.

On her deathbed she told Mincey her secret. His secret. Mincey
was royalty. He was the bastard son of King Zendar. He had never

known his "father." His mother had told him his father had been thrown from a horse and broken his neck right after Mincey was born. Zendar and his queen, Anya, had never had any children, and Zendar desperately wanted an heir.

Mincey's mother, in exchange for her silence, had extracted a document from the king stating that upon her demise, Mincey would be taken care of and be given a position in the court. Idiot that Zendar was, he made Mincey his fool, telling him that that way he would always be close and protected, and that he would be his informant should any of his courtiers decide to rebel or usurp him. As the king's spy, no one would ever suspect the simple fool of treachery. Mincey understood the logic of it, but it didn't make things any better for him at court. Zendar would never know the indignities Mincey had suffered over these past years from his court: the insults, the thrown food, the kicks and slaps—all at his expense.

But then again, there had been the opportunities for revenge on those that had been exceptionally unkind to him.

Mincey's greatest advantage, other than his handsome features, was that King Zendar was quite paranoid of everyone—everyone but Mincey. Zendar trusted him implicitly, believing that their blood tie meant more than anything and that Mincey would have nothing to gain and everything to lose by betraying him.

More the fool he.

Another advantage Mincey had was that Zendar had a cruel side, evinced by the vast dungeon and torture chamber in the bowels of the castle. Mincey, not one to be squeamish, saw the opportunity. He had always had a penchant for rats and he had collected his small "family" of them. His rats had been trained to have a particular fondness for blood and flesh. Human flesh. He would hold back on feeding them until they were ravenous, then would let them have samplings of blood, his blood at first. He would slice a finger and squeeze the droplets onto morsels of food. They learned well, and soon blood became their seasoning of choice.

The first time he had used his pets was on the king's advisor, Ruttan. Ruttan had been cruel to him. He was jealous of Mincey's fine features—himself having a rather large boil on his forehead, and his body odor only bested by his foul breath—and would demean Mincey and impugn his masculinity, often trying, and sometimes succeeding, in giving surreptitious kicks to Mincey's genitals.

Mincey hated him.

One night after a feast honoring the visiting king of Esdaria and his retinue from a nearby region to the south, Mincey had had enough from Ruttan. The oily, drunken sot had struck true with one of his vicious kicks to Mincey's groin. Ruttan had hollered with glee and ranted how Mincey could not be injured as he was a eunuch and merely everyone's butt-boy. Everyone had laughed.

That night, after the feast, Mincey went to the king's chambers and told Zendar that he had overheard Ruttan conspiring with the visiting king to overthrow him.

Zendar yelled, "We must stop this, Mincey. You must discover the truth!"

"Yes, Sire, we will. Mayhap we should question Ruttan privately, and 'persuade' him to tell us their intent?"

Zendar gave a slow smile. "If you feel that is best."

"I do, but I also think that you should be in attendance to observe the 'persuasion.'"

Zendar maintained his smile. "I am in agreement."

Ruttan was taken to the dungeon. The king's executioner, Grutha, a brooding giant of a man, conducted the inquisition, while Zendar and Mincey looked on.

Rattan started off with indignance, then became more manic, with shouts of "lies" and "outrage."

Mincey had a suggestion. Zendar acquiesced. Mincey, knowing of the king's secret appetite for brutal torture, brought out his favorite pet, Greedy, the largest and blackest of his little family. And the hungriest.

"Grutha, bring the head cage for the king's advisor."

Grutha nodded and produced an iron cage with a small, hinged door on top and a matching one on the bottom. He opened a latch on the bottom and secured it around Ruttan's head. He locked it at the neck. Ruttan sputtered and yelled all sorts of denials and imprecations. He had been bound firmly with ropes in a wooden chair secured to the floor so that a hapless victim could not tip it over during the interrogation.

Next, the voracious rat was placed in the cage where it could devour the feast before him.

Mincey happily recalled the screams and pleas from Ruttan. "Please, I beg of you! I am innocent! These are lies!"

That was all Ruttan managed to say that was coherent before Greedy took the first bite of ear. And at the rush of blood into the hungry mouth, he became enraged with implacable blood-lust.

Mincey and the king watched impassively as the rat bit and gnawed at the man's face. It finished off an ear then moved to the nose and lips. It seemed to Mincey that his rat had a rhythm going: a bite of nose, a bite of lip—as if one taste complemented the other.

Ruttan's screams rose to a peak, then slowly began to fade to whimpering as his face became deformed from the torn pieces of flesh from his skull, revealing the sinew and bone beneath. His head would jerk periodically as each new piece of flesh was ripped away, followed by a mewling yelp—that is until one particular bite tore half of his tongue from his mouth. Not long after, the only sounds in the cage were from the rat tearing another succulent piece of flesh and slurping it into its still unsated maw.

Mincey had loved every agonizing moment and knew the king had as well. Grutha remained silent and stoic throughout: the ideal executioner. Unemotional. Mincey had found a friend.

Not only had he ingratiated himself to the king, but he had the ear of the queen—and more—as well. Queen Anya, who, while from a small kingdom herself and being quite a bit younger than Zendar, had aspirations of her own.

Mincey had noticed her secretly eyeing his fine form and strong features on several occasions. He kept his fine figure from hours of tumbling exercise and performance. Many a courtesan had paid him notice, and the occasional dalliance was common for him.

Until the queen came to him one night.

She was dressed in a light wrap, the evening being quite warm. There was the lightest of knocks on his chamber door.

Mincey often slept unclothed—his small chamber could get uncomfortably warm on hot nights—and tonight was no exception. He clutched a pillow to his midsection and cracked open the door.

Anya thrust the door open and rushed in. "Close the door quickly, lest I be seen," she said.

Mincey complied and turned to face her, his naked backside to the wall. "Milady, what brings you here?" he asked innocently, fully knowing the reason for her nocturnal visit. Is everything all right with the king?"

"Yes, well, the king…" she let her voice trail away. She raised her eyes to meet his. Her hands went to the silk ribbons securing her wrap. A bold look came to her face as she undid the ribbons and let her sheer gown puddle to the floor at her bare feet. The rest of her was bare as well. "The king does not know how to pleasure me. He is too old. You are young. Virile. My body is feverish." She ran a hand between her legs and slowly rubbed herself.

Mincey felt himself stir. Her body was lean and white, like the purest of cow's cream, with medium-sized high breasts tapering to voluptuous hips and the dark triangular thatch of hair between them.

She ran her tongue over her lower lip. "My ladies have informed me that you are quite skilled at pleasuring a woman and are favorably gifted as well." Her eyes lowered to the pillow Mincey clutched before him.

Mincey knew the queen well, and this happening was as he had expected. He was prepared for this to his utmost advantage.

He dropped the pillow.

The queen's eyes grew large with desire. "My ladies were not just in their assessment."

Since that first night, Anya had come to him many times. Each time he had expected her to exact a favor from him, a boon from the king. But it did not happen.

Several months later, another great feast was held to welcome back King Justus of Esdaria. Justus's purpose, Mincey discovered through listening at doors, was to unite their two kingdoms, something Mincey most decidedly did not want. He needed sole control of Zendar for his plans to work.

Mincey spoke to King Zendar before the feast. "My King, there are rumors of King Justus's ambition."

"What do you mean, Mincey? What are they saying?" Zendar instantly gave Mincey his full attention.

"I overheard King Justus's royal commander telling some of his men how easy it will be to wrest your kingdom from you once an alliance is made. 'A simple usurping,' was how it was said. Possibly as soon as a month."

"You are certain of this?"

"They spoke freely, not thinking I was paying close attention, Sire. And there is yet more."

"More?"

"The commander also plans to remove King Justus from the throne and take it by force for himself."

"The commander… what is his name?"

"Borkin. He has an unfriendly countenance, one not to be trusted."

"Something needs be done with this Borkin."

"Yes, Sire." Mincey gave a slight smile. "My pets would be most pleased to show Commander Borkin the error of his ways."

"Quite so. A visit to the dungeon seems to be the only way. How will we accomplish this?"

"Please, Sire, you need not trouble yourself with this petty matter. I will employ your loyal guard to assist me."

"Ah, Mincey, it seems you are the only one I can trust. What would I do without you?"

"It is nothing more than my duty you, My King." He turned away, fearing he would be unable to hide his nefarious smile of glee.

*

"What are you doing to me? My king will hear of this!" Commander Borkin yelled, the spittle catching in his bushy beard while he lay bound and recumbent on the large, solid wooden table.

"Your king did hear of this… and of your plot to assassinate him and usurp him from his throne. And the throne of my liege as well," Mincey said, staring down into the burly man's furious visage. "But we are not unjust, and mayhap a full confession will garner you some mercy and a more expedient end."

"I have done nothing! I am loyal to my king!"

"Ah then, perhaps my friends can aid you in restoring your obscured memory, your braggadocio about becoming the ruler of both our lands."

Grutha aided Mincey in affixing a large metal cage over the hirsute, naked, lower belly of the commander.

"What are you doing?" the commander yelled once more. His renewed effort to break his bonds proved futile. His hands and feet had been securely bound to the sides of the table. He lay naked and helpless. The cage was now firmly fixed over the man's lower abdomen and genitals.

Mincey stood straight and gave the cage a firm pat. The commander involuntarily jerked. "Before I introduce you to my friends, I will ask you a final time: Were you plotting to murder both of our kings?" Mincey had his face mere inches from the commander's face, the fetid breath making him draw back slightly.

"No! I would give my life for my king!"

"As you wish." Mincey gave his most cloying smile, then reached beneath the table to produce another metal cage. In it was an ebony-colored rat a foot in length, with a tail to match. It had large jet eyes that issued malevolence. Its crowning glory: two prodigious fangs protruding nearly an inch in length, the tips honed to fine points, capable of piercing the hardest of woods—let alone soft, human flesh.

"Ah, Percy," Mincey cooed to the rat. "Are you hungry? Well, your father always takes precious care of you and this night I have some tasty morsels for you to munch." He held the cage over the commander's groin. The rat's nose and teeth thrust anxiously through the small metal bars. Its nose and whiskers worked in a feverish manner. "A couple of tasty bits and a juicy sausage to whet your appetite for the main course, my pet." He set the cage between the bound man's spraddled legs. The rat pawed at the fleshy inner thighs, barely able to make a scratch on the tender flesh—but it was enough.

The commander screamed.

"Hush now, Commander." Mincey once again leaned into the man's face. "You profess that you would give your life for your king? What about your man parts?" He chuckled softly.

"The king will have your head!" Borkin spat a large gob of mucus in Mincey's face.

Mincey slowly wiped the thick gob away. "You have made your choice. And after my pet is done with your man bits, which shouldn't take long, he will gnaw his way into your bowels. My Percy is quite hungry and I always take care of my pet." He opened the cage at the commander's waist, then proceeded to open the door to Percy's cage.

The rat darted forward into the open cage. This was not its first time at the human buffet. It sniffed, momentarily, at the man's scrotum. Then opened its mouth wide, bit down, and tore into the delicate flesh.

Commander Borkin screamed a scream the likes of which Mincey could not recall hearing before. It was deep, yet high-pitched. An agonized sound from deep within.

He smiled.

"Commander, I will return later," Mincey said between Borkin's agonized outbursts. "It pains me that I cannot remain; I do so enjoy watching my pet enjoy himself."

Another scream of torment was the only response Mincey received from the man whose entire body was a mass of corded muscles as he tried to wrest himself from being devoured alive.

"If there is anything you need, Grutha, my stalwart companion, shall remain, and he may inform me of your needs when I return." He gave a small giggle and tapped on the cage. "Feast, my pet."

Mincey returned to the feast. A bard was singing an epic ode of some battle or other. Both kings appeared to be enjoying the entertainment while they quaffed their flagons of mead.

The Queen gave a frantic wave to Mincey. He gave her a nod of acknowledgement, then made his way along the many long tables, stopping to give the king a small bow. "All is right, My King."

King Zendar nodded in return. "Enjoy yourself this fine night, Mincey. Share a cup of mead with King Justus and myself. You have earned it."

"I will, My King." He reached for a goblet the king's manservant proffered. "To your highnesses, may your kingdoms always enjoy prosperity as long as you shall live." He raised his goblet to the kings, also including the queen in his toast.

The queen's eyes flared. "My lord," she said. "I fear the festivities have proven too much this eve. I would take my leave to lie down."

"As you will," Zendar responded, being used to her bouts of headaches, fatigue, and the like.

Mincey knew better.

The queen rose, gave a slight movement of her head, urging Mincey to follow her.

Mincey winked.

"Your fool is a fine figure of a man," King Justus said to Zendar. "How has he achieved this?"

Raising his flagon to Mincey, Zendar said, "Mincey, show our esteemed guest why you cut such a fine figure."

Mincey drained his goblet and inverted it onto the table in front of King Justus. "Sire, your goblet, please." Justus finished his draught and handed it to Mincey. "Thank you, Sire." He inverted the cup as well next to his own about a foot apart. He lithely sprang onto the table. He placed one palm on the base of one cup, then onto the other. He bent over the two cups and slowly brought his feet up into the air until he was completely balanced on them, legs straight up to the rafters.

The dining hall became silent. All two hundred guests stared at the feat being performed.

King Justus broke the silence by clapping his hands together.

The entire hall erupted in shouts and cheers.

Mincey hated the cheering and applause. They only reinforced the idea that was all he was good for was entertaining them. But let them laugh. His time was coming.

*

Mincey's chamber door was flung open. The queen flew into the room. "Mincey, you have to help me!" Zendar said that if I don't produce an heir..." She paled. "...he will cast me out!"

"But you are with child, Anya."

The queen's jaw dropped. "How do you know?"

"I am rather well acquainted with your body, My Queen. I have noticed the small bulge."

"But I do not want it," she wailed. "I cannot endure the pain. You must help me get rid of it."

"But that makes no sense. The king says you must produce an heir—" He thought for a moment, knowing the queen had not bedded the king for some while.

"Why, whose child is it, Anya? The magician's? Sir Paltrey's? Father Morel's?" He couldn't help the bitter tone in his voice.

Her voice became small. "It's... it's... yours."

Mincey drew back. "Mine? How can you be certain? You have bedded so many..."

"I have bedded no other these past months, save you," she professed.

"The king?"

"No, he has not desired me—nor I him," she added.

"You have no choice. You must bear the child. The king demands it or you will be cast out. Anya it is the only way." His thoughts were in a whirl. A child? His child? A scheme began to form.

"Mincey…" Anya went to him and began to trace her fingers across his neck and shoulders. "Mayhap, now is the time? The king? He is getting old and feeble. He has no heirs…"

Mincey thought, *He does have an heir… Me!* "What are you saying?"

"If Zendar comes to some misfortune, I would become queen. You could become my prince consort and we could rule Boldovia together. Now is the time to seize this opportunity." Her robe had fallen open and she leaned into him, pressing her nude body against him.

He pushed her back and lightly rubbed his palm over her soft abdomen. My baby. My heir. Yes, the time is right!

He continued rubbing, moving his fingers lower. Anya arched her back. "Yes, My Queen. Now is the time."

*

After the departure of King Justus—who was truly grateful for discovering his commander's deception—Mincey set his plan in motion. He convinced Zendar to wait on the alliance, telling the king that the commander divulged Justus's true intentions.

The second part of his plan was to have the queen reveal to Zendar that she was finally with child. The king would have to hold off the announcement until they were sure she would deliver a healthy heir. Zendar, having become somewhat senile as well as distrustful of everyone, would try to remember the conception. Mincey would fabricate a story of a past time when the king had been imbibing a little too vigorously and had bedded the queen, producing the result. Zendar, not wanting to appear the fool or thought to be a cuckold, would aver Mincey's recollection.

Anya told the king of the incipient birth as Mincey had instructed her to do, and Zendar ordered a repast to celebrate, even though no pronouncement was made for the reason of the gathering. The court always enjoyed a feast for any reason. And if the king wanted a feast, he got one.

That night, being in the highest of spirits, and having indulged in a large quantity of spirits, Zendar was now primed for Mincey's request.

"My king, all these years I have served you well and done your bidding, protecting you from insidious plots and those who would wish ill on you—despite the indignities I have suffered from your soldiers and courtiers. If you would grant this one boon, a document alleging that I am your son, a bastard one, but a most loving and loyal one, I would be so proud and eternally grateful. This would not be revealed, of course, until after such time as you had left this world, which I hope will not be for many years," he quickly added. "It will give me the protection I would not otherwise have. In addition, if it your wish, I will serve your heir as I have you. What say you, my king? Such a small boon for my years of service and loyalty."

Zendar narrowed his gaze. "Mincey… I will grant your request. You are correct on all matters. My loyal son! I am all too aware of how my men treat you… Well, no more. They will not take advantage of you after I am gone. Ah… would that you were my legitimate heir. Alas, it is not to be. I will draw up the document this very eve and seal it with my signet." He held up his left hand to display the enormous ring on his middle finger.

Mincey's eyes lit up with greed, thinking, That will be mine all too soon, My King. He said, "Thank you, Sire. You will never know what your magnanimity means to me. Shall I retrieve the parchment for you?"

"If you would. I am suddenly feeling quite fatigued. Let me have done with it and I shall retire."

A short while later, Mincey clutched his future in his hand, pressed over his heart. He crept down the cold stone hallway to the far end where the queen's chamber beckoned him.

As he neared the wooden door, he noticed the door had not been shut tightly: She was waiting for him.

He pushed the door open enough to see the enormous bed on the far side of the chamber. And what he saw on the enormous bed was a very white derriere thrusting hard into the queen, who was on all fours. The man having his way with her, Mincey immediately realized, was Rathben, the king's magician.

"So… my child, eh, Queen Anya?" Mincey whispered, backing away from the door. He would not be telling his good news to the queen this night… or any other. He clutched the scroll hard. "My plans will have to change, I see. Now the question is: Should I wake the king from his drunken stupor or wait until the morrow when he will be thinking more clearly? No question—the sooner the better."

The king's chamber was unlocked. *The fool. Anyone could enter and assassinate him while he slumbers. Truly, no one protects him as I do. My father! At last."* He had the proof in his hand.

The crown would fit him beautifully.

He entered the chamber and was greeted by raucous snoring. The king, fully clothed, was supine on his back, a flagon precariously dangling from a finger and thumb. It appeared to be empty. The chamber was lit and the candles flickered from the draft caused by Mincey opening the door. Mincey closed it.

He went to the king and removed the flagon and set it on a small side table. "Sire," he said, giving the large man a strong push on the shoulder.

The king growled and moved his bulk slightly. Mincey pushed harder.

"What?… Go away." His eyes remained shut.

Mincey persisted. "Sire, you must awaken. A matter of extreme import. It concerns the queen."

Zendar's eyelids fluttered. "The queen? What?… What is the matter?"

"I fear what I have to say is not good."

The king stirred now, rising up on his elbows, eyes open—if somewhat bleary. He struggled to an upright position. "Needs tell me, Mincey. Is the queen injured?"

"Nay, physically she is fine—mayhap too much so," he added. "It grieves me to tell you this. The queen's door was open a crack, I noticed as I made my rounds of the castle, as I do every night. I heard a moaning from her chamber. Thinking the queen might be experiencing difficulties being with child… or worse, I peeped into the chamber and was met with the most heinous of visions. *That was most definitely true.* The queen was engaged in flagrante delicto with—"

The king roared, "WHAT?" He was fully awake. "This cannot be! You lie!"

"My King, I do not. It grieves me so to be the bearer of these ill tidings. But it is so."

"Who? Who would *dare?*"

"Rathben, Sire." Mincey bowed his to conceal his smirk.

"My magician? It cannot be so."

"I was as shocked as you are, Sire. But I saw them engaged in the act, naked as two newborns. They were on the bed, the queen on all fours, and Rathben from behind was—"

"NO MORE!" Zendar was in a rage. "I will have him tortured, beheaded—" He froze. "The queen... My child!" His head fell into his hands in despair. He began to weep. "I thought at last to have an heir... but now... now... How I can I know the father?" His head rose. "How long has she been cuckolding me? Perhaps the child is mine? We must discover this. Mincey, you must help me. My boy, you are the only one loyal to me. Please, you must help. Do what needs to be done. I must know."

Mincey had to quell his enthusiasm. "You know you have my allegiance, My King. As much as it will grieve me sorely, I will do as you ask." He bowed his head, and once again smiled.

*

The magician lay on the wooden table, hands and feet bound to the sides. A leather band circled his head securing a wooden ball in his mouth, spittle dribbling from the corners.

Queen Anya was strapped down similarly, her table at a thirty degree angle positioned perpendicular to Rathben.

Both were naked.

Mincey stood between them, looking from one to the other. Grutha stood off to left. Silent. Awaiting his orders. Mincey spoke, "You have both betrayed the king, and for that you must be punished. King Zendar has entrusted your care to me, and with some small aid from our Royal Executioner, Grutha, and, of course my pets, we will discern the truth." He picked up two cages from the floor. The cages rocked back and forth in Mincey's hands. The large rodents anxiously scrabbling in their small cells.

He set them on the table between Rathben's splayed legs. The magician could only make a pathetic, choking, gurgling sound. But his eyes were wide with fear.

Queen Anya was mewling; tears streaked her cheeks. "Why, Mincey, why? Please do not do this."

"Why? Why? You dare to ask? You did not only betray your husband and king… you betrayed ME!" He calmed his voice. "Have you told your lover here how often you have spread your legs for me? You are naught but the king's whore!" He spat on her bare breasts. "How many others have had your well-trod quim?" Abruptly, he turned from her and walked to the far wall where dozens of menacing-looking instruments hung. "No matter. I will soon know the truth. We have all the time I need. My pets are quite ravenous this eve. With all the feasting in the castle, they deserve their share."

He returned with two more cages, empty, their hasps undone. "Decisions. The lady or the magician?" He snapped his fingers. "Ah. A little of one, a little of the other. That satisfies. You will be able to enjoy each other's misery, as you seem to enjoy each other's pleasures." He gave a low stertorous laugh.

He approached the queen. Reaching out a hand, he caressed her stomach. "A shame. I was not enough for you. Do you have any idea whose child you carry? The king's? Rathben's?… Mine? Or is it another of the court? His valet? A stablehand?"

The queen's head shook violently back and forth. "No, I swear on my honor, the child is yours."

The magician, with the wooden ball gag securely in place, struggled to speak, his eyes darting to the queen.

"Something to say, Rathben? And what would it be? A trick perhaps?" Mincey released the cord from the ball gag. Rathben spat it out and it fell to his chest.

"You vile bitch! You said the child was mine! That we would rule together!" Rathben pleaded to Mincey, "Please, I knew nothing. She never told me she had bedded you. I would not have touched her."

"Ah, but you did. No matter, Rathben," Mincey said airily. "I thank you most fervently for your confession that you and Queen Anya were plotting to kill the king, just as I had suspected." He put his hands together and drummed his fingers together. "Now, what to do? So many choices…"

"Mercy, I beg of you," Rathben squealed. "I have told you all."

"Be silent," Anya interjected. "You are the fool! Did you think a confession would warrant you any mercy? You have confessed to treason! *Imbecile!*"

"Enough, both of you. You weary me with your prattling. I have made my decision. You are both guilty of high treason. Rathben, for your confession, I will be more merciful with you."

"Thank you. Thank you," Rathben mewled.

"I will spare you the agony of watching your death. It can be most disconcerting to watch your entrails being devoured while you look on helplessly." Mincey moved to a recessed grate in the wall, where a fire blazed. Several metal prods protruded from it.

Rathben's eyes once again grew large. "No, I beg of you…"

"I fear I will need to employ the ball gag again. This can be most unpleasant, and your pleas for mercy have grown tedious." Mincey replaced the gag in Rathben's mouth. "Much better." He returned to the fire and withdrew, not a poker, but a long iron rod with a small cup forged on the end. It glowed orange-red. Also hanging above the fire was a small pot. Mincey dipped the cupped end of the rod into the pot and slowly withdrew it. "Silver. Such a versatile metal. He approached Rathben and held the glowing cup over the magician's face. Terror filled Rathben's eyes.

"You will want to remain quite still for this, Rathben," Mincey said, jiggling the rod. "If you move your head, the silver will injure other parts of your face… not only your eyes."

If possible, Rathben's eyes grew ever wider. His head and body shook violently.

"If you would not be still, I cannot be held accountable." Mincey brought the cup close over Rathben's right eye and slowly tipped it. The shimmering metal poured out.

Rathben shut his eyes and his movement ceased.

The molten metal found its target.

There was a sizzling sound as the flesh burned and the silver filled the eye socket.

Mincey inhaled the smell of seared flesh.

The magician's body stilled.

"Oh, it appears to have been overmuch for the tricky magician. No matter. It eases the problem of the other eye." He glanced over at the queen. Her face was turned away, eyes tightly shut. "My queen, the other eye will go much more smoothly, I promise."

"Monster," she muttered.

"Monster? And was not your deception monstrous? How did you plan to eliminate me, eh?"

Silence.

"I will learn all. Never fear." He turned back to the magician, then repeated the procedure with the other eye. The magician's body, while he was still unconscious, jerked as the molten metal filled the other socket. Mincey once again breathed in deeply: metal and burnt flesh.

He returned the metal rod to the fire and walked over to the silent Grutha. Grutha leaned down and picked up a wooden bucket of water and handed it to Mincey—a ritual between them.

He went over to the unconscious Rathben. "I do not have all night, Magician," Mincey said. "I require your full attention for our next game." He removed the ball gag and threw the bucket of water over the magician's face.

Rathben sputtered and moaned as he awoke. "What?… Where?… Help…" The last word said in the most pitiful of tones. Mincey chuckled and replaced the ball gag.

"I do not want to hear your pathetic pleas. We must continue." He reached between Rathben's legs for one of the cages. It contained a large, dark-brown rat, its claws scrabbling between the bars of the cage. He set it on the magician's stomach and Grutha stepped over and threaded a long leather strap through a ring on the top of the cage, then secured it to either side of the table. Rathben squirmed, only succeeding in agitating the rat more.

"Patience, my pet." Mincey wagged a finger at the rat. He reached to the underside of the cage and pulled a small strap. The bottom of the cage slid free. Rathben's jiggling stomach clenched as the rat's claws clenched his girth. His stomach clenched again as the rat's teeth ripped away the first piece of his flesh.

Mincey watched for a while with fascination as the rat frantically ripped, chewed, and swallowed, its blood-covered paws leaving tiny footprints on untouched sections of stomach. Chomp. Rip. Chew. Swallow. A natural repetitive process. *Almost hypnotic*, Mincey thought.

The queen remained silent throughout and refused to look at the carnage being wrought before her.

Mincey noted that the rat was well into the magician's innards and the blood had stopped flowing. He was dead. "Ah, one entertainment finished. Feast on, my pet. It is your brother's turn now. I fear he has grown quite impatient. I have been a neglectful father. This must be rectified at once." He took the other cage and went to the naked queen. "I have saved my little Percy for you. He is very dear to me. I am sure you will enjoy him. I am *certain* he will enjoy you."

The queen squeezed her eyes shut and turned her head as far away as possible. Mincey could see the tears leaking out. He brought the cage close to her face. The rat's claw swiped through the bars and scored her cheek. The queen screamed and a line of blood began to flow. The flowing blood caused the rat to become spasmodic and it violently thrashed back and forth, looking for egress to the juicy flesh just out of its reach. Mincey held the cage firmly.

"Please, no… Mincey… I will do anything… please… my love…"

Mincey spat in her face. "*My love*! How dare you! How many *others* have you said that to?"

"Only one," she pleaded.

"Liar! You will tell me… or do you want to end up like your lover here? Whose child is it? Whose? TELL ME!" He shook the cage in her face.

"Yours," she whimpered. Her eyes opened.

He leaned in. "LIAR!"

She screamed, "I don't know!" Then softer, "I don't know." The tears flowed again, choking off any other words.

"We could have had everything… a child… and heir… a kingdom!" Mincey was swept up in rage, the cage swung wildly in his hand.

"Please, Mincey… the baby," Anya tried to calm him. "Have mercy…"

Mincey's head jerked to her. "Yes, the bayyy-bee." He looked into the cage, then made a decision. He turned to the dead Rathben and put the cage on the man's chest. "I will assuage your hunger, my sweet little Percy." The ebon eyes of the rat glistened in anticipation; its claws scrabbled frantically. And as he had done with the first cage, Mincey slid the bottom hatch away, allowing full access for the rat to Rathben's chest. "That's it. Feast, my beloved pet. There is certainly more than enough to sate your hunger."

He turned back to the queen. "And you, my queen, will get to meet my horse."

Anya gave a sharp intake of breath and let out a sob.

Mincey untied her, and with Grutha's aid, led her to a large, long, wooden, triangular stand set on four wooden legs. Anya pled and cried all the while, struggling to get free. The stalwart Grutha held her fast, as if she were no more than a babe in his arms. "My horse, my lady." Mincey gave an exaggerated bow. "Grutha, please assist me to help our queen onto her mount."

They guided her to the small step next to the "horse."

"Do not do this, Mincey… What must I do?"

The fear in her voice made Mincey smile. "Mount the horse… as you would mount one of your lovers."

She tentatively raised a leg, putting a hand on the back of the pyramid.

"Grutha," Mincey said.

The big man stepped forward and grabbed Anya's waist. She put her hands out to brace herself on the sharp apex of the horse as Grutha set her upon it.

Mincey scurried away to retrieve two more cages, similar to those that held his pets. Grutha maintained his grip on the queen, steadying her, while Mincey scampered around affixing the two iron cages over the queen's feet. When that was done, the queen struggled to reposition herself but the cages proved to be too heavy and weighed her down—the exact intention of the cages. She moaned or cried out with every effort.

"One final touch," Mincey said. He was manic with excitement. He extracted a rope hanging from a wall. "Her hand, Grutha."

Grutha grabbed one of the queen's hands and extended it to Mincey.

Anya screamed as her weight pushed her down onto the sharp wood. "The pain!" she screamed.

Mincey put her hand behind her back. "The other one. Behind your back. NOW!"

When she didn't respond. Grutha grabbed it and gave it to Mincey. Mincey tied them together.

The queen slumped forward, but was unable to ease herself. Her crotch took her full weight and the point of the pyramid began to press up into her. She cried out.

"Can you feel the cages pulling you down, my queen? Now, you will answer me truthfully." He came around from behind the horse to face her. He kept Grutha in place, lest she fall from her perch. "How many lovers have you had?"

"Only you and Rathben… I swear!"

"Liar!" Mincey hissed. "No woman can be trusted. You are like my whore of a mother. You will tell me!" He went over to Rathben's mutilated corpse and fiddled with the rats' cages until he had them secured back inside. He brought them over to the queen.

"It seems I have lied as well. I have decided to use my pets on you."

"No!" Anya involuntarily jerked. She winced and gasped in pain.

Mincey bent down and opened the cage on Anya's right foot… and inserted the first rat.

"NOOOOO!" Anya was out her mind with panicked screams.

"How many others?" Mincey demanded.

"Three," was her screamed response.

"WHO?"

"Sir Galen." Another scream.

"Who ELSE?"

"Jeston…"

"Who?" Mincey paused, bloody rat in hand, trying to recall the name.

"The king's footman. And… and a friar… I do not know his name. Only once."

"*You are a whore!*" he spat out. "*Whose* child is it? *Whose?*"

"I do not know." Her voice was high pitched and shrill. Apparently his pet had found an exceptionally tender toe to nibble.

Mincey moved to her other foot.

"Rathben! Rathben!" the queen shouted. "Rathben is the father! Stop…"

Her screams and cries became muddled in his ears as Mincey sorted his thoughts… and his pets fed on her feet.

He had to know. "Were you two plotting to kill the king?"

No response.

He grabbed her bound arms and pulled her back.

This time her scream was ear-splitting. He noted the blood running down the "flanks" of the horse. *Splitting indeed,* he thought. Once the tender flesh of her nether regions began to separate, the severing of her body would not take long. "Tell me! You were plotting to assassinate the king… and then me!" As he said the last word, he tugged her back hard. A steady stream of blood flowed now.

She screamed and screamed. "YES! YES!"

"As I thought," he said calmly, more to himself than to her. I will now leave you to your thoughts of deception and treachery. You will join your lover in death. And your hateful spawn!" He gave a final harsh tug, hoping the horse had now penetrated her womb and destroyed the vile unborn child within her.

The queen's head lolled back and forth, her moaning had ceased. Mincey listened closely. Silence.

Silence, except the slurping, tearing gnashes of his pets as they gorged themselves on the dead queen's feet.

"Thank you, Grutha, for your excellent assistance. A fine job, as always. I will report your loyalty to the king."

Grutha said nothing.

*

"Sire, it is done." Mincey gave a small bow to Zendar. He and Grutha had cleaned up the remains of the queen and the magician and burned the corpses. His sated pets were returned to his bed chamber, flesh and blood engorged.

They sat in the king's private chamber. Two flagons and a tankard of mead sat on the small table between them. King and fool. Father and son. Zendar handed Mincey a flagon and took the other himself. He raised the flagon high. "You have done well, Mincey. We will announce that the queen has run off with Rathben and that they will be executed forthwith if they are ever found again." They both took a long draught.

"A fine solution, Sire. Have you thought about an heir, now that the queen will not be producing one? You have no queen or progeny…" Mincey let the implication linger in the air.

"I have thought, Mincey, and I have learned many things which were not known to me before. Without you, I would never have known of the deception surrounding me at every turn. I know of no other way to repay your loyalty…"

Mincey's breath grew faster at the anticipation of the king's next words. At last! *I will be given my just deserts. King. I will be king!* His mind reeled at the thought. He felt light-headed. His mind fuzzed. He grew dizzy. Intoxicated with the thought of all that power.

Zendar reached for a small piece of thick parchment Mincey had ignored, lying on the table. "This is for you," Zendar said. I had it especially created by one of the monks. A fine job, I must say."

Mincey's curiosity was piqued, noting that the piece of parchment Zendar held was about three inches wide and six inches long, a plain brown back.

"I must also give laud to our fine executioner, Grutha. He has also been most loyal and has kept me informed in other goings on in the castle." At the mention of his name, Grutha stepped forth from the shadowed corner of the chamber. Mincey started at his unexpected appearance.

"Yes, My King, Grutha has been most loyal in aiding me in culling your betrayers," Mincey said, his attention returning to the back of the parchment the king still held before him. He recalled a visit by an Italian prince, who brought several of these parchments— cards. What was this one for? A gift, Zendar had said.

"Yes. Loyal..." Zendar said, nodding. He waved the card back and forth. "...as I had thought my son would be..." The statement hung in the air.

Mincey tried to focus on what the king was saying. He blinked hard. The card began to blur. What was happening? He'd only had a small amount of the mead. There was still half of it left. The mead. The taste. Not quite right. A bit bitter.

He'd been poisoned.

The king.

He rocked on his stool. Grutha took a step toward him, his hulk appearing larger than Mincey remembered.

The king slapped the card down, face up before him. "I wish you to keep this with you for the rest of your life... as a reminder."

Mincey stared at it. It was a drawing. A drawing of... Him! He stared at his own likeness. There was inscription scrawled across the top. He tried to focus.

The words: The Fool.

His head fell forward and struck the table.

*

Darkness. He was dreaming. He was bound tightly with leather straps. He struggled to free himself.

His eyes were open.

He wasn't dreaming. He was in some sort of wooden box. There was no sound. In his hand… something? The card. The card Zendar had given him before he—

He felt a movement. Heard a… scratching sound.

Something brushed his leg.

Then something brushed his head.

A sharp prick on his ear. Pain. Something had bitten him!

Another sharp bite on his ankle.

They were in the box with him.

No! The rats. His pets.

His coffin.

What had he done? Zendar… Grutha… His carefully thought out plans. All those years. How could he have been so foolish?

THE FOOL.

He screamed.

THE MAGICIAN

2

THE MAGICIAN

HAL BODNER

Upright: Power, skill, concentration, action, resourcefulness
Reversed: Manipulation, poor planning, latent talents

Just because I'm different from the norm doesn't mean I'm crazy.

According to an IQ test I took in the fourth grade, I'm much smarter than the average person. Given the current state of television and modern politics, I tend to agree. A few years ago, a Scientologist was handing out pamphlets and enticed me into taking one of their personality tests. Until then, I had no idea it was possible to fail. But I wasn't offended. If anything, I was amused that they thought I was potentially too much of a sociopath even to join a religious cult.

Often, I've seen crazy people standing in front of convenience stores and talking to themselves. If you bother to stop and listen, they make no sense. And if you make the mistake of getting too close, the stench of their unwashed bodies is enough to make your eyes water. It takes a certain kind of crazy to let yourself sink that low.

That's not me.

Obviously, I'm not like that at all. I take great pride in my appearance. I dress well; certainly, I bathe regularly. Thanks to a combination of good genetics and wanting to get my money's worth out of a gym membership, I'm in great shape. And while I may not be movie-star handsome, I can compete with the guys on the soaps.

Were it physically possible, even I'd fuck me.

So, you see, I'm not really crazy.

Here's the thing...

I've seen the news footage of thousands of people starving in Somalia. It seems like a terrible waste. In the Middle East, they keep tossing social undesirables off of buildings or, worse, beheading them. Where's the fun in that? A single suicide bomber can kill hundreds of people in seconds. With all of that going on, it seems clear that human life is pretty worthless.

Think about it. Even the most infamous serial killers in the US, men like Ted Bundy and John Wayne Gacy, murdered less than a few dozen people apiece. There was all that fuss over Jeffrey Dahmer, and he only killed eighteen. Manson's total was even less.

It's not like they committed genocide. The impact was minimal. When it came to Gacy and Dahmer, most of the victims weren't even missed. Take a look at the scumbags Aileen Wuornos killed. It was only seven men, but some people might think she was doing society a favor.

If only people in general, and the police in particular, weren't so touchy about it, my burden would be a lot easier to bear. Even if I truly was mentally disturbed, self-denial would be the cause. And there's absolutely no reason for it. Only someone who's truly sick could get turned on by the idea of snuffing out another human life. If it were up to me, everything would miraculously heal between sessions, nice and neat, leaving me with an unblemished, blank canvas to start with the next time. I'm *not* a homicidal maniac; death gives me no pleasure.

Pain, on the other hand, does.

When I was about eleven years old, I was obsessed with a slightly older boy. Danny was physically mature for his age, a sturdy child who excelled at sports. I suppose there was a bit of hero worship on my part, made even more acute by the fact that Danny barely acknowledged my existence.

One day, right in front of our house, Danny took a spill from his bike. As I was the only other person around, I came running. Unluckily for him, he'd been wearing shorts, and the sidewalk scraped the first few layers of skin from one knee. Where a tree root had taken a nice gash out of his scalp, he bled freely. Poor Danny clutched his skinned leg and cried, but it wasn't until he wiped away the blood dripping into his eyes that he discovered the loose flap of skin on his forehead. I suppose it was one of those injuries that was painless until you knew it was there, and once you did, it became agonizing.

Danny started screaming.

"It hurts! It hurts!" he bawled. "Make it stop!"

As I stood by, helpless and not knowing what to do, I saw that the fall had also torn his shirt and exposed part of his chest. One nipple peered through the rent in the cloth, and to my astonishment, I noticed there were a few hairs growing around it.

Something clicked inside me. I shuddered, and I think I even moaned. Danny's sobs made my knees wobbly and I had to grab onto a fence post to remain upright. The sound of his pain bounced around inside my head until it was the only thing I could hear. I wanted to capture each cry as if it was a physical thing I could hide in a secret place and treasure.

At the same time, I could not tear my eyes from the line of perspiration, tinged pink from the droplets of blood, that trickled down from his scalp and onto his chest. I yearned to lick it away, to press my face to his naked skin, to take the plump little nubbin of the boy's nipple gently between my lips...

...and to bite down on it as hard as I could.

The mental image caused the pit of my stomach to twist. I struggled to inhale as if the wind had been knocked out of me. There was a building pressure in my groin, like I had to pee worse than ever before. Something released, and horrified, I thought I had wet my pants right in front of Danny. A wave of incredible pleasure washed over me and my crotch pulsed with something that was both warm and wonderful. I cried out, half a moan half a shout.

My very first ejaculation.

Momentarily, Danny forgot his tears and looked up at me with an uneasy expression. I guess my reaction had been pretty extreme. I could not take my eyes off the bit of bare flesh revealed by his open shirt, and once he was back on his bike with his feet on the pedals, a horrible fear seized me. That delicious feeling—what if I never felt it again? What if it was inextricably connected to Danny himself? Until the accident, I'd always been a non-entity as far as he was concerned.

Once he was gone, would he once again relegate me into invisibility? Worst of all, what if he hurt himself again? What it he hurt himself so badly that he was in excruciating pain? And what if I was *not there to witness it?*

I ached at the thought. I grieved that I might only have one chance to experience bliss like that, and that I'd already used it up. How could I spend the rest of my life never knowing that indescribable pleasure again? Once Danny pedaled away, was it gone forever?

So I pushed him off the bike again.

To my delight, when he thrust out his hands to break his fall, he misjudged. His elbow smashed into the pavement and he let out a howl that started my groin tingling all over again. When his right arm collapsed and he landed, face first, on the concrete, my penis instantly stiffened. Had I been another year into puberty, I daresay I might have been able to cum a second time.

Much of my life since then has been shaped by that experience and my quests to recapture it—preferably as often as possible.

Naturally, while I was a youngster still living at home, my options were limited. Though I was certainly willing to go around pushing other children off of bicycles—opportunities were rare. Instead, I spent quite a lot of time, mostly in the privacy of my bedroom with my dick in my hand, reliving the incident. I needed to recapture that exquisite thrill, but I was smart enough to understand that there could be grave consequences should I involve another of my schoolmates.

I set out to experiment, reasoning that if it was the pain that turned me on, maybe I could achieve my goal without involving anyone else at all. Could I get the same result if I intentionally hurt myself? There was so much about my condition that I wanted to know!

I was soon to learn, however, that if there was a Kinsey equivalent for sadomasochism, I was as far away from the M side of the scale as it's possible to get. Even the thought of experiencing pain myself made me queasy. But the memory of my first orgasm proved impossible to resist, and when, after a dozen false starts, I was *finally* able to pierce my own thumb with a straight pin, the tiny wound caused an indescribable agony that I could barely endure.

I also discovered an embarrassing tendency to faint at the sight of my own blood.

My reaction confused me. Had I been a budding serial killer, things would have been easier for me. I would have had a mold to fit into, something to aspire to. But how many homicidal maniacs pass out at the first sign of gore? Besides, all the books I read said that most serial killers start their careers by practicing on small animals. I'll admit that I *tried*, but it was a dismal failure.

Shortly into the process, the kitten started mewling piteously and my heart broke. I was immediately aghast at myself, and to this day, it is difficult for me to look at certain power tools without shame. Worse, no matter how gentle I tried to be, I couldn't remove the duct tape without hurting the poor thing even more. My only option was to use the hammer to put the creature out of its misery as quickly and mercifully as possible. When it was over, I collapsed to the ground and vomited.

I dug a grave for the sad little corpse in the back yard, but I was unable to also bury my guilt. It still haunts me. Every year I make a sizeable donation to the local animal shelter. Nothing will ever truly atone for what I did, but it's the best I can do. For awhile, I actually considered joining PETA as well, but I thought that might be taking my penance to an extreme.

Still, I craved pain with the kind of insatiable lust that causes some people to claw their way to the top of the corporate ladder, while others compulsively collect Disneyiana. At an age where there were few other outlets available to me, I became a horror movie fanatic. As long as a film showed attractive young people slowly dispatched in creatively gruesome ways, you could bet that I'd be in the audience, shoving popcorn into my mouth with one hand and stroking my penis through my pants with the other.

Like most adolescent males, onanism became my main avocation. Unlike other boys, however, my masturbatory fantasies became darker and darker. Not that they were ever particularly jolly to begin with. I managed to get my hands on a few bondage magazines, and though they were good for a couple of orgasms, I quickly grew bored by the staged, artificial quality of the pictures.

Though Danny starred in a lot of my fantasies, I often replaced him with handsome movie stars or a model I saw on a billboard or in a magazine ad. Eventually, I realized that the subjects of my sexual fantasies had become almost exclusively male. If anything, the discovery that I was homosexual eased my mind. I'd started feeling uncomfortable whenever I jerked off to a movie or photo that showed a young woman being tortured. Focusing on a female seemed gross, even dirty. I wanted a man, a man in the prime of his youth and strength. I loved the idea of watching him struggle against the ropes or chains, cursing me defiantly at first, all too soon to be whimpering and begging.

Would his charred flesh smell sweet? If so, could I resist a tiny taste? Could I find what I needed at the local hardware store? Or would I have to design my own specialized tools? Would I need to muffle his screams, or was there a way to soundproof the location so that I could enjoy both the sight and the sound of his agony without disturbing the neighbors?

These were important questions, I felt, and I devoted a lot of time to considering them. But I didn't allow the uncertainty of the answers to detract from my fantasy. Even as I vowed to one day have the answers, I feared I would never follow through. A catharsis of the imagination might be beneficial, but to carry out these impulses would not be indicative of stable mental health.

Once I was old enough to be on my own, I searched the Craigslist personals and began haunting the various underground bondage clubs for real life partners. I found a surprising number of takers, other men eager to be tortured and abused by a good-looking, superior young man like myself.

I discovered a problem with that.

Ironically, their very *willingness* to suffer kept me limp. It simply wasn't a turn on for me if my victim submitted voluntarily. Even when I ventured into more extreme sexual practices, I was disappointed to find out that most men who advertised "no limits" quickly called a halt as soon as the barbecue skewers got hot enough or when I started to slice into something interesting.

A few times, I'll admit, I was tempted to ignore their silly little safe words. But during all those adolescent years I spent dreaming up the most creative and exquisite tortures to inflict on helpless flesh, I also considered the practical ramifications–just in case I ever had the gumption to take the plunge. Were I truly insane, I doubt that I would have thought things through so thoroughly and reached the conclusions I did. No, if I were crazy, I simply would have taken the risk and I would have been caught in a heartbeat.

Hiding the evidence after an actual torture session had to be a terribly involved job. Not only would it cost a small fortune for all those cleaners and disinfectants, even if only half of what they show on TV is accurate, the marvels of modern forensics made getting away with it nearly impossible. I couldn't chance it.

Judges do not grant probation to people who did the things I wanted to do. They throw away the key. And prison would definitely cramp my style. You see, even though I was still afraid to take action, the idea that one day I *might* find the courage was omnipresent. Behind bars, there was no chance at all.

I bided my time and prepared anyway. When I bought my house, the real estate agent was baffled by my obsession with basements. He was exceedingly handsome, and when he casually mentioned that he'd both been captain of his college swim team and had rowed on the crew, I was barely able to retrain myself from knocking him unconscious and nailing him to his own For Sale sign in an impromptu crucifixion. He had no idea that while he was touting the benefits of gas cooking and the place's curbside appeal, my fertile imagination was picturing his blood-streaked torso as I flayed him with twisted lengths of barbed wire.

Once I owned the place, I installed sound proofing in the basement – just in case. I even managed to wangle some chloroform from an acquaintance who had medical contacts. The small brown bottle stayed in my freezer, unused. As best I could, I sketched out some wicked torture implements, and came up with a concept for my own rack—complete with an extra winch for the victim's genitalia—and I enrolled in a Home Improvement course at the local community college so I could learn something about how I might build it. But as time dragged on and my fevered dark desire remained unsatisfied, I was left frustrated, like my balls were soaking in a perpetual ice bath.

Depression took hold of me. I still went to the leather bars and kept up my memberships in the online bondage sites so I could look at the pictures, but nothing I did was truly fulfilling. In the midst of my black mood, I became conscious of certain gossip flying back and forth between the more serious players at the S&M clubs. I suspect that's where I first heard about the magician and his performances, but I don't remember specifically; my hopes had been aroused and dashed too many times for me to get excited about mere rumors. In my experience, there was always some leather-clad peacock strutting boasting about his new "dungeon" which, more often than not, turned out to be nothing more than handcuffs affixed to his bedposts or a few chains dangling from his garage ceiling.

So, I foolishly discounted the early murmurings about the unusual and forbidden pleasures offered by the man who styled himself as the Magician, and the exclusive show he put on for select audience members.

It may have been the name that eventually penetrated my depression and caught my interest. Magic acts have always intrigued me. There's something about sawing a helpless captive in half that I find appealing. I saw an act once, where a volunteer from the audience was already confined to a box before the magician told him he would be skewered with swords. The look of fear on the man's face made my testicles throb. Go figure.

The magician's act was rumored to be all that... and much more. My interest quickened and I was able to pick up bits of information in dribs and drabs, most of it titillating and none of it confirmed. I learned that his performances took place in what was supposedly a real dungeon. Getting onto the guest list was a rare and exclusive privilege. Though I was wary of being disappointed once again by some poseur, the more I heard, the more I was inclined to believe that Julian offered something that might appeal to a man of my peculiar and rarefied tastes.

Six months passed. During that time, I stayed on the lookout for opportunities to make contact with anyone who might pass the message back to the oh-so-mysterious Magician. I took special care to make my interest known subtly, as I sensed that Julian would not approve of someone who appeared overly eager, or who was too brash, or even worse, a boor. Most of my inquiries met brick walls. But one, at least, seemed to have pierced Julian's veil of secrecy.

I have no idea how the Magician got my home address. The card inside the envelope was simple and unassuming. Embossed in black ink were the words *The Magician Requests Your Presence* in an easily readable cursive. Below it, in graceful calligraphic handwriting, someone had written an address, a date and a time on the blank line. The cardstock felt strange, a trifle stiffer than a normal business card, and yet still flexible, with an odd texture. It seemed to be a wafer-thin piece of hide, yet when I held it to my nostrils, I couldn't detect any traces of the distinct scent often left behind by the chemicals normally used in tanning.

Curious, I examined it more closely. The grain was finer than anything I'd ever seen. And though the card had evidently been sized in order not to warp its shape, it was still softer and smoother than even the highest quality kid. I don't know why I found something as mundane as a business card so fascinating, even if it was made of an unusual material—but I did. I spent some time fondling it and rubbing it between my fingers. I rubbed it against my cheek like a silk handkerchief; there was something almost erotic about how soft it was. For no earthly reason, I even touched it to the tip of my tongue, as if to taste it.

I reveled in the strange sensuality of the little card, until a bizarre thought occurred to me. I gasped and shook my head. Yet, suddenly, I somehow knew what it was about the Magician's invitation that captivated me so.

It was made from human skin.

I placed it in my mouth—not just the tip this time. I closed my lips over one corner of the invitation and moistened it with my saliva. As I moved my tongue across the surface, the sensitive organ could feel the tiny, uneven pebbling of pores that had been too small for my eyes to easily see. A little drool dripped from one corner of my mouth and I slurped it back in, not wanting to waste any of the card's essence that might have mixed with my spit. Though it had no true flavor, I found it delicious.

Even the thought of what I held in my mouth was sublime. After years of denying myself, I dared to hope that I might find someone who might understand the figurative demons that possessed me and help me to either exorcize, or even better, to embrace them.

Of course, there was never any question of my *not* going!

My entire body tingled with anticipation as I approached the building where the Magician's performance was to take place. The area was heavily industrial, not at all the kind of place where I'd normally feel safe walking at night. But euphoria had me in its jolly little grip; I had my invitation clutched in my sweaty hand and very soon I would discover whether the whispers I'd heard about Julian's particular—and peculiar—kind of magic were true.

My pace quickened when I spied the weathered steel door with the address numbers painted above it. They seemed to shimmer, as if I glimpsed them through a haze of heated air, until I realized that I was hyperventilating and had made myself dizzy. About twenty feet before I reached the door, all my excitement drained away and I stopped dead, suddenly consumed with doubt.

What if everything I'd heard was urban legend? What if tonight was nothing more than a garden variety orgy with some leather and a whip or two thrown into the mix? Or, I thought as my insecurities got the better of me, what if I was indeed on the cusp of a sadism far beyond what I'd ever dared to dream, and what if, in the eleventh hour, I discovered that I didn't have the stomach for it?

I panicked, and for the briefest instant, I wanted to flee. But I didn't.

Instead, I saw that there was no bell nor buzzer, nor any intercom. When I forced myself to knock, the door felt more solid than it looked. It soon became obvious that there was no way to make myself heard unless I pounded on it and risked injuring my fists. I gave up, and annoyed, waited for another guest to show up— but no one did. Ironically, it was the thought that I might be denied entrance that annoyed me enough to banish my remaining doubts.

I fumed. I would have yelled and cursed, but even though I saw no one around, it wasn't the kind of area where it was wise to start a fuss and possibly attract the wrong kind of attention. My frustration grew, and just when it was about to spill over into that horrid, let-down feeling, I spied a small vertical slot in the door, effectively masked by the heavy door handle just above it.

It seemed perfectly natural for me to drop the invitation into the slot. I did it without thinking, and with only the briefest pang that I might lose my precious piece of tanned hide. It turned out to be the right move. With a click, the door automatically swung open onto a long corridor lit with low-wattage bulbs, which ended in a flight of stairs. In turn, they led down to a round gallery, much like the operating theaters in films set in Victorian England.

All but one of the chairs was already occupied. I counted twelve spectators in the room already, which made me the unlucky thirteenth, but for two attendants. With the sole exception of one incredibly unattractive young lady seated almost directly across from me, I don't think any of the men or women were younger than sixty.

None of them bothered to glance my way. Either they were supremely confident of the Magician's ability to keep out anyone who didn't belong, or they just didn't care. All of their eyes were fixed on the stage below us; several of them leaned forward impatiently, but by and large, the atmosphere in the room was expectant, but with a certain arrogance as if the audience was demanding to be impressed.

Someone behind me cleared his throat, almost demurely, and I turned to find one of the ushers was standing next to my chair.

"There is the matter of the fee, sir. " He said it as if reluctant to broach such a tacky subject. "Might I see your invitation?"

"No one said anything about money," I complained, as I handed it over.

His face brightened when he saw it and he cut me off.

"My apologies, sir. This is a personal invitation from Master Julian. No payment is due at this time." With that, he returned the card to me and resumed his former position.

I'd no sooner returned my attention to the performing area when the lights dimmed in the gallery. Next came a sustained hiss, and the little arena below us filled with smoke. It wafted upward and I discovered it had been oddly perfumed. I inhaled, trying to zero in on the elusive scent, but the nearest I could come to defining it was as an odd, sultry combination of musk and a smell somewhat like sweat, only cleaner. Then, the mist parted to reveal the Magician himself in the center of the stage.

The muscles of my chest tightened until it was painful; only then did I remember to breathe. I have, as I've already mentioned, a fairly extensive fantasy life. Yet never in my most creative imaginings could I have created a man as perfect as Julian.

He stood with his feet slightly apart, his legs firmly planted to display thighs as sturdy as California redwoods, and he held out his arms, palms up, as if inviting us into his embrace. He was bare-chested, lean but exquisitely muscled; even a competition between Michelangelo and Praxilites might not have done him justice. Every movement was broad and sweeping—theatrical, yet elegant. And when he welcomed us to his show, a rounded baritone seemed to fill both the stage and the gallery, no matter that he had not raised his voice.

His face was obscured by a handsome, but cruel-looking mask. The nose was perfectly formed, aristocratic, yet not overly aquiline.

The eyes, deep cisterns of obsidian, lay between sharply defined cheekbones and a coldly noble forehead. The impression it gave as a whole was enticing and beautiful, yet frightening. One would not want to caress such a face for fear their fingers might be bitten off.

It was not until Julian spoke a second time that I realized that the alluring but strangely off-putting construction was not a mask at all. It was his actual face. Then I saw what Julian had bound, spread-eagled, to one of the glossy, black painted, wooden frames on the stage. And the thought of what that visage of haughty cruelty might be capable of doing sent a frisson of erotic anticipation surging through me. My dick stiffened to bronze hardness.

The captive was probably in his late twenties and though, in comparison, few could compete with the Magician's physical beauty, the youth was certainly well built enough to grace advertisements in any number of fashion or physical fitness magazines. He was nude, of course, and his body gleamed with the greasy sweat of terror. When Julian removed his gag, he began to cry and beg. Gently, the Magician stroked his face, murmuring soothing words that were too low for the audience to hear. Gradually, the young man's blubbering subsided, and once it was reduced to low whimpers, Julian removed a thin wand from where he'd concealed it inside his cape.

For a moment, I thought he would use it to somehow free the prisoner from his shackles, perhaps tapping it to the restraints to elicit some dramatic explosion or flash of light. Apparently, the young man did too because his face was hopeful and he sobbed with relief.

The Magician waved the wand and the tip began to glow. And when he touched it, just barely, to the man's naked chest, the reaction was... impressive. His back arched and a high, keening wail tore from his throat. Every muscle contracted and his body began to shake. At the same time, all of the watchers leaned forward to get a better look, me included, and we all uttered a collective moan.

Though it was the first time the Magician forced a scream from his victim, it was hardly the last. For close to an hour, Julian used wands and steel rings, lengths of knotted handkerchiefs, knives and fire on the young man's helpless body, in ways that would have made Houdini writhe in his grave. The gaily painted boxes and cabinets were put to fiendish use. When the Magician sealed the youth inside one and thrust swords through it, there was no trickery involved;

when he briefly set it aflame, we could clearly smell the boy's crisping skin and sizzling fat. Nor did he ignore the more traditional implements of torture; he made sure to vary his act and, in one case, demonstrated a truly innovative use for fishing line and pliers, that even I at my most creative, hadn't thought was possible.

Eventually, when the young man's shrieks faded into moans, and the moans subsided into faint whimpers of agony, Julian delivered his own version of the coup de grace. To share the details would be to profane the most sacred of mysteries. Know only that my memory holds each spurt of blood, each nugget of flesh, like a treasure.

Nor was he the only victim. The night held increasingly agonizing fates for three others, all male, all attractive enough to quicken my interest. Every scream set my penis to pulsing. Each second of writhing and straining was seared into my memory. Throughout, I sat as awed as any saint in religious ecstacy, as emotionally devastated as if I were viewing the very greatest work of art. By the time the Magician reached the climax of his show, his torn and scarred victims decorated the stage, and it was a miracle that I had not climaxed myself.

Oh! Those handsome faces twisted by more pain than the human body was designed to withstand. The sweet, buttery smell of charred skin when it rose in waves into the gallery of spectators. And the sounds? My god! The delicious, devastating screams as pieces of the men were ripped or sliced or sawed or seared away!

To have it happen right before my eyes, was the most exhilarating experience of my life. But more than that, those few hours were even more holier to me, rendered even more sacred, because of the knowledge that... *it was possible!*

How Julian got away with it was still a mystery to me. *But he had!* And if the rumors I'd heard during the preceding long months held even a scintilla of truth, he'd been getting away with it for a long time. There was no question in my mind that I had to meet him, no doubt that I had found a kindred soul at last, and if I were to be so blessed, perhaps even a mentor.

After Julian took his final bow and the lights in the gallery came up, while the others were gathering their things to leave, I barely restrained myself from leaping over the railing and onto the stage. I shouldered roughly past the surprised ushers and bolted from the room. There had to be a way down to the performance area hidden somewhere, and beyond it to the dressing room or wherever the Magician was relaxing in what I imagined was very close to a post-coital bliss.

When the two ushers caught me roaming the halls, I found they were a lot beefier than I'd thought. Though I struggled and pleaded, I couldn't break their grip when they "escorted" me out of the building. I was horrified at myself; I though that my brashness had ruined everything, that I'd never be invited back. I wept at the thought.

Just before they showed me the door, the one who had asked for my invitation smiled and whispered, barely loud enough for me to hear, "A man must earn the right to become the Magician's apprentice."

I went back the next night. And the night after. The mail slot was blocked and no one answered my timid knocks. I tried pounding on the door but the hard steel bruised my hands and I risked passing out from the pain. I sank to the concrete outside the warehouse, weeping.

Am I crazy? Insane? No. But having Julian dangle what I so desperately desired just out of my reach, drove me very close to the brink. Once my roiling emotions settled so that I was able to think clearly, I saw the solution to my problem. The usher had said I must "earn the right." How to do that was obvious.

I found the young man on Craigslist. I was pleasantly surprised by how easy it was to cover my traces, and how well all those empty years of plotting paid off. Just as I'd envisioned, I was able to mask my trail with a bulwark of phony email accounts and by logging in from computers at different libraries.

The S&M clubs promote check-in calls and advise meeting in public for a reason. Some even advise bringing along a friend for safety's sake. Nevertheless, it's astonishing how shame can induce people to keep their darker sexuality a deep secret. Even better for my purposes, most young men assume they are immune, and that horrible things happen only to others.

My first potential victim was gorgeous, but an idiot. He had no problem meeting in the parking lot of a shopping center that had closed for the night. He even allowed me to drive us both back to my house; it never occurred to him that he might be in danger, that it would be easier for me to clean my car than to dispose of his. He failed to notice how carefully I kept a watch to make sure no one saw us together.

The experience was... sublime.

Several hours into it, I began to regret having to kill him. No matter how he pleaded and promised not to tell anyone, I knew he lied. If I was foolish enough to let him go, there would be police and lawyers and proverbial peasants with torches to deal with. Unfortunately, the reality of body disposal was far more gruesome and inconvenient than I'd anticipated.

For weeks afterward I masturbated to the memory of that night, to every slice, every burn, every scream and whimper. Once again I felt the rasp of his body hair against my tongue when I lapped away the perspiration, and relived my surprise when I discovered that blood tasted even more salty than sweat. Within a few months, my memories were no longer able to sustain me and I longed to do it again.

I picked up a hitchhiker next. After that, I met a young man in a wooded area that was notorious for what happened in the bushes. One of the highlights for me was an ex-military lad who, it turned out, had undergone training in resisting torture. It did him little good.

All the while, I'd arrogantly convinced myself that I could do without the Magician. How dare he snub me? He was a tease, no better than a whore who flaunts herself while sneering at a client who she knows could never afford her price. I was perfectly capable of satisfying my own desires with no help from *him*!

And yet...

Julian was truly a master of his art. My acts of sadism, though they satisfied me at first, were those of a talented amateur by comparison. Watching the Magician perform had opened up new vistas of human pain, exotic lands of agony that I had only aspired to explore. When Julian inspired me to act, I hadn't realized that assuaging one forbidden desire, I would find that I needed even more.

I returned to the warehouse, many times. Though I tried to convince myself that Julian could rot in hell for all I cared, I still wound up slumped against the steel door, my hands swollen with futile pounding. One night, casting all of my dignity aside, I shouted into the little door slot, begging to be let in with a fervor that was unmatched by any of my victims. No one answered.

I was left feeling jilted and spurned. To compensate for my the rejection, I threw myself into my own endeavors. Several victims later, I began to suspect that I was out of control. The intervals between my little liaisons had grown dangerously short. And though *I knew* I needed to pay careful attention to misdirecting the authorities and erasing the evidence, very often I had barely dispatched one playmate before I was preoccupied by devising new torments for the next one.

I grew impatient and rushed the clean-up. I no longer took the necessary time to be absolutely *certain* that there was no connection between me and my victims. I was careless.

When I saw on the news that the first body parts had been discovered, I knew my time was limited. Always, my best hope of avoiding capture had been to avoid becoming a suspect in the first place. But if I'd overlooked any clues—and in my fevered haste to try out new things on a fresh subject, I was almost positive that I had— the police had all sorts of technology to lead them to me.

The old terrors returned. I could not—*not!*—return to an existence of unfulfilled longing. My darkest imaginings could never come close to the rush I got from the real thing. I no longer merely craved the satisfaction of causing pain, I was addicted to it. Incarcerated, with no outlet for the pressure building within my soul, the deprivation would push me over the brink into true insanity.

How did the Magician do it? How had Julian gotten away with it for so long? How had he managed to control himself, to hide his traces, to entice his victims, to find his audiences without risking exposure? I agonized over dozens of questions like these, but above all, I wanted to know why he had taken the trouble to lure me in, only to abandon me.

In despair, I returned to the warehouse for what would be the last time. I was so depressed that it was some time before I realized that the door had been left ajar; even then, it failed to cheer me. I entered and wandered aimlessly through the halls. I sat in the gallery for awhile, listless, unable to spark any enthusiasm for life even though I had never lived as intensely as I had the last time I was in this exact same spot. Later, I plodded down a flight of stairs and trudged down an arched corridor, until, through no intention of mine, I found myself on the stage.

The Magician awaited me, sitting in silent judgment.

"What did I do wrong?" I asked.

He shook his head and his stern expression melted into a smile. His arms swept through the air in a grand gesture and the temperature dropped, as if he had summoned the chill. The objects around me seemed clearer, with sharper edges. When I peered more closely, I saw the flickering outlines of people strapped to the tables, sealed into the cabinets, spun on the wheels.

Unless I was horribly mistaken, they were the very same men I had witnessed tortured to death. As I watched, they became corporeal, as real as they had been during the performance.

"But... but..." I stammered. Then, a groan welled up from the bottom of my soul as I understood, at last. "I *am* insane after all."

Julian's rich, deep chucking echoed from the gallery. Had he been mocking me, I would have crumbled. But he was merely amused at my naiveté. He opened his arms, and willingly, I entered into his embrace.

Julian claims that there is as much magic, as much art, in enduring agony, as there is in causing it. He claims that sadism leads to power. In time, he says, I will master the skill, and once I do, I will become his full apprentice. I'm not sure I believe him, but I have little choice. Until then, he insists I pay my dues. At every performance, I stare up at the gallery and try not to scream.

But it hurts.

Oh God, it hurts.

II

THE HIGH PRIESTESS

3

THE HIGH PRIESTESS

MICHAEL A. STACKPOLE

Upright: Secrets, mystery, the future as yet unrevealed, silence, tenacity, wisdom, science
Reversed: Passion, moral or physical ardor, conceit, surface knowledge

She used only the barest of nods to indicate assent, but the men cranked the wooden winch furiously, acting as if she'd cracked a burning whip across their broad backs. The block and tackle suspended from the ceiling above the oubliette rocked and clattered. Thick cable groaned as it wrapped around the winch's barrel.

A man hung limply at the end of the rope, suspended from a chain linked to manacles. Fine, silver mesh gloves sheathed his long-fingered hands and forearms. Filth sheeted off his naked body. Though she had not ordered his keepers to divert a sewage flow through his prison, nor had she disciplined them when she'd learned what they'd done. He slowly spun over the hole, fetid liquid replete with unidentifiable chunks dripping slowly from his slender body.

She flicked a finger. Two men splashed buckets of water over him, exposing pale flesh. The pallid hue suggested he'd dwelled years in darkness. A third bucket, this one aimed by her lover, Marcus, caught the prisoner in the face. His head snapped back, but he did not sputter nor seem to notice as a long lock of white hair plastered itself across cheek and nose. A moment later, as his sharp chin again rested on his chest, his eyelids flickered and opened.

Yes, yes, it is you. The eyes, so dark one could be forgiven to think they were nothing but pupil, had the tiniest hints of reds, golds, greens and blues. It was as if the irises had been seeded with fragments of black opal—though she knew the flecks to be something else entirely, and the product of a process far more painful than grinding pulverized gemstones into his eyes.

She allowed herself to feel pleasure, but only manifested it as the faint twitching at the left corner of her mouth. "It is good to see you again, my friend."

The hanging man simply closed his eyes.

Marcus backhanded the man across his lean belly. "You will show Countess Dyre respect. Answer her."

The countess spitted her lover with an arctic stare. He withdrew a step and lowered his eyes. She looked again at the prisoner. "Despite your circumstances, I do yet consider you a friend. A fondly remembered friend. I would address you as befits you, but the last name I had for you is old."

The prisoner remained silent.

She looked at Marcus again. "Clean him up, feed him, then bring him to my Temple chambers. Use the Penitent's stairway. You have an hour."

*

Marcus dragged the prisoner into her chambers by the chains securing his wrists. "Here you are, my lady. He is clean. He refused to eat. He drank, but complained about the wine."

She smiled easily, ensconced in an oaken throne within the stone-walled chamber. "You never were temperate, were you, Idris? I may yet call you that, may I? Idris Rake."

The man's head came up. His white mane had been gathered into a ponytail and secured with a black ribbon. "As the Countess desires."

Marcus raised a hand, but Rake stopped him with a sidelong glance. "'ware, fool. These silver gloves will come off eventually."

"Wouldn't matter if you could work magic."

Rake looked back at her. "I had supposed you chose intellectual lovers by preference, Ariadne."

"You'll address her as Countess Dyre or…"

"Marcus, please, come here. Attend me." Ariadne gestured toward Rake. "No need to be jealous. Idris and I were friends in days long past. He will not hurt you."

Rake smiled coldly. "Take no heart in her assurances, boy. I find you boring and I owe *her* for killings past."

She stroked a finger along the scar that played over the right side of Marcus' cheekbone. "I never slew your lovers, Idris, just your apprentices. Well, except, perhaps, for that special young man. He was both, was he not?"

"Deimos?" Rake shrugged. "I doubt I am here to satisfy your curiosity about someone centuries in the grave."

Ariadne laughed lightly, and Rake's eyes slitted in reflex. "You are here precisely concerning someone in the grave for many years." She rose from the wooden throne in a rustle of black satin, and crossed to the large door set in the room's interior wall. "When I was your student, you said I shouldn't waste my time pursuing a particular area of study. I think you will find my time was far from wasted."

She opened the door, stepping through onto a balcony thirty feet above the temple floor below. Far to the left, nearest the tall entrance, lay a rectangular pool of a dark liquid. The surface undulated, revealing no discernible hue and remaining utterly silent. Beyond it, filling the largely open center, tables and chair of uniform but utilitarian manufacture oriented themselves toward the altar on the right. Varicolored marble floor inlays depicted symbols odd and arcane, from astrology and alchemy through passages writ in alphabets ancient and powerful.

As she gazed upon the altar, pride swelled her heart. Black stone, fitted and trimmed with gold; it had been styled after the stepped pyramids found everywhere from Babylon to the Americas. Beside it rose a tower of skulls, their empty eye sockets staring intently in all directions. From that pulpit she shared the wisdom of her Lord and Master; as well as dispensed orders to her most ardent congregants.

Carved out of the stone forming the temple's rear wall—seventy feet tall, if an inch—stood the temple's crowning work of art. The skeletal representation of Death exuded strength and a sense of inescapable finality. Absent was any cloak to obscure his nature. His scythe had shrunk to a sickle in one hand and he held a bouquet of nightshade in the other.

Rake leaned forward, resting his hands on the balustrade. "Magnificent."

"Thank you."

"Magnificent evidence that you completely ignored my advice."

"I told you that you doubted me at your peril. This is, of course, the most grand of my Lord's temples, and fitting that we built it beneath the world's greatest city. Please, let us go down. It is more impressive from the floor, and almost time for evensong."

Rake shook his head. "I watch cheap theatrics, I do not participate in them."

Marcus stepped forward. "Tell me your will, my lady, and he will abide by it."

She found Marcus' comment laced with jealousy—and decidedly more revealing of his emotional state than she expected. She considered, just for a heartbeat, granting him permission to do whatever he wished to Rake. She feared Marcus might pitch the man over the balustrade, dashing his brains out on marble floor. That would have been an inconvenience, and caused a delay which, however brief, would have been intolerable.

"He will come along, Marcus. No need for force."

"He does not scare me, Countess."

"But I should." Rake straightened up. "I say this to you less in any belief you will heed my words, than my desire for them to ring in your ears as you die. Run now, Marcus. Run away and live a long life away from her and her madness."

Marcus' resolve locked his features into an iron mask.

Ariadne Dyre laughed. "Your charm, dear Idris, lay always in your brooding taciturnity. Marcus is mine, heart and soul. We have no secrets. As you raised me up, so I have done with him. A person cannot love and fear another at the same time."

Blue sparked in Rake's dark eyes. "Oh, he really *is* a dull boy. No matter." He offered her his elbow.

She slipped her hand through the crook, and guided him back through her chambers and down a wider set of winding stairs. Rake had to duck his head, and walked on the outside. Their descent, his closeness and the hint of his scent took her back to their time together. As lovers, they would have hurried. As a student, she'd always trembled, because often such descents would end in Rake inculcating her in some new occulted truth.

And now, I will reveal to him mysteries he has never dared to explore. Her stomach tightened, hoping for wonder on his part, and yet fearing derision and rebuke. As a Master he had always been stingy with praise, and yet generous with discipline. She'd never sensed any desire to hold students back in this, but more to remind them that the forces with which they worked were dangerous. Now that she had surpassed him, a trickle of annoyance played through her. She did not need his approval, but she found herself desperately wanting it.

They stepped out onto the floor and she turned him to face the wall with the balcony. "Again, more impressive, no?"

She caught his nod from the corner of her eye. "Quite. The windows… intriguing."

As the temple had been constructed underground, the addition of stained glass windows had been a cosmetic choice. Sorcery had kindled eldritch flames in niches carved out behind the glass. Their light illuminated scenes from Apocryphal scriptures, depicting stories of alternative creations. Fittingly, no snake appeared in the Garden of Eden, but Death himself usurped that role. God had trapped him in the Garden out of fear, hoping that harvesting human souls would distract Death sufficiently that he would forget that God's time was at hand. And, later, Death granted Jesus resurrection and ascension to remind His father that Death had not forgotten.

"Your invention, interpretation or…"

"I have uncovered many things since we were last together. I should love to claim creation of that story, but I have merely restored what the Church shunned." She led him toward the heart of the temple. "Mortality so terrified men that Church fathers transformed Death into an infantile surrogate over which God had dominion. Yet even His son died, accepting my Master as his Master."

Rake smiled slyly. "Yet, if I correctly recall, Jesus resurrected multiple people. Likewise Simon Peter and even Paul. So who, truly, was the master?"

"Fanciful stories. Slanders transformed into libelous gospels." She glanced at him. "Unless you know a different truth."

"Truth and religion have always been contentious bedfellows."

"But when they are one and the same, as they are here, reality is unlocked." She freed her hand from his arm and clapped once. "And this is the Truth you must understand."

From somewhere high up, in a chamber hidden beyond the ceiling's vaults, bells began to toll. Not too loudly, nor brightly, but deep and resonant enough that they sent vibrations through her chest. Though she had heard them ring countless times, they never failed to thrill. They celebrated her success, in sharp contrast to the stony silence Rake had spared her efforts.

Drawn by the tolling bell's echoes, people gathered in the temple. They entered through the large doors for the most part, proceeding in a stately and measured fashion around the dark pool. A few came through small doors from adjoining chambers. Most all wore somber clothing, many adopting raiment styled after that worn by Puritans. A few chose finer clothes, complete with high boots, quilted waistcoats and long jackets or gowns—yet of subdued colors. Some came as couples, and a few approached as groups, but the majority came alone.

She wondered how long it would take for Rake to notice the difference between himself or Marcus and her congregants. Though she watched closely, she missed the point where he must have realized what was going on. It should have been simple, really, since the temple was something she'd always described as a consequence of her studies. His delayed reaction she put down to his utter disbelief at her success, and then his stubborn refusal to give her the satisfaction of acknowledging it.

He gave no outward sign until one man walked past close enough that Rake could have reached out and touched him. Rake's eyes tightened. He stared hard, then failed to suppress a shiver. "That cannot be."

"But it is. The Conqueror himself. He is not the oldest congregant my Lord has given to me, but is one of the most treasured."

Rake fixed her with his obsidian gaze. "But he appears..."

"As he was? Yes." She spread her arms to take all the congregants in. "My Lord Death has graced me with a community of wondrous people. Some have returned to prove His power and beneficence. Others—you will see them later—have yet to enjoy His embrace. They fervently believe, however, and worship wholeheartedly."

"And their donations fund your work."

"Their generosity is a testament to their faith." Ariadne couldn't help but smile openly. "You would be more than welcome to enter fellowship with us."

"I was always more inclined to be a hermit than a High Priest."

Marcus snorted. "That's not a position needs filling."

Rake turned his back toward her lover. "If that is so, why am I here?"

"My congregation is full of the best and brightest of human beings ever to stride the world beneath stars, moon and sun. Philosophers, astrologers, artists and writers, conquerors and kings, generals, chieftains, emperors and empresses—separated by centuries, yet all united in the bosom of my Lord. All people so vital, with so much strength of mind and personality, that though my Lord took them at their appointed time, He cherished them enough to restore them to the world. In his judgement, their lives had been so exemplary that the only justice was to bring them back."

Rake shook his head. "How is it he manages the choosing? The spin a wheel of good fortune or...?"

"He whispers the name to me, in those quiet moments, when I think of nothing at all." She brought her hands together as if in prayer, stilling their nervous flutter. "He made a choice, a recent choice, and this is why you are here." *One of the reasons, anyway.*

Rake arched an eyebrow. "Your lord regrets that Deimos died prematurely, then?"

"My Lord makes no mistakes, has no regret." Ariadne, unable to conjure up even a faded image of the dead apprentice's face, waved away Rake's comment. "No, He desires the Bard of Avon to enter into our fellowship."

Rake's laughter filled the lugubrious cathedral. Fury flashed through Ariadne. Marcus' lips peeled back in an unvoiced snarl. None of the congregants seemed to recognize the laughter for what it was, nor did they even try to locate the source. For them it was purposeless noise, but it lashed her.

Rake sighed. "Your lord wants him resurrected, or is it you who wants him back? Your cheeks yet burn because you talked yourself into believing that sonnet was written about you."

It was! Mortification curdled in her stomach. "You paid him to deny it and publicly humiliate me."

"By all things holy, woman, that happened well past a century ago. You will resurrect him to do what? To tell you that, yes, I did pay him to lie? He was a writer. He would have written anything I paid him to write." Rake hugged his arms to himself as much as the manacles would allow. "His grave is cursed, it is writ plain in stone. Nothing good will come of disturbing his bones."

"I made no choice, Idris Rake. This is the command of My Lord Death." She smiled easily. "And I know of that curse. I have been to the church. I sensed the curse's nature. The unique peculiarities of your magic alerted me to your role. My Lord wishes the Bard's brilliance to affirm His beneficence and mercy through fellowship, and you are the means of accomplishing His will."

"Thus your master requires I remove the curse on the grave."

"No, my friend. That has been done."

Marcus laid a hand on Rake's shoulder. "I managed that myself. Rather easy."

"She has taught you much." Rake nodded once. "Then you need me for…?"

Ariadne waggled a finger at him. "The *other* curse. The one on the leaden casket holding his remains. Remove that."

"Happily." Idris held up his hands. "Remove the gloves."

She stepped close and stroked a hand over his cheek. "Even were you to promise to do nothing untoward, I shouldn't return to you the means to work your magic. No, reveal the key to me and I will do Marcus the honor of letting him remove the curse."

"And the benefit to me?" He looked her in the eyes and her heart quickened. "Recall that I do not fear your master."

"Nor do I."

"You deceive yourself, Ariadne. Again. You have always feared Death. What you first sought to appease, you now worship."

She turned from him. "We both worship Death."

"No. My mastery of necromancy concerns death only in that I desire to know what the dead have known." Rake spread his hands to the extent the chains made possible. "You, this…"

Ariadne spun back. "This, Idris, is my Lord returning the dead to us so they can continue to create and think and guide. You want information they knew. Here they discover new things, they produce new things. Artwork and concertos, new plays and poems and potions which make life more enjoyable. My Lord does not enjoy suffering. He dispenses the mercy that God dictates we should show one another, yet He denies to us all. My Lord Death not only ends suffering, but returns to us those who will relieve it, not just tell us to endure it."

Rake shrugged. "This is your new Truth. So be it. But, again, what benefit do I reap by helping you?"

"I have discovered answers to questions which greatly concerned you before."

"Such as?"

"I realized you had authored both curses, not just because you had been my teacher and my lover, but because of tiny little aspects of your thaumaturgy. I found those peculiarities, traces really, elsewhere." She watched his face and how his expression froze. "Not left behind by someone you mentored, but someone with whom you shared a mentor."

"Impossible."

"Why is it impossible for me to have uncovered something for which you have searched for eons." She opened her arms to take in the temple. "This here, these people, a century and a half ago, you thought would never return from their graves. I have accomplished one impossibility, why not another?"

"Point taken."

"And I shall reveal the information to you, happily; and even assist in your assessing its import, in exchange for this one, tiny favor."

Rake's eyes focused above and beyond her. He had not changed since she last saw him, so recognizing that expression came by reflex. Once she'd marveled at the way he shut out the world, letting his mind devour a problem. She felt a touch of the exhilaration she'd known, and its potency surprised her.

Yet now, it seemed like such a waste. Idris Rake had once traveled the same path as she, but had balked at the single-minded devotion and dedication she'd lavished on Death. At first she believed his aversion came from a refusal to acknowledge anything being greater than he was. But as his attitude soured and he withdrew, she discovered the true reasons. *Jealousy. Envy.* He would never enjoy the close communion she had cultivated with Death. To avoid facing the truth, to avoid acknowledging that he had lost her forever, he'd denigrated her work and abandoned her. That she had murdered his new apprentice and had caused the deaths of others close to him had not been to anger him, but to prove her devotion to her Lord and Master.

Rake stroked his chin. "Very well. I agree to this bargain."

"As I knew you would." She looked at Marcus. "Fetch the casket and place it by the Resurrection Pool. Get everything else ready, please."

"I should remain with you, my lady."

"Run along, puppy. I shan't hurt her."

Marcus looked from him to her, but Ariadne waved him away. "Quickly now."

As her lover departed, Rake returned his attention to the gathering of the dead. "Have you a service to conduct. Do they sing at evensong? Take communion? What is it they eat?"

She followed his gaze. The dead had seated themselves in chairs and at tables, most facing their god's terrible visage. A few had bent their heads in prayer, while others sat in silent contemplation. She wished she knew their thoughts as they came into the Temple, but that remained a mystery to which her Master had denied her access.

"They do not eat as a rule, though they may, and those who had a passion for food and drink, yet indulge. Such consumption does not sustain them. For that, they undergo a Ritual of Renewal in the Resurrection Pool. Their need for it differs, largely based on how long they have been cradled to my Master's bosom. Some, very recently dead and regrettable experiments, have become apostate and sustain themselves by drinking blood from the living. They are not true vampyr, but close enough to be mistaken for same. More, really, like the *ghul* of the Arabias."

Rake stepped closer to one of the seated congregants. "Time in the grave equates to a diminution of their skills and abilities, yes?"

"Actually not."

"Truly?"

"Your work, my dear Idris, does not recover memories, it *plunders* them. Your magics destroy the fragile structures that defined them. The sacrament of Revivification rebuilds the congregants physically and since there is only ever one soul for one body, that soul reenters immediately. The process of active cognition takes some time, as if they are waking from a long nap. If one is patient, one gets more than information, one gets a person who is capable of thought."

"How is it that the Conqueror appears here as he did in life? No one alive today has seen him, so to sculpt his likeness so faithfully…"

Ariadne laughed indulgently. "I do not sculpt…"

"Your master, then."

"No, they do it themselves. You'll see, they are a bit Protean at first, but over time they grow into their new bodies. The sacrament returns to them the essence of who they are, and that includes what they appear to be. Their bodies mold themselves to those conceptions."

"You make it sound as if they return to life perfectly. Perhaps in a state of grace."

She ignored his mocking tone. "Not quite." Ariadne pointed to one man seated alone. "That is Sixtus Cerialis. He served with Legio IX Hispana, fighting Boudica. He died beneath the wheels of her war chariot, and even now is unnaturally skittish around horse-drawn carts."

"Passions and fears linger, then?"

"Traumatic death does leave a scar, as so often seen in ghosts. But here, made flesh again, most can get beyond that and return to the passions which made them worthy of resurrection." She pointed toward the Resurrection Pool, where a handful of living acolytes had made preparations for the sacrament. "Come. When I had confided my plans to you previously, I had not anticipated this level of success. And I understand your skepticism, which is why I am pleased to have you here today."

He did not offer his arm to her, and she chose to take no umbrage at the slight. That had always been his way—cold silence masking resentment. She still felt its hurtful sting, but muted, because she understood. Her former master, brilliant as he was, had never accepted the need to adapt his thinking to changing realities. Instead, he sought to bend reality to his will, and spurned any evidence which indicated he had failed in those attempts.

Several female acolytes—as were their male counterparts, clad only in plain loincloths and equipped with small, ceremonial daggers—arranged tall, gold candlesticks in a circle at the pool's narrow end. They reverently set thick red candles atop all dozen of them. Symbols cast in gold—this time in the Enochian script John Dee had claimed to discover—had been affixed to the candles and other arcane scripts decorated the candlestick shafts. Male acolytes laid a stiff, rectangular canvas sheet at the heart of the circle, with the foot pointing toward the pool.

Two other men carried a lead-gray box between them. It measured a yard on the longest side, two feet high and two wide. Brass caps reinforced the corners and heavy iron chains wrapped it twice round in each direction. A heavy padlock gathered the chains on the top and secured them tightly. Marcus, following them closely, directed them to set the box down outside the circle of candles. They complied, then withdrew.

"Please, Idris, the key to unbinding the curse."

He nodded assent. "A kitten sleeps in sunlight."

"*A kitten?*" Marcus snorted and advanced toward the box. "It'll be open in no time."

"Wait, Marcus."

"I know the unbinding, my lady, have no fear."

She considered for a heartbeat letting him reap the whirlwind his confidence had sown, but she stayed him with a hand on his shoulder. "This, Marcus, is Idris Rake. You have never met a warlock of his skill, and never will again. To work with his key, you must feel the kitten's fur soft against your skin. Likewise, the warm sun. You must hear the contented purring."

Marcus, being far from a complete idiot, brought his hand back to his belt.

"How can words convey all that?"

"They cannot." Rake's lips pressed into a thin smile. "You must touch the lock and weave your sensory perceptions into the unbinding. Silently."

Marcus looked at his mistress.

"Yes, Marcus, you are capable of this"

Marcus dropped to a knee beside the box. He touched his index finger to a rivet on the lock, as if a child poking a dead animal to see if all life had flown. He closed his eyes and began to work. He'd never been a strong magician—were it not from the way he moved his lips as he worked through the disenchantment, Ariadne would have had no indication that magic was in play.

The lock clicked. Marcus jerked his hand back. The lock clicked and a sliver of spring-steel curled out the keyhole. It glistened with a crystalline fluid.

Marcus paled noticeably.

Rake smiled. "Kittens have claws."

"But *poison*, Idris? Is that not beneath you?"

"I was pressed for time safeguarding the bones. You were hunting me, if you will recall. Poison was the quickest and most efficacious manner I could assembling for dispatching a meddlesome witch."

Ariadne arched an eyebrow. "And the poison, yet viscous after at least a century?"

"Urchin."

"I would have thought you had time back then to gather a sufficient supply of sea urchins."

"True. I defaulted the more plentiful and locally sourced alternative." Rake flicked a silver-sheathed finger at the box. "Go ahead, Marcus. Nothing lethal remains therein."

Marcus carefully freed the chains from the lock and gingerly set aside the latter device. With the help of his two, half-naked aides, he freed the box from the chains. The one who carried the chains away returned with a small pry-bar. Marcus worried a hole in the casket's lead sheathing with it, then peeled the soft metal away. The oaken box beneath had weathered the years well beneath a slab in Holy Trinity Church, with the general hue only slightly darkened with age.

Ariadne raised a hand to her throat. "Gently. Carefully."

Marcus rolled the lead sheets down, and momentarily set the pry-bar down. He gently hit the box along the lid's base with the heel of his hand, then repeated the process using the pry-bar. A small crack appeared between lid and the box. He inserted the bar's tapered edge and worked at opening the box with a gentleness he'd never exhibited outside their lovemaking. He worked his way around, then signaled his two aides to remove the top.

They did so, revealing a tattered cloth lining and a withered corpse of a man laying on his left side. His knees had been drawn up to his chest, and his head bowed to rest on them. His clothing, of much rougher manufacture than the box's lining, had survived well in the grave, with only the odd stain to hint at time's passage.

"That is as I left him." Rake's smile betrayed an uncommon affection for the man in the box. "He'd specified how he was to be buried next to his wife, recalling his early days as a conjuror's assistant at faires and entertainments. She relayed his wishes to me— she believed he'd modeled Prospero on me…"

"An honor you purchased."

"All great artists rely on patrons." Rake sighed. "No money changed hands. He asked that I guarantee his bones would lay undisturbed for eternity. I gave him my word."

"And now you break it."

Rake shrugged. "To you goes the shame for that, Ariadne. Had I foreseen this day, I should have made other arrangements."

"Had you not doubted, you would have foreseen. The shame is yours once more." Ariadne clapped her hands. "Now, ladies, prepare him."

Two acolytes lifted the body from the casket. Another came behind, scooping up all the bits that fell away. Quickly and efficiently, they laid him on the canvas. They straightened his arms and legs. Ancient ligaments popped and parted, but the women carefully returned scattered bones to their proper positions on the canvas. They tucked dried muscles beneath flaps of leathery skin tanned with age. One even combed wisps of brittle hair into place with her fingers. In very short order, the body stretched out as if he had lain in a full length casket.

While they worked, Marcus' aides carried a small table to the side of the pool. On it, Marcus arranged a golden chalice, a sharpened goose quill, a brass key and a razor-edged dagger. He moved with a solemn efficiency which pleased her. She even encouraged him with a smile when he looked back, seeking her approval for the way he'd placed her tools. He beamed, then lit a taper. Ariadne nodded and he proceeded to light the candles, starting nearest the pool, then working his way around widdershins until he completed the circle.

Rake yawned. "That they require such sanctimonious mummery is why I have always had contempt for the gods."

Ariadne stopped Marcus with a simple gesture. "What vice is ritual which allows you to perform miracles?"

"Gods want what gods want." Rake stepped back. "I shall say nothing more."

"That would be appreciated." Ariadne kept her tone even. Now that the bones had been freed from the casket, she did not need her former master. In fact, slitting his throat and adding his bits to the pool would doubtlessly make the ritual much easier. Marcus would have happily killed him for her—yet one more act of undying devotion.

The same devotion the Bard should have for Death. And should have had for me.

But she didn't order Rake's death. It wasn't even that she wanted to kill him herself—while quite willing to do so, she had no burning desire to murder him. What stayed her hand at that very moment was her desire to watch his face as she did what he had thought impossible. She wanted to see his expression, as he realized not only had her powers vastly outstripped his, but that he was entirely in her power, and yet lived only at her whim. *Only then will the doom his arrogance has so long demanded crush him.*

Ariadne moved to the corpse's feet, standing between them and the pool. She raised her hands and immediately the resurrected congregants ceased their mutterings. A few—those most in need of renewal—stood and turned toward the pool. None approached. The acolytes formed a living screen to keep them back. Marcus took his place at her side.

"We gather here, brothers and sisters, beneath our god's black gaze, to accept from Him another of our brethren. Our brother William, who had the gift of composition."

She paused and Marcus handed her the quill. She ran her fingers over it, then returned it to him. Marcus bent and tucked the feather beneath the bones of the corpse's right hand.

She continued as Marcus again stood. "Our brother William had more, and it is this greater gift for which our Lord returns him to us. As with all of you, William had the key to the mysteries of the human heart and mind and soul. He could see what so many others could not, and shared his vision of those mysteries with us."

Marcus gave her the brass key, which she caressed. Her lover took it from her, then placed it in the corpse's left hand. He stood again, and took up the chalice. He knelt at the pool and dipped some of the dark liquid into it. Though no mist rose from the pool, the liquid steamed in the gold cup.

Ariadne accepted the cup from him. "In this cup, Brother William, you shall find all that you once were, and all you shall be. This is the cup of mysteries. This is the cup of Death's blessing. Drink of this, and know you drink of His favor."

Ariadne advanced and lowered herself at the corpse's left shoulder. Marcus knelt at the right and slipped a hand under the corpse's head. He lifted it carefully, as one might raise the head of a person deathly ill, so they could drink more easily. Ariadne tipped the cup, allowing the black liquid to pour through the open mouth and spread out on the canvas. Marcus set the head back down, and the liquid slowly flowed back to seep into the bones.

Marcus took the cup from her and returned it to the table. He picked up the knife. As Ariadne bared her left wrist, he offered her the dagger hilt first.

"Oh, Brother William, you have drunk of His favor. Know that we, your brethren in His Worship, also welcome you. I welcome you." Ariadne drew the knife over her wrist lightly, barely feeling the sting. She held her left hand out, and let a single drop of her blood flow down. It splashed onto the skeletal breastbone and sank in immediately.

Marcus bared his own wrist as Ariadne walked around the skull to his side. He cleared his throat, then spoke in solemn tones. "Oh, brother William, you have drunk of His grace. Know that we, your brethren in His Worship, also welcome you. *I* welcome you."

"Thank you, Marcus."

In a flash of silver, the blade came up from his wrist. Without hesitation, Ariadne stroked the blade across Marcus' throat. She grabbed a handful of his curly black hair and yanked back hard. The wound gaped, bright arterial blood spraying gloriously. She caught her dying lover's shoulder as he sank to his knees, twisting his body so the blood would splash the Bard's face, then directed the flow over his chest and abdomen. By the time she turned him the blood pulsed more weakly, but still drenched the body's legs and feet, pooling on the canvas.

She let the body slump to the floor, willfully ignoring the surprise contorting his features. She wiped the blade on a tiny but dry bit of Marcus' shirt and looked up. "Do not judge me harshly, Idris. Though eager and quite faithful, Marcus did not understand all that my Lord would demand of him. He will be remembered amongst our martyrs, which is considerably more than he could have ever expected had he continued to draw breath."

Rake wiped a smear of blood from his cheek. "Doubtless, you are correct."

"Now, brothers and sisters, your work."

The acolytes now fell upon Marcus. Enthusiastically employing their ceremonial knives, they quickly took Marcus to pieces. While the women minced his flesh and carried away the offal, the men produced hammers to shatter his bones. They scraped out the marrow and, in concert with the women, sank it and the other traces of their comrade into the pool.

They then positioned themselves as would pall bearers and took hold of the canvas. They marched into the pool, which rose to mid-thigh on even the smallest of them, and laid the Bard's blood-soaked corpse on the surface. It did not sink, nor did the dark fluid cling to or stain them as they emerged. They each took two candlesticks and sank them into the Resurrection Pool, again surrounding the corpse. They returned, pristine, to flank Ariadne, facing the pool and the floating corpse.

Ariadne raised the knife overhead, holding it such that it unmistakably resembled a sickle. "By this, Your sign, the blade which cuts all threads of life, we ask you, Lord and Dread Master, to fulfill Your promise to Your brother, William. Life for life. A gift of love so that you may reveal Your love. That all may know the truth of Your love of those who fall before Your magnificence, grant William your favor. Thy will be done."

"Thy will be done."

The tingle began in her belly as the fluid's undulations rippled out from the corpse. As she felt the presence of Death sizzle through her, little waves splashed against the pool's edge, then lapped back onto the canvas. The Bard's corpse began to rise and fall as ripples built into waves beneath him. As the head and feet dipped, they vanished for a moment. They returned, covered in dark red, which froze as if wax. Layer by layer it coated the bones.

The sheer weight of the hardening liquid drew the corpse down. It sank beneath the viscous fluid, which once it had flowed over the body, sealed itself seamlessly and ceased all motion. If not for the beating of her heart and the flicker of candle flames, she could have believed that time itself had died.

Ariadne caught Rake's doubtful expression again. Just wait, just wait.

The Bard burst up through the congealed surface, as if shattering ice on a pond. The whole of the liquid became fluid again, yet remained quite turgid. It flowed slowly down his body, but never off. It molded itself to him, melting into flesh, sinking even deeper. It covered his face in a featureless mask. Waves returned, crashing against him, rocking him back and forth. With each wave that covered him in spray, his appearance became sharper, his muscles redefined, his bones clad again and his skin made whole.

His old rags had fallen away in the pool, but his hands still clutched the quill and the key. The Bard took one staggering step toward the pool's edge, then another. The liquid dripped from the tokens he held, then from him. His flesh became transparent for a moment, then took on the innocent pallor of a newborn's skin.

As he rose, coming up hidden steps inside the pool's edge, the fluid finished renewing his legs. The mask into which the liquid had hardened finally cracked and fell away. The Bard sucked in a huge breath, the gasping breath of a drowning man having finally struck to the surface. His eyes snapped open. He glanced at his hands, then down at his body and finally up at her.

Victory blossomed hot in Ariadne's belly. She smiled, forcing herself to smile triumphantly for Idris' benefit, and opened her arms. *My lord's will is done.* "Welcome, Brother William. We rejoice that you have been returned to us."

The Bard stepped from the pool, pale and naked. "You... did this... to me?"

Ariadne stepped toward him holding out a blanket she'd accepted from one of her acolytes. "By the Will of our Lord, yes."

The Bard smiled, opening his arms so she could wrap the blanket around him. He took another step toward her, more steady by the moment.

She approached, the blanket ready to accept him. "Come, Brother, and be welcome."

The Bard nodded, then buried the key in her throat, and tore it out sideways.

Pain ripped through her. Blood gushed into her shredded windpipe. She coughed a crimson fountain. She wavered, then hit the floor, banging her head on stone. Shimmering lights exploded before her eyes. Panic quickened her heart. More blood spurted.

Then Idris was there, on a knee beside her, his right hand closing the wound and pressing firmly. "You did not heed the warning."

Ariadne stared up at him, bloody hands grasping his shirt tightly. *How?* Her lips moved, but only red bubbles emerged. *Why?*

"When I warned you off this path, it was not because I feared you would surpass me. Nor was it fear you would spend centuries in folly." He stroked her hair with his other hand. "I never doubted you would succeed. Succeed beyond your wildest dreams."

You believed! A smile rose to her lips unbidden, the pain banished for a heartbeat.

"Your success was Death's nightmare." Rake looked over toward the congregants and the idol beyond. "Death did not give you these people out of *love*. They were to appease you, to sate you, to blind you. You did not need to worship Death. You surpassed Death. You could have taken the sickle and sprig yourself, become Death yourself. And when Death realized you would soon understand that truth, retaliation was the only recourse."

Confusion knitted her brows.

"I kept my word to the Bard. His bones are safe, elsewhere." Idris sighed. "Knowing you would eventually want to punish him for the jest, I buried another in his place—one who had cause to hate you. Deimos."

The revivified man grunted at the mention of his name.

Ariadne stiffened, and cold stole into her bones. She met Rake's dark gaze and tried to rise. I *must...*

"Do not struggle, Ariadne. I would remember you as being peaceful."

This is not my end.

"Would that I could save you." Rake, his gaze frigid, raised his blood-stained, silver-gloved hands from her throat. "Alas, right now, you have made my working magic quite simply... impossible."

III

THE EMPRESS

4

THE EMPRESS

HEATHER GRAHAM

Upright: Fertility, femininity, beauty, nature, abundance
Reversed: Creative block, dependence on others

Max Thibault reset the last of the connections for his "Rue Morgue" collection in his family's "Monster Manse" attraction. His older brother, Ethan, who was actually going to take over the business, nodded with satisfaction.

"Love this rogue's gallery!" Ethan said, smiling in admiration of their attraction. Then he looked at Max again. "Thanks for the help. Dad hasn't been up to the manual stuff for a while, and for a last minute adjustment... well, I'm glad you could come by on a break."

"Not to worry; I'm legit. I called it in, I am on break and my partner—you've met him, Dale Hickman—is a great guy, and he's representing our shift, just in case of anything," Max said.

Ethan nodded. He would be playing a vampire count—host of the place—when they opened tonight. He was great for it with his dark eyes and refined features. "Dale is a great guy," he agreed. "As for the manse this year, this gallery... creepy as can be, yes? Darkness, black lights, the fog machine rolling away—it's going to be amazing. Better than ever. Really—thanks for the help!"

"No problem," Max assured him. "Dad is in his sixties now—I guess he kind of gets to slow down, even though I wouldn't suggest it to him!"

Max gazed over their handiwork. He loved the family business; the haunted house had made him and his brother two of the most popular kids in school when they were growing up. Everyone had wanted to come then—and still did.

Ethan had grown up to major in engineering and architecture, Max had gone into criminology. After a few years working for the police in New York City where he'd elected to go to college, he'd come home to become a detective with the NOPD. Max loved his work; he also loved being home. Especially when it was fall—and "Monster Manse" opened for the season.

Monster Manse was housed in a building that had once been a rectory—which meant it sat near one of the oldest churches in the area, St. Maria of the Glen, a church that still maintained the centuries-old burial ground that sprawled around it on all sides. It didn't hurt that their haunted house was next to the burial ground at all.

The rector, Father Sebastian, was a friend. He and Ethan had gone to school together and been friends—which Ethan said hadn't been an easy thing. Father Sebastian had always known that he wanted to be a priest. That meant lectures when they wanted to stay out late, drink, carouse—in other words, behave the way that older teenagers had a tendency to behave.

Sebastian was great for them now, though. He was loved by his congregation, and because he was so human, he had a very active church. He told his flock to enjoy the theatrics—but remember where they could find real demons—and real love and forgiveness. He'd even shown up for their opening the last several years.

Max took another step back.

He set the final cable for their motion activated Jack the Ripper, and took a step to the side. Their eerie Jack—with his top hat, cape, and diabolically evil face—looked up and lifted his blade. The blade was made of plastic, but it had a sheen in the black light that made it appear sharp, real, and lethal. Of course, the fake blood falling from it added to that appearance.

H. H. Holmes—the Chicago mass murderer who had killed dozens, perhaps hundreds, of people during the World's Columbian

Exposition—stood next to him, tapping a hammer he held with his left hand in his right palm. Behind him a bit, and on a pedestal, Countess Elizabeth Bathory looked out benignly, a smile that was purely evil lining her lips. On either side of the carpeted trail on which the brothers now stood, killers looked on, and the Countess Bathory clapped each time one of them lifted a weapon.

"We're ready. You going to be off work in time for the opening tonight?" Ethan asked. He smiled. "We are sold out."

"Of course, we are," Max said, grinning. Life was so odd. He and Max had managed to fight a lot when they were kids. They were just two years apart. From the moment Ethan had left home to go off to Boston for college, however, they had been best friends. Since he'd come back three years ago, Max loved to work at the place whenever he could. He loved helping out. They opened for a number of seasonal events—Christmas, Easter, the Fourth of July, and here and there for special events—but Halloween was their main event.

"Montana and I will be here by six—we're letting the first arrivals in at 7:00 PM, like usual, right?" Max asked.

"Yep. Montana got the night off?" Ethan asked.

"Yes."

Max smiled. Life was really pretty good for him at the moment. Being a homicide detective wasn't easy—but it was something that he felt was important. He loved New Orleans, and working a job he considered to be a way to help his city meant a great deal to him. You didn't have a city like NOLA—wonderful, historic, diverse, and ever growing—without dissension and crime. So he was here, he was home. With a damned good job he loved—and Montana.

He'd known Montana since they'd been in grade school. He'd known her so long that t was difficult sometimes to remember that— once—she'd been a creepy girl. Then she'd been the tomboy that had played with him and Ethan, and then they'd been in high school, sent out of the city after the storm, and then back, and working together on all kinds of projects to bring NOLA back to life.

Then, they'd both gone to college in different states, and drifted apart. Eventually, when he'd made the decision to come home and take work with the NOPD, he'd been out on Frenchman Street with friends, and he'd seen Montana once again.

That had been two years ago. They'd both been twenty-seven at the time, older, and maybe—just maybe—wiser than what they had been as kids. Still, it had taken him some time to get Montana to really be with him. They'd dated forever before they'd moved in together. She had a problem with commitment—something she admitted. She'd almost gotten married once. Her fiancé had been killed in the service, and Montana had told Max that she'd nearly fallen apart; she'd really had to learn to live again.

Live on her own.

He knew she never wanted to feel that broken again.

Montana was a musician and played guitar with a group called "Three Men and a Girl." She was a talented musician; she always had been. She had really grown up, as well. Her facial features were fine and angled and beautiful; her eyes were, of course, the same deep blue they had always been. They just seemed to look at him so differently.

At first, of course, there had been a lot of laughter, a lot of wow! Old friend back in town, let's rehash some of the past and find out what we've each been doing. Then he'd thought that she might be with one of the "Three Men" who formed three-quarters of the band, but she was not. Pete and David were each married, and Justin was gay and just about to marry his partner, as well.

She had just needed to keep something of a distance.

But, still, they'd finally gotten together, and even though they should have been a little bit old-hat by now—they'd seen each other almost every day for the last two years—he still felt that he was just about the luckiest man in the world. Montana was beautiful, fun, vivacious—and she loved him. Now they were going to be married—one day. She told him she really believed that they would do it, that she was ready to do it—she did love him, so much. Yes, definitely, as soon as they figured out just exactly how and where they wanted to do the deed. It was important to both of them, and they'd mulled over different churches and venues. They'd even considered the Monster Manse—since it could be used for many different things. It did, after all, even substitute for Santa's Workshop every season.

He was lucky; he needed to remember to simply thank God for what he had.

She was quick to say, "I love you."

She never said, "I need you."

Max's phone buzzed; it was his partner, Dale Hickman.

"Just making sure you're doing okay at the old manse," Dale said. "I'm invited, right?"

Max grinned. "Yeah, you're invited—and I'm on my way back right now. We'll head out right after our shift."

"Yeah! Our shift is over in about an hour, thank the lord, today. Bunches of crazy stuff with people seeing things. Halloween is on the way."

"I haven't been gone that long—did anything else happen?"

"Patrol has been getting a lot of calls about kooks—and drunks. I've just finished up the paperwork on the Watford case. D.A. told me no problem. No jury would believe that Alma Watford accidentally shot her husband with a shotgun—five times."

"You were worried? Never mind. No one ever knows a jury, huh?"

"What about Montana?"

"She's meeting us at the manse with a friend."

"Cool. Tell me the friend is cute?"

"She is. See you soon."

Max hung up his phone.

"Gotta go; I'll see you at six," he told his brother. "Not long now—I'm betting some people will already be parking and getting into line."

"Yep—and thanks!" Ethan called.

Max turned to leave.

Creating motion.

Jack the Ripper raised his bloody knife again.

Countess Elizabeth Bathory offered him her evil smile.

They were amazing electronics, or whatever one wanted to call them.

They looked real.

He was a hardcore cop, but…

Something about the knife…

About the countess's smile…

He actually shuddered as he walked out, a chill racing through him.

Someone walking over his grave, his mother would have said.

He hadn't realized until he was older that it was an odd saying for someone who had hailed from NOLA where most interments were above ground, in the "cities of the dead,"—and like the one by the manse, attached to a church. Places where families were buried in small mausoleums that resembled little houses—above ground burials. He would never be in the ground; his family owned a vault at Lafayette Cemetery in the Garden District.

But, in a way, the saying made sense.

Because he felt cold and clammy… as if he lay among the dead!

He gave himself a fierce shake. He was a cop. He-Man cop, as Montana liked to tease. And he sure as hell wasn't frightened by any Halloween attraction owned by his own family!

*

"Hey, it's New Orleans, and it's something that people just do in New Orleans!" Brenda Smyth said with determination. "I've done a lot of research. Read about the best people. There's one in particular. She's got raves on all the tourist sites—the Empress! She's great. New to the city. She'll read tea leaves, or your palm, or your tarot cards. And it's a great tea shop as well. They have coffee and cookies and the like, too. You said that you were thirsty."

Montana Gautier sighed inwardly.

She loved Brenda, but like most of her friends who visited her here, there was no such thing as a simple lunch, dinner—or a quick drink.

Everyone wanted voodoo, magic, vampires, or seers.

And it all made her so miserable!

Then again, what could she say? Max and his family did own the Monster Manse, and they would be heading there soon.

"I know the shop, Brenda," she said. "I live here, remember?"

"You live in the Garden District—not the French Quarter. I, on the other hand, am a tourist—and therefore, probably much better informed on what's happening locally than a local. And I have done extensive research on the French Quarter!" Brenda announced. "I know you—and what you said to me over and over again a zillion times. You love the French Quarter, but that's not all there is to New Orleans. Yes, you come in, but you go everywhere else, too. So, indulge me! Let a tourist tell you about the French Quarter."

Montana smiled. She and Brenda had been roommates all through their years at Carnegie-Mellon. Brenda was a fantastic violinist—she now played for Broadway and Off-Broadway shows. This was the first vacation she had taken in years, and her first trip—ever—to New Orleans.

During the day, they'd seen the Audubon Zoo and the Aquarium of the Americas. It was almost time to head over to the Monster Manse to meet up with Max and Dale Hickman.

"Okay, okay, you want to go to the shop. Great. We'll go. I'll have tea—but I'm not having anything read."

"Oh, come on!"

"No!" She didn't mean to snap the word the way she did. She just liked to avoid fortune tellers of any kind.

She'd never forget that, right before she heard the news about Brody, she'd laughed with friends at Jackson Square, and seen a palm reader there who looked at her and told her that she'd have a long and happy life. That everything was wonderful.

She'd still been smiling when the news that he had been killed had come.

Brenda was oblivious. She grinned brilliantly at Montana. "Great! I love it. Oh, I love New Orleans! I love all the decorations out for Halloween. I love the voodoo shops and the costume stuff and the masks and… tonight! Tall, dark, and studly really owns a haunted house? By a church and a graveyard. Oh, that is too… too cool!"

Montana managed a smile as well. Brenda was always so full of life; she was great. "Max's family owns the attraction; his brother, Ethan, is actually going to take it over soon from their father. He's an electronics genius. They buy most of their animatronic characters, but Ethan actually created a lot of the effects that help make it so amazing. There's a dining room set-up where a mummy and a bunch of other creatures—vampires, werewolves, ghosts—appear to be having a celebration dinner, and they move, and do all kinds of cool things. Ethan is pretty amazing and really works the place. Max… well, Max really loves to be a cop."

"Very, very cute cop—and young for homicide, huh? Now I know why you were never that into anyone in school—you were waiting for him."

"Nope. I'd forgotten about him until he showed up one night when the guys and I were playing. Anyway, let's get tea. We'll go through the manse. Then we'll take you to a place where you can get the best crawfish boil, shrimp and grits, and bread pudding in the city."

"I'm game for that!" Brenda shivered, delighted. "Cool. Lead on."

Montana miraculously found street parking on Chartres Street and she knew the shop that Brenda wanted to see.

"This-away," she said.

In just a matter of minutes, they arrived at the shop.

New Orleans went really crazy every October, but they were still in the middle of September—right when the Halloween antics were all just beginning. She had to admit; she especially loved NOLA during Halloween season. The city truly embraced all that was fun—and creepy—about the holiday. There were all kinds of balls throughout the city, and some of the costuming was absolutely amazing. She loved to dress up herself; now and then, she'd served as a guide for Max's family attraction, but that was often difficult because her band was always playing during the season, as well. And if they didn't play at Halloween, they might not be asked back to play when they weren't in season.

The place was called "Tarot and Tea." And Montana hadn't lied; she had been there before. But only for tea. They carried a really nice selection of teas; you could buy a cup or a bag to take home.

The place was decked out for Halloween. Skeletons hung here and there from the rafters; spider webs covered corners and sconces and other paraphernalia. A little witch on a broomstick advertised that readings were available by appointment.

"By appointment!" Montana said.

"And you think I don't have an appointment?" Brenda asked her. "Oh, ye of little faith!"

"But, I don't want an appointment!"

"And I didn't get you one!" Brenda assured her with a laugh. "Just me."

While she might have been to the shop before, Montana never had met "The Empress." While Brenda headed in for her reading, Montana wandered in the front of the shop. There were charming little wooden "tea" tables all about and a rack that held papers and magazines. She couldn't help but notice the front page of the main national paper. The headline read: "Halloween Horror Killer Strikes in Texas!"

As she was glancing at the article, a young man behind the tea counter spoke to her. "Terrible, huh? Thank God, it's Texas—no offense to Texas—but we sure do get our share of kooks here. I'm

Donald. Donald Levin. Can I get you some tea while you're waiting? Complimentary with a reading—even a friend's reading!" he said with a grin.

She ordered tea. And Donald told her that "The Empress" was actually Tina Mayberry from Williamsburg, Virginia, but she had lived all around the world and studied with some of the best people in the business and knew the cards backward and forward. Even they—Donald, and his wife, Louisa—were astounded by the amount of rave reviews they received on tourist sites since The Empress had come there.

"I'm just not terribly into readings—of any kind," Montana said.

"Afraid of what they might say?"

"No." What difference did it make? Anything learned was a lie! "I don't believe in predetermined destiny in any way, that's all. But, on the other hand, I do believe in people getting carried away in self-fulfilling prophecies. Oh, I'm sorry—I sound horrible. I won't say this to people coming in for readings, I promise!"

At that moment, Brenda came out from the curtained-off back of the shop, her reading having come to an end. She was followed by a slim, attractive, middle-aged woman with pitch-black hair and brilliant green eyes. She wasn't in any kind of a fortune-telling get-up—she wasn't even wearing a Halloween costume or token hat. She appeared regal—and regular, just nice and friendly.

"Thank you! You're wonderful," Brenda said, her face lit up in a brilliant smile as she and the woman walked out. Seeing Montana, Brenda stopped short. "Hey! Montana, this is Tina—"

"Mayberry, yes, thank you. Donald told me," Montana said, reaching out a hand to shake with the attractive older woman.

She realized that the woman had been holding a deck of tarot cards in her right hand; she went to shift them in order to shake hands, as Montana had offered.

But the cards fell to the floor.

It really was quite extraordinary. Most of the cards stayed together in the container. One—just one--slipped from the pack. It seemed to skid across the floor—and land directly in front of Montana.

"Oh, I'm sorry! Go figure on that," Montana said, reaching down for the card.

"Not your fault at all," Tina Mayberry said. "I dropped the cards, and it's not as if they were heavy or anything!"

She smiled, a great smile as Montana reached down for the card.

"The Empress! How fitting," Brenda said.

Montana tried to hand the card to Tina. It seemed to have a mind of its own and slipped from her fingers again. Once on the floor, it seemed to spin so that the elegant woman on the card was actually staring at Montana.

"The Empress, yes." Tina said.

There had to be a wind—a draft from an air-system of some kind—in the shop. The card suddenly spun around.

"The Empress of the tarot," Tina murmured, looking at Montana. "The card... it's your card."

"My card? Is she some kind of an evil card?" Montana asked.

"No, no—and cards aren't evil. None of the cards are evil, not even death. Death can merely mean one door is closing," Tina said, sounding distracted. She kept studying Montana. "The Empress is a very good card. Usually, she is all about femininity and fertility, love and hearth and home, all good things."

"Usually?" Montana said. She wasn't sure if she wanted to hear good things or bad things.

Either would be a lie!

Tina smiled. "Even inverted, it's nothing bad. It's just..." She broke off "... you know, it's not a bad thing to be dependent on other people, and have other people dependent on you."

"Of course not!" Montana said.

She wondered suddenly if she'd spoken too quickly.

Sometimes, she was afraid. She really, really, really loved Max. She worried that she loved him more than he could possibly love her. She worried that she was a musician. A pretty good one, yes, and she wasn't bad to look at, but...

Max was beautiful; tall, broad-shouldered, with a strong jaw and handsome features, dark eyes and dark hair, a full and generous mouth, and a killer smile. He was always confident, always in control; he could laugh so easily, but take charge of any situation in a heartbeat...

But she had already lost out once. Lost out to another time when she had really loved someone, when she had dared to live with another person. Have another man so entangled in her life that life itself was nothing without him.

Tina reached for Montana's fingers, ready to finish the handshake that had never happened. She'd been about to smile or laugh.

But then...

It was simply uncanny. Eerie. Montana was convinced that the woman had a *buzz-shock toy*, or something else in her hand. When their palms connected, it seemed that a jolt went through Montana, a sizzle of lightning throughout her.

Then Tina spoke swiftly, earnestly. "He needs you as much as you need him. But, tonight…call for him! You will need him. Don't hesitate; it's not a joke. Do it."

Montana jerked her hand back. Instinctively, she went for the card on the floor again, trying to pretend that nothing had happened, nothing at all.

Somehow, she refrained from stomping on it. She caught the card firmly between her fingers and handed it the tarot reader.

"Not to worry—we're just out for a fun evening at a family place," she said. "And, actually, we'd better get going! Thank you all—thank you. Brenda, let's head on out," Montana said.

"Yes, thank you—" Brenda began.

Montana had her arm. She was determined. She had Brenda out of the shop, down Chartres, heading for the car.

"Hey!" Brenda protested. "She's really nice—and good! You should listen to her. We should go back. She seemed to be concerned."

"Oh, Brenda, come on! She makes her money that way! I have nothing against anyone making a living, really, but I'm not going to fall into that kind of… bull! We need to get going, really. I'd like to be there when Max and Dale arrive. You're going to like Dale; he's a great guy."

Brenda had fallen silent. "Whatever," she said after a moment.

When they reached the car, she was still quiet.

As they neared Monster Manse she turned to Montana to speak. "You had a bad deal, but that was five years ago now. You have a great guy. Let it go; let it be. Open your mind—you don't have to believe in any of this, but, at the least, you can be polite."

"I wasn't rude!"

"She said something about depending on people and you went ballistic. The Empress! There's good in the card, too, you know."

"It's just a card! It isn't good or evil."

"No, the card isn't good or evil. And I don't think that I believe in telling the future, either. The future is what we make it—that's what you've always said, and it's what I feel, too. But, sometimes, something like a tarot deck and a good reader can beat the hell out of hours with a shrink. The cards can make us see things in ourselves. Hey, that particular Empress even looked like you."

"Brenda!"

"Gorgeous! Really, she has a stunning deck. And the Empress is gorgeous!"

"Flattery will not get you anywhere," Montana assured her.

Brenda smiled, but her smile faded quickly. "I'm afraid," she said softly. "I'm afraid for you. You're not scared?"

Scared? She was miserably terrified. Damn, but she hated fortune-tellers, palm readers...

And tarot cards.

"We're going to a haunted attraction—we're supposed to be scared."

Brenda threw her hands up in the air. "All right. Okay, forget it all. Yep, fun. We'll have some fun. Eek! Creepy fun. Yeah, that's the ticket! Good old creepy, bloody, ghoulish fun!"

*

Max and Dale were about to leave for the day and head out to the manse when Sergeant Jeffries came in and asked everyone to stay for a quick meeting; actually, they weren't so much asked as they were told—the meeting was mandatory.

The whole precinct seemed to have gathered for a meeting; not just the detectives, but every officer who wasn't on the street. Lieutenant Deauville had gathered them and he had a PowerPoint on the screen, showing them crime scene photos from Baton Rouge and Houston.

"They're calling him the Halloween Horror," Deauville said. He was a lean, fit, hard man with a bald head, a man who was great in a leadership position. He had the ability to wield firm authority—but do it with complete courtesy. "I think you all heard about the attack in Houston a week ago. But, this is just in from our fellows over in Baton Rouge. His last attack was at Jumpin' Jack-O-Lantern's there; he hid out with the automated Halloween displays. He managed to take down a store manager to kidnap a young woman; she was later found dead in the river." Images flashed on the screen. "Prior to that," Deauville continued, clicking a button that brought another image up on the screen, "he struck at a costume shop in Houston; three dead, slashed to death in the animatronic monster session—which is where he earned his media moniker. Here's the thing: he's in Louisiana, folks. And he likes big cities. He might have headed to Mississippi, or even back Texas way. But he might be here."

He might be here. Here. In NOLA. And Max's family owned the Monster Manse, a perfect venue for the sick son of a bitch!

"We have to go now," he said quietly. He was standing next to Dale, his partner since he'd joined the NOPD, a man who made up for his medium build and stature with long hours at the gym and the shooting range. They were friends as well as partners; there was no one else he'd rather have guarding his back.

"What?" Dale, frowning with his concentration on what they had been seeing, turned to look at him.

"Now, now, we have to get to the manse. I'm going to call Ethan; stop the opening until I can get there."

"Oh, hell, yeah. I'll tell the sergeant why we're slipping out!" Dale said.

While Dale moved around the precinct room, Max slipped into the hall, dialing his brother's number.

"Hey, where are you?" Ethan asked him. "Montana and her friend are here. She's so amazing, by the way. We had to cut the ribbon for the season and start. Montana led the way in."

"No, no, Ethan," Max said. "Get everyone out… there's a killer on the loose."

"A killer?"

"The guy from Texas—the guy who killed the people in the costume shop in Texas," Max explained quickly. "He struck in Baton Rouge now," Max explained quickly.

"That's Baton Rouge—"

"About a two hour drive! Ethan, a haunted house like ours is perfect for this guy. They haven't caught him; he moves quickly. Please! I'm on my way with Dale. Get everyone out. Get them all out, now. Please!"

*

Okay, it was going to be great, ghoulish, creepy, bloody fun!

Max and Dale were running late. That happened. They were cops.

Montana didn't mind. She loved Ethan—he was a great brother to Max. And she loved the attraction. There were a number of costumed "ghouls" running around, mainly to keep people in order as they went through the house—and through the little café/bar and gift shop.

And so—in her creepiest voice—she welcomed people to the first night of Monster Manse for the season, cut the ribbon, and walked in first.

Ghouls cut the others off right behind her—including Brenda. She was to be swallowed up first—and then the others could enter in groups. A grand opening was always a good idea. And it was also important that they keep crowd control if the motion-activated monsters were going to have their desired effect on the guests. But, as the door shut behind her, she found herself hugged by one ghoul—Sydney Hold, with whom she'd gone to high school—and then another, Tracy Latham. They laughed and chatted for a minute, and then a very tall vampire—a new hire, a young man Montana hadn't met—urged her to start on through and get some of the noise makers going as they opened the doors.

"Hey, Connie Levine is halfway through!" Tracy told her. "She'll be thrilled to see you."

"Great!"

Montana hadn't thought that she could be really frightened; she'd been to the manse dozens of times. In fact, she'd gone with Max and Ethan on one of their buying trips out to Hollywood, California. She'd discovered that she loved "Monsterpalooza" where Ethan often shopped for makeup and fabricated pieces or creatures. She was not frightened by the fake.

But there was fog whirling around in the corridors. And out of the fog, a giant werewolf suddenly lunged at her, growling and snapping its teeth.

She jumped. High. And a scream escaped her. The thing was in an alcove and it was really, truly scary.

She kept walking. Imps, demons, devils—scenes of ghoulish torture surrounded her. She went through the dining room where the mummy and friendly ghosts and skeletons sat down to dine together. The next room was geared toward the rougarou—a Louisiana swamp creature—and in the next, cackling witches worked around a bubbling cauldron.

It wasn't until the next room—which had Rue Morgue emblazoned in red on the identifying sign above the door—that she found Connie Levine. Her friend was standing in a little statuary niche, just inside the door. She was dressed in a maid's uniform a-la *The Rocky Horror* Show. Her head was down; her little white maid's cap dipped low on her forehead.

Connie seemed to be indicating the rogue's gallery before her that included Jack the Ripper, H.H. Holmes, Charles Manson and a few of his family members, and--swirling around to stare at her with an evil smile as she entered the room--Countess Bathory.

Montana smiled. The animatronics weren't half as frightening, she thought, as Connie Levine—and the way she stood in the niche... just waiting to move, too.

Jack the Ripper let out a frightening whisper of sound.

"My dear... a moment of your time! Only a moment!" He raised his knife.

Montana hadn't known that the animated characters spoke. Eerie music played throughout, and sometimes, a voice over.

Nothing like the whisper of this Jack!

She looked back; she was still ahead of other people. She could risk a minute to say hello to Connie before hurrying on to allow her friend to scare those on their way.

Connie's head was bowed; her neck was twisted eerily to the side—that indicated that they had, indeed, reached the rogue's gallery!

That was surely for show. Even in high school, she'd been the consummate performer. Now, Montana was certain, Connie could look up suddenly and scare the bejesus out of someone!

She felt her phone buzz in her pocket as she headed toward Connie.

She'd turned off the sound for the grand opening, before making her show of boldly and bravely entering the house.

It was Max. But, even as she answered it, she smiled. She heard delighted screams as others came in behind her.

"Hey! Get here!" she whispered. "The place is nuts—fun nuts!"

"Montana, get out. Get out now. I'm on my way. Get out of the house."

"Max, this is me, Montana—"

"I'm serious; I'm begging you. I've told Ethan to get everyone out. No joke, Montana, no Halloween prank. A killer in Texas moved on to Baton Rouge. That was last night. This is the perfect venue for him. Get out, please. I'm almost there… just a few minutes. But, get the hell out—now!"

She had reached Connie. Her friend still hadn't lifted her head; hadn't moved.

"All right; I'm actually with one of the actor-slash-guides now," she said. "Connie. Come on, Connie, look up, quit with the scare tactics—it's just Montana!"

She touched her friend's face.

She felt something sticky and then smelled the coppery scent around her friend at the same time. It took only a moment to realize that she was dead. That her throat had been slashed ear-to-ear.

"My dear! A moment of your time, only a moment!"

The whisper came again.

Montana turned.

Jack the Ripper had spoken.

He had come down off the pedestal.

He was standing in front of her, and his knife was dripping blood. Real blood.

Montana let out a shriek—and ran.

*

Max reached the place just as Ethan was trying to make his way through the crowd that was spilling out of the house.

"Where is she? Where is Montana?" he asked his brother.

Ethan looked like hell. He shook his head. "Someone said that they heard her screaming, shouting for everyone to get out. And someone else said that one of the creatures was coming after them, and Montana tripped the creature. I don't know what's true, I don't… I'm trying…"

"Has anyone been hurt or killed—seen anyone? Anything weird?"

"It's—it's a haunted attraction!" Ethan said. "Seen anything… weird? Like what?"

"She's in there!" A young woman suddenly shouted, beating on Max's arm. Max looked at her, distracted.

"I'm Brenda—and she's in there," the young woman said. "Montana is in there! You've got to get her... she'll die, oh, God, the tarot card... said that she'd need you, she needs you... get the hell in there!"

"We can't reach two of our employees on the radio system." Ethan said.

"Get the lights on!" Max told his brother.

"I can't! Someone messed with the fuse box. I've been trying!" his brother told him.

"The card! The tarot!" Brenda moaned.

He didn't need any tarot card to tell him what to do; nor did he need Montana's hysterical friend. He needed to find Montana.

"I'm behind you!" Dale shouted.

Max barely muttered, "Excuse me!" as he made his way through the people pouring out. A lone girl—shrieking her head off—raced by him, and then he was alone in the vestibule. He pushed open the door to the gauntlet of rooms that stretched out before him. The music was silent,

He knew the rooms—and he knew the creatures. Ethan had apparently turned off the fog machines, but fog still whirled low around the floor. He raced through one room and a werewolf jumped out at him, fangs glistening, a roar of sound coming from him. He passed through the dining room where creepy creatures gathered for a meal.

"Montana!"

He shrieked her name. Nothing.

And then, he heard her call his name.

"Max!"

She was ahead, past the dining room, past the rougarou... in the room where the witches stirred away at their cauldron.

He burst into the room just in time to see her.

She was fighting with the Jack the Ripper motion-activated character.

Except, of course, it wasn't any kind of a machine or fabrication; it was a man, a real man, dressed up in a Victorian frock coat and a tall hat.

And carrying a very real knife.

He drew his weapon and shouted out a warning. "Stop! Let her be!"

The fighting pair swirled around; he couldn't shoot. He could hit Montana.

He raced toward the two of them. The man held a knife high. Montana was holding her own, fighting, kicking, writhing, trying to escape the madman's grasp. But the man seemed to have the strength of a zillion tons of adrenalin.

Max caught his arm.

The arm that wielded the knife. Montana shrieked, breaking free, and then… the knife was turned toward Max. And despite his shouts for Montana to get out, she wasn't doing so. With a scream of rage, she hurtled herself back on the man with the knife. To Max's astonishment, the knife went clattering to the floor as Montana bit the man's arm, hard. But still, the madman seemed to have the strength of a dozen men. And with that one arm, he flung Max across the room.

He was flying, and he knew it. Still, he drew out his gun. And he fired. His aim was good.

The "Jack the Ripper" wasn't a rougarou, a machine, or any kind of a monster. He was a man, and Max's aim was true. He saw the man take the bullet dead center in the chest.

And go down.

Then, Max sailed right into the wall—as if he'd been hurtled like a rocket into space—and stars burst before his eyes.

Then there was only darkness.

*

She hadn't been hysterical through any of it; she'd been, Montana thought, logical, at the least. Terrified beyond imagination, but not hysterical.

But, then…

There was Max. On the floor. Crumpled in a ball.

The lights were finally back on; Dale was there, on his phone, getting help, getting back-up, getting ambulances… shouting out that it was a crime scene. Then he was on his knees by Montana, and he was searching for a pulse, some sign that Max was alive.

Montana couldn't even care that Dale was there—or that anyone was there. "No, no, you can't… you can't die on me. You can't save me—and then die on me!" She said.

Not again, God no, please.

She held his hand, weeping.

"I love you. I love you." She whispered it over and over.

Suddenly she couldn't help but remember the tarot card. The way it had spun from the deck.

The Empress. Home, hearth, health, fertility… and reversed. A warning. She needed him, God, yes, she needed him, and she hated it, because she was so afraid of pain. And yet this…

"Please, I love you. I need you. Max, please…"

"A pulse!" Dale told her. "He has a pulse! We've got to get out of the way, the EMTs are here, Montana, come on!"

She moved away. The police were rushing in and medical help was there, too. She knew that the crime scene techs who had arrived would be moving past them.

They would find her friend, Connie. They would take pictures, there would be an autopsy…

She couldn't even weep for her friend, Montana thought. Not now; she was in too much shock. She could only pray for Max.

Dale saw to it that she could ride in the ambulance with Max. Ethan would come behind them, with Dale and Brenda.

The police would handle the haunted manse.

And the corpse of their far-too-real Jack the Ripper.

*

It was almost an entire day before Max opened his eyes.

Montana was there. She jumped up, tears springing into her eyes again. She spoke incoherently.

"I thought I'd lost you; I think the doctors thought we'd lost you, too," she said.

He smiled and he touched her cheek gently. "I thought I was lost myself, for a bit," he told her. He had a strange reflective look in his eyes.

"What? What? Max?" she asked him.

"I felt I was in some distant land… or an alternate universe, maybe! I thought that I had to leave, that I knew you couldn't see me, but, I somehow had to say goodbye. But, then there was this woman. She walked toward me as if she was nobility… she was very regal. And she said, 'no, Max. You can't go. She needs you. She said that she needs you.' And then I felt myself coming back, as if whisking through time and space… opening my eyes, and seeing you."

Montana started to shake. She tried to sound light, as if she were joking, as if it was all part of the hospital and the knock on his head and the fact that she might well have died herself.

"Did she have a tiara or a crown?"

"She did! In fact, she kind of resembled you. Maybe she was you, deep in my heart, calling me back!" he said.

"Maybe," Montana whispered. "Maybe she is me, and what is in my mind, and all my fear… and what faith I need to have. I'm not at all sure, Max. I think she was the Empress."

"The Empress?" he murmured.

She shook her head. "Doesn't matter," she told him softly.

And it didn't.

But later—weeks, later, actually—when Max had long been out of the hospital and they were finally planning their wedding at the cathedral, she went back to the teashop.

Donald was still there; the Empress had moved on.

"Where is she?" Montana asked.

"I believe she went on to Salem. You know, after all that craziness at Monster Manse, she said that she was done here, that she'd done what she'd come to do. She had to move on.

"Do you have an address for her?"

"I do—but, you know what? I asked friends in Massachusetts— this address is actually out in the Atlantic Ocean. I'm sorry. She's just… gone."

Montana thanked him and left. She hurried down the street; Brenda was back in town. She and Dale—left together while Max was in the hospital—had become an item.

They were all due to have dinner at *Antoine's*.

A nice thing to do in New Orleans!

As she hurried down Chartres, she passed a window that displayed tarot cards. In the fan of cards, she saw the Empress.

And she paused.

"Thank you!" she said softly.

She didn't know if she was foolish or not. She didn't know if the woman she had met had been some kind of a strange adult Mary Poppins, or if she hadn't really existed at all—if she had only been the reflection of what was inside each person she saw.

Didn't matter.

She smiled at the card.

"Thank you, thank you!" she repeated.

Then she hurried on, ready for her future, whatever it might bring.

5

THE EMPEROR

LINDA J. PARISI

Upright: Stability, power, aid, protection, a great person, conviction, reason
Reversed: Benevolence, compassion, credit, confusion to enemies, obstruction,
immaturity

Settling Station, NY 1983

"S-s-so, Trembles. Who'd you pick?"

Normally, ignoring Hugh Devlin was easy. But not this time,
Alan Trembley thought.

This time he knew the Triumvirate would really laugh at him.

Thwack! The slap on the back of his head stung. He sat down,
rubbing the abused area. Poor Ollie. They both suffered the
ignominy of brains instead of brawn. Poor Ollie.

"I asked you a question, Trembles."

Alan hated being smart sometimes, hated that he was always in
classes with older boys. And now even a girl. Funny, they picked on
him way more than they picked on her.

Deciding silence was the better part of valor, Alan ignored
Trevor Chadwick as he sat down next to him. "Ooooh," Trevor
mocked, throwing up his hands and feigning terror. "He's too
frightened to answer."

Jasper Niebold stopped in front of his desk, looming like a large bear. The assignment was to choose and "become" a Roman Emperor for their Ancient Civilizations class. "I'll bet you didn't even pick one," Jasper said, the disdain in his voice pricking him deep inside. Most of all he hated the Triumvirate. Devlin, Chadwick, and Niebold.

Niebold sat down in front of him. Alan wondered if that was to allow him to hide, or so as not to be seen. Did Mr. Strickland share their sentiments? After all Alan was the anomaly, even more so than Christine.

"Lay off him," Christine Hathaway ordered.

The Excelsior School, with deep roots going all the way back to 1829 and a proud heritage for the young men who graced its hallowed hallways; men who became the movers and shakers of this country. How they must mourn for those days. Alan knew Mr. Strickland did. His voice caught as he acknowledged Christine, forced to accept that she even existed. But money talked. The school was in financial trouble from what he'd heard his parents say. And besides, the times they were a-changing.

"All right, ladies and gentlemen. Take your seats please." Mr. Strickland waited as the room quieted down. "Good. Let's begin. I hope you all took my request seriously and selected an Emperor." He glanced around the room. "As moderator of the class," his teacher continued. "I've chosen Julius Caesar. I'm sure you'll all agree that's appropriate."

No one would dare disagree. Despite the changes in the student population, teachers still ruled at The Excelsior.

"Excellent. Should there be any duplication, the first applicant wins." He paused then pointed. "Mr. Devlin? You start."

Of course. The Triumvirate would go first. Always Devlin, Chadwick, and Niebold.

"I chose Augustus," Hugh began. "Because he was considered to be the first Emperor. His reign lasted from 27 BC to 14 AD."

"Good choice, Mr. Devlin," Mr. Strickland nodded. "Let's keep this short. Just an introduction. You'll all need to go into depth later." He looked around the room. "Mr. Chadwick?"

"I chose Vespasian, sir. For his military prowess. 69-79 AD."

"Not surprising, Mr. Chadwick, considering your family history." A long line of West Point graduates. "Mr. Niebold?"

"Hadrian, sir."

"Ms. Hathaway?"

Wow, Alan thought. That was an unexpected honor. Right after the Triumvirate.

Christine rose, flashing him a little grin. "Marcus Aurelius, sir. For his dedication to duty. 161-180 AD."

"Indeed," Mr. Strickland murmured. "Impressive choice."

Alan listened to others then started as his name was called. Dead last. "I chose Antonius Pius. He had the most peaceful reign of all the Emperors. 138-161 AD."

"Figures," Trevor sneered, not trying to hide his contempt.

"Too afraid to fight," Jasper agreed.

Strangely enough, Mr. Strickland supported his choice. "Gentlemen. Be not so quick to judge. Antonius Pius is considered one of the Five Good Emperors."

Before anyone could answer, the bell rang, saving Alan from more ridicule. "A brief history and lineage for tomorrow's class," his teacher called out. Several classmates groaned. There was a Physics midterm tomorrow. But Alan smiled to himself. He'd anticipated the request and already had the assignment put together.

Hurrying out of the classroom, Alan caught up with Christine. "Tha-Thank you."

Her smile warmed her soft brown eyes. "It's okay Alan, I get it."

"Ignorance is bliss."

"You hardly ever stutter with me. Do they frighten you that much?"

"The Triumvirate?"

She laughed, getting his reference immediately, and nodded.

Alan loved the sound, crisp and clear like music. "Not really," he answered honestly. "Something just stops inside, like a connector that won't quite make contact."

She turned to go to Political Science and Alan had Physics. "See you later."

As he walked down another hallway toward the front offices, Alan saw Mr. Strickland talking to some parents. Had they found Ollie? Alan missed his friend. They'd gone to sleep five days ago, and when Alan awoke, Ollie was gone. Alan didn't think much of it at first, but as the day wore on and Ollie wasn't in class, or at lunch, he began to worry. The next day he got up the nerve to approach Mr.

Pickering, the Headmaster. Oliver was missing, he was told. He wasn't at school and he hadn't reached home yet.

The day droned on and the hole inside Alan grew. His classes complete, he walked into his room feeling very alone. Ollie was a good kid and made Alan laugh. Placing his books on Ollie's desk, he walked over to the window, watching some boys play soccer on the green, sleeves rolled, ties flapping in the wind. For a moment he wished he was strong instead of smart. Then he'd be able to fit in. With a heavy sigh, he wondered yet again. *Where are you, Ollie?*

The next day, after class, he summoned the nerve to ask Mr. Strickland. "I-I s-s-saw you with some parents yesterday. Were they Oliver's, sir?"

Mr. Strickland sat back in his chair, his usual stern visage softening. "I'm afraid so, Alan." He watched his teacher rub his face with his hands, and then drop them with a sigh. Sorrow reflected in his gaze.

"You think s-s-something's happened to him too, don't you?" Alan asked, twisting his hands in his pockets, dreading the answer.

"Yes, yes I do." Mr. Strickland leaned forward in earnest. "Do you have any idea why he might run away?"

"N-n-no sir. I swear. W-w-we'd been studying for our Physics midterm. He was talking about going home for spring break."

"Did he seem terribly homesick to you?"

Alan shook his head, that emptiness filling his belly again. Mr. Strickland nodded. "Very well, Alan. Thank you. Now I must warn you. The police are coming back again. They're probably going to be more forceful when they speak with you this time. Answer their questions as honestly and as best you can."

A prediction of bad tidings, the police did exactly that right after his Physics mid-term.

At first, they were polite. "Where were you five nights ago?"

"In b-bed."

"And did Oliver go to bed too?"

"Y-yes."

Then they got angry. "That's all you remember? You didn't hear anything? You didn't wake up? How could you not have woken up? He must've made some noise."

"N-NO! D-d-don't you think I w-wish I h-had?"

"You were good friends. Why didn't he tell you anything? He told you something. He must have."

"H-he did-dn't!"

But Alan survived the interview. Wrung out, he skipped dinner and lay on his bed wondering where Ollie could be and what could've happened to him. Was Ollie lying in a ditch somewhere? Could he have gotten kidnapped trying to hitch a ride to the train station?

Christine stopped by after dinner with a smuggled piece of chocolate cake. His favorite. "Thank you."

"Are you all right?" she asked, sitting down on Ollie's bed.

"Something's happened to him," Alan said, sitting up across from her and placing the cake on his night table. "Something bad. I just know it."

She nodded. "If he did try to get home, it could be anything. I mean, he'd have had to walk five miles to town then get on a train."

Alan slammed his hand down on the bed. "Why didn't he just say something? I could have... I could have tried to talk him out of it."

"Maybe he didn't want you to," Christine answered softly. "Maybe he wanted it to be a surprise for his parents. I don't know."

"But he's smarter than that, Christine," Alan protested. "To just up and leave? Without a word?"

"Alan, c'mon. You've got to stop this. You'll make yourself crazy."

Christine was right. "Thanks. And thanks for the cake."

She rose, squeezed his shoulder lightly, smiled, and left. But Alan knew. Something inside wouldn't let him go. He had to find the truth.

*

Mr. Strickland wasn't at his best the next morning. His pets, the Triumvirate, weren't prepared and Alan showed them up with his presentation despite his delivery needing a bit of work. Mr. Strickland motioned for him to stay a moment after class.

"Thank you for being prepared, Alan," he praised. "How did everything go with the police yesterday?"

"I-I did exactly w-w-what you told me to do. I told the truth."

Mr. Strickland nodded. "They're doing everything they can, Alan."

"Not enough," he protested. "Sir? S-s-something's not right. He wouldn't just l-l-leave without saying good-bye or leaving a note."

"I'm sure he meant to, Alan."

Footsteps drew his attention to the door and he turned. Christine was there giving him a brave smile.

"I'm late for Physics," he mumbled.

Mr. Strickland nodded then reached out and squeezed his shoulder, just as Christine had the night before. Maybe he felt as bad.

Some of the emptiness dissipated. "Thank you," Alan said, and then he walked out.

"How are you doing?" Christine asked as they continued down the hallway.

"I don't know," he answered, still miserable inside.

Hugh spied them from down the hallway. "Oooohh, look at you making goo-goo eyes at a girl, Trembles."

"Think he'd know what to do?" Trevor asked.

"All of you, stop it!" Christine's face reddened.

Professor Brooks insisted on telling everyone in Physics about Alan's perfect score again. Crawling under his desk sounded mighty good. As his classes droned on, Alan wondered why the Triumvirate were riding him so hard. Had they done the same to Ollie? Had Ollie not told him because he was embarrassed? Scared? Or resigned, because he knew there was nothing he could do about it?

After classes were over and he was in his room, Alan walked over to his window but this time he didn't see the Triumvirate on the green. Curious, he walked past Devlin and Chadwick's room. They weren't there. The same with Niebold.

Alan knew lots of hiding places in their dorm, had used many of them to get away from the very boys he now sought out. He checked them one by one until he came to the last and best. The storage room behind the boiler in the basement. As he approached, he heard voices he recognized.

"Did you see his eyes? It was sooo cool."

"Pissed himself. Disgusting."

"Squirmed like a worm on a hook. Sweet."

Alan had heard enough. No wonder Ollie ran. They'd been torturing his friend.

Gathering his courage the next day, Alan asked to see Mr. Strickland after classes were over. "S-s-sir? I-I think I n-n-know why Ollie ran away, sir."

"You do?" Mr. Strickland asked with a frown. A combination of alarm and concern filled his gaze. "Are you quite certain? This is very important, Alan. I have to know the truth. Don't forget, the police are involved."

He couldn't forget. Besides, Mr. Strickland had just called him by his first name. And his teacher never did that. Ever. Not with any of the boys. Or girls. "Y-y-yes, Mr. Strickland. It's the Triumvirate."

"Triumvirate?" his teacher asked.

"S-sorry, sir. Messers Devlin, Chadwick, and Niebold. Th-th-they were hiding in the s-s- storage room behind the boiler. I-I overheard their conversation."

"Overheard a conversation," Mr. Strickland repeated, a frown of consternation growing on his brow. "Go on."

"Th-th-they'd been teasing and torturing Ollie, sir. That's why he ran away."

His teacher didn't answer right away. "Are you sure?"

Alan nodded. "I'm sure. They've done the same to me," he confessed, his gaze falling to the floor. Then he looked up in earnest. "N-n-not as bad as this sounded, but bad enough."

"I see," Mr. Strickland murmured. "This is a dangerous accusation, Alan."

"I know, sir."

"Right now this is simply hearsay. Can you get anyone to corroborate?"

"You know they won't, sir. Th-th-they're too scared. They only pick on the younger boys."

"All right," his teacher told him. "You leave this with me for now, do you understand? Not a word to anyone else. I need to figure out the best way to approach Mr. Pickering. With the police involved…" A flicker of horror ran through his gaze. "Their parents could destroy this school."

"Yes, sir," Alan answered, hope lifting a thousand-pound weight from his shoulders. At least someone was listening. "Thank you, sir."

Alan read commiseration in Mr. Strickland's gaze. "I was like you, Alan. I know how it feels. I'll get to the bottom of this. I promise."

*

A week went by. Then two. Alan struggled to get back into some kind of routine. But coming back to an empty room each day after class served as a grim reminder that Ollie was still missing. And that he might be dead.

The police questioned him again, their questions growing more desperate. They searched for clues, tearing his room apart, even brought in dogs to search the grounds. All the while, Alan waited for Mr. Strickland's promise to be fulfilled.

He heard nothing. The police found nothing.

Life went on. Weekends were the hardest. Without Ollie, time dragged. Alan spent most of his time in the library to avoid the Triumvirate and prayed Mr. Strickland would use his discretion.

Alas, that was not to be. Very late on Saturday night, Alan awoke to rough hands, a piece of duct tape being slapped over his mouth. He watched them shake out a pillowcase that served as a hood as it shut him in darkness. Shards of terror slithered through his veins, his heart pounded so hard he could feel the beat in his ears, the roar drowning out everything else.

They'd been drinking. Alan could smell the sour staleness of beer.

Oh God! Oh God! What were they going to do to him?

He found out soon enough. They carried him, kicking and trying to scream, up to the third floor music room. There, they yanked off his hood.

Devlin paced, nearly beside himself as he hissed, "Rat on us, will you?"

The blade of a pocket knife glinted eerily in the light of the candles in the room. "You little prick!" Chadwick added.

Niebold simply pulled the tape off his mouth with a malicious grin.

"You're bullies, all of you!" Alan cried. Anger pushed away his stuttering. "Damn you all."

They laughed.

"Gentlemen. Court is in session. Roman court. What say you?"

They all called out, "Aye!"

Forcing Alan to sit in a chair, Chadwick asked, "So, Augustus?"

Devlin smiled. A shiver ran down Alan's back. "Let's begin, Vespasian."

Smack! Pain radiated through his cheek.

Bam! Niebold's backhand sent shards of glass through his face and made his head spin. They fired questions at him, yet Alan refused to answer. All the while, he heard a strange creaking behind him. Finally Augustus asked, "Hadrian. Are you ready?"

"Yes, Augustus."

They yanked him out of the seat. Shaking, eyes wide as fear skittered through him, Alan turned. A slow hollow began to build in his stomach. The riser floorboards had been removed. Just enough room to…

The room tilted then Alan screamed. A hand clamped over his mouth as he began fighting back. Buried Alive!

Heart pounding, nostrils flared, he kicked and flailed to no avail. Tape replaced the fingers that crushed his cheeks and Alan fought and fought until exhaustion set in. Then they lifted him and pushed him into the tiny crawlspace. The first outer plank was nailed in. Hadrian laughed, enjoying each pound of the hammer on another nail. Alan whimpered, begging for mercy. They showed none.

"You see, Trembles, we weren't kidding," Augustus told him.

"No one rats on us," Vespasian added.

"Little coward." Alan could hear the sneer in Hadrian's tone.

The last two floorboards were screwed in place. Alan kicked and pounded on them to loosen them. But he was too small, too weak to get them to budge. The walls began to close in. His heartbeat raced, his head pounded. He cried. He begged some more. Darkness descended. They were gone.

Not the light. Oh, God, don't take away the light!

Alan shut his eyes, breathing deeply, trying to slow his heart. He couldn't. *All a bad dream. All a bad dream.* The floorboard was an inch away from his nose. He felt it. Terror slithered through his veins. He kicked. He pounded.

Then the sobs came.

The walls continued to shrink. His throat closed. Mummified. Entombed. He was going to die. Encased in a coffin. Time passed without meaning.

What was that? Alan strained to see. A glimmer of light? Yes! Yes! Light. Just a flicker.

The creak of a floorboard. Oh joyous sound! Alan began to scream beneath the tape. "Help me! Help me!"

All of a sudden another sound. The screech of a screw being turned. Relief flooded his being. Alan sobbed like a baby when the first board was lifted, sobbed even harder as she ripped off the tape. "Christine!"

"Oh my God, Alan! What? Are all right? Who?" Her gaze hardened. "Those bastards! Those filthy, dirty bastards!"

She helped him sit up and get out. He sat on the edge of the stage shaking while she replaced the floorboards. Cool air washed over him. He gulped it in as if he'd never be able to breathe again. "H-how did you find me?"

"A bunch of laughter woke me up. I followed it to Devlin's door. They were boasting about what they'd done."

"Thank you."

"We'll get them for this," she promised.

"No!" he cried. He gripped her hands and begged. "No. Please. No. They'll do it again. No more! Do you hear me? No more!"

"All right, Alan," she soothed. "All right. Take it easy."

"I-I told Mr. Strickland. Even he won't help. He's too afraid of what they'll do to his precious school. No one will help."

"What about Mr. Pickering?"

"Alone. All alone."

Christine stared at him as if he'd cracked. Well, hadn't he?

"Let's get you downstairs," she said.

Alan stayed in his room all day Sunday, not eating, barely sleeping, and nearly freezing with the window wide open, terrified to turn the light off.

On Monday he went to Mr. Strickland. "Yes, Antonius?" his teacher asked, thinking it was about class.

"Please, s-s-sir." He could barely get the word out.

"Slowly, Alan."

"Want… you… to stop. D-d-did not see anything."

His teacher frowned, concern rampant in his gaze. "Are you sure, Alan? They didn't do anything to you, did they?"

"N-n-n no, s-s-sir."

"Alan," Mr. Strickland continued, his tone gentle. "If they've used force in any kind of way, you need to tell me."

Alan shook his head and ran out of the room. He couldn't breathe. His chest locked. He ran to his favorite tree and fell to his knees gasping for air. Chris found him there. Alarm filled her gaze. "Aren't you supposed to be in Physics?"

"Ca-ca-ca-can't go inside. N-n not yet."

"Maybe you should go to the Infirmary. Tell them you don't feel well. C'mon Alan," she continued. "I'll help you."

Alan stayed in the Infirmary until the doctor came, followed by Mr. Strickland and Mr. Pickering. The doctor examined him and asked questions. Then he moved off to speak to the two men. But Alan could hear. Trauma. Panic attack.

"Alan, we're going to call your parents. You need to go home and rest," Mr. Strickland told him.

"No! I'm all right! Please," he begged. "I can't go home!"

His parents would never forgive him. They'd beggared themselves to get him into The Excelsior. They knew how smart he was. They dreamed of what he could do with his life using those brains.

Mr. Strickland seemed uncertain. "Are you sure?" He bent down and whispered to him, "I know you're lying about being bullied, Alan. I want to help. But I can't do that unless you tell me what happened."

Help? The man wanted to help? That was funny. Alan had trusted him once. Did he think he could trust him again? And what if he did go to Mr. Pickering? Would Mr. Strickland back him up?

Alan knew the answers to those questions.

"No," Alan insisted. "I'm…" He swallowed but didn't stutter. "All right. I'll be fine." He sat up. He prayed the connectors in his brain would work and he wouldn't stutter. "May I go back to my classes now?"

Mr. Strickland nodded and shrugged. So he did. He went to class alone. He sat alone, ate alone, studied alone, and finally the Triumvirate left him alone.

*

They found Ollie on a bright spring Tuesday morning. The police, using dogs, followed a short-cut Ollie might have taken to go to the train station through the woods. They found him crumpled on the ground, his suitcase next to him. The autopsy revealed a heart defect. On his way to the road, Ollie'd had a massive heart attack.

But Alan knew something else that would cause that kind of heart attack. And he knew better than to go to Mr. Strickland or Mr. Pickering with his suspicions. So he turned to the last remaining friend he had. Christine. And told her to meet him down by the lake.

"They killed Ollie," he announced once she got there.

"No, they didn't, Alan."

"Just as if they'd put a gun to his head. They locked him under the stage and the stress caused his heart attack."

"You can't prove that," Christine insisted. "And you can't accuse them. Not after what—happened."

Alan grimaced but stood his ground. "I'm going to gain their trust. Slowly. So they relax around me. And then I'm going to gather the proof I need."

He offered his brain in return for entry into their club. Homework, reports, test answers. So did Christine. They didn't accept right away, which gave him time to get to town and purchase small tape recorders. He and Christine recorded each conversation, gathering enough evidence to have all three boys expelled from the school.

During the conversations, Alan realized they were referring to some kind of club. An inner circle club. He told Christine about it.

"They call it The Emperor's Club," she told him.

Stunned he asked, "You know about it?"

"Sure. Mr. Strickland's project for his little 'pets.'"

At first Alan felt betrayed. Christine knew this and he didn't. But then he rationalized there was no reason for Christine to tell him. But what if he could use it to his advantage? Perhaps he could *prove* all of his suspicions. That afternoon, he caught up with Mr. Strickland at the end of the green.

"I want in," Alan stated.

Taken aback, his teacher stared. "In? I beg your pardon but in what? In where?"

"The Emperor's Club."

"Of course you can join," Mr. Strickland told him with a quick laugh. "It's open to all students."

Alan took a deep breath and looked the man straight in the eye. "No. I want into the one the others don't know about."

With a skeptical glance, his teacher said, "I don't know what you're talking about."

Alan stepped forward right into the man's face. "I think you do, Caesar. And the Ides of March are almost upon us."

Alan whirled on his heel, walking briskly back toward his dorm. He began to shake as he walked, alternating between terrified and euphoric.

He'll tell them. They'll put me in there again.

No, they won't. Because I'll go straight to the police.

Mr. Strickland will protect them. He'll tell them I had a breakdown.

I'm going to expose them once and for all.

Later, before bed, he told Christine what he'd done. "You didn't," she breathed.

Proud of his newfound courage, his chest puffed out. "You should've seen the look on Mr. Strickland's face."

"Do you think this will work?" Christine asked.

"Worst case it will keep us safe."

Christine didn't sound so sure. "I suppose so."

He'd figured it out. Mr. Strickland was terrified of change, anything that would make The Excelsior different than the way it used to be.

Finally, Mr. Strickland took the bait. He asked Alan to stay after class on Friday. All he said was, "The meeting will be held Sunday night. The other members will come and collect you."

Careful, Alan thought. Nothing admissible. Good. A worthy adversary.

While they studied in the library, Alan passed Christine a note telling her to take her tape recorder too.

Sunday night, Alan made as if he were going to bed but kept his clothes on. Very, very late, to the point that he actually fell asleep for a while, the Triumvirate finally came to get him. They were all wearing sheets made into togas and circlets made of leaves on their heads.

A pillowcase covered his head like before but this time, Alan's heart nearly exploded. Sweat pooled on his chest. *No! No! The darkness!* He begged them to take it off. They laughed.

Finally, they stopped. The pungent decay of the woods filled his nostrils and he could hear the tiny lap of the lake against the shore.

They ripped off the hood. He stood on a grassy area by the lake surrounded by torches flickering eerily in the wind.

"So," Mr. Strickland began. "We have a new guest."

The Triumvirate didn't look happy. Devlin scowled, Chadwick's fingers curled into fists. Niebold's stance filled with menace.

"We learn history for a reason, Alan," his teacher said softly. "We study Roman Emperors and their civilization to understand their greatness, to make ourselves great, to make this school great."

"C-caesar was great," Alan agreed. "B-but in the end, he was assassinated. B-because absolute power corrupts absolutely. Didn't you tell us that, sir?"

Alan held his ground as righteous anger burned away his fear.

"Indeed I did, Alan. But the Roman Empire survived because of that power, because it wiped out any threat. Change is a threat to the status quo, is it not?"

He held up the note Alan passed to Christine in the library. "You may come out now, Marcus Aurelius."

Christine stepped hesitantly out of the bushes. She mouthed the words *I'm sorry* to Alan as she stepped into the torchlight.

At first Alan wasn't sure what was going on.

"I'm sorry to say your plan was a failure from the very beginning," Mr. Strickland told them, his golden circlet gleaming in the firelight. "Because you never understood. You cannot beat an enemy that is more powerful than yourself."

"The truth will out," Alan countered. But even as he said the words his heart sank. Could he be right? Could absolute power corrupt the truth?

"The only constant in life is change," Mr. Strickland continued. "But not here. Not on these grounds. Here we defend time, defend honor, defend what is rightfully ours? Is that not correct, gentlemen?"

The Triumvirate agreed with nods, growls, and chest thumps.

Mr. Strickland turned, his face growing cold as he faced Christine. "The Excelsior is a boys' school, Ms. Hathaway. Always has been, will forever be."

The Triumvirate closed in around Christine. They grabbed her and began shoving her toward the lake.

What?

Alan followed, not sure he wanted to. By the edge, fairly close to the water, in the soft ground, they'd dug a pit at least ten feet deep.

What the hell was going on?

Mr. Strickland turned to him. "Well, Alan? Time to decide."

Unsure of what was going to happen he answered, "Decide what?"

"Are you going to join us or not?"

"Join you?" Alan asked, still not quite processing what was happening. He hated these people, his teacher most of all. Become allies? He'd rather…

Mr. Strickland nodded. "Which emperor will you be? Antonius or Caligula?"

Christine, realizing what was about to happen, began to fight them with all her might. "No, Alan. Please. Don't do this," she begged.

Be a friend and end up with Christine or be an ally and finish his time at the Excelsior untouched, without further incident. The easy way or the hard way.

"Your choice."

In those moments of deadly silence, Alan realized a very important lesson. If you can't beat them—join them.

*

Twenty years later…

The Excelsior wasn't even a school anymore. The buildings, untouched and devoid of care, withered in the damp fall air. The place brought back too many memories, memories he'd tried to bury. But he'd accepted Christine's invitation because he owed her that much at least. He'd turned on her.   In the years that followed, he'd had too much time to think about what could've been. In the end, self-preservation simply won. But that didn't make what happened any easier to bear.

A student out running in the early morning found her. She didn't speak, didn't acknowledge anyone. Catatonic, they said. With her fingertips raw and bleeding from trying to claw her way up the side of the pit.

How he'd hated himself.

The rain didn't help. It was so muddy, she couldn't get out. At night, he'd wake up from nightmares trying to claw his way out of the same pit. Only his wasn't real. Hers was.

He heard later, she also ended up fighting off pneumonia. She nearly died.

At times, Alan wished he'd died too.

Of course, Strickland planned everything that way. To ensure their silence. Divide and conquer, right?

He parked his car and got out, pulling his trench coat tight. He walked along the path to the lake wondering what it was all for. It seemed so far away, so long ago, like a play tucked into memory.

He saw her standing staring out at the lake. Taller, a woman, slender and statuesque, her auburn hair lifting with the wind gusts.

"Thank you for coming, Alan."

He didn't even say hello. "Christine, listen to me. I can't make up for what happened. But I'm sorry." The pent up words simply spilled from his mouth. "I should've stuck with you. I should have gone into that pit with you. I was a coward."

"Yes, you were." She turned and her gaze blazed with remembered torchlight. "I couldn't get out! I couldn't get out! You were supposed to come back for me. I came back for you," she accused.

"They wouldn't let me. They tied me to my bed and kept guard outside my door all night! I wanted to but I couldn't!"

She nodded, but the hurt and betrayal of that night sat on her shoulders like a mantle. "I've spent ten years trying to understand, Alan." Her arm swept wide encompassing the failing grounds of The Excelsior. "My only crime was that I was a girl."

"My only crime was that I was smart."

"So petty. So insignificant," she murmured so he could just barely hear.

A long silence stretched between them. "Why didn't you tell the police?" he finally asked.

"No one would've believed me. I couldn't even speak when they pulled me out. I-I wandered in a strange darkness for a long time." She turned back to stare out over the lake.

"You seem to have succeeded quite well. I've read all your books. New York Times bestselling horror author. I guess you're a millionaire now too."

She shrugged. "Funny, without The Excelsior I would never have been a success, I would never have been able to tap into that darkness." She turned. "Strange how things work."

Her gaze snared his. "You haven't done so badly for yourself either, have you, doctor?"

A PhD in Physics. "I suppose."

She turned away again as if looking at him sickened her. Looking in the mirror sickened him at times too.

"Strickland's dead. Stabbed to death. Multiple times. They said he was mugged."

Surprised Alan answered, "I didn't know." Just like Caesar, he thought.

"Niebold's dead. Afghanistan."

"I'd heard."

"You probably didn't hear how." Alan shook his head. "They said it was locals. Retribution. They left him in a pit. Twenty feet deep. In the middle of the desert. He couldn't crawl out. He died of exposure."

Exposure? Wait a minute. A pit?

"Chadwick had a severe intestinal virus," she continued, her voice completely monotone. "Vomiting. Diarrhea. Went on for months. To the point where he burnt out his esophagus and ruined his entire digestive system." She paused. "Do you know how Vespasian died?"

"No."

"Diarrhea," she stated as if it were an ordinary fact. "Chadwick's permanently disabled and in a wheelchair now. I checked up on him recently. He's about 90 pounds, soaking wet. The feeding tubes don't work anymore."

Alan frowned. "Are you telling me this so I'll feel sorry for them?" He started breathing heavily. The air became thick and too hard to draw in.

Her features registered pure innocence. "No. I thought you might like to know, that's all."

"So, go on." Fair enough. He'd go along with whatever game she was playing. Again, he owed her that much. And she seemed hell bent on making sure he knew all the details. "Devlin?"

"It was rumored that Augustus was poisoned by a fig."

All of a sudden it dawned on Alan. She wanted him to know what happened to them all because… "You did it." He drew in a deep breath. "You-you killed them."

Without a drop of emotion she simply answered, "They killed me. The night they left me in that pit. And so did you."

His insides hollowed. The thick air began to choke him. His throat closed. "I'm sorry, Christine. S-s-s-so very s-s- sorry."

She smiled. "There's the Alan I knew."

Alan shook his head and clamped his lips together until the shaking stopped. "Are you going to ruin me too?" he joked.

She didn't smile this time. "I purchased the property, Alan. I own this whole place now. I can do anything I want with it. Even make a new school."

Bewildered, he asked, "You'd do that?"

"No. Of course not. You see, it's about power. Just like Strickland said. You never grasped that. You kept thinking the truth would win." She stared at him, pity in her gaze. "But Strickland knew. So did the Triumvirate. It was always about power. And I have the power now."

She wasn't making sense. A strange light grew in her eyes and Alan realized that in order to write the books she wrote, she'd gone a bit mad. His heartbeat sped up in his chest again. Realization dawned. She wanted revenge.

Alan turned to run. His feet slipped on the damp grass and he stumbled. His legs churned as he tried to get a grip, but she was fast. The needle pierced his neck with a faint pinch, and the world faded.

When he awoke, they were in the third floor music room. This time the room blazed with light. His hands and feet were zip-tied together. Fear spread like a sickness inside his belly. "C-c-c-Christine. Please. You've made your point. I was a little r-r-rat bastard. But I was a kid. A terrified kid. You have to understand."

"I understand, all right," she answered, her tone gentle but hurt. So very hurt. "Yours was the worst betrayal of all, Alan. I thought you were my friend."

"B-b-but I was, Chris. I w-w- wanted to be. I-I…"

She almost looked sympathetic. Almost. "I couldn't take it anymore. The-the-they broke me."

"Yes. They broke me too. And now I've healed. And so will you." That strange light was back and burned even brighter in her

103

gaze. "I want you to understand. I want you to feel the abandonment. I want you to wallow in every moment of torment."

"Christine, please. You're talking crazy. Stop. I was always your friend. Honest. I swear."

She continued as if Alan hadn't uttered a word. "I own this property. No one will ever find you. I won't come to rescue you. Just as you didn't come to rescue me. And as the darkness closes in and you realize that I'm not lying, remember what you did. Remember how it felt. As the last breath of your life leaves your body, remember what you did. Remember what a coward you are."

She began to screw in the last plank of the riser. The sound of the drill screeched up his spine.

"Chris. No! Please! I beg of you! Have mercy!"

"Why should I? You showed me none."

"CHRIS! PLEASE!"

The last screw drove home with sickening finality. Alan pounded on the panel with all his might. He kicked, he fought, but the boards wouldn't budge.

"Goodbye, Alan."

The lights went out.

Alan screamed.

6

THE HIEROPHANT

MATHEW KAUFMAN

Upright: Religion, group identification, conformity, tradition, beliefs
Reversed: Restriction, challenging the status quo

Saint Augustine Church, Key Largo, Florida—Friday, August 14, 1992

Ten days before…

Vivian Hampton, thirty-four-year-old single mother of two, pulled into the church parking lot. She had spent a lot of time speaking with God ever since she was diagnosed with breast cancer last year. She pulled the silver Volvo into the first available parking spot and slipped the shifter into park. Fumbling, she retrieved her purse and rummaged through the contents before finding the aluminum flask.

Okay. So God wasn't the only thing she was turning to these days. But cancer was wrecking her life, not to mention her perfect tits.

"Jesus, please forgive me," she said, before taking a long slug of the Five O'clock Vodka inside. She grimaced, forcing the liquid down with a hard swallow. One more burning gulp later and she returned the shiny, metallic container back to her purse and pulled her keys from the ignition.

She stepped out of the car and forced on the best fake smile she could muster. *Here we go. Please, don't let me die. I don't want to die. I have already lost everything. Why are you doing this to me?* Vivian tried her hardest to clear her mind and walked to the church.

She opened the front door with a metallic click. The foyer floor was a beautiful white marble with golden cross inlays. The walls were coated in a multitude of colors, the majority a bright red. Vivian followed the stone pathway into the massive worship room. Beautiful stained-glass windows lined the walls, depicting various scenes from the Bible.

Light shone through the multi-colored windows, illuminating the church's extravagant interior. A life-size golden Jesus on a cross hung directly above the pulpit. Vivian approached the prie-dieu and again fumbled through her purse. This time she retrieved the new-looking Bible, and after setting her purse on the floor next to her, she knelt.

She placed the book on the rail in front of her and lowered her head to pray. She quietly mouthed the words even though Saint Augustine was currently empty.

"Dear Lord, please… Please, please let me live. I am on my knees for you. Please," she said.

Footsteps clacked on the hard floor; she looked toward the sound.

"Vivian, welcome back. It's good to see you," Father Marcus said. "I'm sorry I interrupted you."

"No, Father, no interruption at all. I'm glad you're here."

Vivian stood and greeted Father Marcus. Her arm snapped out clumsily to grab hold of his hand. A small pair of skeleton keys fell from his grasp.

"Oh, please, forgive me, Father," she said, grabbing his hand and kissing it.

"Please, my child, relax. Would you like to go to confession? There are two others waiting. I would be happy to hear you out."

"That would be wonderful, Father. Thank you."

Truthfully, she loathed confession. She hated everything about churches and the people that went to them. She would much rather be getting laid, but none of that would happen if she died. Come on

Vivian… You can fake your way through this. Soon, you'll be back to normal.

They quietly left the worship room and proceeded to the confessional booth at the side of the room. Vivian sat on the bench outside, next to two other middle-aged women waiting for their turn to confess. They quietly greeted each other with nods and smiles. Vivian didn't recognize either of them, but she was relatively new to religion. Religion was a common side effect of cancer, and it was no different in her case.

Roughly thirty minutes passed before it was her turn. The previous woman exited the booth and departed. Vivian stood and entered the dark-brown wooden booth.

Hearing her enter, Father Marcus began the typical prayer. "Please begin," he said.

"Forgive me, Father, for I have sinned. It has been over twenty years since my last confession."

"That's quite a long time. I am sure you have much to confess."

"I do. You see, I have recently been diagnosed with breast cancer. I am very scared. I don't want to die. I want so many things from my life."

"Aye. Have you prayed on it a lot? Have you been a good Christian?" he asked.

"I have prayed every night of my life," she lied, rolling her eyes in disgust.

There was no reply from the Father. A wooden door clacked shut, somewhere close. Vivian jumped.

"Father Marcus?"

Again, no reply. The sound of keys jingling broke the silence. The lock on her side of the booth clicked as the key, now inside it, turned.

"Father? What's going on?"

Vivian grabbed the handle on the door and began to turn it. The door wouldn't budge.

"FATHER?" she said, panic stricken. "Father… What the fuck is going on?"

She heard the other door open and close again.

"Oh thank God. I'm stuck in here. Please get me out." Stricken with panic, Vivian pounded on the door.

She screamed, "LET ME OUT! GET ME THE FUCK OUT OF HERE! HELP!"

Suddenly the lights flickered before dying completely. The confessional wall between her and where Father Marcus was supposed to be slid open. The booth was pitch black and suddenly very hot inside. Vivian stood and slammed her shoulder against the door. Her heart pounded rapidly, forcing her blood through her veins.

"FATHER MARCUS, HELP!"

"There is no use screaming," a voice whispered right in her ear. "This is what you get for being a whore. *Voluptuous Vivian*. Isn't that what they called you after you got your new tits?"

"Fuck off! I don't know who the hell you are, but I am going to call the police! FATHER MARCUS?"

"No. No, I don't think you are," the voice said as Vivian rattled the door.

Unable to open the door, Vivian searched through her purse in the dark. Her hands glanced over the contents. *There. There it is.* With the flick of her thumb, a spark jetted from the top of the lighter she had retrieved. The flame illuminated the blackened room like a can light at a rock concert. Unfortunately for Vivian, the light impaired her already night-adjusted vison. Fuck.

A long, slender finger slid out from behind the flame.

That wasn't a finger… That was a claw. A claw with a very long, very sharp nail.

"Oh, Jesus Christ!" she screamed.

"At least your tits won't kill you! Goodbye Vivian."

As the voice spoke her name, the claw closed around the flame and extinguished it. The lighter ripped from her grasp. The thick, hot air began to fill her with panic. Her heart pounded. Something clacked against the booth's wooden floor, moving closer to her.

"Oh Jesus."

Sharp claws struck her arms. Blood escaped the new wounds wetting her clothes. Pain rushed in and took the blood's place.

She screamed—

It was too late. The claws ripped through her skin, through the muscle in her neck. The creature grabbed hold of the spine buried deep in her neck. She felt the fingers grip it tightly. Vivian stood frozen, only able to blink as the life drained from her body.

The creature pulled, breaking her neck. The grip released at the sound of the snapping bones. Vivian's body slumped to the floor, her eyes filled with eternal darkness.

*

Vivian Hampton's home, Key Largo, Florida—Tuesday, August 18, 1992

Six days before…

Dex sat conversing with his sister, Mary, in the kitchen of their beachfront home.

"What the hell are we going to do, Dex?" Mary asked.

"Nothing. Mom has done this before. You know how she is. I'm sure she'll be home soon. I'm sure she is just out with the dickbag of the week," Dex replied.

"I get it… Mom's a whore. But still… she's never left us alone during hurricane season. Hurricane Andrew is only a few days out. We can't stay here. I don't want to fucking die, asshole!"

"Oh my God… Over-react much? I'm seventeen, Mary. If she isn't back in a couple days, we can just get in the Jeep and I'll drive us out of here. I have a few hundred bucks saved up so we can eat and stuff. Relax already. You're such a drama queen."

"Fine but…" Mary said anxiously.

An emergency alert warning broke over the television.

"Yeah, yeah. I get it. It's windy. Stop playing that annoying sound," Dex said.

Mary slammed an elbow into his ribs. "Shut up. This is serious."

A computerized voice spoke as the words scrolled across the screen. The two, now silent, leaned closer to the TV

"The U.S. Weather Service has issued a severe storm warning for areas in the southern panhandle of Florida. Expect winds of up to forty miles per hour tonight growing to fifty tomorrow," the voice said.

"The U.S. Weather Service is issuing an evacuation for the following counties: Miami-Dade, Broward, Palm Beach, Martin, St. Lucie, Indian River…"

"Dex, I really think we should go. They're evacuating the whole coast," Mary said.

"I know but I'm not leaving Mom here and spending all my money for no reason. It isn't even that bad out. Look."

He stood and walked to the sliding glass door. The sky was a bright blue and peppered with clouds. They were moving relatively fast, but all of the trees were still upright. So how bad could it really be?

"It's not even bad. The waves are still below the seawall. We are good for another couple days. Trust me."

"Fine, but you are getting us pizza for dinner tonight! And I want mushrooms!"

Dex laughed and messed up her hair with his hand.

"Stop… Stop!"

*

Vivian Hampton's home, Key Largo, Florida—Friday, August 21, 1992—5:00am

Three days before…

Waves crashed violently over the concrete seawall. Set after set bashed against the concrete, sending hundreds of gallons of saltwater flying into the air. The wind had been howling since late Tuesday night, but not like this.

Dex awoke to the sounds of rattling siding and the whir of wind whistling through the cracks in the closed windows. He was nervous about getting trapped in the storm but had been through worse. The last hurricane had been just like this and then drifted away into nothingness. He hoped that hurricane Andrew would do the same, even though the likelihood of that was small.

Dex rolled over in his bed and reached for the remote on his nightstand but discovered the whole stand was empty as he swept his arm across its surface. A fresh blast of sea air ripped in through his window, flying across the stand.

Jesus, that's some strong wind. It knocked all my shit onto the floor.

He reached down and poked around in the darkness, like a blind man, before he found it. Gripping its rubber keys and plastic body, he flipped himself back into bed. He fumbled for a moment before finding and finally pressing the power button.

The television clicked on. MTV raged to life. Ugly Kid Joe's *Everything About You* blared. He'd obviously forgotten to turn the TV down before he crashed. His thumb jammed on the volume button and began flipping through the channels, searching for news.

He found the local ABC news channel. Peter Jennings was intensely reporting on the approaching hurricane.

"Overnight the wind speeds have seemingly increased exponentially. Andrew wasn't expected to make landfall until August twenty eighth. In an unprecedented manner, Andrew has now morphed into a Category Five storm. The latest analysis now puts Andrew crashing onto the shore near Homestead, Florida, sometime on the morning of the twenty fourth. If you haven't already begun your evacuation, I urge you to do so now," Jennings said.

Water splashed against the window of Dex's room.

Maybe this was more serious than he thought. *Where the hell is Mom?*

An emergency alert came over the TV, interrupting his train of thought. It reiterated much of the same information Peter Jennings had already gone over, but then a familiar face filled the screen.

Father Marcus?

"Citizens of Key Largo," he said, "I have prayed for all of you. You are my flock, my friends. I care a great deal for you and wish to open my house to you. For those of you who have not yet evacuated, I fear that moment for escape has passed. There is no Ark from Noah to save us from the Devil's fury that is surely inbound.

"Please, wait no longer. Come join me in the storm shelter beneath Saint Augustine's. There is plenty of food and water for all those left in Key Largo. Wait no longer. The storm is coming."

The feeling of impending doom scared the shit out of Dex. Alone, in his room, he sat staring at Father Marcus' face. His crooked smile was untrustworthy, like that of a used car salesman. But at least the church was an option. He rose from his bed to peer out the covered window.

Before reaching the window, the glass exploded. Shards of the sharp glass flew through the air. Some of the pieces struck Dex in the face, ripping gashes both large and small, and Dex screamed. Blood trickled from the wounds. More glass shards pounded his body.

Something crashed repeatedly into the house. *Thud. Thud. Thud. What the fuck?*

Dex wiped the blood from his face, and a flash of red smashed into the broken window, stopped only by the thick wood frame of the small window.

He flinched. "Holy shit!"

Pinned to the window was a STOP sign. Its reflective white letters lit up from the light of the television.

"Fuck—I think we waited too long."

"Mary! Mary! Get up!" Dex yelled.

"What the hell, Dex? Leave me alo… Holy shit! What happened to your face?"

"The storm busted out the window and I got all cut up. Listen, there is no time to argue. Get up and pack a bag right now. You have to HURRY!"

"Oh my God! Alright. I'll hurry. Are you going to be okay?"

"I'll be fine. The cuts aren't too deep I don't think. I'll go clean up in the other bathroom," Dex said.

"Where are we going?"

"There isn't time to talk about this right now. Please Mary, go!" he screamed over the howling wind.

Dex saw the worry on Mary's face. What thirteen-year-old wouldn't be? After all, they were trapped in the path of an impending hurricane and their mom had been gone, presumably fucking some random dude, for almost a week.

Dex waited until Mary left the room to go clean himself up. He slowly pulled a few pieces of embedded glass out of his face and chest. His face contorted in pain as he tugged on each piece. Blood trickled down his face. He grabbed a white hand towel and soaked it in hot water. After he removed each piece, he pressed it to the area to help stop the bleeding.

More often than not, the pressure from the towel revealed another piece of glass hidden under the skin's surface.

"Ouch. FUCK!" he yelled as the towel revealed yet another shard. This one required a pair of tweezers to remove. Carefully, he plucked out the shrapnel. More blood leaked from his face. He thought that was the last one, though, and at least that provided a small bit of relief.

He wrung out the blood-soaked towel, re-wet it with fresh water, and gave his face one last rub, just to make sure he got everything. Just as he finished, the lights went out.

Fuck.

"Mary! Hurry up. The power is out and we need to get out of here now!" he yelled up the stairs.

Another sound of breaking glass came from upstairs.

"Mary?" he yelled up the stairs.

Footsteps pounded down the stairs and she flew into view.

"You ready?" he asked, relieved that she was okay.

"Yeah, that was the window in my room. Are we going to be okay?

"We'll be fine. You just have to do what I say. Can you do that? Can you be brave?"

Mary nodded, her bag clasped tightly in her right hand, a teddy bear clutched tightly in the other.

"Good girl. Let's go," he said.

They rushed through the house, making their way to the garage, and Mary followed closely behind Dex. Things slammed into the exterior of the house. Dex hoped they could get to the church okay.

Seconds later, the two leapt into the front seats of Dex's Jeep. It was nowhere as nice as his mom's, but it was his and he liked it. He reached up and clicked the button on the garage door opener. Nothing happened. He clicked it harder, a few more times.

Nothing…

"Shit. The power is out. Hold on, Mary, I have to get out and open the door."

Mary clung to the stuffed bear in her lap, squeezing it so tight that it looked like it might pop at any moment. Dex patted her head and hopped out. He rushed to the door and ripped it open, revealing the fresh load of Hell outside.

Water flew sideways through the air, bringing with it debris of all shapes and sizes. A palm frond whipped in front of his face. He leaned out of the garage, tracking the larger pieces and was promptly struck by another. He returned to the Jeep and looked at Mary.

"Hold on, kiddo. This is going to be a rough ride."

"Where are we going?" she asked again.

"Oh, sorry. Father Marcus was on TV and said Saint Augustine's had plenty of room in the shelter and loads of food and water. I think it's too dangerous to leave the Keys, so…"

"Oh, good. That's not too far, either."

"That's a good thing too."

Dex turned the Jeep over and it roared to life. With one more rev, he slammed the stick shift into first and dumped the clutch. The Jeep lurched from the garage as the tires broke and regained traction.

Once out of the safety of the garage, the Jeep bounced over the piles of debris that covered the ground. Dex gripped the wheel, white-knuckle tight. He swerved rather expertly around the larger objects while busting through the others.

As the vehicle changed direction, so did the rain. The open-topped vehicle quickly soaked with a mix of rain and the salty seawater. Mary was now pleading to hurry. Dex could see that she was soaked, as was he, but she was shivering already.

He shifted and slammed his foot back onto the pedal, bottoming it out on the floorboards. The engine revved. Dex reached to turn up the open-top vehicle's heater just as a telephone pole cracked under the pressure of the wind. The pole toppled and slammed to the ground directly in the Jeep's path.

"Shit!" Dex screamed, jerking the wheel hard to the left and slamming on the brakes. "Hold on!"

The Jeep slid, hydroplaning across the water's surface. It spun out of control and slammed violently into a yellow curb lining the road's edge. The rear passenger's side dropped down, stopping the Jeep. The vehicle rested awkwardly, the nose perched much higher than the rear.

Dex checked to make sure Mary was okay. She was, so he unfastened her seatbelt and they jumped out. He grabbed their bags. And they ran. Just a few blocks from Saint Augustine's, they ran hard. Occasionally they tripped and stumbled, but neither fell.

Before they knew it, they were standing in the parking lot of the church. They pushed on, scanning the lot for flying debris, ducking what flew near them. Then he saw it.

"Oh my God. Look, Mary. Mom's Jeep."

"Awesome, let's get in there and find out why the hell she left us at home ALONE!"

"Relax. First let's get safe, then we'll deal with the other stuff."

"Fine," she said, picking up the pace.

They burst through the church doors with a percussive bang.

*

Dex and Mary were welcomed into Saint Augustine's with open arms by Father Marcus. They were issued a cot as well as a few towels and some snacks to tide them over until dinner. The shelter was not much more than a large concrete bunker underneath the church. It served its purpose, though. It felt… safe.

Dex and Mary set up their cots together. There must have been a couple hundred other townsfolk there already. Many were settled in and sat conversing with each other, talking about all manner of things.

Prior to setting up their cots, both Mary and he had searched the area for their mother. Neither found any sign of her. They decided that she had to be here somewhere and they would take turns searching for her after they dried off and settled in.

Shortly after they were dry-ish, Father Marcus paid them a visit.

"Welcome, my children," he opened with. "I trust you are settling in okay?"

"Yes, Father," Dex said. Without hesitation he blurted, "Have you seen my mother? Her Jeep is outside, but I can't find her."

"I did see her, several days ago. Around the fourteenth, I believe. She was here for prayers and confession. I waited for her to finish praying, but she never showed up for confession. I assumed that she left afterwards. Ask around, though. This shelter is large and I don't get around well. It is possible that I missed her."

Father Marcus retrieved something from his pocket. He opened his hand and presented his open palm to them. Two butterscotch candies and a pair of skeleton keys lay in his palm.

"Please, have a piece of candy," Father Marcus said.

The children obliged and took the candies, leaving the keys.

"Thank you, Father," they said. They hurriedly unwrapped the sweets and popped them into their mouths.

Over the next couple days, Mary and he took turns walking around the shelter, looking for their mother. Unfortunately, no one they spoke with had any recollection of seeing her. At least they were warm, dry, and safe.

Until the generator stopped. The lights flickered, and… died.

*

Saint Augustine Church, Key Largo, Florida—Sunday, August 23, 1992

One day before…

Father Marcus spoke, "Fear not, my parishioners, candles are being distributed as I speak."

Sure enough, candles began to light tiny patches of the shelter one or two at a time. This didn't stop children from screaming and crying. No, it incited the raucous noise. Sounds echoed deafeningly off the cold stone walls.

A scream resonated off the high ceiling. This one wasn't from a child, but rather, from a man. It was immediately followed by a loud *snap*.

"What the hell was that?" Dex asked.

"I don't know. I think it came from somewhere above. Maybe up in the ceiling supports," Mary said.

Sounds of wood creaking filled the air. And a gust of wind ripped through the basement shelter, blowing out all of the freshly lit candles. Several more *snaps* came from above, frightening the parishioners. Dex heard them gasping.

"What the fuck?" Dex said. "Let's move to the walls in case the ceiling collapses."

He stood and felt Mary do the same. The air was again still inside the room. Something dripped down Dex's left, arm and he instinctively reached out to wipe it off.

A viscous liquid with a new, strange odor filled his nostrils. *What the fuck…*

The candles in the room lit, one at a time. He fumbled with the packet of matches they'd been given and struck a match and put it to the wick. A small area around them illuminated. Mary gasped.

"Look at your arm, Dex. Is that blood?"

"What? No. Don't be stu…" his voice trailed off. The liquid that dripped down his arm was a deep red. Not like a nose bleed. He'd had his fair share of those. This red was different. Darker. Thicker.

Another volley of drops struck his arm. Shocked, he jerked it away from the drips. He raised his candle up and looked into the darkness. He couldn't see a damn thing.

"Shit. Can you tell where it's coming from?" he asked.

"No. I can't see a fucking thing," she answered.

"Mary… Watch your mouth. The Father is in here somewhere," he reprimanded.

"Sorry."

"I have an idea. Stand up on your cot. I'll give you my candle and raise you up on my shoulders. I don't want whatever this shit is dripping on me all night."

"Okay, I'm ready," she said.

Dex hoisted her up and she raised the candles high and waved them around searching for the source. They lit up very little.

"What do you see, Mary?"

"Nothing. It's way too dark. OH FUCK! DEX! HELP ME! PUT ME DOWN NOW!" she screamed.

Dex dropped her. She was still screaming and shaking violently.

"What is it? What did you see?"

Mary wrapped herself tightly around Dex's torso, bawling.

"Mary, tell me what you saw."

"There is a man—HANGING—up there," she sputtered.

"What?" he asked.

"A fucking dead guy, Dex. Some dude hung himself and is swinging up there," she cried.

"Then this is *blood*? Oh, Jesus!"

"HELP US!" Dex screamed. "Father Marcus!"

More and more candles were lit, illuminating the room better. Dex hugged his sister tightly. Both of them tucked their heads into each other, blocking out the horrific sight of the dangling man.

Screaming filled the room as the brightness increased. Dex pulled Mary closer but raised his head to look at what had caused the commotion.

"Oh God! Don't look, Mary."

Three groups of men hung some fifteen or so feet above the crowd's head. Dex felt sick. The men swung back and forth, occasionally bumping into one another. Dex counted six. Six men in each group. Six in each. Six, six, and six.

Parents all across the room covered their children's eye. These were not just random men dangling from the ceiling. Dex recognized them as fathers, brothers, and sons to some of the others.

Chaos erupted. Those with sense charged the steps that had brought them down into the shelter. Two or three wide, they ascended the stone steps. Panic filled their candlelit faces.

The room was deafeningly loud and filled with the sense of impending doom. Dex watched the first few reach the top of the stairs. They fumbled with the knob, but it didn't open. They slammed their shoulders into the door. The door stayed sealed shut.

Several new men took the others' places, beating on the locked door. They slammed and kicked at it. Some hit it so hard they broke bones. Those injured were carried down the stairs, back through the crowd below. Back to where their families were, where their cots sat. Back to where the bodies hung.

Dex and Mary watched as the men's injuries were treated as best they could be with no medical supplies. What kind of shelter has no medical supplies?

A new voice shouted over the roaring crowd.

"Stop, please. Stop! STOP!" the man's voice screamed.

Somehow, it gained the attention of the entire room, even over the banging and panicking.

"This isn't working. The door is stuck. Likely from something above. Probably the storm. We can't just sit here and let the kids see these men hanging from the ceiling. Let's cut them down and get them out of sight."

"Has anyone seen Father Marcus? He may know if there is a ladder down here," the man said.

No one answered him.

A woman from the crowd brought the man a long fiberglass pole.

"This was in the back. I think they hang Christmas lights with it," she said.

"Thank you," the man replied. "This helps, actually."

Dex watched him pull a large pocket knife out and unfold it. The man cut a strip of sheet off of the cot next to him and used it to secure the knife to the pole.

"Grab a few blankets and the strongest of you will have to get under the men one at a time and catch the bodies as I cut them loose.

They are already dead," the man said. "So it won't hurt them if you miss. Just don't get caught under them."

Horror filled Dex's eyes and the men took their places. The man raised the pole toward the first rope. He touched the knife to the rope and pushed the pole forward.

"ENOUGH!" a voice said echoing through the room. The church bells began to clang, signaling midnight. The sound was deafening. The candles flickered. Another gust ripped through the room and extinguished the flames—*again*.

*

Saint Augustine Church, Key Largo, Florida—Monday, August 24, 1992

The day of…

A glow of fire illuminated the area around the top of the stairs. A man clad in a dark robe entered the room and walked down several steps and stopped. A large orange flame engulfed his right hand. It danced back and forth, casting horrifying shadows over the room.

Shit… Dex eyed the staff in his left hand. It was a long golden rod with three bars crossing it at the top. Each bar was slightly shorter than the one below it. The staff itself was nearly as tall as the robed man that possessed it.

"Let us begin," the robed man said.

The man raised the staff high into the air and clacked it onto stone steps. A dark wave of energy shot out across the room. The bags of flesh hanging from the ceiling exploded into a fine, red mist that rained down onto the crowd below them.

Dex and Mary screamed, as did the rest of the crowd. The red liquid rained over everyone and covered them from head to toe in blood.

"SILENCE!" the robed man commanded. "Kneel before me."

Some of the crowd did just that as looks of terror covered their faces. Others froze in place.

Dex was one of the latter, Mary the former.

"KNEEL!" the man commanded again, striking the stone with the heel of the staff.

That was all it took. Another wave of the same dark energy ripped through the crowd, much lower this time. It tore their legs out from under them, causing them to fall onto the blood-drenched floor. A second wave of energy crashed into Dex's body and was quickly absorbed.

Where the man once stood, Dex watched as the robe fell to the floor, empty. The fire dropped to the floor as well but still burned brightly.

Dex stood. He saw Mary look up at him with a what-the-fuck look.

"What are you doing?" she asked him.

Dex simply raised a single finger and pressed it across his lips. "Shhh."

Dex walked to the front of the shelter and ascended the stairs to where the staff stood glimmering next to the flames. He knelt and retrieved the two skeleton keys from the pocket of the robe. Dex clutched the staff and looked over the crowd of kneeling, shuddering heathens.

He took the keys and separated them from the ring.

"These keys were once *my* keys. My keys that opened the gates of Heaven. Now they are the keys to *your* Hell!"

One at a time he slid them into the two keyholes in the staff and gave each a quarter turn, locking them into place. Dex raised the staff high into the air and continued to speak.

"I was there for the massacre of Matthew. I was there for the obliteration of Sodom and Gomorrah. I was there for the torment of Job. I was there for the massacre of the Innocents. I was there for the ten plagues of Egypt. I was there for the flood of Noah. I was there for God's judgment against Jerusalem. I was there for the crucifixion of Christ. And I will be there for the Lake of Fire, when Hell comes to Earth. I will be there long after you have perished.

"FOR I AM ABADDON. I am destruction. I am Lord of the Pit. King of Locusts. I am the Destroyer!"

Fire rose and covered Dex. It swirled around him, engulfing him in his entirety. His human flesh melted away leaving only Abaddon.

The fire died down around Abaddon's hooved feet. His scepter now blackened, glowed a fiery orange in places. He stood some nine or so feet tall now. A set of giant bat-like wings sprang out from his back. Claws replaced fingers. Red, veiny skin replaced pale flesh. The only thing that remained from where Dex's body once stood was charred stone.

Abaddon leapt from the great stone stairs. His wings flapped, cushioning his landing. Abaddon kicked those close enough to kick. Their puny human carcasses crushed like balsa wood. He raised his fiery scepter above his head and swung it. It crashed into five, six, seven at a time, their bodies breaking and instantly set ablaze.

"Your kind will never survive. You are far too trusting. Look at me when I kill you. You trusted me when I looked like your beloved Father Marcus." Abaddon smashed a wriggling carcass next to him with his great hoof.

"Mary. My dear fool, Mary." Abaddon clomped over to her. "You trusted me too. Just as your filthy whore of a mother did. You believed that your frail shit of a brother, weak little Dex, would save you.

"Let me say this… Much like your mother, and all the humans that have had the displeasure of crossing my path, you were wrong."

Abaddon raised his great staff above Mary and paused briefly, "Goodbye, Mary. Say hello to your mother for me!"

The staff swung down, chased by a flaming comet. It smashed into Mary, making her head explode. A fine, red mist sprayed across the already grim room. Abaddon swung time and time again, his staff colliding with those in its path. The carnage was nothing short of complete destruction.

Abaddon wrecked on until the entire shelter was completely ablaze, while outside, hurricane Andrew did the same, smashing and crushing all of southern Florida.

*

What was left, Key Largo, Florida—Wednesday, August 26, 1992

Two days after…

From above, rescue workers dug into the pile of rubble that was once Saint Augustine's Church. Rescue dogs barked at the smell of a human body trapped below. A male voice called for the workers.

"Help me. I'm trapped down here," the voice shouted.

"We are coming, son, hold on," the fireman shouted back.

They broke through to the entrance of the shelter several minutes later. There, on the steps, lay the body of the trapped teen. He coughed as the debris rained down on his battered body. The fireman reached in and pulled the boy out.

"What's your name, son?" he asked.

"Dex," he replied.

Dex sat up after they pulled him out. He clung to a broken scepter in one hand and a pair of skeleton keys in the other. He scanned his surroundings and found only four firemen and a search-and-rescue dog for as far as he could see.

He stood, gripping the scepter tightly ,and plunged its jagged end into the neck of the closest fireman. Blood sprayed from the man's neck as he collapsed to the wet ground. Fast as lightning, Dex did the same to the other three firemen. They were all dead in less than a minute.

Dex looked at the dog. They locked eyes for a moment. The dog whimpered and sat, submitting to him. Dex walked over and knelt next to it. He ran his bloody fingers through the German shepherd's soft fur. The dog began to pant happily.

Dex grabbed its head and twisted with all his might. The dog's head separated from its body. Blood sprayed through the air and the dog's body collapsed.

*

What was left, Key Largo, Florida—Wednesday, August 26, 1992

A news helicopter flew over what was left of Key Largo. The pilot communicated with the cameraman in the back via headset. Both scoured the wreckage.

"Hey, Carl. Look over there. What is that?" the pilot asked.

"Looks like a dog. Maybe a German shepherd," Carl said.

"Shall we set down and save it?" the pilot asked.

"Hell yeah. That would make great news."

The pilot began to lower the chopper. The shepherd stopped and sat, looking up at the helicopter as it landed.

"Go get him, Carl. I'll film."

The pilot grabbed the camera, switched it on and placed it atop his shoulder. His eye pressed tightly to the viewfinder; he zoomed in on the pup. Steadying himself, the camera lens whirred, focusing.

The coarse fur whipped to and fro, like tall grass in a summer breeze. The dog locked eyes with the pilot through the camera lens. It crouched, eyes changing from blue to blood red. A smile spread across its face.

"Carl, stop!"

7

THE LOVERS

LORI AVOCATO

Upright: Love, union, relationships, values alignment, choices
Reversed: Disharmony, imbalance, misalignment of values

A Pauline Sokol series novella

Pauline Sokol stared at her sleazy boss, Fabio Scarpello, and said, "A mental institution, Fabio. Not a *lunatic* hospital. That term went out with lobotomies and massive jolts of electric shock."

He took a long draw on his unlit cigar (because the fabulous office manager, Adele Gerard, who kept him, no, put him in his place, would not let him puff smoke into the air at Scarpello and Tonelli Insurance Company). Although she smoked cigarettes when he was out of the office. Adele was a pip. A gorgeous woman with the body of a Victoria's Secret model, and she always wore polka-dotted something. And gloves. Usually black to match her hair. "Whatever. Lunatic, mental house, you call it what you want but that's where you're headed."

I gulped. Not again. I'd been sent to a mental institution a few years ago; no, I was kidnapped and taken to one where I investigated medical insurance fraud. Now what? More fraud "Over the Cuckoo's

Nest?" "I can't be locked up there again, Fabio. Use someone else."
This time I shuddered at the thought.

He shoved a folder toward me. Another reused one from a
previous case. The info was blackened out and written below: *Lunatic
Hospital. Pauline. Somewhere in New England.*

"Somewhere in New England? What the hell does that mean?"

"Ask Adele. She's got your envelope of goodies." With that, he
took a long drag and inhaled nothing but the stinking smell of a half-
used cigar. "You have to be there tomorrow, so pack fast." Help me
Saint Theresa.

My favorite saint, me being Catholic. I relied on her numerous
times and something told me I was going to need her again. I looked
up to Heaven, trying to ignore the stains on the office ceiling, and
mumbled, "Give me strength, St. T."

*

The drive took nearly an hour. If I were in Connecticut, I would
be in another state in that amount of time. Instead, I followed the
directions to Batesville, which Adele gave me for my GPS. It landed
me in the middle of the woods in the furthest (as far as I could tell)
southwest section, which was near the shore. Long Island Sound.
How bad could it be? I'd read somewhere that being near the ocean
caused our bodies to secrete extra serotonin from negative ions that
we inhaled in certain environments. Think mountains, waterfalls, and
beaches. Some biochemical reaction increased levels of serotonin.
The mood chemical, which helped to alleviate depression, relieved
stress and boosted energy, was something I could use right about
now. Who wouldn't benefit from more serotonin? I caught a glimpse
of the water off to the left, slowed, opened my window and inhaled
deeply.

I felt better already.

Then, I remembered Fabio had sent me here as a nurse, and not
a patient this time. A nurse. I had burned out of that profession long
ago, but he kept getting me back into it by default. I was the only
medical insurance fraud investigator with real medical knowledge—
and no real investigative skills. But, I told myself, I had been learning.
And I had helped solve many cases and earned the insurance
companies gazillions of dollars back and criminals behind bars.

But not alone.

I rounded the curve to see a long driveway, weeds poking through the broken cement, several large red brick structures with white trim, looking very much like an old factory from the early 1900s, and off to both sides white clapboard houses and some weathered cedar shake ones, whose grayish shakes were blowing in the wind. Dilapidated with a capital "D."

I inhaled even deeper because the site before me decreased my serotonin level to about zero.

Then I shivered. It had to be eighty today with oodles of ocean humidity, yet, I shivered. Hm. There weren't any cars in the front circular drive, and I didn't want to go find a place to park and have to carry my luggage for miles. So I pulled up there and left my luggage on the curb. Thanks again to Fabio, I was staying in the staff quarters. Lovely. I'd suggested I get a room at a nearby Marriott or Red Roof, or looking at the campus surrounding me. Any place but here. After parking, I decided to go check in before I committed to any lodging.

Committed.

Oops. Not politically correct for a mental institution. Before I left, one of my darling roomies, Goldie, the dearest transvestite in the world and married to our other roomie, Miles, a RN like me, I had learned this place was very old. The second oldest in the country. A place in Hartford was the first. He also said they used to be called "lunatic" hospitals, and I said that was horrible. Mental health was like any other health problems and should be treated as such, I had argued. Goldie had agreed with me, but that didn't change history or his many horror stories. So, I pulled over, turned off my car, grabbed my purse and stepped out.

'Geez," I said out loud, after another chill chased up from my toes to my head. I felt as if I had something wrong with my brain and no amount of negative ions was going to cheer me up. As I walked around the side of the car, I looked up to the second floor of the adjoining brick building, and although there were no lights on in any windows of that floor, a figure stood where I could see. Not sure if male or female, but I waved anyway.

No response.

Good thing I'd brushed up on my psychiatry with my books from nursing school before coming here. I'd also downloaded some articles to be current. I hoped I wasn't going to have to do much hands-on nursing care, and, since I was working alone, I hoped the case wasn't too difficult either.

The figure opened the window for a few seconds… then was gone!

Oh, geez. It seemed as if it had *flown* out of the window. I scanned the ground below to see if it had jumped, but I really never saw anyone fall out the window. I needed a beer. Coors. Usually light, but right now, I actually needed the real thing—damn the calories. Goldie's stories were playing havoc with my imagination.

Until I got to the front door. *Gulp.* The gigantic worn wooden structure looked as if I was stopping by for that beer with Stephen King. Along both sides of the door were cracked cement flower pots, huge ones, with ivy hanging over all sides. Dead ivy. Soon I expected to hear shrieks coming from the floor above, until I thought, *cut it out. Act professional. You are fine. Everyone knows you are here even, (sigh) Jagger. It is a hospital, for crying out loud.*

Ah, Jagger. The thought of the gorgeous hunk/investigator calmed my nerves but riled up my hormones. Still, I would be safe knowing I wasn't that far away, and I could text in seconds. I found myself yanking my cell phone out of my purse and texting him a "Hey, I'm here."

Red letters filled my screen. Message not sent. Great. No good cell service near the water. Why couldn't they stick cell towers out on floating barges? Before I could continue my thought, the door swung open with a thud when it hit the wall, which had lost chips of paint already, and now a few more.

A very good looking man in a tailored navy suit and red tie walked out. "Ma'am."

I looked behind me. "Oh, me. Hello."

He continued on and didn't offer help, although he looked rather confused at seeing me. Maybe gawking near the door had something to do with that. The door remained open to the dingy lobby with no one around so I turned and called, "Excuse me!"

He stopped, but didn't turn. "Go to the desk and ring the bell, Ms. Sokol."

If I thought those earlier chills were chilly, these right now were freezing. I watched him continue on. *Okay. Okay. He knows who I am because clearly they don't get a lot of drop-ins here. Yes, that's it. Of course he knew they'd be getting a new temporary nurse today. He must be a doctor.*

As I made it across the large lobby toward the unattended reception desk, my mouth dried. Probably from fear as the place had this haunted look about it. A large, worn, red Oriental rug covered more worn wooden planks throughout the room, which had a mezzanine-like area three quarters of the way around behind a railing that looked a bit rickety. I shook my head. My mind was zooming to the worst-case scenario since I arrived at Amity by the Sea Hospital. Amity? What a misnomer. Besides, there was no way I could tell the railings were rickety from merely looking at them, despite the fact that the floors squeaked. Oh, how cliché. I hoped no one noticed I'd left the front door open—for easy escape if need be.

At the desk, I leaned over and called out, "Hello," then searched the cluttered mess for a bell or something to notify someone I was here. "Hello."

"Hellllllloooooo!"

I swung around to see a woman, dressed in a white robe, coming down the gigantic wooden staircase and grabbing onto the carved lion's head at the end. Her hair looked like mine one time when I had to hurry off to work and the stylist couldn't finish my perm.

"Janet, go back to your room."

I swung back around the other way to find a young man sitting at the desk, handling papers as if he'd been working there for hours.

Maybe lunatic hospital *was* the correct term?

Shame on you, Pauline, I thought, then said to the young man, "Hello. My name is Pauline Sokol.

The nurse you were expecting."

He looked at me as if to say, "No, I wasn't," but instead said, "Kirk," while he shuffled more papers around. "Kirk. Kirk. Kirk, I tell you."

After a few more minutes of waiting and hearing some odd sounds, like calls from a distance, I decided not to mention them because Kirk paid no attention. I knew patients in a psych hospital could get noisy, have behaviors and some needed close watching to prevent self-harm or harm to others, so staff probably learned to tune them out so they could do their jobs. Suddenly, I felt a tap on my shoulder, but, again, Kirk paid no attention.

I swung around, saying, "Yes?"

No one was there.

But just as I was about to question Kirk, that snappy dressed doctor hurried through the door I'd left open and up the stairs. Even though they didn't squeak this time, I thought he seemed a bit odd, not even telling Kirk he was back.

"Here."

I turned back to see Kirk handing me a folder and a very old, large key. "Room 113. Second floor."

I smiled. "You mean first floor."

"No." He got up and turned his back to me as if to say "get lost."

"Kirk, was that nicely dressed man a doctor?" I stuck the key in my purse and the folder under my arm.

Without turning around, he said, "Don't know what you are talking about. Get out of here! Go!"

Just then another gentleman came from the back room to the desk and stood shaking his head. "Kirk. Kirk. How many times have you been told to stay away from the front desk?"

"None," he mumbled.

"Baloney. Go to treatment room 120 on the first floor. Nurse Waring is waiting for you."

Kirk never turned back to face me but eased himself to the side and walked toward the stairs backward until he caught my gaze, swung around and hurried up the stairs, which creaked and squeaked like an un-oiled Tin Man!

"Ma'am."

I looked back around, feeling a bit unnerved.

"Sorry, he's a good lad, but so wants to be useful around here. I am John Valeri, the receptionist. And you are?"

I wanted to scream, "Outta here!" but said, "Pauline Sokol. A nurse. Your nurse. Well, not your nurse unless you, too, are a patient." I started to chuckle but John looked rather serious. So what was new? "I am the nurse. Well, the temporary nurse. I'm not planning to be here too long."

"Who is?" John looked at me then the folder under my arm. "Looks as if you already have your info."

"Oh, this. Well, Kirk gave it to me, so I wasn't sure—"

"Kirk knows his stuff." With that he turned and started shuffling papers on the desk behind him.

Oh… my… god. Was he a patient *too*? I waited several minutes to have him turn back, but he wasn't budging and no one else miraculously appeared, so I turned around, grabbed my suitcase and started to say. "Is there an elev…?" Never mind, I thought. I'd take the stairs. This place gave me the creeps, and I was going to call Fabio and give him a piece of my mind as soon as I got cell reception.

If I got reception.

But no way would I confine myself in some old, rickety elevator in this facility.

*

My room was rather New Englandy quaint. It overlooked a few overgrown gardens, but further in the distance I could see the water. I opened the window and inhaled to replenish my serotonin. After that bizarre arrival, I needed it. Several people walked in the dilapidated gardens, and I thought it a shame that no one kept up the flowers and bushes. Several men in navy scrubs where out there too, so they must be staff.

I stuck my head back into the room, which had a brass bed, a real old one, and a twin, no less, a small rocking chair with a side table holding a candle. Geez. I thought that's dangerous in a place like this, but looking closer saw it was a fake battery one. Somehow that made me feel better even if an odd thing for this old decor.

One would expect chipped paint on the walls, but the coat appeared rather fresh, although a drab gray. If I was a superstitious person, I'd think this place haunted. Instead, I said a few prayers to St.

Theresa and a back-up "Hail Mary." Couldn't hurt. The breeze from the water filled the room, so I sat in the rocker—without a soft cushion I might add—and started to look through the file Fabio had given me and the one from, well, Kirk.

Someone was sending bills to Atlas New England Insurance Company from here. Didn't seem any big deal, until I looked at photo copies of the bills.

Nineteen fifty seven.

I held the bill closer to the light, although I'd never had vision problems. Sure enough, all the copies had dates back before I was born. Back before my mother was born! How odd and why would Fabio give me these? Was I supposed to solve some case that was over sixty years ago?

These patients were probably not here any longer or they would have passed away by now.

My head pounded, so I decided to take a walk and clear my thoughts. I grabbed my cell to try to get service outside, although the way things were going, I wasn't too hopeful.

I took the gigantic key from my purse, left the purse on the bed and tucked the cell into my pocket. Once outside the door, I shut and manually locked it. Oh, how very old fashioned. Down the hallway I started to turn toward the stairs but heard a shuffling, a bang, and saw the doctor in the blue suit run out of a room.

"Hey! You okay?" I shouted and ran toward the room.

Room 120.

I looked in the doorway to see Kirk, sleeping on the treatment table, no one else in the room. A tongue depressor sat on the stand nearby and a syringe. Oh, dear. What had they pumped into poor Kirk, and where was a staff member?

With his hands and feet restrained, Kirk looked safe enough from falling as he snored softly, so I went to the door.

Down the end of the hallway after the staircase, was that doctor. Facing me, but not moving.

"Hey, sir! Doctor!" I hurried toward him.

He didn't budge.

Since I didn't see him up close and personal, I hadn't noticed before, but his eyes were rather glassy when he looked at me. No, through me. He stood still, staring, then turned, and over his shoulder said, "Only concern yourself with the lovers, Pauline. *The lovers.*"

"What the heck does that mean?" I yelled after him, but he kept going, and soon, as if he just disappeared, I could no longer see him. Of course, he hadn't just disappeared, however, the hallway was long and dark and had several doors off of it. As I got closer, I noticed all were closed. He must have sneaked into one, but I wasn't about to open any doors in this place unless it was part of my job.

My job.

Geez, I had no idea what I was supposed to do or when.

"The lovers," came from nowhere in a rather deep, scratchy voice.

I swung around but that didn't sound like that doctor or John, and I could hear Keith still snoring away in the distance. Chills ran up my spine in the humid air. I hugged my arms around myself and said, "Damn." Knowing I should go back to my room and read more about this case, I couldn't help myself, so I walked further down the hallway—away from my room.

You have no business sneaking around, Pauline, I thought, however, I had to keep going. Guess my investigator juices were flowing. When I got to the end of the hallway, there was a door. Not just any door. It was so institutional, with a frosted glass window and lettering that had withered and faded with age.

Thirteen.

I could make out a thirteen. How corny. Above the number was the word "Ward." So that door led to Ward 13. Corny, yes, but enticing nevertheless. I had my phone with me, so I'd take some pictures to, perhaps, use on this case. Not much made sense around here, so I reached for the handle and turned it downward. With a click and a squeak as I pushed the door open, I felt a rush of cold— really cold—air, smack me in the face. Who would have thought part of this old place was air conditioned?

When I stepped through the doorway, the air smothered me in humidity. Hm. I was guessing it wasn't air conditioned at all. Very dark, except for the light through the extremely dirty windows, I took out my phone to use as a flashlight. I slid my finger across the bar on the phone, pressed the flashlight symbol, and suddenly regretted doing that.

As if I'd stepped back in time, the furniture in the room looked like it was from the fifties. Much like my mother's nostalgic house. But Stella Sokol's house always had a warm, cozy feeling with delicious food aromas. This place was hot, humid and confusingly cold feeling. The furniture was filled with cracks in the vinyl, holes in the carpet and scratches in the woodwork of the doors and tops of the tables, as if someone had tried to scratch messages into them. Patients? The aroma was certainly not food but more medicinal. Institutional, if that could explain a scent. I held my phone up to see farther into the room.

The doctor stood in front of a distant window.

"Hello. I seemed to have lost my way."

As I cautiously walked forward, I realized it wasn't a figure of a man but the gentlest of breezes that had the worn blue curtains spinning upon itself to trick my mind. "Oh." I had to either find my way back or go out of one of the side doors that, hopefully, led to the courtyard where I might find a staff member.

This place gave me the creeps, and the worse part was how empty it was.

So far I'd only seen two patients here: Kirk and the lady in white on the stairway. It hadn't been that many years since I worked in a hospital, and no unit at Saint Gregory's was ever empty. Mental health has made leaps and bounds over the years, so many patients were treated as out-patients, but there still were a number of institutions with the more severe cases. Why would they need my help here if there weren't hardly any patients? Wait. There were several outside my bedroom window that I'd forgotten about, but still not many for a place this size.

Amity by the Sea was making me feel nuts, and I was a logical person. Nothing logical about this ward, the doctor, poor Kirk or a slew of oddities around here. *Enough.* I had to get back to my room and some sanity. I turned to go back to the door that I'd come through, and it was then I heard a scream.

"Help!" a female voice cried out. "Please!"

Damn. My Catholic-school-induced conscience would never allow me to walk away from helping someone, nor would my years of being a nurse. "Yes? Hello!"

Silence.

I ran toward where I thought the sound came from. Of course, the way things were going, maybe I imagined the voice. "Is someone there?" Three corridors came off the main room I'd landed myself in, so I turned toward the one on the right. That had to be where the person was. "I can help you if you tell me where you are!" I shouted.

This time the voice came out considerably weakened. "Help." A deep sigh followed. "Here.

Here."

"Okay. I hear you. Bang something so I can follow the sound."

Clang. Clang.

It came from the last room at the end of the hallway. I had a pretty good sense of direction and realized that was the room that I

135

NEVER FEAR – THE TAROT

thought I saw someone in earlier. I'd managed to get myself into the older, more dilapidated building when I came through the door. Before me, the hallway ended with an Exit sign and probably a fire escape. I hurried into the room.

A beautiful, and by beautiful I meant creamy white skin, black hair piled high in a bun and dressed in a white johnny coat, yet looking at if she were in the nineteen-fifties, woman lay on the bed— in restraints much like Kirk's.

"Oh." I came closer to her. "I am a nurse, but don't think I should undo the restraints until I talk to a staff member—"

If I thought the doc's eyes looked through me, this gal's burned into me.

I reached out to touch her, but before I could… a card fell from her hand onto the floor.

"I'll get that for you." I reached to pick it up, and when I stood, she was gone. Gone.

I never heard a sound. And the restraints were gone too. Someone was trying to fool me. Or *scare* me.

I turned and ran to the exit door, pushed the door till it creaked on its hinges, and I flew down to the last stair of the fire escape, which was several feet from the ground. "Oh, hell!" I jumped, landed on my feet and ran toward what I thought was the courtyard.

My sense of direction was correct. The courtyard lay ahead, but no one was around, so I flopped onto the closest bench and tried to breathe slower. Then I fell back, shut my eyes for a second and let out a gigantic sigh. I needed to find my way back to my room, pack my bags and get the hell out of Amity. With that plan in mind, I looked at the card still in my hand. Much larger than a playing card, it was rather worn, but I held it out to the sunlight to see two naked figures, male and female, with what looked like some angel behind. The label on the bottom read: The Lovers.

On the top of the card, in a very female handwriting was written, My Lover. And that made my heart skip a few beats.

*

Taking slow, deep breaths till my heart beat in a regular sinus rhythm, I stayed out in the open and out of the buildings, and pulled my cell from my pocket. Damn. I hadn't taken any pictures, but then again, I was fleeing for my life. Or, at least, my own mental health. Only two bars on my phone. I put Jagger's name into contacts and pressed the green button until it became red and shut my eyes. "Please answer. Please, Jagger." But nothing. I waited to leave a message, but the phone conked out before I could. Damn again. I tried to text and that didn't work either. So, I got up, walked away from the water and tried the office. If anyone knew where Jagger was, it would be Adele. No answer, and again, as if someone had control over my phone, the reception died.

I made my way around the buildings to the front door, since I was familiar with how to get to my room from there. If I had my purse and car keys, *I think* I would have high-tailed it to my car and peeled out of the weed-infested driveway to get back to the safety of Hope Valley.

Yanking the huge door open with little difficulty, I assumed my adrenaline was pumping from my "fight or flight" response to this place. I had no intention of fighting. Flight was my first choice.

John was behind the desk. Great. I'd have to explain to him that I needed to leave.

When I walked closer, he turned around. He'd been reading a paperback novel and had a stack of five or six in front of him. Good for him. He looked up and said, "They have been waiting for you."

If "they" were all the ghostly weirdos I'd run into already, I was about to tell him they could go jump in the sound. I was leaving. But curiosity and logic got the best of me. "They?"

He turned toward the back table, rifled around with some papers, then turned back only to hand me one—that was blank.

Oh… my… god.

"I don't see anything on this." Yes, I felt stupid saying that, but it kept getting weirder and weirder around here, so stating the obvious was logical to me right now. "Nothing. Look." I held it out toward him.

"Room 213." He turned his back toward me.

I knew he wouldn't answer anything so I turned toward the stairs. As I walked up, they creaked as if I'd fall through any second. Nothing would surprise me. It bothered me and yes, made me curious and curiouser to know what John meant by "they." Guess I'd find out in Room 213, but what the heck floor was that on?

Maybe I'd stick around a bit more and try to find out more about the insurance fraud. Since John seemed the most normal of anyone I'd met, he kind of gave me a false sense of security. Okay, I'd give it a shot. I stopped mid-stairs, leaned over the railing and asked rather loudly, "What floor is that on, John?"

"The one you just left."

Gulp. He knew I'd ventured into the other building, but how? Maybe they had a system of cameras around here? Would make sense, except that I never saw a camera on the ceilings nor did I see monitors near John's desk.

I turned toward the stairs and walked slowly to the top. I figured I would need my strength if I ended up in some weird time warp as I had before. But John said they were waiting for me, and he was certainly real.

I think.

*

I managed to make my way through to Ward 13. A nurse sat at the desk this time. She actually wore nurse's whites, a cap, and if I could see her feet, I'm sure she had old Clinic White Nurse's shoes on! Oh well, to each her own. It did make her look more professional than scrubs and clogs.

Those were the days. "Hello, I'm Pauline, the new nurse."

"Room 213." She quickly bent her head to the left and back upright.

Okay. I guess that was down the corridor on the left. A few patients sat in the chairs of the common area this time, watching TV. I couldn't believe my eyes. The TV was tiny and the picture in black and white. They didn't seem to mind, though, as they just sat staring. Sad, I thought. How very sad when one's mind goes. Mental health was a difficult field. How much easier to treat people with stomach or heart or muscle problems. But not the mind. Much more difficult, and it seemed, when one's mind became lost, it was very difficult to get them back to reality—if they ever could.

I looked at the top of the doors to see the numbers and found myself at Room 212. Then the hallway ended. Strange. I was certain she meant this corridor. I started to turn around and noticed a very tiny sign above a doorway. Two hundred thirteen. It must have been through the doorway. I opened the door only to see a set of stairs. Great. I held onto the railing and walked down. This place now had creeped me out so much that I feared I'd do a nosedive down if I wasn't holding on.

At the bottom of the stairs, I froze. Ahead of me was a long tunnel. I'd walked down below the ground level and the tunnel had no windows. But on the side wall was 2-1-3, with an arrow pointing—toward the tunnel.

Pauline Sokol was no fool. Pauline Sokol was an investigator, and if she doesn't do her job, thousands suffered with higher insurance premiums because of all the fraud. *I have to help,* I thought after that little pep talk. For a few seconds, I stood staring down the tunnel, felt my phone in my pocket. If nothing else, I could use it as a weapon. Maybe. Then, suddenly a figure walked down at the other end.

"Oh, hey! Can you help me find Room 213?" I ran forward, but the figure, a woman in a johnny coat again, walked away from me. "Damn it." Hurrying faster, I got to the end of the tunnel, and naturally, another door. I never saw the figure leave through the door, but she was gone, so that had to be where she went. "I feel like damn Alice in Wonderland," I mumbled.

I opened the door and stood, shocked.

Not only was Room 213 probably in here, but first, it was also another common area. No nurses or other staff were around, and this time, no patients either. The décor was similar to the one upstairs, aquamarine vinyl chairs and couches, purple walls with black trim. Yikes. Suddenly I remembered one of the nuns back in Catholic grammar school telling us that if kids wore purple and black, that was a sign of mental illness. I chuckled. I'm sure the nun said that so we'd be glad to wear our gray plaid uniforms.

I heard a woman yell out again. Oh, dear. She kind of sounded like the one I saw, or thought I saw this morning. I touched my pocket. I still had her Tarot card in my pocket. I guessed she'd want it back, so I followed the voice and turned into what looked like a treatment room.

She stood there, this time her bun was undone to reveal long, flowing dark hair. Her patient gown was much longer when she stood, and a gentle sea breeze blew it and her hair in a very sensuous way. No wonder. I could see she held the hand of a man who lay on the treatment table.

I hoped they hadn't overly medicated him.

The woman sang softly into his ear. Maybe he was her lover.

How sweet. I couldn't see past her, though, to see if he were awake or zonked out, like I'd found poor Kirk. "Excuse me," I said as softly as I could. I stepped forward but didn't want to startle her with my touch, so I repeated, "Excuse me."

She swung around, glared at me until I shivered, and ran past me. No, she kind of floated past me, but at warp speed! In her haste, I had been spun around as if the ocean breeze had turned into hurricane force winds. "Geez!"

I swung back around and walked toward the bed—then froze. "Ja... Jagger?"

*

It couldn't be! What would Jagger be doing in this lunatic bin? Now I decided that term was truly appropriate. I tried to shake him. He had been drugged, and hopefully, not received electric shock therapy. I cringed at the thought. I bent toward his ear. "Jagger. It's me, Pauline. You know, Sherlock?" He'd given me that endearing term way back when we worked cases together, but back then I'm not sure it was endearing. I reached out to touch his shoulder for a gentle shake.

My hand went right through to the table.

I yanked it back. What the hell was going on? I couldn't bear to think something had happened to Jagger! Not Jagger. There was no one like him. I couldn't look at him, so I turned away to face the doorway. Oh, God, what was I going to do? My hands shook, my heart broke, and I shut my eyes to tell myself I must be dreaming. Suddenly a cold wind blew into my face.

My eyelids flung open to see that same woman standing in the doorway. "He is *mine*," she growled.

"You keep your hands off of him!" I readied to yank out my phone to clobber her if she tried to get near Jagger. But, I wasn't sure she was even real.

"Emily," a soft, raspy sound came from behind me.

I swung around. The man lying there was not Jagger at all! Oh, God. *What is happening?* This man was very old, white hair and glassy blue eyes. Not Jagger at all.

Emily flew past me. "Joshua. Joshua. Joshua Mendelson. " She leaned toward him and started singing again.

That was my cue to exit.

I didn't even remember running through the tunnel, but found myself in the common area where patients had been watching TV. No one around. No great surprise. Even the nurse was gone. I started to head toward the door out of this hell, but stopped. The nurse wasn't around. So, I decided to go behind the desk and see what I could find for my case.

Patient records were held in silver metal, flipchart-type records. This place was back in the fifties for sure. I opened several, read through notes and found bills. Bills that were over sixty years old!

Someone was still billing the Atlas Carrier Insurance Company from this unit. I'd have to ask John about that. When I went to stick the flipchart back into its holder, I noticed a name on the lowest chart. Joshua Mendelson. I grabbed it and sat to read through it.

Joshua Mendelson was being treated for a psychosis. He'd received massive doses of antipsychotic meds. Even I knew the doses were way too high. He also received electric shock therapy several times a week. Today must have been one of those days. I could only guess that those doses were also way too high. I thumbed through to find out his history. Joshua had been institutionalized since he was seventeen. His parents reported him seeing a woman who was not there. "A visual hallucination," I mumbled. He had tried to hurt his parents, so they had him committed to Amity by the Sea—in 1956.

Nineteen fifty six.

I shook my head and continued reading. Joshua was a wild patient, often needed to be restrained with cold wet packs to calm him down. Back in my student nurse days, I remember the instructor telling us how patients were stripped of their clothes, wrapped in cold, wet sheets much like a mummy, with only their head sticking out. Apparently, the archaic swaddling calmed them down and they remained that way until the staff felt them ready to go back to their ward.

Upon further reading, I learned that Joshua had formed a relationship with a female patient who had been suicidal. Emily? I could only guess. As I read further, sure enough, Emily and Joshua had fallen in love. She became pregnant and the nurses took her son as soon as she gave birth, sending her deeper into her psychosis.

Neither Joshua nor Emily were ever the same nor were they allowed to be together. I touched my pocket to feel Emily's card. When I pulled it out of my pocket, it came out upside down. Now I had to know more about the meaning of the card.

I heard shouting in the distance, and since it wasn't a cry for help, I stuck Joshua's record back into the holder, got up and hurried out of the unit.

If it even was a unit.

The entire place was so weird that nothing made sense to me.

What was real and what was not.

Joshua and Emily *were* real, but now…

*

Once I was safely back in my room—if I could be safe anywhere around here—I held my phone toward the window. More bars. Great. I Googled The Lovers tarot card. When I picked it up after Emily had dropped it, I held it upright. That meant love, trials overcome. Maybe that's what made me think I saw Jagger lying there instead of Joshua. On the other side, the reversed side, it meant failure and foolish design. Poor Emily and Joshua fell right into that one. How sad.

I tried to call Adele to find out where Jagger was. This time she answered. "Hello, *Chéri!*"

I loved the way the French Canadians spoke. After a bit of chit chat, I asked, "Adele, do you know is Jagger on a case? Do you know where he is?"

"With you, Chéri, with you."

The phone fell out of my hand. I collapsed backward onto the bed. With me? He couldn't be.

Not in this lunatic asylum. Quickly I got up to clarify with Adele, but the phone was dead.

Oh… my… god.

I packed up my stuff, found my pink pepper spray, which I'd gotten as a gift from Jagger, and stuck it in my pocket. Maybe that's why I saw him here. A premonition. My mother swore by them but I'd never had one… until now.

Sneaking down the creaky staircase, I looked to see John not at his post. Great. Hurrying across the room as if my speed would make it creak less, I got to the front door, yanked it open and out I scurried to stick everything into my car. I'd find Jagger and get us both the hell out of here. Fabio could balk all he wanted about the case, since I'm sure neither he nor the insurance company would believe me about them getting billed from a ward that was stuck in the fifties. Right now, I could care less. I had to find Jagger.

After I'd locked everything but my phone and pepper spray in the car, I headed back inside. Despite my determination, I didn't feel quite that confident. I mean, I could hold my own against criminals committing fraud, but I was guessing this time I was not playing on an even field. Being Catholic, I don't think I was supposed to believe in ghosts. But damn it, there sure was a lot of proof in this nutty place.

John was at his desk. Great. I went over to him, once again interrupted his reading, and asked, "Is there a male unit here at Amity?"

Without looking up, he mumbled, "Ward 313."

I shook my head, "I should have guessed that." If Jagger were undercover here, he'd probably be assigned to a male ward. At least I hoped so. "What floor—"

"White house by the beach."

Now that I couldn't have figured out by myself. I swung around, hurried toward the door and turned toward the water. That house had to be one of the little white cottages with the shingles blowing in the wind. When I got close enough, I saw the doctor in blue standing in the doorway. He quickly turned, went inside and shut the door.

He must have seen me. Did he know I'd been snooping around? No matter. I ran up the steps onto the porch and tried to open the door. Locked. "Damn it." I started to pound on it, half expecting the doctor to open it and chastise me. But that didn't matter. If Jagger had come to help with this case, I needed to hook up with him and maybe, just maybe, tell him about the weirdness I'd been through.

A young guy in blue scrubs opened the door. "Yeah?"

"Hi. John told me to come here. I'm the new nurse." I bit my lip and waited for him to tell me to get lost. But he didn't. Without a care, he stepped aside and let me come into the shabby living room where a few men sat, once again watching TV. Color this time. Poor things. Not much mental stimulation around here.

He pointed toward what looked like a makeshift nurse's station. I went behind the desk and looked for the flipcharts, but there was a computer here instead. Interesting. Made Ward 213 look very retro. No charts had billing information on them. I guessed there was a separate department for that, unless John Valeri did billing too. Before I could get up to look around more, I heard talking down the hallway.

I remained silent for a second, then heard a deep voice say, "Yes, Doc."

Leaning as far over as I could without being seen, I saw the guy who let me in talking to the doctor in blue. "Give him another shot of propranolol."

The guy hesitated, "But, Doc, isn't that way too high of a dose after the previous ones?"

"Where's your psychiatric degree from, Bryan?"

"I don't have one, Doctor Mendelson. I'll get the shot ready."

Mendelson? Oh… my… god. He was Joshua and Emily's son! The nurses must have secretly raised the baby. Maybe that's why they hung around here after I'm sure they had passed on. I got up and stood near the desk. Too much propranolol could cause memory loss and plenty of heart problems. Whoever they were giving it to, could be in serious jeopardy. I was ready to head down the hallway to talk to the doctor, when his words stopped me cold.

"At least he'll forget all about the billing issues, Bryan. You don't want to go back to prison, do you?"

Before I waited for Bryan's response, my intuition kicked in. Jagger! They had to be talking about Jagger. I saw Bryan turn into a room, which was probably the medication room and the doctor went down the hallway. Within seconds, I silently walked down the hall, looking into each room.

In the second to the last room, a man lay on a treatment table. Not just any man… but Jagger!

"Oh, no!" I ran in and leaned over a passed out Jagger. "Jagger, wake up. It's me, Sherlock. We have to get you out of—"

"He ain't going anywhere and neither are you—nurse whoever you are," Bryan said, holding a syringe out toward me.

"I think this patient has had enough." While I spoke, I touched the pepper spray in my pocket and wrapped my fingers around the container. Please, God, let it still work.

As Bryan came around the treatment table toward me, I pulled it out and sprayed the crap out of him. Despite his screaming and falling to the floor, Jagger remained silent, but the doctor came rushing in.

"What the hell?"

I stooped down, grabbed the syringe from Bryan's hand and stuck it with all my strength into the doctor's arm. Since it would take a bit to work, I sprayed him too. A lot.

Then I leaned over, shook Jagger several times and said, "Come on, Jagger, wake up. Wake up!"

His eyelids fluttered open, I leaned forward and kissed him, then looked to see a card sail to the floor from *his* hand, landing upright. *The Lovers*. I stared in disbelief as Jagger mumbled, "What the hell took you so long, Sherlock?"

With tears of joy running down my cheeks, I realized The Lovers apparently led me to the man who made me quiver so I could save his life this time.

And Emily and Joshua helped.

VII

THE CHARIOT

8

THE CHARIOT

TARA NINA

Upright: Succor, Triumph, Providence, War trouble, Presumption, Vengeance
Reversed:Riot, Quarrel, Dispute, Litigation, Defeat

Chapter One

It was a dark and stormy night. Lightning flashed. Thunder rolled, rattling the windows of the abandoned warehouse. Agent Josie James drew her gun, eased along the darkened corridor and readied for whatever lay in wait. Her muscles tightened, fingers whitened with her grip on the weapon. Wind whistled through broken panes, making it difficult to determine which noises the fugitive made and which belonged to the gust of cold air laced with rain.

Each step brought her closer to the dim light at the end of the long hallway. Her heartbeat increased. Pulse thumped through her veins. Someone hid in that room. She heard the shuffle of feet and the scrape of a chair. Had they somehow sensed she was there? Josie froze, watching, waiting for a sign, some signal giving her the advantage she needed to take her prey by surprise.

*

Anora reread the first words she'd managed to write in over six months. With the stress of her divorce and the battle with Tony in court over the rights to her novels, it was refreshing to at least be in front of the computer. All that "he said, she said" scenario had torn her apart. His claim to have been instrumental in the creation of her Josie James mystery novels was ludicrous. The judge initially leaned in his favor. Thank God, her smart attorney requested proof of Tony's knowledge of the storyline, without using any media devices to retrieve information, while in court. When he couldn't give basic particulars concerning the characters, titles, or plots of any of the thirty-six best sellers in that series, the judge was forced to reconsider.

Since there was no prenup, the ass was awarded a decent chunk of her money as reimbursement for all the years he'd worked to support her writing "hobby." If the judge had known the amount of verbal abuse, the lies, and the humiliation she'd suffered in silence… It didn't matter. It was over. It wouldn't have made a difference in the judge's decision. He was a man, and men stuck together. Tony hadn't been a controlling, manipulative monster when they met, but he turned into one the instant she created a formidable name for herself in the publishing industry. Anora kicked herself daily over that mistake made while wearing the blinders of love and stupidity.

Hobby! She snorted. The judge called her work a hobby. Her lawyer had soothed her anger by saying he was just jealous that one book alone made double the benchwarmer's yearly salary. That still made the edge of her lips twitch into a small smile.

She leaned back, staring at the blinking cursor. Here she sat working on book number thirty-seven. Words whirled around her brain, trying to form a blockbuster start to her latest creation, but what she'd written didn't ignite her imagination or make her fingers itch to burn up the keyboard.

"Pure crap," she muttered under her breath. Her finger hovered over the delete key, but never landed.

She jumped as a bright flash of lightning filled the room, illuminating the shadows that had taken over. Thunder rumbled across the slate shingles of the old cabin on Chariot Lake at the same time a hand landed on her shoulder. Anora screamed as she shoved away from the desk, spun the chair and leapt simultaneously. Her IPOd headphone cord caught on the arm, snatched one bud from her ear while the other remained steadfast, causing her head to swivel in the direction of the intruder. Laughter pealed, breaking through the writer's fog, which consumed her brain mere moments earlier. Recognition sank in as the man switched on the overhead light.

She snatched the ear bud out, freeing herself from the tangled mess of her headphones. "Dammit, Elijah! I should kill you for that! Haven't you ever heard of knocking or at least calling before you scare the bejeezus out of someone?"

He straightened his glasses as he cleared his throat, stilling his laughter. "I did. Check your cell phone. There should be three missed calls and two voice mails from me. Got nervous that an ax murderer or something up here in the boondocks had killed you, so I took the three hour drive, thank-me-very-much, to make sure my number one author wasn't chopped to pieces. And as for the door," he continued, pointing a finger toward the opened wooden door, "I knocked. You really should lock that thing when you're sitting with your back to it, lights off, and music blaring through your headphones. You never know. Next time it really could be an ax murderer. Then, where would I be?"

"Looking for a new number one," Anora practically growled, staring at him. Part of her was excited to see him. He'd been on her mind a lot lately, and not in a professional manner. The other half was trying to regain a normal heart rate.

His black hair hung sexily over one eye before he brushed it back into the funky hipster style he wore. Those big brown eyes of his were hidden behind the popular black plastic rims every male member of the hipster community donned, and his clothing was straight from the pages of GQ—straight-leg jeans, white button-down with the sleeves rolled to the elbows, topped with a deep green sweater vest and cool, cutting-edge loafers on his feet—no socks. With his tall, leanly-muscled frame, he'd be the perfect poster child for the casually dressed business male. Elijah was dreamy to say the least. He'd been her agent for seven years and had been behind her every step of the way. Not her ex. She breathed deeply, calming the nerves he'd frazzled. When he turned away, it didn't last. Her gaze landed on the mold of those jeans to his ass and her heart rate spiked again.

"Ah, yes. But I wouldn't like it." He walked to the door, stepped outside for a moment then returned with a large carryout bag. Shutting the door, he smiled. "I brought food from the only open restaurant in this town. Joe's Fish Shack or something like that. The young lady behind the counter swore they made the best coleslaw." He tilted his chin, poking his nose in the air comically. "I'll be the judge of that. You know how I loves me some coleslaw. Which way to the kitchen?"

She pointed. The scent of fish wafted to her nose as he walked past her to the kitchen. Her stomach groaned, reminding her the last meal had been breakfast. Anora hurried behind him, images flipping through her head. Had she or hadn't she cleaned? Were there dishes in the sink? She hated not being able to remember if there were or not. Ask her anything about one of her novels and she could spout it accurately without a second thought, but day-to-day life, well, that was a different genre entirely.

She caught the swinging door, entered and released her breath. The kitchen wasn't a disaster. Her cereal bowl and spoon were in the dish drain along with the coffee mug. The glass carafe on the coffeemaker contained one last cup, but had long ago shut off via a timer. So, not bad.

Elijah set the bag on the small stainless steel, square table, which was pushed against a wall in the quaint kitchen. It wasn't a large room, just big enough to suit its purpose. The cabinets formed an L-shape along one side of the room. The sink sat directly in the middle of the stainless steel countertop of the lower cabinets. A refrigerator stood at the end of the L beside the back door. The stove was on the opposite wall and had a shelf above it containing a microwave. A faded shade of yellow covered the walls. The black-and-white, checkered-patterned linoleum had seen better days.

"You want to eat in here?" Elijah unpacked the bag, while looking at her.

"Nah, let's sit in the other room. It's bigger, not so close."

He turned, clipping his hip on the edge of the closest cabinet. "I see what you mean." He gave her an arched eyebrow.

"You want a bottle of water or a glass of wine?"

"Wine, of course, my dear."

She moved to the fridge and pulled it opened. Taking out a bottle, he groaned behind her.

"Red in the fridge?" He visibly shivered when she turned. "Have I not taught you anything?"

"Nope. I like what I like." Anora grabbed two glasses from the top cabinet beside the fridge. With bottle, glasses and a corkscrew in hand, she waltzed past him to hold the swinging door open with her hip.

Holding the takeout metal containers and two packets of plasticware complete with salt, pepper and napkins, Elijah strolled into the main room of the log cabin. "I got you the lemon chicken dish with pasta and me the fried fish of the day with slaw and sweet potato fries."

Her stomach roared like she'd swallowed a lion. He grinned. "Guess my timing couldn't have been any better."

Chapter Two

"Thanks for the meal." Anora poured the last of the wine into their glasses, then took a seat beside Elijah. The log cabin had a wide front porch and a comfy swing hung from its ceiling. They'd moved to the swing to relax after dinner.

The storm subsided to a steady rain. Woods surrounded three sides of the cabin. The front yard faced the lake and it was a short walk across the dirt road to the dock. A pair of rental cars sat in the driveway, hers and Elijah's. Owning a vehicle wasn't necessary in the city with the buses, cabs, and subways.

"Couldn't let you starve." He clinked his glass to hers before taking a sip. "Besides, I wanted to see you, make sure you were okay." He leaned toward her. "You didn't sound well before you left."

Anora rested her head on the back of the swing and stared in the direction she knew the lake sat, though there was no seeing it this night. "I just needed to get away from all that crap, from Tony and his shit brigade. Still can't believe he got almost half my money."

"Consider it well spent if it means he's gone." Elijah took a swig, then added, "Never liked him anyway. He was the load of bricks holding you back."

She sighed heavily. "What if it was the need to prove him wrong that drove me to write, to prove I wasn't stupid and could create a world people wanted to read about? I haven't written shit since the divorce started."

"You've written something. I read it while you threw away the plates."

"That crap?" she gasped. "You shouldn't have read it."

"It wasn't your best, but it wasn't your worst either."

A long silence lingered between them before she spoke again. "I'm thinking of stepping away from the Josie James series. Start something new, different."

"Like what? Any ideas you wanna bounce off me? I'm game." Elijah turned into the corner. He faced her and used his foot to gently sway the swing. Its creak, mixed with the steady cadence of the rain, blended into an unusual background noise, pleasant with an eerie twist.

"Not sure, but this area is full of inspiration. Did you know a gypsy and her lover founded this town? Antanasia and Alexandru. He was a fisherman. Together, they built a store in what is now the town of Chariot. They sold necessities like groceries, fish, bait and tackle. They bartered with the locals, traded goods for furs and deer meat. In the back of the store, she told fortunes. Apparently, she made a unique black raspberry jam, which kept hunters and fishermen returning just to lay claim to a jar."

She didn't give him a chance to speak. "Once they established their business, the town grew and it needed a name. The tale goes, Antanasia set her tarot deck on the counter, tapped it three times and told Alexandru to pull a card. That would be the name. He lifted the top card and it was the Chariot, the card of succor, triumph, and providence or vengeance. In her opinion, it was the right choice. They'd been cast out of their homeland because neither family approved of their union. This card proved they were triumphant in their new life by being successful when no one believed in them."

"That's an interesting story."

"Oh, it gets better yet, sad *and* frightening." Anora wet her mouth with a sip of wine. "Alexandru drowned in the lake while fishing. His boat was found capsized, but his body was never found. Antanasia's heart was broken. She believed he'd been murdered but couldn't prove it. Legend has it her spirit remains in the area seeking vengeance for Alexandru. This cabin was theirs. It's been renovated, given a modern kitchen and plumbing, but the ghost remains, lurking, taking souls in exchange for her lost love."

"Ghost, really? You believe this cabin is haunted?"

"I'd like to think so. It'd make for a creepy setting, don't you think?"

"Maybe." He cleared his throat. "What do you mean by taking souls? Has someone died in this place?"

"Not sure. The real estate agent wasn't specific. She told me there have been multiple unexplained occurrences throughout the years."

"Occurrences? What sort of occurrences? Chains rattling, sightings of ghosts?" His sceptical tone told her he didn't take her seriously.

"People have gone missing. No bodies were ever found, but each one had stayed at this cabin."

"You mean they disappeared while staying here?" His voice deepened with concern. "Did they ever find out what happened? A serial killer possibly?"

Anora shrugged. "It's just a ghost tale. You know, something someone started so far back that no one knows if it's true or not. An urban legend of sorts. But it's the reason the agency has difficulty renting this cabin. No one wants it after they hear the tales."

"No one but you," he noted.

"Yeah, I like the place. Even though it's kind of scary." Thunder rolled as if on cue and the rain increased its pace.

"Has anything scary happened to you since you've been here?"

Was he teasing her? "Not really." She paused. Anora wasn't sure if she should tell him since he didn't seem to take the possibility of the supernatural being real seriously. "It's just…"

"It's just what?" He straightened. In the dark, she couldn't see his eyes clearly, but she knew he stared directly at her.

"I'm probably being silly. I've been here a couple days and nothing bad has happened, but sometimes I feel like I'm being watched."

"Have you seen anyone hanging around the cabin? Maybe peeking in at you?"

"No, it's nothing like that. It's not…" She bit her lip, not sure how to proceed, then blurted, "I'm not certain it's human. It's a sensation, an icy chill, and doesn't seem friendly."

A cool breeze blew across the porch, causing Anora to shiver. Elijah's arm came around her shoulders, hugging her close to him in a warming embrace against his side. This close, she saw and felt him much better. Was that desire she read in his eyes or simply her wishful imagination? His heat him chased away all that chilled her, making her hunger for more. Anora couldn't move. She licked her lips, anticipating what he might say—or better yet, do. But hesitation replaced the flicker, dousing the flame.

"You sure you haven't seen anyone lurking around?" Concern riddled his words as his hand absently stroked her shoulder.

Her brain focused on those fingertips for a millisecond before she responded, "No."

"I think being in such a desolate location as this cabin has set your vivid imagination on fire and rekindled your muse." His tone softened. "So you want to write ghost tales? Then do it."

Her stomach sank. God, they'd been best friends forever. What was she thinking? The recent sex dreams starring Elijah had tormented her nights. Having him here, alone with her in this cabin in the middle of nowhere, this was a fantasy come true. She'd been secretly attracted to him for years, but never acted on it because of her marriage. She believed in those vows, even when Tony hadn't. She straightened, placing a bit of space between them. But was she woman enough to follow through on these feelings now? She hadn't been with another man for almost eight years. Granted, she hadn't had sex with her ex in the last three, not since the night she'd first suspected him of cheating. She mentally shook the images from her brain and forced herself to focus on what Elijah had asked.

"Maybe romances with paranormal elements."

"Everybody's doing it. Not sure I can sell it with the market slush right now." Her eyes landed on his hand as it brushed the renegade lock that had fallen over his brow back into place. Her fingers twitched to do that for him. "How about romance with a murderous element?"

Anora sat upright, a bit too quickly, and her head spun from the wine. She caught the arm of the swing to steady herself and breathed deeply the wonderful scent of the fresh rain mixed with wet wilderness smell. Nothing like a good dose of air to clear the head. A hint of an idea took root in the base of her brain. She could do this. She could write a murderous romance, and she knew just the name she'd give the first character she'd kill off.

She stood, leaned and kissed Elijah on the cheek. Hovering nearly nose-to-nose, she made the mistake of inhaling the essence of the man. Inch a bit to the left and she'd get that taste she desperately wanted. Anora righted, spun, and called over her shoulder, "Let me think on it. You're welcome to use the downstairs guest room. It's the door beside the stairs."

The screen door slammed behind her, making her flinch. Before he followed her inside, Anora hurried across the room and upstairs. Anora flopped across the bed. With Elijah sleeping in the same house, this was going to be a long, hard night filled with frustrated, unfulfilled dreams. She punched the pillow, before she rose and dressed for bed.

Chapter Three

Elijah stood outside the screened door and watched her cute ass until she reached the top of the staircase. *Missed the moment.* Her lips were so close he smelled the wine on her breath. He swore he'd seen desire in those beautiful green eyes. Sitting beside her on the swing, he'd ached to tangle his fingers in her long red hair, especially that lock of natural blonde that ran down the right side of her face. It was a streak of nature making her oddly more beautiful to him. Her ex made her try to dye it to match the rest, but the color never took. Elijah smiled at the memory. It was her body's way of telling her to leave it be.

Thinking of her body had him wishing he'd followed her. She was perfectly rounded in all the right places as far as he was concerned. That damn asshole, Tony, kept her on edge about her weight nearly twenty-four-seven. He snorted. The jerk had a beer belly. What gave him the right to condemn? Elijah had shared that opinion with Anora every chance he'd gotten.

He walked in, empty glasses in hand, and headed to the kitchen. They'd shared a spark. He felt it and he sensed she had as well. For a second, he'd almost acted on it, but sensed her hesitation. He checked the back door to assure it was locked, before stepping through the swinging door. It squeaked sharply, making him cringe. That he would fix tomorrow.

Longingly, he stood at the base of the stairs, contemplating his next move. Follow her, or wait. Hell, he'd gotten good at waiting— years of it. Elijah resolved to stick to his plan as he walked out, retrieved his overnight bag from the trunk and locked the door.

From its solitary location, he doubted anyone would break into the car. On the ride here, he hadn't seen many neighboring houses and almost missed the narrow driveway in the pouring rain. He squinted in the direction of the lake but couldn't see it. The continuing storm made it difficult. Trees lined the small front yard. Their moss-covered limbs hung low, weighed heavy by the rain as they danced freakily in the wind. Elijah shook his head at the thought. Damn! He'd been hanging around authors for way too long.

Even though he held an umbrella, he hustled back inside before getting completely soaked through. He shook it closed and leaned it against the outside wall beside the front door before entering.

Looking around, he noted the log cabin wasn't huge. If he had a guess, it was nearly a hundred years old. Someone renovated it and turned it into a vacation rental by the lake. It had two bedrooms. Anora had told him the second floor consisted of the master bedroom, bathroom and a closet. The main floor had an open floor plan. The front door opened into the main family room, complete with a fireplace, big comfy couch and chairs. A desk sat in the far corner to the right of the door and had an an old swivelchair. An antique grandfather clock stood watch beside the front door. The stairs ran along the wall to the second floor. At the back of the first floor, from left to right, was the small kitchen, beside that a full bath with a shower, no tub, and on the opposite side of that the guest bedroom, which just to the left of the staircase.

Elijah opened the door, flipped the light switch. Nothing fancy inside—a queen-size bed, nightstand and an old wooden armoire stood in the corner. A small lamp on the nightstand barely lit the room. He wouldn't be catching up on any reading by that. Something banged against the cabin and scratched along the solitary window of his room. The wall shook. Elijah dropped his bag on the bed, zipped it open and withdrew the one thing his grandpa had left him, a Colt forty-five. It was probably the storm causing branches to knock against the cabin. He eased his shoulder against the wall and peered out the corner of the window into the darkness of the roaring storm. Nothing. What the hell did he think he'd see?

Had to be those stories of unexplained disappearances she'd shared that had him spooked. Guess coming from a long line of cops gave him a suspicious mind. And a weapon. He'd never fit the mold for a cop. He remembered telling his grandpa. He loved books. Fell in love with the whole publishing industry in college. He shook his head as he checked the safety and placed the gun back in his bag. If it wasn't for his grandpa's encouragement, he wouldn't have started his own literary agency, and he wouldn't have landed his finest client. The woman he…

He eyed the ceiling, knowing her bed probably sat directly above this one. When she'd told him she was leaving the city to gather her thoughts, he'd expected her to disappear to a spa somewhere, not a log cabin by a lake deep in the woods. A spooky damn cabin at that, he snorted. The divorce took its toll, wore on her soul to the point she'd lost weight and her muse had taken a dive into hiding. It was his job to bring it back. The world deserved more stories from A. G. Barrett.

Something thumped behind him. Elijah straightened, turned. Had a shadow moved in the corner? What made the noise? Eek, eek, eek, whoosh. He stalled. That he decided was the wind and a limb hitting against the window and the cabin. The lamplight flickered. Power surge. He hoped the storm wouldn't take down the lines. *Squeak. Scratch. Thump.* He moved around the room, honing in on the noises. His heart raced and he breathed deeply, trying to steel his nerves. Standing in front of the large, wooden, ornately carved, tall armoire, he grasped the handle.

He tugged. It didn't budge. With both hands, he pulled the jammed door until it flung open. He stumbled, off-balance, as something black and large flew out at him. The dark shape surrounded him, covering him from head to toe. The more he struggled with it, the tighter it wrapped around him, confining him, suffocating him with its musty, putrid smell. Elijah tripped, landed hard on the floor and rolled around until he won the battle. He freed himself from his adversary, stood, then burst into laughter at his stupidity. A blanket had attacked him and nearly won.

A creak overhead stilled his laughter. Was she walking about or was that the mattress while she got comfortable? Elijah scrubbed a hand down his face. This was going to be a long weekend, knowing she lay above him and not in the fashion he'd fantasized about for years.

He stripped down to his boxers, kicked the blanket into a pile in the corner and crawled into bed. He plumped the pillows behind him and caught sight of a mouse scurrying from the armoire. Well, that explained the mystery noises as far as he was concerned.

Complete darkness filled the room when he switched off the lamp. This was definitely not like the city where the billboards acted as a nightlight even with the window blinds shut. Elijah shifted, settling in the bed. This reminded him of the backwoods swamps of the Carolinas where he was raised. Dark nights, no lights, and the beauty of a sky filled with stars. Maybe tomorrow they'd see the stars because tonight was all about the storm. Thunder rumbled while the deluge of rain pounded the roof slates.

Coldness brushed his cheek. Elijah opened his eyes, disoriented for a moment, before he remembered his location. Feeling for the watch he never removed, he touched a button, lighting the dial. Two a.m. Why was he awake? He rolled onto his side as the light faded, and he froze. Something caught the corner of his eye. Blinking, he adjusted his vision to the darkness, turning toward the object. A low shimmering glow hovered in his doorway. It flickered in a series of long, then short bursts of levels of brightness, beckoning him to watch. He didn't believe what he saw.

Elijah pinched the bridge of his nose, closed his eyes, then reached for his glasses. Once his vision adjusted, the image remained; yet now it traveled, moving in his direction. It had to be the wine combined with Anora's ghostly tale about this cabin that created this surreal dream. He tired to convince himself his imagination was running rampant. He shook his head against the pillow, attempting to clear his thoughts. When he opened his eyes, *it* had grown.

The object spun, casting rays of sparkling white light, dispersing them like arrows bouncing around the room. Elijah ducked as these beams whizzed dangerously near his head. His earlobe stung when one zinged past. He touched one, looked at his fingers but saw no blood. The temperature dropped, making him shiver. What the hell was this thing? He inched lower on the bed, trying to work his way to the overnight bag and his gun. Seconds before he reached it, the bag forcefully launched across the room into the armoire and the doors slammed shut.

Elijah prayed this was a nightmare and he'd wake soon. Then it hit him. What if it wasn't Anora! He couldn't let this thing go after Anora. He attempted to roll away from the spinning ball of brightness, but his body refused to move. It was as if unseen ties suddenly bound him to the bed.

The shadow spiraled closer, molding into a womanly form, until it floated inches above him over the bed. Long black hair cascaded around her thin, veiled face, features hidden by a dainty piece of lace, which hung from a thin, beaded band around her head. Pure ice coated his flesh, as a sheer hand stroked his bare chest. Bangles around her wrist jingled with her touch. A whispered word filtered through his muddled thoughts.

Come.

His brain burned from the worst case of brain-freeze ever. Against his will, he was compelled to rise. When it turned and floated from the room, his legs acted of their own accord and carried him after it. An invisible icy claw wrapped around his soul and dragged him forward. Conscious thought attempted to shut down. Nothing existed but this being—this woman. Entranced by the ethereal beauty, he trailed behind it, snatched open the front door, and followed without haste. An image struggled to surface, slapping a smidgeon of his brain, begging him to stop. Someone needed him. Something familiar warred within him, demanding he stop. Stop. Go. Stop. Go. The need to catch her overwhelmed his common sense, making him run to keep up.

Dampness lingered in the air from the recent rain. The sound of his name called from somewhere behind him. He wanted to stop, to answer the call, but he couldn't turn, couldn't look to see anything but the beauty before him, who guided his every move. This heavenly beauty needed something from him. But what? Though he tried, the ability to focus had been short-circuited. This creature controlled his will and his body.

Through the yard, down the driveway, and across the road, he bypassed the dock and stood at the water's edge. Wetness soothed his aching feet. He trudged farther into the icy coldness, reaching for her. She wanted something from him. A kiss perhaps?

Come closer.

Elijah stretched upward. Part of him wanted only to learn what she needed, while the rest of him desperately warred to be set free of this icy cold death-grip she held around his being.

Closer. I need you to…

Wetness soaked him to his hips. He didn't care. This woman needed him, but he wasn't sure for what. Just as the veil started to lift, something grabbed him, jerked him backward. His feet slipped and he sank, arms flailing about, reaching for something, anything to stop his descent. Inhaling a breathtaking cold, Elijah gasped, sucking in even colder, life-stealing liquid. Unseen arms jerked him upward, breaking free of the ice-cold water. Scrabbling to gain his footing, he slipped in the muck. Someone grabbed his arms.

"Elijah! Please wake up!"

Her voice startled him. Elijah sputtered and coughed, fighting for a clean breath of air. Hands held onto him, shaking him until his muddled thoughts cleared and he pried his eyes opened. Shivering, his voice quivered, "Where am I?"

"Thank God, you're awake." Anora hugged him. "A few seconds more and you would've drowned."

"What?" He glanced around. The lake! They stood in the water. "How the hell did I get here?"

"Sleepwalked, I guess. Let's get you inside. Get you warm."

He held onto Anora as they trudged from the icy coldness. A shadow hovered near. He spun to see it. For a split second, a woman's shape floated above the lake, beckoning him. When Anora turned, it vanished. "Did you see her?"

"See who?"

"The woman who led me here."

Anora's brows pursed. "What woman? I didn't see a woman."

Chapter Four

She'd wanted to call an ambulance or take him to a hospital, but he'd refused, claiming he wasn't injured, just wet. She'd even suggested they pack and move to one of the motels over near the highway, but he'd said no.

Anora handed Elijah a hot cup of tea as she sat beside him on the couch in front of the fireplace. The minute she'd gotten him inside, she'd wrapped a blanket around him, had him remove his wet boxers and built a fire to warm him, then changed into dry clothes herself. Knowing he was naked beneath the blanket sparked her desire, but having seen him waist deep in the lake spiked her concern.

"You're lucky you didn't lose your glasses going for a midnight swim like that," Anora said in a teasing tone, trying to lighten the mood.

Elijah recoiled deeper into the couch corner and shrugged. "Keep a spare pair in my bag. *And* I wasn't going for a swim. *Not* of my own accord."

Anora arched an eyebrow, kept her eyes on him, and saw confusion muddle his gaze. Teasing probably wasn't the best idea right now. What she'd just witnessed was difficult to describe. He'd been the victim of something odd happening to him, and she knew he suffered a traumatic blow emotionally. "How long have you been prone to sleepwalking?"

"I don't sleepwalk."

"Care to explain what happened then?"

His set the cup on the end table and positioned himself facing her. His features darkened and his eyes held a look of lost befuddlement. "I can't explain exactly what happened." He paused, shaking his head. "Even if I told you what I think I saw, you wouldn't believe me. I'm not even sure if *I* believe me, and I saw it."

She slid closer to him, laying her hand on his on the back of the couch. "Saw what? What do you believe you saw? You can trust me, Elijah. I won't laugh. I will believe you."

He breathed deeply and stared directly at her. Anora read his angst, the indecision that tore at him, before he finally blurted, "Something came into my room—a bright light. It spun, shooting sparks all over the place. I thought it was dangerous and wanted to stop it before it hurt you, but somehow it bound me to the bed. It compelled me to focus on nothing but it as it shifted into this woman. This vision had long flowing hair, and dressed like a gypsy, with bangles dangling on each arm, which jingled when it moved. It put me in some sort of trance and led me to the lake. I tried to stop, but I couldn't." He shoved forward, leaning his elbows on his knees, sinking his face into his hands. "I wanted nothing more than to follow her. It kept whispering 'come' and I did. I'm not sure what it wanted. If it wanted me to help it, or kiss it, or whatever." He groaned in frustration.

Anora moved beside him, rubbing her hand along his shoulders, hoping to soothe his angst. He was visibly shaken. All she wanted to do was hold him, ease his pain. She'd been scared shitless seeing him standing in the lake. Now, she had no clue what to say. This whole supernatural stuff was new to her. Could a ghost lead people to their death in a lake? Was it even possible? She pulled him closer and figured the best they could do was talk it out.

"Are you sure you're not hurt anywhere?"

"No," he replied, shaking his head as he pulled from her touch and sat back. "Just embarrassed that I let something like this happen. I've never considered myself a weak minded person, and now this, this—" He thrashed a hand through his hair. "Ugh, I don't even know what this *is*." His eyes widened. "The thing threw my bag across the room, into the armoire and slammed the doors. Didn't you hear the noise?"

Anora shook her head, "No. I didn't hear anything until the front door opened."

Elijah stood, marched to his bedroom door, and switched on the light. His shoulders slumped, and he looked back at her. "My bag is still on the foot of the bed where I left it." He returned to the couch and flopped down beside her. He laid his glasses on the end table, rubbing his eyes. He shook his head. "This isn't right. I know what I saw."

She huffed, not sure what to do or say. For a moment, she sat silent. "I don't think this makes you a weak person, Elijah. There's something going on here and we've just got to figure out what it is."

"Not sure what you mean by that."

"Well, think about it. Apparently, there have been disappearances over the years. Let's research this as best as we can." She walked to the desk, retrieved her laptop and logged on, then looked up the town, its founders and the local legend.

Elijah slid close to her, reading over her shoulder as they discovered a few interesting bits of information. She noted he didn't have his glasses on. "Don't you need your glasses to read?"

"Not when I'm this close. I see okay without them. It's a weak prescription." He leaned back. "That's a lot of men who've simply disappeared from this cabin over the past seventy-seven years."

She sat shoulder-to-shoulder with him while they studied the computer screen. "Odd, they were all men. No women. You said the ghost wore a veil. Did you get a look at her face underneath?"

"No."

"I wonder if she'd lifted the veil, you'd be dead, like what happened in that old horror movie I watched years ago." Anora slipped her tone into a creepy voice, trying to make him smile. "The creature was so hideous when it lifted its veil, the mere sight of it shocked people into instant death." When she wagged her eyebrows and giggled, she achieved lightening the mood. Elijah snorted and smiled with a shake of his head.

"What would've happened if I'd kissed her?"

Anora didn't skip a beat. "You'd most definitely be dead."

"Dead, huh?" His smile slipped away suddenly. "You think that's how the others disappeared, a ghost led them to drown in the lake?"

"Not sure," Anora considered as she leaned back, pointing to the screen. "Don't you think there would've been some bodies found?"

"Not if she's somehow managed to secure them to the bottom."

"I bet, they were lured into the lake, woke up in the water, got scared and ran off, never to return to this area again." Anora tried to play devil's advocate, ease his concerns, but her mind filled with phenomenal plot twists as she spoke, and her eyes widened. "But then again, what if the stories have a hint of truth? What if the ghost of Antanasia has been leading lonely men to their deaths all these years as revenge for Alexandru's death?"

It made her smile when Elijah picked up on her vibe instead of thinking she was making fun of him. "I think your author brain has kicked in and is running wild with the possibilities for a new paranormal series."

"Me thinks you may be right." She grinned and was happy to see him relaxing a little bit. She knew this had been a hell of a scare for him—and her.

"I told *you* what I *saw*." He crossed his arms over his bare chest, and she couldn't help but let her gaze dance across that tautly toned flesh for a moment. The blanket pooled around his waist. Anora's eyes darted down, then snapped back to his face. His eyebrow arched, amusement glistened in his gaze and she knew he'd caught her looking at his lap. He challenged, "Tell me your version of what you saw me doing. I'd love to hear it. What made you come outside after me?"

"I heard the door. When I came downstairs, it was wide open and I saw you going down the front stairs. I followed you. Several times, I called your name, but you acted like you didn't hear me. I thought something was wrong with the way you were moving, like an invisible rope was pulling you along. Your head was tilted upward, as if you watched something intently. I couldn't see it. I tried to reach you, but as I ran, you ran faster, headed straight for the lake." She leaned, touching his cheek. "I believe you. I may not have seen her, but I felt a presence in the air, and it wasn't a friendly one." She shivered. "I thought I saw a dark shadow flowing around you, and it scared me. It had no particular shape, just energy, strong, seemingly violent in nature. It's the feeling I got, real or not."

Elijah took the laptop, set it on the end table and pulled her into a hug. She snuggled against him, tucking her head in the crook of his neck and shoulder, laying her palm on his bare chest. "It's the vibe I got as well. She's one angry woman. Thankfully, I've got you watching my back."

"I'd rather be watching your front," she mumbled, softly. His hand cupped her chin and lifted her face to meet his gaze.

"What was that?"

She hadn't meant for him to hear. Heat filled her cheeks and she knew she blushed. Anora tried to sit back but he tightened his arm around her. Elijah kissed her. The intensity grew, tasting each other, pulling closer together, arms wrapped around tighter, holding on, not wanting the kiss to end.

The couch vibrated and bounced violently, forcing them apart, as if being jostled about by an earthquake. Losing her balance, Anora fell against him, clawing at his shoulders for support. Elijah grabbed her arms. Anora shoved upright and rolled from the couch. The movement stopped instantly.

Something popped loudly in the distance. The lights flickered, then shut off. "Great. Storm must've blown a transformer," Elijah stated the obvious about the lights.

Breathing heavily, she gained her balance. "That was some kiss."

"Earth-shaking to say the least," he added weakly as he stood, grabbing the blanket before it slid completely off his hips. "This area isn't known for earthquakes, so what the hell was that?"

Anora shook her head. "I've got no idea."

The glow of the burning logs gave the room minimal light. Elijah fashioned the blanket into a toga of sorts, tying it in place, making him look like a drop-dead, gorgeous, Roman warrior, or a frat boy.

She leaned more toward the hot Roman. Frat boys never were her thing, even in college.

"Nothing's knocked off the shelves, so maybe it wasn't an earthquake." Elijah dropped to the floor and lifted the end of the couch, looking under it. "I don't see anything that could've caused it to move like that." Releasing the couch with a thud, he stood, facing Anora. "As much as I'd like to say, my kiss moved the earth for you, babe, I've a freaky feeling that bitch is back."

Something moved in the far corner. Anora couldn't take her eyes off it as the shadowy image thickened, took shape, becoming brighter and shiny. She nodded toward it. "You're right."

He's mine. I need him, came the whispering soound of a frail feminine voice. The shimmering form shifted into a woman, with long black hair, flowing wildly around her in the air, even though there wasn't a breeze. Her clothing was archaic and faded. The blouse held a hint of tan in color, and the full-length skirt appeared to be a faint shade of purple. Bangles hung around both wrists, jingling with each movement. A veil concealed her face.

Anora moved in front of Elijah. Fear trailed up her spine, but she managed to stand steady with him near. They had to protect each other. "He's not yours. He's mine."

Elijah didn't cower behind her. He gently squeezed her waist, as if letting her know she was right, and then stepped to her side, taking her hand in his.

"I'm not yours. What the hell do you want?" Elijah's voice deepened and his grip tightened on her hand as they formed a united front against this entity.

A high-pitched screech filled the air as the shadowy figure took flight straight at them. Anora leaned against Elijah, yet stood her ground, even though fear coursed through her veins and her knees wobbled. "You've led your last man into that lake. Elijah is mine."

Frigid cold coated her from head to toe as the ghost halted within millimeters of her. Elijah released her hand and snaked his arm around her waist, tugging her closer to him. Warmth from his body was the only heat she felt at that moment. She stared directly where she thought the woman's eyes should be, but couldn't see them through the veil. The smell of black raspberry jam swirled in the air between them. Anora knew whose spirit she faced. Though her mouth had dried, she managed to speak, keeping her tone even keeled, while her insides quaked.

"I'm sorry for your loss, Antanasia. I'm sure Alexandru was a good man, who loved you deeply."

Anora's hand lifted as if the ghost inspected it, singling out her ring finger from the others. Bare but signs of once a ring upon it. The veiled head nodded toward Elijah. *He is not your husband. You cheat.*

Anora shook her head. "No."

He's mine. Antanasia's hands lifted to her veil. Anora couldn't let this happen. She wasn't losing Elijah to this creature.

"Elijah, don't look at her. What if that's how she's able to control men, through her stare? Please don't look at her!"

He cupped her cheek, turning her face to his. "If you haven't guessed, you're the only woman I want to look at. Together, we'll think of some way to beat her."

Her heart stuttered at his words. This bitch of a ghost wasn't winning. "Don't look at her." He nodded and closed his eyes. Anora stared directly at her as the veil lifted, unveiling one of the most beautiful women she'd ever seen. Digging deep, Anora leaned in. "He's mine."

The stench of burnt black raspberry jam singed her nostrils. The face contorted into a gruesome vision of flesh melting, dripping away, leaving a distorted skull with sharp teeth, and the red glow in the sockets where eyes had been moments before. Her stomach churned, bile rose in the back of her throat. This wasn't at all what she'd expected. Hell. She had no idea *what* she'd expected. Boney, skeleton hands reached for her neck. Anora screamed.

*

Elijah reacted on impulse, lifted her and spun Anora around, placing his back to the creature. The smell had him gagging, tears leaked from the corners of his closed eyes and his heart pounded, but he wasn't loosing his hold on Anora no matter what happened. He screamed, "She's mine. I've waited seven years for this, and I'll be damned if some bitchy spirit is going to ruin it."

Keeping one hand gripped firmly on Anora, he swung to face the ghost. Cracking his lids open just enough to get his bearings on its location, he foolishly thought he could tackle it. He let go of

Anora, and rushed it. Instead of hurting it, he ran through it and smacked face first into the wall behind it. Dazed, he sank to his knees, rubbing his forehead. Slowly he stood. The worst case of the dry heaves hit him hard and fast, wracking his body until he was weak and sweaty. Then the next wave hit. Invisible knives tried to cut their way out from the inside. He froze, grasped the wall with both hands and tried to focus as the worst sensation he'd ever experienced shot through every cell of his body from the roots of his hair to the tips of his toes. He couldn't move. A bony cold hand slithered across his shoulder, untying the blanket. It fell to the floor.

Look at me.

Elijah forced his lids to remain sealed shut. No way in hell was he looking at that thing. Icy fingers trailed all over his flesh. It turned his stomach knowing he couldn't stop this creature from exploring his nakedness. Damn, why hadn't he put on clothes? *Because he wanted to snuggle with Anora, and wearing nothing but a blanket seemed like a good idea at the time.* Now, with this ghost caressing him, not so much sexiness in that. He cringed when it cupped his balls.

*

Her eyes widened. Anger outmatched her fear.

"That's it. I told you, bitch. He's mine."

Anora grabbed the closest weapon, the poker from the fireplace. With both hands, she swung it, not knowing what else to do. Antanasia's shrill laughter was like a banshee's, rattling the windows. Anora arched her shoulders in a desperate attempt to shield her ears as she kept swinging. Swoosh. Swoosh. The poker slashed through the ghostly being. In frustration, she threw it, hitting the wall directly behind the ethereal bitch.

Elijah's flesh held a bluish tint. The bitch was freezing him with her touch. She had to do something. Anora wedged herself between them, even though it meant stepping into the ghostly figure. Icy shards coated every aspect of her being. Fear twisted her gut as she wrapped her arms around his waist, tugging him tightly to her. She moved her whole body side to side in a slow rhythm, attempting to warm his flesh. The frigid temperature of the spirit's touch had them both shivering. Her teeth chattered, everything hurt. Each intake of air was filled with cold moist crystals, but she held on to him. She

167

knew it worked, because as he warmed, he regained function in his arms and gathered her closer, holding her tighter, confining the limited body heat between them. His lips met hers in a trembling kiss.

In a fit of rage, Antanasia turned into a spiraling mass of dark matter. The whole house shook. Pans and dishes rattled in the kitchen. Books fell from the desk. Something crashed upstairs. The air whirled around them with tremendous force, lifting them as they broke apart from their kiss. They clung to one another. Fear held them gripped tightly together.

A thick substance bubbled and spurted from the walls, stinking of burnt black raspberry jam, oozing from every crevice, dripping on them and singeing their flesh. Neither could see the ghost clearly in the whirlwind of violence that lifted them higher until they smacked against the ceiling. As quickly as it started, it ended. They dropped and landed in a heap of arms and legs tangled together, coated in globs of a thick gooey, sickening-sweet burnt smelling substance.

Elijah and Anora struggled to their feet to face the hissing figure crouched in the corner. They held onto each other, not letting go no matter what the creature did next. Both of them shook as they stepped backward away from the thing.

Elijah steeled his legs to hold them both up, since he felt Anora's wobble as they moved. Were they going to die? Did this thing have the ability to kill? Then an idea hit him, and he figured, what the hell, throw it out there.

"You can't have me. But if you need a man, take her ex-husband. He's all yours. No contest there."

Chapter Five

Deathly silence hung in the air. Unified, they faced the shadowy figure of Antanasia. A bone-chilling shrill cut the air, seconds before the dark image thrust forward. It slammed into Anora, tearing her from Elijah's grip, sending her skidding in a heap across the floor. Antanasia twisted her distorted face and grinned at Elijah, keeping him momentarily pinned in place with an unseen force. His gut roiled with anger and hatred for this thing. His fists balled at his sides while he struggled to move, to get to Anora. Pure evil washed over him and he swore he tasted black raspberry jam. He was done with this bitch. He knew he wasn't supposed to look at her, but there was no chance in hell he was going to let her control him. He didn't dare blink, no matter how disgustingly horrible the ghost's face became.

Antanasia formed into a column of black vapor and shot directly into Anora's nose and mouth. Anora gasped, gagged and coughed, then shook violently. Her eyes rolled back in her head, her eyelids fluttered closed and her legs kicked rapidly. Elijah panicked. That bitch was inside Anora. That *fucking bitch* was inside his woman, killing her from the inside out. Damn. Damn. Damn. Seeing her body slither across the floor in severe pain tore at his soul, knowing she suffered ten times the agony he'd experienced earlier. He had to stop this before that bitch of a ghost ripped Anora apart.

With every ounce of grit he could muster, he fought the invisible bonds Antanasia placed upon him. Sweat beaded upon his brow as he dragged his legs and forced his body to move toward her withering body. "Hold on, Anora. Fight the bitch. Don't let her win. Fight her!"

When he was close enough, he rocked forward, using gravity to lunge him toward Anora. He landed hard, knocking the wind from his lungs, causing him to gasp, but it broke the creature's invisible lock on his body. Elijah scooted over to Anora, cradled her in his arms. Her face had gone pale. Her lips were bluish.

"Noooo! Anora! Fight. Please fight." He hugged her tightly against him, rocking her like a child.

Kiss me, graced his ears. He knew the words were not Anora's. Her beautiful face warped into the hideous creature of the dead. Was this some sort of gruesome test? Elijah didn't falter. He grasped hold of the love he held in his heart and lowered his lips toward hers.

"Anora, I love you. I always have."

The instant their lips touched, the blood within his veins ran ice cold,shaking him from head to toe. With arms wrapped around his Anora, determination held him in place, his lips firmly pressed to hers, willing what was left of his body heat to warm her. Her frosty skin frightened him beyond belief. He pressed his mouth harder to hers, delving his tongue inside, even though the sensation of freezing from the inside-out threatened to turn him into an iceberg. He'd give her every ounce of heat he had if it meant saving her life over his. He broke from the kiss, holding her, cradling her in his arms, wrapping his body around hers, doing everything he could to warm her, save her.

He murmured, "Don't let the dead bitch win."

She shook so violently, he could barely hold onto her, but he wasn't letting go. Anora's head lolled back, mouth opened and an ear-piercing scream exited as putrid, black fumes smelling of burnt, black raspberry jam funneled from her throat. Elijah held on, stroking her hair from her pale face. For what seemed like an eternity, they huddled together on the floor. He was afraid to look at her, to see if the love of his life lived or died. Elijah simply held her pressed against his chest; his chin rested on her head, his eyes closed, as he prayed.

*

Her hand shook as she touched his cheek. She twisted in his arms, drawing from his strength. Elijah loved her. If she'd heard him right, he'd been waiting for her since they'd met. Why hadn't she seen it before? Because she'd been trapped, blinded by a sweet-talker and stuck in a loveless marriage.

Elijah held her tightly. Heat from his touch warmed her, knowing he cared made her fight the ghost that had invaded her body. She now knew what they needed to do to end this. She opened her eyes and stared at the man she'd come to realize she loved.

"You love me?"

"Yes." He nodded. "Are you okay?"

She cupped his cheek. "Other than feeling like my insides have been tossed around in a blender, I'm going to be fine. You?"

He leaned into her hand. "Yeah. Bruised a bit, but breathing." He looked around. "You think she's gone?"

"No," Anora shook her head and answered sadly. "But I know what she wants, and I think it's up to us to help her. It's the only way this will end."

"Doesn't require killing anyone does it?"

"Nope. You still remember how to dive?"

He sat back eyeing her suspiciously. "Yeah, but…"

Anora placed her palm on his chest. "Trust me."

He thumbed her eyelid, lifting it as if looking for something. "That bitch isn't still in there is she?"

Anora slapped his hand away. "No, she's not."

"Good, cause I really want to kiss you and only you, this time."

Elijah kissed Anora, soft and gentle, tasting every nuance of her mouth, relishing her flavor and the touch of her tongue against his. This woman had been worth the wait.

One week later

Anora and Elijah sat cuddled together under a blanket on the swing. Her head rested on his shoulder. "You think she's finally at peace?"

"Since she hasn't made any more nasty appearances and we did what she told you she wanted while she was inside you, I'd say, yes, she's at peace." Elijah toyed with her hair while they gently swayed, enjoying the early evening, watching the sun set on the lake.

"It had to be horrible trapped in spirit form for seventy-seven years, unable to be reunited with your soul-mate in the afterlife. And all this because of a curse placed on an amulet by your pissed-off mother and mother-in-law." Anora twisted on the swing, facing Elijah more.

He liked the way she looked wearing nothing but his T-shirt. Elijah lifted his gaze to Anora's beautiful green eyes. "What I don't understand is why her brother made them matching gold amulets in the first place if the family didn't approve of their union? Why such an extravagant gift just to curse it? Can we go over her story again? I'd like to get a better understanding of the why she was haunting this place. It might make for a new series for you."

Anora nodded. "He wasn't against them. He was the only family member for their love. He secretly forged the amulets, but somehow their mothers found out and cursed the amulets without his knowing it. According to what I learned from Antanasia, they didn't approve of their union but couldn't stop it, so they wanted to make things horrible for them, especially when they died. Neither would find peace without both amulets being buried together. It wasn't until she was very old, when she received a letter from her brother telling her of the curse. By then, it was too late. She spent her afterlife searching for Alexandru knowing he wondered, lost just as she was because the amulets weren't together. She lured men to the lake to use them to find the amulet, not to kill them. Most woke when they got wet and ran away scared. The others packed and left the instant she made an appearance. Over the years, the legend simply grew. We were the first who listened to her plea for help instead of running scared."

"That was because of your author's open-mindedness to all things being possible," he said. "If this happened to just me, I'd long been gone."

"Nah, I don't believe that. You're just as open-minded as me. If you weren't, you wouldn't be my agent. Thanks to your diving skills and Antanasia narrowing the field down for it's location, we found the amulet and it's where it belongs buried beneath their combined headstone. So hopefully, they found one another and they've found peace. I think this calls for a glass of wine." She crawled from under the blanket and stood. "I'll be right back."

When Anora returned to the porch carrying two glasses of red wine, Elijah was on his cell phone. She handed one to Elijah, then snuggled into place beside him under the blanket on the swing.

"Thanks, Uncle Hank. I appreciate the call. We'll see you as soon as we return." He pressed the disconnect button and laid his phone on the porch rail along with his wine glass.

His brows were pursed and his expression one of indescribable confusion.

"You okay? Did someone die?"

He took her glass and set it beside his, before gathering her hands in his, and turned catty-cornered in the swing, facing her.

"That was Uncle Hank."

Anora's heart skipped a beat. From the look on his face, something bad had happened. Elijah's Uncle Hank was her consultant on all things police protocol. He'd been on the force for over twenty years. "Ohmygod, is he okay?"

"Yes." Elijah nodded. "He called to tell me…" He paused, took a breath as if what he was about to say was the hardest thing ever. "Tony is dead."

"What?" She couldn't be sure she'd heard him right. "Which Tony?"

"Your ex. He was found dead in his apartment. Uncle Hank was assigned as the investigator for the case. Saturday night, a neighbor heard screams coming from his apartment and called the cops. According to him, the body was found sitting in a chair at the desk in his home office."

"What?" she cleared her throat and tried again. It wasn't as if she was upset over his death, just stunned. Forty-two wasn't old. "Why's he assigned to the case? He's homicide. Do they suspect murder?"

"They found a handwritten note on his desk proclaiming you as his beneficiary. That's why Uncle Hank was called. Your assistant, Maxine, told him you were on an extended vacation. He tried your cell phone, left a message, then called me. I told him we are here together. He asked if we could prove our whereabouts Saturday night around seven p.m. I said yes. We were at dinner at a restaurant in town. I gave him the link to my Instagram account. The selfie we posted proves our location, date and time. Considering we're a good three-hour drive outside of the city, we've got a solid alibi."

"They think he was murdered." She spoke the words softly as the situation sank in. "And they think I had something to do with it. Him leaving me as his beneficiary makes it look even worse for me."

"They don't suspect you of murder. He was simply tying up loose ends."

"Do they have any idea of what happened?"

"Not really. From the preliminary report, the coroner suspects a massive heart attack." Elijah shook his head. "Uncle Hank said, from the expression on his face, it looked as if he died painfully. They found him with his eyes wide opene and his mouth ajar, as if he'd been screaming or yelling. That's probably what the neighbor heard. He was probably screaming for help, in too much pain to move. His cell phone was in his bedroom on the charger, no landline. But that's not the oddest thing. A tarot card was found in his jacket pocket."

Anora sat back. A knot formed in her chest and her eyes widened. She knew Antanasia had traipsed around her memories. She'd commented on the vile husband of Anora's past, that he treated women poorly. Anora swallowed hard. Anora hadn't asked for anything from Antanasia. Anora just wanted to help end the other woman's reason for being without her soul-mate in the afterlife. She expected no reward, especially not something like this. It was all she could do to push the words across her lips. "Which tarot card?"

"The Chariot."

VIII

STRENGTH

9

STRENGTH

ED DEANGELIS

Upright: Strength, courage, patience, control, compassion
Reversed: Weakness, self-doubt, lack of self-discipline

"You're a bum, Jimmy, a bum!" Tino shouted at the wheezing, middle-aged man who was throwing varying punch combos at a two-hundred-pound heavy bag.

"Shut… up… Tino!" Jimmy said through gritted teeth and labored breaths. His body ached and his arms burned, but he had to push himself; he had to be ready. *Jab, jab, left hook, body, back step, right step, fake, right uppercut.* Jimmy cycled through his opening combo list, his body weaving into a pattern that after years was deeply ingrained in his muscle memory. Despite those years, Jimmy could feel himself wearing down: his body ached and he had only been practicing for fifteen minutes, only five rounds, not even half the fight. If only he was ten years younger. But Jimmy knew he was past his prime. He had just celebrated his fortieth birthday, and his little girl Ginny's eighth birthday. His hair was turning grey, and although he knew he was still strong, he was slowing, and some days his entire body would shake uncontrollably for short periods of time. He should have stayed retired; he should have listened to Audrey's advice. He smiled despite his fatigue and allowed his mind to slip back into days past, while his body shifted to autopilot.

"Jimmy Flannigan Thacker, ye must be daft in the head if ye think this be a good idea! Ye just turned forty, and ye think to go strutting back into the ring like some young cock trying to prove yeself! Eight years ye've been retired! Ye have a family to think about now!"

Jimmy wanted to smile as he watched his wife storm around the kitchen table, Audrey was pitching an awful fit. But he couldn't blame her, nor could he grow angry. The way she stomped around, her slender five-foot frame, her tousled blonde hair flying every which way, she was beautiful, even if her face was currently redder than the Devil's arse. And he knew she had a right to be the way she was right now. "I know, darling, I know. But that is why I do this, for my family. I squandered most of our money when I was young. Trying to prove things to people, trying to make us look good. When all we really needed was one another. This fight, this one fight could secure our comfort for years to come. I need to do this. Not to prove something myself, or to others. But to provide for you and Ginny."

Audrey was not even close to being convinced, although his words had lessened the fire in her blood, if only slightly. "We been having enough to make do. Ye can teach boxing to the younger generations and while Ginny is in school I can pick up spare work till I find something more permanent." Audrey sighed, concern now replacing the anger on her face and in her voice. "Ye can't be going back into the ring, Jimmy. You're hurt. I know ye don't show it, but I see you shaking. Yer whole body shakes as if the chill o' death is upon ye. And then there are the blackouts. I know you have them, those moments when ye looked confused and can't remember what ye had just been doing or where ye ha—"

Jimmy slammed his hand down so hard on the table, an audible crack resounded in the tiny kitchen. "I won't hear any more from you, Audrey! I am doing this for you and Ginny. Ain't no shakes or my rattled brain gonna stop me from providing the good life for my wife and child." Jimmy stood and, reaching down, he grabbed his small duffle bag that held his gear. "I'm going down to the gym to train with Tino. I'll be back in time for dinner."

As the door closed, the last sounds Jimmy heard were the soft sobs of his wife.

"Focus, Jimmy, yah damn bum! You're slacking," Tino shouted as his hand lashed out to slap the back of Jimmy's head.

The painful slap broke Jimmy out of his reminiscing. He shook his head and redoubled his efforts, his thoughts turning back toward his combinations, allowing his muscle memory to take over as he settled into his routines.

Tino did not, however, relent with his verbal assault. "How do you expect to even last a single round in the ring with Magnus 'The Mountain' Magni? He is six feet, four inches of solid massive muscle. He is undefeated and has sent *twelve* of his last twenty opponents into the hospital. Jimmy, he is not just looking to beat you and claim your undefeated record. He wants to destroy you, to show everyone that he is the best." Tino paused for a moment, concern filling his wrinkled face. "You were the best, Jimmy. Anyone dumb enough to jump into the ring with you would get pounded. No matter their size and skill. Yah know why? Because you wanted it more! You had fire in your gut! But that was eight years ago. Now… now you could die, Jimmy, if you go through with this. I know the pay is a lot, even the loser's cut is plenty. But what's the point if you lose your life?"

Tino gently placed his hand on Jimmy's shoulder. "Cancel the fight. You know I'm retiring. You can take my position as coach at the gym. It don't pay much, but with you coaching I'm sure it will draw boxers from all over, and business will skyrocket."

Jimmy's shoulders slumped, and he turned, flashing Tino that crooked smile with a few missing teeth. "I know, Tino, and I will love the job, but I have to do this first." Jimmy hesitated, his eyes flicking away from Tino's as he paused for a moment, finally after a protracted pause he spoke. "I need to fight—I need to win."

Tino shook his head, chuckling softly. "Lad, you have no idea what you're getting into. I've seen Magnus. There is almost no—"

Raising his hand, Jimmy Stalled Tino's counsel. "You don't understand, Tino. Almost all the money is gone. I trusted the wrong people, and… now it's almost all gone. I haven't told Audrey. She just thinks I lost a little. But in truth, Tino, we're just a few months away from the poor house. And even if I took the coaching job, all that will do is allow us to survive. That's not enough for me, Tino. I wasn't ever a person to settle, to scrape by. Audrey wants more children, but I won't bring any more children into this world. Not until I know I can provide for them properly. I need to do this. Not for myself, but for Audrey and Ginny." Jimmy yanked his gloves off, flexing his wrapped hands a little, frowning as he gazed at them. "If only I was ten years younger. Or stronger. If only for this fight, just for this fight. I would be done; no more fights, no more gimmicks. No more dumbass decisions made behind my wife's back." Jimmy sighed the sigh of a man who knew defeat, but still hoped for victory.

Tino's grip on Jimmy's shoulder grew tighter for a moment, before going slack. "You mean that, Jimmy? You swear to me that if you win, you will be done with boxing? Other than coaching?"

"I was done eight years ago, Tino, when Ginny came. I knew in my heart I was done. But I was stupid, and because of it I jeopardized my family's future. All I need is this one last win. The odds against me are so high that if I took what savings I have left and placed it on myself to win, and I actually managed to win... my children's, children's, children would be set."

"Do you swear it, Jimmy?" Tino's voice rose in intensity. "Swear to me if you won this fight, it will be your last."

Jimmy turned. Confused, he gazed at his friend and mentor, who had just turned a few shades paler. "I swear, Tino, that if I win this fight, I will never box again." Jimmy smiled, his wrapped right hand moving up to rest upon Tino's. He could feel and see his friend's hand trembling. It made him think. *This is what it must look like when I get the shakes. Audrey and Tino are right, I need to stop. This will be my last fight!*

The pressure from Tino's hand finally lessened, and his voice steadied. "All right then, I think I can help you, Jimmy. I know a man, one of those Chinese mystics. Me and a bunch of my buddies once saved him and his family from a lynch mob, back during WWII. It was when the country was rounding up all the Japs and re-settling them in camps across the country. Back then, any Asian was considered a Jap. Gang Liu and his family had come here before the war. They were nice people, they just looked like the enemy, and that alone after Pearl Harbor was as good as a death sentence. Gang's family had been driven from their small apartment and were cornered down in 42nd street. Me and my buddies saw what was going to happen. We knew Gang was Chinese, so we intervened on their behalf. We were able to convince the group to take their racial-fueled bloodlust elsewhere."

Jimmy groaned. Crossing his arms, he turned to face his friend. "You're rambling, Tino. What does some Chinese man you saved a few decades ago have to do with helping me win a fight?"

"If you would let me finish, I was getting to that!" Tino snapped back after Jimmy's interruption. "As I was saying, we save Gang and his family. Later he approached me and the guys while we were getting a drink down at O'Rileys. We were confused about why—"

Jimmy's eyes rolled as Tino's story once again began to go off the tracks. He uncrossed his arms, rolling his now open hand in a simple "get on with it" gesture.

Tino's face turned a light shade of red. "Fine, Fine! Turns out Gang was some kind of Chinese Mystic. Or so he claimed he was to me and my buddies. Told us he would grant each of us a gift for saving him and his fam—"

"Tino, I ain't going to no Chink magic—"

"Shut yer fucking mouth and listen to me, boy!"

Tino's sudden outburst came so unexpectedly that Jimmy rocked back an inch.

"I'm trying to do you a favor here. I know it sounds strange, almost crazy. But this man… he knows things, strange things. Remember Jack's daughter? She got all sick, doctors said she had cancer."

Jimmy nodded.

"Well Jack took her to Gang, and within a day she was already getting better. I saw her just last week, all strong and healthy looking. Doctors could not explain what happened to the cancer. And then there was Finn. He started to lose his sight, went to Gang, and within a week he could see better than any twenty-year-old. I have never used my gift. My life is good and I don't need no celestial magic used on me. But…" Tino paused, that same hesitant tone once more entering his voice. "…you need something that I can't give you. A chance, a way to win. But perhaps Gang can. What do you say? Come with me and we will go visit him."

Jimmy laughed softly and shook his head. He began to unwrap his hands, peeling the tape off quickly. "OK, Tino, I'll bite. Let's go see your old slant-eyed warlock buddy."

Tino flashed a glare toward Jimmy. "Watch your tongue, boy. You better show this man respect in every way when you see him, or else he won't help"

Jimmy held up both hands, one now unwrapped, with a placating motion. "OK, Tino, I'll be good. But we gotta hurry. Audrey won't be happy if I'm late for dinner." Jimmy tossed his gloves and wraps into his gym bag. Moving toward the exit, he tossed it over his shoulder and waited as Tino shut off the lights and locked up. They headed out the door. Instead of turning to go north, which was the normal route, Tino headed south, heading toward Chinatown, which was only a few blocks away.

*

    Chinatown was a sea of people and a bouquet of exotic smells. Jimmy and Tino waded through all of this, weaving down crowded alley after alley. Jimmy was lost after the fourth turn down some alleyway stuffed with various shacks selling all kinds of things, most of it strange looking and odd smelling. But eventually Tino turned and stopped in front of a small store set within a brick building. Jimmy could tell by the different-colored patchworks of bricks that the building was old, perhaps from the early 1900s, maybe even late 1800s. There was no window, only an old door cracked with age and covered with an unaccountable number of paint layers, the foremost of which was a dark green, which in turn was covered in strange, painted symbols of gold and red. A small, dirty window sat toward the top of the door, thick smoke curling behind it. A sign hung above the door, but the words, like the symbols upon the door, were Chinese, so Jimmy didn't bother thinking on it. Tino seemed to know where he was going and that was good enough.

    Tino strode through the doorway. The interior exhaled a thick cloud of incense smoke. At least Tino hoped it was incense. "Better not be some opium den, Tino."

    Jimmy's quip was quickly answered. "Shut yer mouth, Jimmy! Don't say anything unless you're spoken to, got it?"

    Jimmy nodded. He needed to win this fight, and if this crazy Chinese wizard could help him, then shut his mouth he would. Jimmy reached up to wipe his fingers through his greased hair, slicking it back as he strode behind Tino into the little shop.

    The smoke was so substantial he couldn't see past his own nose. His mama's tales of the Tiber valley back in the old country came into his mind. *"And I swear, Jimmy, the fog was so thick when I was walking home, I always would get lost. That is how I met your father, stumbling up to his family's farmstead after being lost in the fog."*

    But as quickly as the fog had surrounded him and his mama's voice had filled his ears, it was gone, replaced with Tino's old but strong grasp yanking him forward, a harsh whisper emanating from

Tino. "Jimmy, what's the matter with yah? I said don't open yer mouth, not stand around looking like you're funny in the head."

Tino let go of Jimmy's shirt and stalked off down a narrow aisle. Jimmy shook his head, blinking rapidly as his eyes teared up from the incense that was now seeming to recede from around him.

The small room was packed from floor to ceiling with all kinds of oddities. They were stuffed in old wooden shelves and cracked display cases in such a manner that only a madman would have been able to know what was where, much less do any sort of inventory.

Jimmy could not make out what many of the oddities on the shelves were: strange, unfamiliar objects made from all different kinds of material alongside jars filled with only God knew what; strange hanging plants, which somehow seemed to thrive despite the room being devoid of sunlight; and above all else, strange figurines and statues. Hundreds of them, all shapes and sizes. Some of people as well as all kinds of creatures, from dragons to turtles to monkeys. They were scattered all over the shop. Jimmy glanced up as he passed another hanging plant—or what he thought was plant at first.

"Holy fuck, is that a shriveled monkey hand?" Jimmy leapt back, bumping into a solid display case, but thankfully not knocking anything over. He grimaced as he took in the gruesome sight of that furred little hand, tiny shriveled fingers curled into its own palm but a few still stretched outward.

"Ahhh, I see you have taken notice of a most obscure item."

Another shriveled hand rested upon Jimmy's shoulder, but as his head snapped to the side in an almost frantic pace, he saw that this old, shriveled hand was not a monkey's and was most certainly still attached: long curled fingernails, white pasty flesh, and blue veins that Jimmy thought he saw wriggling under that white flesh. Yes, this hand was most certainly alive and attached, which in no way calmed the tough boxer but only caused his instincts to kick in as he spun around to face the source of that voice and skeletal hand.

The old man that greeted Jimmy had not been behind that counter a moment ago. But now he stood there. Dark eyes glinted with a life unmatched by the withered body that held them. The old man wore an elaborate robe made of silks dyed red and gold, with strange patterns woven with green thread. When Gang smiled, Jimmy winced at the combination of his missing teeth and the rotten ones that were left.

"Hello, Gang." Tino's voice was calm and toneless, his face a stone mask devoid of emotion as he spoke to the ancient Chinese man behind the counter. "I trust you know—"

"Yes, I know why you are here. My body might be old, but my mind is not. You have come to call upon the debt owed to you. Very well, what is it that you need?" Those skeletal hands slowly folded back toward Gang's body, disappearing into the large sleeves of his ornate robe.

Tino glanced at Jimmy, and when their eyes met he jerked his head slightly toward Gang. "I pass the Debt to you, Jimmy," Tino declared firmly before looking back at Gang, whose white, bushy eyebrows rose at his statement. "Tell him what you need."

"I... I..." Jimmy stuttered, a momentary welling of uncertainty causing the verbal skip. "...need to be strong."

"Ha!" The barking, short laugh of Gang filled the room like thunder for a split second. "You are already strong. Look at you, built like an ox."

"I need to be stronger, stronger than any man has or ever will be. Just for a short period of time... please."

One of Gang's massive bushy eyebrows rose once again and those sharp eyes bore into Jimmy for what seemed like an eternity. Finally, Gang nodded his head. "Very well, a debt was owed and I shall repay it. You shall have what you desire. Wait here."

Gang turned, his robes seeming to billow despite the lack of flowing air, and he pushed his way through a curtain of beads behind him. The sound of glass clinking together as well as other strange unidentifiable noises were heard along with strange guttural chants. The chants began to crescendo until, with an almost strangled cry, they ended and the air seemed to hum. A minute later Gang returned, his ancient hand gently grasping a small vial filled with a clear, red liquid that seemed to shimmer for just a moment as it shifted inside its glass container.

"What is that?" Jimmy asked. Fear mingled with revulsion filled his voice.

"It is what you asked for. But if you want specifics, there is some yak-blood, some crushed elephant tusk, some rhino horn, the eye-juice of a tuna..."

Jimmy raised his hands quickly, stalling the ancient man's foul list before he named something that would make him mess up the shop's floor with a potion made from what was currently in his stomach. "No, no I'm good." Jimmy reached out his trembling hands. One of his episodes. He gritted his teeth but right as he was about to grasp the red vial of liquid the old man pulled his hand away.

"There is a price for magic, boy. I told all those who came in before you, and since the debt is now yours, I shall explain the same to you as I have to the others before you. There is always a price you pay for this. Be sure that you are willing to pay for what you take."

Jimmy's calloused hand snapped back to his body, and within a second he had made the sign of the cross. "I ain't sellin my soul!" He began to backstep, but paused as laughter rich and loud echoed from the man before him, like the short barking laugh from before. The noise did not match the mouth that it issued from. It was rich and deep, full of life, but life of a younger man, not the skeleton before him. The old man laughed without breath or pause for what seemed like forever before he calmed, his remaining yellow teeth now exposed as he grinned widely. "I am not your white Devil, boy. I do not want your soul, nor would such minor magic ever cost such a terrible price. I do not know the price, for the magic determines what it is. All I can tell you that the price for each man is always different. If you drink this, you will pay a price. But it is yours alone to discover, and to live with." His gnarled hand extended once more, and curled fingers and long yellowed nails unfolded, offering once more the potion.

A voice deep inside of him whispered not to take it. That voiced found its way out as Jimmy turned his head toward Tino. "Tino, what happened to Jack and Finn? What price did they end up paying?"

Tino's faced scrunched, his eyes glazing over in thought moments passed before he spoke. "Last I heard from Finn was he was heading west to live with his brother. His house had burnt down; he lost everything he owned in a few hours."

"As for Jack, a few months after his daughter got better he was run over by some crazy driver on his way home. Poor bastard will never walk again. But his daughter's doing well. Gonna be heading to college come summer." Tino's voice became distant. His thoughts surely mimicking Jimmy's as he thought about his friend's miraculous blessings followed by their untimely tragic misfortunes.

Jimmy's head snapped back toward Gang. "So that was their price? One lost his home and all his worldly possessions, and the other his legs?"

Gang lowered his extended arm and merely shrugged. "The magic chooses the price, not I. Nor do I know if those things that happened to them were indeed the price they had to pay. I only know that the price was paid. I can sense such things, but nothing more." Gang lifted his arm again in offering, the potion sitting in his now open palm as his fingers uncurled from around the vial. "Take it or not, I have made the potion and my debt is now settled. Drink it and gain the strength you desire, but also gain a debt that the magic will call upon. Or don't, and you will owe nothing. The choice is yours and yours alone."

Jimmy should have left, should have turned tail and run out of this smoke filled shop of mysterious and horrors. But there was more at stake than his own well-being, or his crappy possessions. Images of himself in a wheelchair or watching his apartment complex burning down filled his mind. But he pushed them deep down with thoughts and images of his wife and child. *This is for them, and I will pay any price to get money I need to secure our future.* With that final thought Jimmy reached up and snatched up the vial.

It was time to leave. The smoke was causing his skin to itch, and it felt as if he could barely breathe.

Right as he reached the smoke-covered door, Gang spoke out once more. "Drink it right before the fight, and for an hour you shall have what you asked for, strength beyond that which any man has, or ever will have."

Jimmy heard, but was already plunging into the curtain of smoke that concealed the doorway, before exiting through the small, painted doorway outside. A moment later Tino followed. They stood there, not saying a word, until Jimmy reached out to place his hand on Tino's shoulder. "I just wanted to say tha—"

Tino jerked his shoulder away and looked up into Jimmy's eyes, his own filled with sorrow and regret. "I should have stopped you, Jimmy. Who knows what that price is? This was a mistake, and I am sorry. His old voice cracked with barely contained sorrow before he jerked his shoulder away and stalked off down the street, calling out after a few paces. "I gotta think, Jimmy. Just go home. I gotta think."

And with that Tino turned down another random alleyway filled with people and vanished from Jimmy's sight.

*

It had been two days and Jimmy had not seen heads or tails of Tino. He was beginning to worry, as it was the evening of the fight and Tino was nowhere to be seen. The weigh-in and physicals had already occurred, and now Jimmy paced back and forth in his dressing room, his hands wrapped by some strange new guy, a young kid named Nicky.

"Where the hell are you, Tino?" Jimmy mumbled to himself, eyeing the clock. "Christ! It's almost fight time. Where are you, old man?"

Jimmy's eyes flickered over to his gym bag, the small potion sitting right on top of his regular clothes. *"Drink it right before the fight, and for an hour you shall have what you asked for, strength beyond that which any man has, or ever will have,"* the old mystic's words echoed in his ears.

Jimmy shook his head to remove the last traces of the old man's warning. He rolled his shoulders and clenched his fists before striding over to his gym bag. Reaching down, he grasped at the vial, and with a flick of his thumb, popped the cork. He brought the vial to his mouth and swallowed.

The taste was horrid, like gritty, salty iron with some other taste he could not identify. Beyond the taste was the burning. It coated his tongue, filled his mouth, and burned down his throat into his belly where it felt like fire now swam. He doubled over, the vial dropping onto the carpeted floor. Jimmy's arms cradled his burning gut. But the fire within him was not content with just his mouth, throat, and stomach. It began to course through his body, slowly at first, then more rapidly as his heart rate skyrocketed, until with a simpering whimper Jimmy collapsed. His vision filled with black spots. But just as quickly as the burning had come, it left, leaving on a throbbing sensation.

Jimmy reached out, gripping the sofa to raise himself. A ripping and crunching sensation greeted his ears and his hand as his fingers ripped through the upholstery and cracked the wooden frame beneath. Jimmy staggered to his feet, eyes wide and mouth open at the damage his grip had caused. Stepping backward, his feet stumbled across one another. He began to fall.

His hand shot out to stop his descent; his open palm thudded into the painted cement wall. An audible crunch filled the room. Splintered cracks formed around his hand, which was now sunk slightly into the wall. As Jimmy pushed himself away from the wall, dust and chunks of the wall came along, clattering to the floor. He looked at his wrapped hand, now coated in grey dust.

"Holy Mother of God, the old chink wasn't fooling." Jimmy's voice was barely a whisper as he spoke. The sudden rush of that knowledge and what it meant caused Jimmy to thrust his fist high into the air in a sign of victory, his mind racing. *There ain't no way that stinking Norwegian is gonna win now! I'm gonna crush him like Grandma used to crush grapes in the old country."*

The door burst open. Scrambling into the room came Tino's temporary replacement, Nicky. He was scrawny young man with a beakish nose and a mop of brown hair stuffed under his hat. "You alright, sir? I heard you yell." Nicky stood nervously at the door, eyes wide.

Jimmy could see him shaking. *Poor kid doesn't have a strong bone in his body.* Jimmy waved his hand and glanced up at the clock, 6 p.m. on the nose. "I'm good, kid. Let's get going, I got a fight to win." Jimmy held his hands out so Nicky could put his gloves on.

Nicky waved his slender hand toward Jimmy. "Nah you're good. Yah still got a few minutes. The clock's ticking a little fast." Nicky smiled, showing his large, bucktoothed grin.

"Get 'em on anyway, Nicky. It's time to go show this upstart who the real champ is."

Jimmy spent the next few minutes shadow boxing, aware of the minutes ticking away. A sudden knock at the door startled him out of his thoughts and routine. "Come on in, Nicky, yah don't need to knock." The door creaked open, but instead of Nicky, Jimmy's friend Liam stepped in, an Irish buddy of his from the gym. Liam was also the middleman for Jimmy's bets. Jimmy had sent him out earlier with the rest of his savings to place the bet. Liam was a good, honest Catholic so Jimmy knew he wouldn't cheat him. Jimmy sauntered over about to clap his buddy on the back, but faltered when he saw the drawn look on his friend's face.

"What's wrong? Did something happen with the money?" Jimmy's voice rose in pitch as panic began to creep into his voice.

"No, no, the money is fine. I placed the beat. It's Tino, Jimmy—they found him this morning at his loft. He's dead."

Jimmy had lived a life of taking blow after blow. And he had learned how to handle them and come back swinging. But this was a sucker-punch to his heart, a part of him that was not hardened. It hurt, terribly. He was staggered physically at the words, his body rocking for a moment before he tried to compose himself. A million questions surged through his mind, but only one escaped past his lips in a pained whisper. "How?"

Liam reached out to steady his friend, but Jimmy pulled away. "Well, they aren't sure since they just found him, yah know. But it looks like it was his heart."

"It wasn't his heart," Jimmy mumbled. A wrenching sense of guilt began to spread throughout his body.

"What you say, Jimmy?"

"N-nothing, nothing." Jimmy knew what had caused the old man to die—it was the price the old man had spoken about. If he had known, he would have never taken the potion. Tears began to line Jimmy's eyes. "Oh, Tino, you damn old fool. Why…"

"Sir." Nicky poked his head into the doorway. "It's time."

The roar of the crowd, thundering; the flash of cameras, blinding. It fell upon deadened senses as Jimmy made his way to the ring. Overwhelmed with guilt and sorrow for his lost friend and mentor, he walked in a daze. The voices of all those around him were like distant whispers, the people nothing more than fading shadows.

He moved without true thought or purpose, until the loud ding of the bell brought his mind racing back. It just took a few seconds too long to finish that race. As Jimmy's eyes grew unclouded and sharp once more, they saw a massive gloved fist heading straight for them. A split second later the impact came and he was sent hurtling backwards into the ropes. His years of training worked into his muscle memory thankfully worked a little faster as his arms shot up to cover his face just as a barrage of savage punches were thrown. Even with his arms absorbing the blows he could feel each one. *Holy hell, he hits like a fucking brick shit-house.*

Jimmy's thoughts were interrupted by sudden jabs to his gut and sides. *Come on, Jimmy, you gotta focus, gotta anticipate.* Jimmy managed to break away, moving to the side and quickly outpacing Magnus "The Mountain" Magni, who roared after him like some mythical beast of old. It was then that Jimmy got his first real look upon Magnus. The beast towered over him, and beast was the only word that Jimmy's mind could conjure to describe the hulking behemoth before him. It was as if a chiseled statue of Mighty Thor had come to life and put on some boxing gloves.

The hulk that was Magnus rushed at him, the ring shook under each massive stomp.

Jimmy braced himself as the berserker raced toward him, Magnus's eyes wild with bloodlust and rage, right arm raised back to deliver a punch that Jimmy thought for sure would knock him out of the ring if it landed. *Well if David did it, so can I.*

Jimmy's body grew tense as time seemed to slow down, his eyes growing sharp as he watched his destruction approach, and as that massive tree-trunk limb began to descend, he stepped to the right and brought his right arm up in a savage upper-cut. Magnus was not expecting the punch, his own self-confidence assuring him that he could never lose to such an old man.

Magnus would never get the chance to regret that pride-induced assurance. As Jimmy's fist connected with that massive jaw, Magnus's head snapped back, his entire lower body lifting up into the air before slamming down onto the ring like a falling meteor. The roar of the crowd became deafening as Jimmy stood there in stark disbelief, seeing Magnus "The Mountain" Magni lying before him, out cold.

Jimmy roared his victory as he bounced around the ring, arms raised in triumph. *I did it! I did it! Thank you God! I did it!*

Through his victory-fueled haze Jimmy noticed the cry of the crowd had not died down but had changed in tone and intensity. He stopped jumping before looking around, before his eyes fell upon the still-unmoving form of Magnus. The ref was standing next to the kneeling ring doctor. Who had quickly jumped within the ring upon Magnus failure to stand, or even move after the fight was over. His fingers quickly reaching out to touch the side of his neck. Jimmy knew something was wrong. *Why does his neck look so funny?* The thought was answered as the ring doctor sadly shook his head and looked up at Jimmy.

"He's dead; neck's broken."

Dead? But how? Jimmy knew. He looked down at his gloves and mumbled softly, "Strength beyond that which any man has, or ever will have. Oh Lord, what have I done."

He turned and fled, leaving the ring with the snapping of metal as he ripped two of the ropes from their post before making his way into his dressing room, collapsing against the closed wooden door once inside.

*

"Jimmy Flannigan Thacker, you move away from this door right now and let me and yer daughter in!" Audrey's voice had risen finally after almost thirty minutes of banging on the door. "It not be your fault that the man had a weak neck. Now stop being daft and open this—"

"No! I… I can't yet, just a little while longer." Jimmy's voice was ragged with guilt. He had killed Tino because of his greed and vanity, and now he had killed Magnus. He hadn't known Magnus, but he knew that no man deserved to die just because he wanted to prove he was the best. The ref and others had come by to try to convince Jimmy that he was not at fault, but he had been inconsolable because he knew the truth. He had asked for this power, and in doing so he had doomed two men to die. Jimmy blinked through teary eyes up at the clock. It was two minutes until seven. *Two more minutes and this curse will finally be over.*

Audrey's tone changed suddenly. "Ginny, dear, cover yer ears." A moment passed before a tirade of profanities assaulted Jimmy through the door in such magnitude that if those words had been capable of asserting physical force, the door would have been blasted apart, as would have Jimmy.

Jimmy winced at the verbal assault. Blurred, puffy eyes once more moved to the clock on the wall, just in time to see the clock tick to 7 p.m. Jimmy pushed himself up and off the ground. Legs trembling at the effort, slowly he staggered away from the door, his body sluggish, worn from sorrow.

Audrey's verbal attack finally ended with a kick to the previously blockaded door. Slowly it creaked open. Audrey peered inside the room at Jimmy. He stood a few feet away, slumped. She froze, no doubt seeing his broken heart through his swollen eyes. "Oh, baby."

Her voice, her soft tone was a balm upon his aching heart. Blinking, his blurred vision finally began to clear. A moment later he could see perfectly once more and before him stood his wife Audrey and his little girl and Ginny—the reason he had done all of this, the reason he would be able to go on. His broken heart began to mend at that simple sight and thought.

He saw the bluster leave her as she gazed upon him. He opened his arms, needing to feel them, to hold and cherish his loved ones. They rushed to embrace him and Jimmy began to weep freely once again as he cradled his loved ones tightly. His eyes closed, and his soul and heart rejoiced in the feel of them so near… until he felt them break beneath him, felt their bones shatter, felt them stiffen for a split second before they both went slack.

Jimmy collapsed. Sorrow and anguish swelled within him for a split second before bursting free in a soul-wrenching wail. His heart broken, Jimmy's shuddered as sobs and other unintelligible noises of grief continued to usher from his shaking body. Holding the limp bodies of his wife and child, Jimmy's heart shattered, never again would, or could, he feel joy or love. As overwhelming misery settled within Jimmy Thacker's soul, a soft whisper filled his ears and his mind.

"Your price has been paid."

IX

THE HERMIT

10

THE HERMIT

LISA MANNETTI

Upright: Soul-searching, introspection, being alone, inner guidance
Reversed: Isolation, loneliness, withdrawal

"Anchorite: A type of hermit who does not wander or roam, but instead permanently seals herself up, literally, by being walled inside a tiny cell (an anchorhold, q.v.) attached to a church.

Anchorhold: Sometimes there was a door that was much too heavy for the anchorite to move, but typically, there were only two or three openings: a small shuttered aperture facing the altar called a squint or a hagioscope where Mass could be observed and Holy Communion received; another tiny flap-covered rectangle to permit the passage of food, water, chamber pots, etc. and, occasionally, a third window high up on the outer wall which faced the street and was covered with translucent cloth to permit the entry of light."

—Roman Catholic Encyclopedia

"My dear sister anchorites, love your windows as little as you can. For from sight comes all the misery that there now is and ever yet was and ever shall be..."

—From the Ancrene Wisse, 13th century

192

Northern Scotland, circa 1560

Prologue

There was the stone circle dream again; the same one Catherine had been having since earliest childhood. They say those are the dreams one never forgets, never gets over. *They say those dreams are warnings,* she thought, *but that couldn't* be because the gray stone tower that was a-building ever higher and higher in her dream, enclosing and encircling her until she could dodge the narrowing sunlight and crouch in the widening shadows had always made Catherine feel so very safe.

No, it was the *other,* more recently borne dream that disturbed her: A woman held down fast to a chair in a white lime-washed stone cellar. On her face and head sat an iron device like a mask, known as a brank or a scold's bridle. Two long thin horns rose up from the metal neckband, went curving high up—past the cheekbones and eye sockets—and higher still past the crest of her skull, their ends terminating in small bells that would tinkle every time the woman moved. That jingle, a mocking sound to further her sense of humiliation.

But, far worse were the rows of sharpened triangular teeth lining the slit mouth—

teeth that prevented talking, teeth that, if she tried to speak, would eat the wearer's own tongue.

*

"Bishop Anderson is here to see you, ma'am," said the girl—recently chosen according to custom by Catherine's husband Lord Barclay as a lady-in-waiting. She gazed briefly at the slate floor and, at the same time slid back her left heel so her knees bent slightly and her narrow hips and flat midriff tilted, giving the smallest fraction of obeisance—a courtesy, Catherine surmised, that might have been for the bishop's notice instead of her own; she could hear him breathing heavily just beyond the open parlor door. The former prelate—his predecessor—had been such a braw fellow, a good heart. This one—well—she had her doubts about him, but he was here.

"Thank you. Show him in, Margaret."

Catherine could guess why he'd come to the gray stone manor house for the second time in less than a fortnight; there might be a certain amount of unrest, but Mary Queen of Scots was still on the throne and this fat bishop wanted to polish up his dusky granite church near Aberdeen until it gleamed—a Catholic gem above the highlands.

"Quite a few of the nobles here and in the shire have made substantial donations already, my lady," the bishop said around a mouthful of scone, at the same time he brushed a few errant crumbs from the puddle of his black robe in the center of his lap.

"My husband has been very generous with St. Anselm's."

"Oh, certainly, Lady Catherine, without a doubt. Ah, but an anchorhold would be just the thing. Give us a sterling reputation for housing our very own wise woman or pious man—think what might be given to the church in the future, based on the holy one's followers."

"To be sure," Catherine said. "But who will inhabit the cell and dispense all this wisdom and piety?"

"Only let it be begun to be built, and surely our sweet Savior and his Holy Mother will send us such a one."

"Lord Barclay is at court, but let me think on it and when he returns presently, I will make mention of your… architectural plans."

"Most bounteous," he nodded. "Thanks and blessings upon you and your household."

The raisin-flecked scones, black tea, and whisky were by then gone, and Catherine wasn't sorry to see the acquisitive bishop depart as well.

"I think the bishop has eyes for you—maybe for both of us," Margaret said and they both laughed.

*

That night Catherine dreamed of a gentle woman lying on her back and so heavily veiled nothing could be seen of her pale face except her eyes—which seemed full of terror; when they weren't wide with fright, they shifted rapidly and anxiously back and forth from side to side. The red-mitred archbishop suddenly stood alongside her, his hand above her head, his fingers poised to make the sign of the cross. Surely, Catherine thought, now the poor woman would find calm and peace in the blessing. Instead, underneath the thick linen cloth, she saw the woman's mouth open wide to scream.

*

Margaret. Marge. Grete. Peggy. Peg. *Meggie*. With a great deal of shared mirth they'd settled on Meggie as a sweet diminution, and Meg, too, and today was Meg's birthday. Dear girl. Catherine had a surprise for her. A lovely dress—a gown made for dancing—that Catherine secretly ordered from Annie Duncan in the village instead of the Aberdeen seamstress she usually hired. But Annie was more than adequate and the yellow dress the color of gold proved it.

The friendship between them truly began, Catherine recalled, just after the dream about the women lying supine in terror of the unknown red-robed archbishop. "I can make nothing of it, Lady Catherine," Margaret said, "but if you wish, I can consult the cards."

"Cartomancy?"

"I learned the art at court. There was a copy of an old book— *The Oracles of Francesco Marcolino da Forlì*—that my kinswoman Lady Ashcroft studied and taught me. The cards can be very instructive—"

"Is it not forbidden?"

"The symbols—I swear it—are more Christian than Rome itself. And anyway, we can treat it as a game, a mere amusement."

Catherine never noticed that Meg contradicted herself. (Were the shifting, subtle time-worn cards a game or divination?) Never agreed to the suggestion to read her own cards, and never taught Catherine the meanings of the faded polychrome pictures drawn on the cards. Catherine never noticed that their daily play grew longer and longer and passed, on her part, from keen interest to obsession. Margaret (Meggie!) had something—information—that Catherine wanted, no, began to hunger for. Catherine still loved William, Lord Barclay. The marriage had been arranged; she had the money, he had the title, but she loved him. What, Lady Catherine pined to know, did he feel about *her*? The cards were not always clear according to Meggie, but Catherine wanted—needed to know and she kept asking for another layout, a different spread. Time after time, day after day.

It never occurred to her that she, Catherine, had something that Margaret wanted even more.

*

In the early 1550s when Catherine had been a budding pre-
pubescent girl of not quite ten, her father had had three priest holes
secretly built inside the estate her paternal grandfather named
Wellbridge Manor House. With the advent of Protestantism, it was a
common practice in England and, her father reasoned, who knew
when Scotsmen might also need them to hide vestments and
tabernacles, holy water or even holy men themselves? One—the
smallest—was revealed when the riser of a step in the grand staircase
was turned, then lifted. A second called for putting out the fire in the
great room, bracing a ladder inside the chimney and accessing a
narrow stone shelf that led to an interior space. The last was
concealed in one of the closets between her parents' bedrooms, a
closet in her childhood that had been her mother's dressing room. A
devout woman, Catherine's mother wanted a place to pray, to keep
holy things and Jesuit priests near her. Perhaps because Catherine
had been punished not a few times when as a nine-year-old she was
caught in one or another of the priest holes playing with her dolls,
dressing them in the clergymen's Flanders lace chasubles and French
silk stoles on rainy days; perhaps because she was so very Catholic
and William was not; perhaps because she liked having a secret when
they married and by law he became the owner of her adored
Wellbridge Manor House; perhaps she had a flash of prophetic
intuition; perhaps for all these reasons or some other unknown even
to herself, she never told Lord Barclay—or anyone else—about the
hidden rooms and compartments.

Cues as subtle as the constantly fluctuating backgrounds and
secret symbols in the cards. Margaret's birthday feast. Sharp—
excited—hand claps and flashing eyes during a Volta. A fan
fluttering, slyly concealing then revealing a white bosom above the
décolletage of a yellow dress the color of gold. Something in the way
two particular wine cups tilted, clinked, and subtly lingered against
each other during a toast. Something—
Catherine was inside the priest hole peering through the tiniest
pinhead roundel of a carved oak floret watching her husband eagerly
strip Margaret, watching Margaret enthusiastically assisting him, and

then pulling at William's clothes, watching them melt into each other's flesh, hearing them sigh and moan.

Shifting embers masked the noise of a panel sliding. Catherine silently padding into the room. Her bare feet warmed against the stone flags in front of the fireplace grate; the orange-gold flames cozened her ankles and calves, then blazed upward toward her heart: She stood immobile until, knife upraised, she lunged.

Her aim was true. The dagger slashed past the thin hanging gauze that curtained the bed; its tapering double-sharpened point entered Barclay's back between the left ribs and punctured his heart.

"Clean yourself up, you betraying bitch," Catherine said, wiping the eight-inch blade on the curtain. Barclay was still sprawled atop his forever-more-lady-in-waiting who'd given a short scream when he'd opened his mouth to cry out; instead, he gushed silent blood over her throat and chin.

*

At first Catherine felt better than she'd ever felt before. A surge of powerfulness, of righteous anger and a sense of utter control coursed through her. No wonder men love war, she thought. No wonder that kind of killing was called the heat of battle. What triumph, what confidence, what a sense of certainty—surer than the constancy of sunrise and sunset, surer than cosmology and the belief that God's ordered universe was nothing short of perfection itself. *God's in His heaven and all is right with the world.*

Catherine was—yes, she was—invincible; nothing worried her. Her demesne—her own private *world*—was rife with potential. The body? Pfft. William Barclay—late of Wellbridge Manor House— could be left in the forest where his remains would be scattered by ravening animals; he could be hoisted into the priest hole above the fireplace where his corpse would be slow-roasted and eventually turned to ash; he could be said to return to court and thence, who knows where? There were so many possibilities: highwaymen and pox, robbers and brigands, accidents and mishaps—any of those might be the source of the fate that made him disappear unaccounted for.

Margaret, the betraying bitch who pretended to be Catherine's friend could also be dispatched—perhaps even to lie eternally alongside Barclay: She could be poisoned or pushed down stairs; or, for that matter, she could be sent away; or branded as a heretic or a witch; or the victim of a hundred varying misfortunes. No question it could be done. Catherine, at first, wasn't the slightest bit worried about getting rid of the treacherous lady-in-waiting whose rank was, of course, lower than her own.

Love drowned, and then died in the well of her rage and their perfidy.

Gone. I will get these letching turncoats gone.
And good riddance to them both!

An hour later, Lady Catherine lay in her own bed listening to the sound of Margaret crying softly while she scrubbed away traces of William's blood from the stone floor, the wooden bedstead and her own treasonous bosom. The sounds cheered her. The slow whoosh of the brush, the small heaving air-gulps and whistling sobs, the rustling of newly-crimsoned curtains and coverlets.

Catherine lay supine on her back, her head on the pillow, rosary beads in hand, saying her nightly prayers when she began to feel the first twinge of unease.

"Hail Mary, full of grace… pray for us sinners," she whispered. "Sinners," she repeated softly. A tiny rill of guilt—wee and insubstantial as a first teardrop—seemed to course down her gullet. *So what,* she thought, shrugging a shoulder, there were worse sins and certainly worse sinners in the world; let Mother Mary see to them.

The phrase "murder will out," rose up instantly—and unbidden—in her brain.

Where had she first heard it? Yes, Chaucer. *The Nun's Priest's Tale.* A story about frightening dreams that were portents, about false flattery *(just like Margaret!)*, about illicit fucking! (Just like Barclay *and* Margaret!) "Murder will out," she murmured, then shook her head. The shame—the consequences! They wouldn't hang her because she had a title; she would be beheaded.

She fell silent. The crystal beads lay dead in her fingers.

She was damned. She was going to hell. Her eternal soul had an ineradicable blot on it. Confession to the priest, even to the Holy

Pontiff (*the pope himself!*) wouldn't be enough—it was mortal sin. Unless—

Unless, she thought, *I can atone—sincerely and completely—through penance...*

But what about their sins, their penance?

Penance must be done....

Penitents, of course, could be bought. It was never Church doctrine, but the history of the thing was there. In this life... even in the *afterlife*, come to think of it... because why else would you say prayers for the dead? Why else make novenas to release sin-blackened souls from Purgatory? Why pay—make a donation—for flickering votive candles or a Latin mass for the dead? Yes, money could do a great deal, and filthy lucre could provide that first, all-important cornerstone for a forgiven—a *cleansed*—soul.

*

It was such a glorious moment in the history of St. Anselm's that Bishop Anderson had summoned Archbishop Stewart all the way from Edinburgh to officiate at the consecration of the new anchorhold. The two clerics—one as tall and spare as birch, the other short and wide like clumped heather—blessed the small trefoil-shaped hagioscope that gave such a limited view of the altar, then they turned and led the procession from inside the church. Now they stood beneath the outside window, vestments billowing in the wind. Deep-voiced singing of the Gregorian chant, the *De Profundus*, the liturgy for the dead. The bronze censors that held the holy incense swayed in the sharp breeze, the heavy smoke shredded away before Catherine could breathe in its essence.

The window was shoulder height. She stared at a bonnie little blond-haired girl with a smudgy face who stood leaning against her mother's skirts sucking quietly at the short finger in her mouth. The child looked enough like Margaret to be hers, Catherine thought. No, that couldn't be. It was just the one time. Had to be. Barclay had been at court—but then again they fell into each other's arms so easily—so readily—

The bishop began to fasten the shutters from outside the anchorhold. Behind them there was only a round, latticed hole (like a smaller version of the grate inside a confessional) accessible when the wooden shutters were open so the anchorite could speak with passersby, perhaps to ask for alms or dispense blessings—

Margaret, of course, wouldn't be doing much talking. Not with the thick metal brank on her head that would be removed only at mealtimes. In winter, according to the prescribed ritual that was only once a day. She was supposed to do nothing but think and pray—and that was fine with Lady Catherine.

Once Catherine had donated the money to build the anchorhold (built in memoriam to her late husband—a nice ironic touch, she thought, which included a bronze plaque screwed into the wall facing the street which, alas, Margaret, that rutting bitch couldn't see) his Excellency, Bishop Anderson had the thing constructed in record time. It wasn't hard to persuade the fubsy little cleric that Margaret would make an excellent candidate for inhabitancy; it was easier still to convince her ladyship-in-perpetual-waiting under threat of Barclay's flintlock rifle to beg this boon of his Grace. ("This kind of play acting should be a skip on the moors for the likes of you, Margaret. If you have any doubts about your ability, keep a lemon in your pocket you can clandestinely touch—then wipe your eyes—to shed tears. Get down on your knees. And don't get up until he agrees, or tonight will be the last night you lay that lively blond whoring head on one of my pillows—or any other cushion. With the possible exception of a dirt headrest. So make it good, Meggie."

Like some other anchorholds, this one had a door that was designed to be too heavy for its inhabitant to move by herself from inside. Door or not, *you were never supposed to leave.* There had been anchorites, Catherine knew, that had burned alive in their cells rather than flee, though she had her doubts about those solitaries—and how much straw they *really* still had up in the old brain loft after years of isolation. Never mind sanity—mentation itself was a difficult thing to hold onto when one lived forever walled off from humankind. There had to be a servant to see to the shut-in's needs: food and water; clothes and bedding; prayer books and chamber pots. Catherine had paid for that along with everything else—that cold and desolate "everything else"—that now comprised Margaret's drab bed and board, her constrained life.

*

The trouble for Catherine began because she couldn't resist visiting the dank, drafty anchorhold. At first she did no more than whisper a few taunting words through the hagioscope after High Mass. "Enjoying the body of Christ, Meggie dear?" It was so pleasant to think that was the only "body" lusty Margaret could enjoy. She could clench her fists, of course, but she could not answer.

Then after a short time, the days were lengthening, spring was in the air and she wanted to observe Margaret's suffering more closely. She'd walk along with the servant carrying the covered dish of haggis (secretly wishing she could spit on the anchorite's dinner or slip in rat's guts when the cook had her back turned, mixing them among the usual sheep's pluck of innards).

She'd watch as the servant girl and the bell-ringer opened the heavy door, removed the mask-like brank and Margaret ate—slowly; as if it took some time for her to recover the ability to work her jaws. Catherine convinced herself she stayed through mealtimes to be certain that Margaret didn't talk to her keepers about the disappearance of a certain local lord and the reason he vanished, while she—for the same reason—had been clapped in a cell to live out her days wearing brown wool rags and shorn blond hair.

But, like all interests—even overriding ones—with time the thrill began to pall; a certain jaded weariness set in watching Margaret eat her food with the slowness of a senile, toothless crone. Catherine decided to begin to pay "midnight surprise" pop visits to her pet anchorite. Yes, she thought, *just to make sure Margaret's belly wasn't popping, too. Besides, it would be fun to scare her out of the three or four hours of sleep she was allowed, or to embarrass her whilst she was squatting on the chamber pot or picking vermin from her crusty scalp.*

*

A full moon rode high above the stone Celtic cross topping the church steeple. It was Midsummer's Eve. Catherine followed the winding path that led to the anchorhold's outer window and opened the wooden shutters. She lifted the lantern and peered between the small interstices of the grate. Instead of spying her quarry lying asleep on the sharp twigs and moldy straw that made the mattress of her bed, there was no Margaret to be seen. *It's impossible. She's got to be there!* In her haste to shine the light into all the corners of the cell, it swung erratically. Shadows shifted eerily and she felt her heart quicken.

She entered the church and set the lantern down on the pew closest to the anchorhold's entryway. Fueled by anxiety, she pushed at the heavy door. It squealed and grated against the stony floor, but finally yielded. Moonlight shimmered and glittering straw-dust danced on the swirling air. She stood blinking with disbelief, then retreated to snatch the lantern. Nothing. *Nothing!*

Her first inclination was to go and wake the sexton—not just to begin the hunt for the missing woman *(missing whore!)*, but to ring the bells, to rouse the bishop, to sound the alarm and wake the very dead!

Catherine stood in that silvery, shifting chiaroscuro, heart beating madly—so wildly that at first she was aware of no other sound. Then, gradually, she heard a noise that sounded like the humming whir of a thousand flying insects. She blinked twice.

Margaret—naked except for a kind of muddy daub smeared from her head to her toes and bathed in moonshadow and moonlight—gently drifted down to the grimy floor from the highest roof beams.

*

"How now, Mistress Catherine?" Margaret walked (sashaying her hips like some incarnation of the goddamn Queen of Sheba) toward the bedstead where she slid her hands under the makeshift mattress and retrieved the filthy rag of a woolen robe. She slipped it on over her nakedness. "Cat got your tongue, Your Ladyship?" She laughed. "Let me help your poor mind—so confused and befuddled even though you weren't the one living in near-total isolation—to grasp the situation." Light and dark played over her. She rinsed her arms and face in the basin, then stood with her thin white moon-witched hands on her flat hips and stared at Catherine. "So uncertain, the cat must have your eyes, too…"

Catherine nodded. True, she was angry, but she was confused as well, and for the moment, her confusion and the resultant curiosity outweighed her irritation. "How…?" she began.

"How? How did I disappear? How did I seem to hang splayed from the ceiling and float gracefully—feet first—to the ground? Hmmm…"

"Yes, how?"

"Well, My dear Ladyship, it's the same answer. In a word, transvection—"

"Trans—?"

"Transvection. Yes. Most commonly achieved by smearing flying ointment into the hair and skin and then… well, flying." She paused. "You look so bewildered. And yet, you were right there—just beyond the squint, if I'm not mistaken—when His Grace and His Eminence chanted the liturgy of the dead. The *De Profundis*. Ringing any bells, Lady Catherine?"

Catherine nodded, and some of the dumb-cow look left her eyes. She was still befuddled, but she did remember the dedication ceremony.

"Good," said Margaret, "because being locked in here liberated me completely. Think of the whole process like the miracle of transubstantiation. The wafer and the wine that become Christ's body and blood." She paused. "Only in this case, one can actually witness the miracle." She gave a little laugh. "Certainly Bishop Anderson would call it a miracle if he could have seen me—not two hours ago—dancing at the very top of the Brocken in the Harz mountains in Germany…"

"Germany?"

"Yes, dancing on the summit, and fucking, too, because Midsummer's Eve always pulls in a much bigger crowd than Beltane, Imbolc, or Walpurgis Night—"

"Walpurgis Night!" Catherine felt herself reeling. "You're a witch!"

"Well, who in hell else would be up there jigging naked in the freezing snow? It feels like you're wearing a goddamn ice-shroud on that goddamn peak from September to May." Her eyes sparkled yellow as the low-slung moon and Catherine suddenly knew she was actually seeing the devil's own hot-eyed mirth glimmering there.

"Get thee gone, demon!"

Margaret began to laugh; her shoulders and midriff shook and the laughter became a whoop. "Demon… ha ha… oh my," she wiped a tear from her eye. "Demon. Oh that's rich. No, Mistress Catherine, I'm not a demon. I'm merely a servant of the Lord—"

"The Dark Lord, the devil you mean—you blasphemer!" She crossed herself. "What's the difference, anyhow? You're a witch—it's the same thing—"

"It isn't. Let me show you."

She saw Margaret wave her hands once, twice, thrice… and the stony throat of the cell seemed to disappear—but gradually—like mist rising off the Dee River then scattering as the sun rose higher on calm summer mornings.

Margaret led her to the street window. She made no movement that Catherine could discern, but the shutters crashed open against the outside stone walls. Catherine winced at the sharp clatter. The carved grate dissolved, and the translucent cloth that let in the light through the tracery vanished—wavering only for an instant before it became glass-clear.

Catherine's vantage point looked down through thick fog to a plinth of square granite boulders. She appeared to be watching the capering fire-lit figures from perhaps twice the height of a man—as if, she thought, she were a guardian angel hovering above an earthbound charge.

But the leering red faces crowding the altar—if that's what it was—were far from angelic. To her ears the sounds they made were growls and gibberish, but now and again, she heard the word "Brocken-spectre"—that eerie wavering human shadow projected through the mist against a light source. To the observer it seemed like an apparition. A ghost. A haunting. But it was a common, well-documented illusion and nothing more, she thought.

Then a low gasp went through the crowd, rippling from the rear of the group toward the altar. In the flickering red-orange light of the fire-glow, she saw the naked people suddenly bowing. Some threw themselves to the ground and covered their heads with their hands and arms.

She heard the ponderous thud of footfalls. And maybe—but, no, her imagination was deceiving her—the sound of weighty hooves striking solid rock.

*

Tambourines fluttered and tinkled. Mockery of the Sanctus bells rung upon the altar as the miracle takes place in the Holy Communion.

An impossibly huge creature with the face of a gargoyle stood wearing a black archbishop's mitre that rose up high between two tall curving horns. Spread in front of him was a young woman, screaming at the sight of his clawed hand lifting to cast an airy pentagram over her white breasts. It was blasphemy… it was worse… it was the dream—her dream!—the one Margaret claimed confounded her! She'd brought out those unholy cards that opened a first portal… and now this sad, terrible travesty, Catherine thought.

The warlocks, the demon—each with his manhood bared, pawing and grunting over the terrified woman—the sacrifice.

And then, all of them began to caress one another; men and women turning to the nearest body, heedless of who or how. The demon thrust himself again and again into the spraddled girl, then suddenly emitted a long shouting howl.

The witches and warlocks stopped all movement at once. Their eyes, red with lust in the firelight, looked up, seeking his muddied citron gaze.

Then—although she saw no outward signal—as if their minds were inextricably linked, all of them turned as one, and baring teeth and nails, they crowded in and fell on the girl.

Soon—too soon—her shrieks bled into silence.

*

Her memories of that hideous Midsummer's Eve were confused with other journeys through the air to the Brocken on Lammas and the Autumn Equinox that Margaret showed her. But Catherine could never be certain if she'd merely witnessed the sickening rituals or had participated. Now Margaret told her the Witches' Year was coming to a close on Samhain—or All Hallows' Eve, as Catherine had known it in what seemed another lifetime. Was another lifetime, she amended, as she sat—dazed and listless—on a crude three-legged wooden stool surrounded by the stone walls of the anchorhold.

Life certainly was—if nothing else—paradoxical, she thought. Six months or so earlier that year, she'd thought it was tremendously ironic that the rectangular bronze plaque that bore her husband's name and had been fastened against the outside stone wall of the anchorhold wasn't visible to the inhabitant when Margaret was the one confined to the filthy, malodorous cell.

Ironic indeed.

"My dear sister anchorites, love your windows as little as you can. For from sight comes all the misery that there now is and ever yet was and ever shall be…"

So said the Ancrene Wisse, the handbook for anchorhold dwellers. And, it was more than true, more than ironic, Catherine thought. Through her little windows she'd seen Margaret having sex on the altar with the short, chubby bishop. It didn't matter, Catherine supposed, that Margaret might've bewitched the poor cleric. What mattered was that afterward when Margaret appeared belly a-bulge (and who knew who—or what—fathered the growing child) the bishop, the archbishop—the whole congregation—believed it was Immaculate Conception. How else to explain the circumstances of a woman barred inside a cell who was pregnant? They were waiting to hear officially from Rome (from the Vatican! From the Holy Pontiff himself!) about whether the whoring witch and her bastard were a genuine miracle. In the meantime, Margaret was regarded as a saint. Saints, according to the clergy, had to be available at all times and completely to their devotees. So Margaret was whisked out of the anchorhold.

At the same time, Catherine had the stone circle dream almost every night. After the terrifying night rides to the Brocken on the Witches' Sabbaths, the refuge the dream offered seemed not like mere escape or safety, but a slice of Heaven itself. It had nothing to do with Margaret's wiles, Catherine told herself, because the stone circle dream belonged to her. She'd underestimated Margaret when her lady-in-waiting read the cards, but she never doubted it was her own idea to return—full circle—as it were to make amends for her crime. For her mortal sin. Penance needed to be made.

She had paid for the construction of the stone anchorhold and, she'd told the bishop, she wished to retreat to the cell to pray ceaselessly for the soul of her husband and all the faithful departed.

Now she moved from the wooden seat to the bed. She knelt to pray. She remembered thinking when they walled her in and she looked toward the street just before they fastened the shutters, *this may be the last time I see the setting sun. The last time I watch wind trammel grass and redden human cheeks.* The same gusty drafts once again billowed the clergymen's cassocks, sent their embroidered silk stoles flying on the horizontal, and fanned the hair of the little blond girl who stood alongside her mother. The only difference was that it was autumn now…

And she was safe for a while.

Until the randy bishop began to visit her…wanting Catherine to supply what Margaret in her hugely pregnant state was no longer able—or willing—to give him.

Catherine didn't care. She'd tried to out-maneuver the wily Margaret, but instead had been broken emotionally on the wheel. Betrayal paled compared to the gloom, the sense of utter helplessness she felt in the face of Margaret's witchery.

And she might have been content. Locked in the anchorhold, forgotten by all from the moment the priests chanted the rite of the dead. But the bishop would not leave her alone. She begged them to brick in the doorway and she had felt something like relief when she heard the thick, slapping sound of the mortar and the last stone was locked into place.

She no longer wished to see *anything* or *anyone*.

They can't get in now, she'd thought. Mistakenly, as it turned out. She heaved a sigh. She was beyond tears… there was only a dull leaden feeling left inside her.

Was there something in that scold's bridle, (*the brank!*), some unknown, unimagined alchemy or power that drew in the world of the occult?

She didn't know.

She only knew that from the moment they intoned the *De Profundis*, she felt an inward trill—and she shuddered; it was then Catherine noticed the metal mask exactly resembled the Brocken-devil's face. The long curving horns, the slit mouth filled with rows of tiny sharpened teeth—

She had taken it off, but it was too late.

Time and again Margaret and the bishop, too, had slipped like smoke into the anchorhold. Gasping, she'd watch the flute of smoke plume between the stones, expand like a pig's bladder, then settle toward the floor. A second later, the sparkling smoke was gone and one or both of them stood in front of her. Sometimes, they came to jeer and taunt. Mostly, they appeared in order to bend her to their will. She was powerless and, whether her head was bent and her mouth full of the fat bishop's manhood, or Margaret laughed while Catherine licked the stone floor, she was their puppet and they did what they wanted. *Sheer deviltry,* she thought.

Once she had wondered if the anchorites who stayed inside their cells even while the flaming rafters fell in on them, had lost the mental capacity to obey the instinct to survive. Now, she thought, it didn't matter. She no longer cared. She was tired unto death of Margaret's humiliations and her blasphemous witchery.

Death, Catherine thought, was sure to bring her respite—release.

She stood up from the rat's nest of a bed and reached into the pocket of the tattered woolen smock she was wearing. Inside was the flint and steel.

She would be steel now.

She stuck them together over and over, and the sparks fell in a glittering shower onto the dried twigs… a little flame…. and then the smoke.

She lay down on the floor at the other end of the cell.

This was smoke she could welcome.

These were flames that would sing her brightly—and inexorably—to her final rest.

11

THE WHEEL OF FORTUNE

JEFF DEPEW

Upright: Destiny, fortune, luck, felicity
reversed: Increase, abundance, superfluity

October, 1944

It was all happening so fast, Captain Heinrich Gruber thought, gazing out at the Greek countryside rolling past. Too fast. Just yesterday,he had been sitting in his familiar office (his familiar comfortable office) in the German Headquarters in Athens, checking over ration reports. Now, here he was, in a four seat kubelwagen, leading a troop transport over a narrow bumpy road towards a village he had never even heard of.

He leaned forward and tapped the driver on the shoulder. "How much farther?"

The driver's eyes never left the road. "It should be just over this ridge, Herr Captain."

It was a nondescript village near the western coast of Greece. In an area called Foloi, known for its woods and oak forest, apparently. This was in the documents that had been hand-delivered yesterday, along with orders to leave at 0600 that morning.

This was all new to Gruber. He was a bureaucrat, not used to the outdoors. He already missed his office with its richly panelled walls and large desk. That's where he should be right now, drinking a hot mug of kaffee while he began his daily paperwork. He was not a field commander. But he wasn't going to say anything. Orders were orders, especially these days.   Since the Allied invasion in France last June, tensions had risen. He had seen the stress in the faces of many of the officers he worked with, and to be honest, on more than one night he had awakened in his villa, heart pounding, to the sound of planes flying overhead. Is this it? He would ask himself, waiting in the darkness for the inevitable explosions and sirens and shouting. *The end is near* was the prevailing unspoken feeling. Between the Allies and the *verflucht* Russian army, it seemed to be only a matter of time. Of course, if you believed Goebbels' propaganda, the German Army would emerge victorious by the end of the year.

And every so often, one of his superiors would not show up for work. No messages, no notes. The rumor was that most were headed for Argentina.

Gruber lifted his briefcase from the seat beside him and opened it, pulling out a thick file folder. The phrase streng geheim was stamped across it in larger red letters. Gruber had never even seen a top secret folder, let alone been given one. And this one... it seemed like madness. He opened the folder and looked through his orders again. *Impossible. The Fuhrer must be getting desperate.* He shook his head. *I know he's been searching for sacred and holy relics...* but this is too much. But if there was even a chance of finding... No. It was impossible. He leaned forward again, turning to Krause, the sergeant he had just met this morning.

"What do you know of these orders? This mission?"

Krause turned around from the passenger seat beside the driver. He was older than Gruber, his face lined and serious.

"I was ordered to give you the file and accompany you to the village. The men and I are to follow your orders for the duration, sir."

Gruber gazed at him a moment. "The duration? Of what?"

Krause remained silent.

Gruber tried another tactic. "Do you know why we're here?"

"No, sir. I only know we need to find a local to guide us to our destination as soon as possible."

Gruber nodded and sat back. "Our destination," he repeated under his breath. He read over the file again. Unfolded a map. Maybe he had missed something. It just didn't make sense. He took out a pack of photographs. There were several grainy images of ancient documents containing lines of Greek letters and symbols. Gruber gazed at them for a moment before he put it all away and closed his briefcase. He glanced up as the vehicle slowed and stopped.

"We're here, sir."

The village of Kavos was smaller than Gruber could have imagined. The main thoroughfare was dirt, now mud, and the vehicles had to stop twice because of goats wandering through the streets. Narrow stone buildings, mostly two story, lined the streets on either side. People filtered out of doorways and stared as the motor cars entered their village. Old women wearing black shawls and men with heavy moustaches gazed with curiosity and, in a few cases, open hostility at the Germans. A young boy shouted something at the vehicles and ran away, laughing, followed by a barking dog.

"Orders, sir?"

Gruber started. He looked around. Krause was standing at attention. He had opened Gruber's door. The other soldiers were climbing out of the back of the truck. They spread out around the transport, their eyes watching for trouble. These were hardened men, Gruber thought. Veterans. He glanced at their field grey uniforms. All of them SS. And he was supposed to lead them? Him? *I don't belong here* Gruber thought again as he turned to face the men. He looked up as rain began to fall. *I should be back in my office.*

Gruber sighed. "Let's get inside."

*

Twenty minutes later, he sat at a rough wooden table in what served as both the city hall and the mayor's home. The mayor, a thin, tired-looking old man with a white stubble on his chin and bushy eyebrows, stared insolently from across the table. Several other villagers stood behind him, their dark eyes full of fear. Gruber played with the small cup of bitter coffee they had offered him. He rotated it slowly around in his hands.

Private Kohler, a slight, short bespectacled private, was serving as interpreter. He stood on Gruber's left. Krause and a half dozen soldiers were standing silently around the room. Two more were standing guard outside.

"Mayor Stavros bids you welcome and requests that you make yourself at home. He has offered his own house to you, Captain Gruber."

"Yes, thank him. Tell him I apologize for not speaking for myself. I can read a little Greek, but cannot speak it very well, I am afraid."

Kohler nodded and translated.

"Hey, Kohler, ask him if he has any daughters to offer us." A burst of rough laughter.

Gruber spun around. The speaker was Werner, a tall, stocky ruddy-faced private. His eyes met Gruber's, he grinned, and muttered something to the man next to him. Before Gruber could respond, Krause rose and stomped over to Werner, grabbed him by a lapel, and led him outside. Gruber turned back to Mayor Stavros.

"Tell him I apologize for... uh my men. I mean no disrespect and want to be as little bother as possible to the mayor and his people. We will not stay very long. We just need some information. And a guide who knows the area around the village. We are looking for a temple."

Kohler translated this and Gruber watched Stavros's expression carefully. The man's lined face paled, and he shook his head and rattled off something in Greek. The men behind him began speaking quietly to themselves. One turned and removed his hat, nodded at Gruber, and quickly left the room.

Gruber turned to Kohler.

"What? What did he say?"

Kohler took off his glasses and rubbed his eyes. He replaced his glasses.

"He says that there no guides here. He says there is nothing to see. They have nothing we want. We are free to search the entire village. But he also said—" He paused, looking carefully across the table at the mayor.

"He said we are in danger if we leave the village to seek the temple."

Gruber's heart leapt into his throat. This was exactly what he didn't want. He was not a warrior, not a tactician. He was a scholar who, because of the war, had become a minor bureaucrat. He took a deep breath and looked around the room. The soldiers behind him were all paying attention now, eyes firmly on the Greeks.

"Ask him," he said to Kohler, and swallowed. "Ask him if he is threatening us."

Again, Kohler spoke rapidly and listened carefully to Stavros's response. The other Greeks behind him nodded. Kohler looked up at Gruber. "He said he's trying to help us. There is something in the forest."

*

The room was small but serviceable. A bed, a small night stand, and a wobbly table which served as a desk. There was no electricity, so Gruber had to make do with several candles and an army lantern. The map lay spread out on his bed. He sat at the table writing, as he did most nights, a letter to his wife. How he missed Truda. And their little house, just blocks from the university. That life seemed so far away now, he thought, gazing at the flickering flame of a candle. Teaching at the university, researching in the library, having friends and colleagues over for dinner. And of course, Truda. And the baby, of course. So hard to think about. His son Hans, whom he had never seen, except in the photographs she had sent. He took one out from his satchel, and smoothed out the creases. Truda, sitting in a rocking chair, her face tired but beaming with happiness as she held their son. Only weeks old. Gruber had been promised furlough so he could attend the birth, but that had been cancelled. And then another furlough cancelled. He hoped to be able to return home by Christmas, at least. He put the photo down and quickly finished the letter.

Gruber rose, and using the lantern to guide him, left his room and descended the narrow staircase. Krause was sitting at the bottom of the stairs, smoking. He stood up when Gruber approached. Gruber motioned for him to sit back down. The other men were spread out on the floor in their rough canvas sleeping bags. Most were asleep, but several were quietly playing cards by the light of the fire. Against the far wall Kohler sat by himself, reading. He looked up as Gruber entered the room.

"Have any of the villagers volunteered to be guides?" he asked Krause.

Krause shook his head. "Nothing. I'll alert you if anything happens."

Gruber nodded." All right. I'll be turning in."

"Sir?"

Gruber turned to Krause. "Yes?"

"Forgive me for asking, sir, but how is it you can read Greek, but not speak it?"

Gruber smiled. "I suppose that's why I'm here. I'm a professor at the university in Cologne. I teach a course on ancient Greek history and mythology."

"That's why you're 'here'?" Krause repeated. "I'm sorry, sir, I don't understand."

The men playing cards had turned to listen. Kohler still sat alone, the fire reflected in his glasses. Gruber nodded.

"You would have found out eventually, and now is just as good a time. May I have one of those cigarettes?" Krause handed Gruber a cigarette, then held out his lighter. Gruber inhaled. Held it, then exhaled. "Danke."

For the first time since he had arrived, Gruber felt at ease. Like a teacher again. All eyes on him, listening intently.

"I'm not sure how much you know about the ancient Greeks, but they believed that their destinies, their lives, deaths, and everything in between were all predestined, even before they were born. And they personified these beliefs with three women. Three sisters called the Fates. Or more properly, the Moirai. The Moirai control the destinies of all men, and even the gods themselves. They measure one's life as a length of thread. And as long as that thread isn't cut, we live.

The first sister was Clotho, who spins the thread of life. She's often shown sitting at a spinning wheel. The second sister is called Lachesis. She measures out the thread. The third sister is Atropos. Atropos has a pair of metal shears, which she uses to cut the thread."

"What does this have to do with us?" asked a voice from the men on the floor. "Are we looking for three women?"

Gruber put out his cigarette in a half-full cup of water. "No, according to our orders, we are looking for the Shears of Atropos. Some say that whoever possesses the shears cannot die. And our orders are to locate the shears and deliver them to the Fuhrer."

*

Gruber slept fitfully. He dreamed he was in a forest and saw a beautiful dark-haired young woman in a white shift. When he approached, she glided away behind a tree. He followed her and as he caught up, he realized it wasn't her, but it was her, only older. She was still beautiful, though. She moved away from him again, stole behind another tree trunk. He followed her around the tree. She turned. It was still her, but she was dead. Her face was an ancient mass of scars and sores, her eyes red, oozing holes. Her toothless mouth gaped open, revealing a black tongue and cracked, diseased gums. She sprang at him.

Gruber sat up, heart pounding. He sat for a moment, getting his bearing and collecting his thoughts. Dim light was forcing its way through the battered blinds. Morning. He dressed quickly, smoothed his hair back, and checked his reflection in the mirror. He had to look his best for these men. He felt better after talking to them last night. Perhaps they might view him as more of an authority figure. He had stuck the picture of Truda and Hans in the corner of the mirror, and he snatched it up and put it in his breast pocket.

Gruber stood in the of the center village square. It was really just a space surrounding a crude stone statue of three weather-beaten figures. Candles and dried flowers littered the ground around it.

Dawn was just beginning to creep over the horizon, a rosy pink in the distance, but the town and surrounding woods lay shrouded in grey. Although it wasn't raining, the air was moist with a constant drizzle. Gruber was cold and wet, and longed once again for his kaffee. He clapped his hands together for warmth and to show the enthusiasm he didn't feel.

The mayor and several of his cronies stood miserably in front of him. Twenty or so villagers stood behind them. Their faces were hostile. There was no fear there, thought Gruber. Just malice. But after all we've done to their country, who can blame them?

Kolher was speaking quietly to the mayor, who was shaking his head. He looked frightened.

Kohler stepped up to Gruber and spoke quietly. "There have been no volunteers to guide us to the site. The mayor says he cannot force his people to help us. And he also warned us again not to enter the woods."

The mayor was speaking animatedly with an old woman who had approached and was tugging at his sleeve. Gruber motioned for Krause to come over and asked quietly, "This is a little out of my … area of expertise. What do you recommend? How can we get a guide?"

Krause looked at the villagers, thought for a moment and spoke quietly. "When we had trouble with the hill people sabotaging our vehicles and attacking us at night, we made examples of them." His eyes met Gruber's. "Memorable examples."

Gruber paced across the square. This was a crucial moment. The wrong decision could cost him the respect of his men or the enmity of the town. He stopped and returned to his men.

"Take the mayor into custody," he told Krause. "Have him guarded. No one may see him or have any contact with him." He nodded at Kohler, then turned and spoke directly to the civilians.

"This village is now under a curfew" He waited for Kohler to translate. "At sundown all citizens are to remain indoors. Anyone caught out of doors, will be arrested and held for questioning. No one is to leave town. All we are asking for is a guide to lead us to the temple of the Moirai. We know it is nearby. As soon as we have that guide, the mayor will be free and you can get back to your lives".

He could see some of his men grumbling, and some of the younger village men began shouting and gesturing but were shoved back by the soldiers. Gruber was about to speak again when the sound of a motor caught his attention. He looked up the road. A military kubelwagen rumbled toward them. Gruber looked at Krause, but he was hurrying towards the cars.

The car stopped and the driver exited and opened the rear door. A black-booted leg exited, followed by a slender man wearing the traditional black uniform of the SS. He looked around at the crowd the way a teacher looks at a room full of disobedient kindergarteners. He shook his head and approached Gruber.

He lifted his hand. "Heil Hitler." Gruber saluted back.

"You are Captain Heinrich Gruber." It was not a question.

"I am, sir."

"I am Sturmbannfuhrer Engels. I am now assuming command of this mission. You will remain as an advisor. I am told you have some background knowledge in the object we seek."

Gruber opened his mouth, but nothing came out.

Engels gestured at the gathered crowd, "What is happening here?"

Kohler approached him, saluted. "Sturmbannfuhrer Engels, the townspeople are not cooperating with our search. The captain has just declared a curfew until we find a guide."

Engels's face brightened at the sight of Kohler. "Wilhelm! How are you?" The two men embraced warmly. Engels held him at arm's length and gave him the once over. "You are looking well. How is your father?"

Kohler smiled. "He is in excellent health, sir. I will tell him you inquired about him."

Engle patted him on the shoulder. "Unfortunately I will not be able to make our hunting trip this year. I will be in Berlin."

"Ach, that is too bad, sir. I know you will be missed."

Engels nodded. "Yes. Now what was this about a curfew?"

Kohler straightened. Back to being a soldier. "Captain Gruber has just set… a curfew." He said "curfew" distastefully.

Enges glanced at Gruber. "A curfew? Really? Apparently, Captain Gruber is not accustomed to dealing with these types of people."

"No, sir," Kohler added. "I don't think he is."

Gruber said nothing, but his thoughts were dark as he glared at Kohler.

Engels put a forefinger on his lower lip and silently scanned the crowd. He motioned for two of his men and pointed at a young woman wearing a red print dress. The soldiers pulled her, one on each arm, from the other villagers. A man lunged forward but a brutal blow from a rifle butt knocked him to the ground. The soldiers brought the woman before Engels and forced her to kneel. She was pleading, reaching out towards him.

"Tell them this is just the beginning," Engels said to Kohler, approaching the woman. "Tell them no one is safe until someone offers to lead us to that temple."

As Kohler translated for the crowd, Engels drew his pistol, pulled back the slide, and shot the woman in the head. She collapsed without a sound. her body twitched once and was still. Blood pooled beneath her.

"Now!" shouted Engels over the cries of the villagers. He reached into a coat pocket and pulled out a steel magazine, full of bullets. He raised his arm, holding the magazine high in the air. Even in the gloom of the overcast morning, the shiny steel gleamed menacingly in his hand. The crowd quieted down as he began to speak. Kohler loudly translated. "As you see, we have more bullets. More, I think, than there are people in this village." Engels paused, let the meaning of that statement sink in. "What we do not have is time. Therefore, if we do not have a volunteer to guide us to this temple in five minutes, I will use another bullet. Five minutes after that? Maybe two." He looked coolly at the shocked, frightened faces. He pulled out a pocket watch and glanced at it. He snapped it shut and looked directly at the mayor. "You have five minutes."

*

Forty minutes later, Gruber was marching. The forest seemed endless; trees after trees after trees. Not enormously tall, or thick, but there was so many of them. Their branches intertwined, often blocking out the sky. It would be easy to get lost in a forest like this. Gruber adjusted his shoulder straps. His pack was too heavy. He was heavy as well. He had put on weight since his assignment to Athens. Sedentary work, not enough walking, he supposed. And now here he was. He was wet, he was cold, he was hungry, he was tired, and they were chasing a myth. This entire mission was a waste of time. He wished fervently that he had been left behind. But no, Engels had told him they might need his "expertise."

Within minutes of the woman's death, an older man had stepped forward and volunteered to be their guide to the temple. There was much shouting and gesticulating by the other villagers, but after Engels fired his gun into the air, they calmed down.

The guide walked purposefully along a narrow, barely noticeable path that led up a slope. Engels followed, speaking with Kohler. Behind them was Krause, with his men, who were spread out in a line, walking easily as they spoke quietly with one another. They soldiers had to keep pace with Engels, who moved very slowly and daintily, often grabbing onto Kohler's shoulder for support.

Gruber brought up the rear. His boot slipped on a wet rock, he fought for balance, stumbled and slipped to one knee in the mud. One of the men turned around but did not bother to help him up. Gruber reached for a limb to pull himself up when a pale shape dashed by just out of his field of vision. He turned, but whatever it was, it was gone. Something white. A goat? A wolf? Did they even have wolves in Greece? He quickly got to his feet and hurried after the others.

*

After an hour or so, Engels requested a brief rest. Gruber gratefully sat down on a large rock. Krause walked around, looking at the soldiers. He seemed troubled.

"Where is Hahn?" he demanded. Nobody answered. Some shrugs, uncertain murmurs. The villager stood off to one side, watching them. His face was impassive.

Werner looked down the path. "Last time I saw him, about twenty minutes ago, he said he had to take a piss."

"HAHN!" Krause shouted. No answer. "HAHN! Where the hell is he?"

The men spent five minutes calling for Hahn until Engels called an end to it. "He will follow our tracks. We don't have time for this." He looked at Kohler. "Ask him how much farther."

After consulting with the man, Kohler reported to Engels. "We should be there by nightfall. If we hurry."

Engels nodded. "Then we hurry."

*

The rest of the day was a blur. Marching. Occasionally stopping for a few minutes at a time. Krause and some of the men shouting for Hahn. Then marching again. Weaving through the oaks, crawling over rocks and fallen tree as they followed the barely perceptible path.

They stopped when one of the men claimed he had seen someone through the trees. Krause sent three soldiers to investigate, but they found nothing.

Gruber passed the time by imagining what Truda and the baby were doing. Noon: lunch of course, and then perhaps a nap. Two o'clock; perhaps a stroll through Geusenfriedhof, the beautiful old cemetery in Cologne. So peaceful and serene. He and Truda would often spend hours among the beautiful monuments and statues. The cemetery always felt more about celebrating life and the living than death. The dead were dead. They didn't care about grand tombs or statues. It was the living who designed and cared for them. The living who visited and remembered them.

As the sun began its slow descent over the western mountaintops, the group reached a small clearing atop a plateau. In the center was a mass of huge boulders, about five meters high. The guide spoke urgently to Kohler, who looked at Engels. Engels, in turn, shouted orders at Krause. Krause called his men to him. Gruber walked toward them, feeling that he should be part of the conversation.

"And what exactly does he say is the threat?" Engle was asking Kohler, although he was staring at the guide, who looked extremely uncomfortable. He held his hat in his hands, his eyes on his feet.

"He's not saying exactly, just that the temple is 'protected'. He wants to return to the village as soon as possible."

"Are we here?" Gruber asked excitedly. "Are we at the temple?"

Engels glanced at Gruber, scowled, then back at Kohler.

"First of all, tell him he's not going anywhere. We may need his help to get back to the village. And second of all…" he turned around, holding out his arms in an exaggerated fashion. "Where is this temple?"

Kohler rattled off some Greek and the guide pointed to the rock mound. Gruber and the others approached it, and sure enough, on closer inspection, it did indeed look like a man-made structure. Roughly rectangular in shape, with vines covering much of it, and the opening blocked with large boulders, almost as if someone wanted to conceal it. As he got closer, he saw carvings in the stone above the entranceway(if that's what it was).Very old, and in disrepair, but definitely there.

Gruber stepped on a rock, balanced himself, reached up and began pulling vines away. He uncovered some carvings and brushed them off. Faded and worn, but legible. He stood back and took out a notebook and began quickly writing.

"What does it say?" Engels demanded.

Gruber looked down at his notebook, back up at the entranceway. He pointed. "That says 'Moirai'." Noting Engels's blank expression, he added, "The Greek name for the Fates. And this…"

he moved closer to the structure. "This says 'infernal goddesses'…
only…" He rubbed his mouth, gazing up at the inscription.

"Only 'what'?" Engels's tone was impatient.

"It's just that the Fates were generally not seen as evil or
'infernal'." That epitaph usually refers to the Erinyes, or the Furies.
They were the goddesses, demons, of vengeance. Three sisters, just
like the Fates. They punished wrongdoers."

"So? What does it matter, as long as the shears are here?"

Gruber shook his head. "But why the Erinyes?"

"Ne! Erinyes! Erinyes!" The elderly guide pointed at the ruined
temple

Engels approached the opening and pulled at one of the
boulders. It didn't budge. He motioned for Krause.

"Have your men clear this opening."

Moments later, three soldiers, coats off, shirt sleeves rolled up,
began prying and lifting the boulders from the entranceway to the
temple.

The guide, who was standing nearby, lunged at Kohler and
grabbed his collar with one hand, pointed at the temple with the
other, speaking rapidly. One of the soldiers pulled him off Kohler
and flung him to the ground. The guide continued to plead with
Kohler, pointing at the temple, then down then the hill.

Engels motioned for one of his men. He pointed at the guide.
"Get him out of here. But watch him."

*

It was now fully dark. A small fire burned near the temple
entrance. Guards were posted, and the men were taking turns eating.
Earlier, a guard saw a figure moving through the trees, and they
thought it might be Hahn, but again, they found nothing. Another
soldier had gone missing, as well. Vogt. Gruber couldn't remember
what he looked like. Krause sent several groups out to find him, but
they came back empty-handed.

"He probably got lost and headed back to the village", Kohler
said. He and Engels sat in camp chairs by the fire, sipping kaffee
laced with brandy. Gruber had not been asked to join them.

He sat on a fallen log by himself, a hunk of bread in one hand
and a tin cup of kaffee in the other. Some dinner, he thought bitterly.

"Jah." Engels nodded. "I will deal with him when we return to the village."

A sudden gust of wind flung powered through the trees, shaking branches and tumbling leaves against the trunks.

"We got through!" shouted a voice from the temple entrance. Gruber put his cup down, tossed his bread aside, and headed up the hill. The men looked up as he approached and stepped away from the narrow opening. Krause held out a pocket torch to Gruber, who grabbed it as he stepped up towards the opening they had made. But it was too small. He couldn't even get in past his shoulders. Cursing, he withdrew and extended one arm into the opening, shining his pocket torch. He then squeezed his head through alongside his outstretched arm, breathing slowly, controlling the claustrophobia.

"Well?" demanded Engels's muffled voice from behind him.

Gruber swung the torchlight from left to right.

It was a indeed a temple. Intricate friezes and other carvings covered the walls. Words, hard to make out in the poor light. Lachesis Atropos… and Erinyes again. The temple extended farther back, into the actual hillside. It was a cave. It was deeper back there, and his light didn't show much, so he focused on what he could see. A thick layer of dust covered everything. A stone shrine, really just a raised platform, stood in the center of the main chamber and on the shrine sat a small bundle wrapped in cloth, linen perhaps. Gruber squeezed forward for a better look. He swept the room with his light again. Some shattered pots, an ancient dagger, a broken spinning wheel... but his light went back to the bundle on the shrine. It was about thirty centimeters long. His mind buzzed with excitement. *Could this be it?*

"Gruber!" Engels was rapidly losing what little patience he had. Gruber slowly pulled himself out of the opening and stepped to the ground. Engels looked frantic. "So what is your impression? Is this the correct location?"

Gruber nodded. "I think this is it. The writing indicates that this is a temple dedicated to the Morirai." He paused, still digesting what he had seen. "And there's a…" He held his hands out to demonstrate the size. "There's a wrapped object on a shrine. It *could* be the shears. But I don't know who can fit through that opening."

Engels reached out an arm and gestured. Kohler, shirtless and barefoot, stepped forward.

"Private Kohler has already volunteered to enter the temple and see what can be found."

"I will do my duty for my country and my Fuhrer." Kohler stood at attention, though he wobbled a bit. His eyes were a little glassy from the brandy. He climbed up to the opening, gauged it, and slowly slithered inside. They heard him grunting, his feet disappeared and then he cried, "I'm in!"

Engels clambered up and stuck his head into the opening. "Do you see the shears? Bring them to me!"

Engels leaned forward, grunting,his feet kicking in the air, then pulled back. He was holding the small bundle close to his chest. Krause helped him step down from the rocks.

Engles knelt and unwrapped the bundle. The linen wrapping was worn and thin, and the edges unraveled as he touched it. The wind picked up again, forcing Engels to hold the cloth down as he uncovered the shears which were amazingly, still bright and metallic. They were fashioned from a single solid piece of metal bent into a narrow U-shape. The blades at the opposite end of the U, so when it was squeezed, the blades would cut. Intricate scrollwork was carved into the metal; Greek characters and figures. This was a find of tremendous import. Gruber hunkered down beside Engels.

"May I see them, Sturmbannfuhrer?" He held out a hand, but Engels slapped it away.

"Nein!" he snapped, rising. "This belongs to the Fuhrer now. I will deliver them personally." He looked around at the makeshift camp. It had grown much darker now, and the temple was just a dark shape against a darker background. The sparse moonlight cast a faint blue glow on the clearing and the men.

"Sergeant Krause!" Krause hurried over.

"Yes, Sturmbannfuhrer?"

"Can you lead us back to the village tonight? Without the guide?"

Krause hesitated. He looked at his men, then back at Engels. "It will be difficult in the dark, sir, but we can do it if we follow the path. We just need to pack up. And some of the men haven't eaten yet."

Engels nodded. "Thirty minutes." He looked over at the soldier standing beside the village guide. He pointed at the guide, who sat on the ground, head down. "Kill him." A shot rang out, and the man collapsed in a heap.

Kohler, still shirtless, approached Engels. "May I see it, sir?" Engels hesitated, but held out the cloth bundle to Kohler, who slowly unwrapped it without removing it from Engel's grasp. He gazed down at the shears then up at Gruber. "What do the stories say?" he demanded. "What powers do these have?"

Gruber shifted uncomfortably. He wasn't used to being spoken to like this by a private, but he could say nothing in front of Engels. "The few stories I know state that whoever controls the shears cannot die. That by possessing them, you effectively stop Atropos from 'cutting your thread'."

Engels quickly rewrapped the shears.

"Get dressed, Wilhelm, we are leaving shortly." Engels stood back and shouted. "Bring only what you need! We are returning to the village tonight!"

Kohler hastened to obey, but froze as a shout rang out.

"There's someone there!" One of the men cried.

"Over here!" shouted another, from the opposite side of the camp.

The soldiers brought their guns up and assumed defensive positions, all the while staring out into the darkness.

"Hahn?" Someone hissed. "Is that you?"

Gruber unholstered his sidearm. He could see nothing beyond the trunks of trees closest to the fire.

"Is it the resistance? What did you see?" demanded Engels from somewhere behind him.

Sauer replied, "I'm not sure, sturmbannfuhrer. It looked like someone running, then they disappeared behind —."

He was cut off by a shrill scream punctuated by a rifle shot. The men froze.

"Who was that?" shouted Krause. "Who fired?"

No answer. The men listened.

A round object landed at their feet and bounced once before rolling to a stop. At first Gruber though it was a rock, but as it reached the light, he realized, to his horror, that it was a human head. The stump of the neck was ragged and torn and still bleeding. The mouth opened and closed once. Gruber looked away as the soldiers sprang into action. Krause barked out orders. Dim moonlight filtered through the clouds and trees, casting menacing shadows.

More shooting. Gruber saw the flash of a rifle muzzle nearby and instinctively ducked. He squatted and made his way to the trunk of a large tree and stayed down. No sense being accidentally shot. He could hear Engels and Kohler whispering nearby.

Shouting. More gunfire. Then a cry for help which was abruptly cut off.

Gruber watched as a soldier on the other side of the clearing sprinted, dodging between trees and simply vanished. A flash of white and he was gone.

One of the men, Saur, approached, body low, eyes focused on the treetops.

"There!" he cried, and fired up into the trees. Gruber watched in horror as a white blur swooped down and yanked Saur up into the dark. His rifle clattered to the ground where he had been standing. His screams echoed through the clearing.

All eyes looked up, but the darkness was immense. It was impossible to tell where the trees ended and the night began. Saur's screams became sobs, pleadings, only broken by wet crunching and snapping. Gruber was reminded of the sound made when a leg is twisted off a roast pig.

Wetness on his face. Rain? But it was warm realization hit as a leg came tumbling down from the trees. *It's still wearing a boot,* he thought crazily. Engels let out a high pitched shriek and pointed his pistol at the sky.

"What is it?" he screamed. "Who is out there?" A soft wet thud as an arm landed beside him. Blood spattered his boots.

More screaming and gunfire. A pale figure zipped between trees, pausing just long enough for Gruber to see it was a woman. An old woman. No, A young woman. It was impossible to tell. She was bareheaded, the tendrils of her hair flowing in the windless night, wearing only a white shroud, torn and stained. Her red eyes blazed. She leapt away. Gunfire from the left, more screaming.

"Did you see that?" Engels gasped. "What was she? Who was she?"

"They. Not 'she'." whispered Gruber, more to himself. "The Erinyes."

"Give me that!" Kohler's voice was shrill. He and Engels were fighting over something. They struggled and swore.

"Nein! It belongs to the Fuhrer!" The two men, both pulling at the small bundle, stumbled into the clearing. Kohler twisted his body, yanking the wrapped shears out of Engels's hands. Kohler fell to the ground and scrambled to his feet. More screaming and gunshots in the distance.

"Now I cannot die! Isn't that right?" Kohler looked at Gruber, his eyes wild." I cannot die if I have these?"

Gruber's mouth opened but he said nothing. None of this made any sense. *I shouldn't be here.*

"Wilhelm, give me the shears." Gruber had his pistol out, pointed directly at Kohler's chest. Kohler's shirt was on, but unbuttoned. He was holding the bundle. He looked at the gun, then at Engels. He shook his head and turned.

"I'm going back to the village. I will leave the shears there. When I'm away from this." He jerked his head to gesture around him.

He headed down the hillside. Engels stepped forward and shot him in the back. Kohler stumbled, but kept walking. Engels fired again. Kohler wobbled a bit, then his legs just gave out. He struggled to his feet as Engels approached. He twisted around. Blood trickled from his mouth. He slowly pointed a shaky finger at Engels.

"I… cannot die…" He started back down the hill. Engels strode forward, walked directly behind Kohler, and shot him in the back of the head. Kohler's neck jerked forward and bits of bone and brain shot out in front of him. He dropped to his knees again, but did not fall. He did, however, drop the bundle containing the shears. It fell from his hands and landed at his feet. As he reached out for it, Engels fired again, and again, and again. Eventually Kohler stopped moving.

Gruber silently watched the scene unfold. He remained silent as a woman wearing a white shroud weaved through the trees towards Engels.

"I am sorry, Wilhelm," Engels muttered as he ejected the magazine from his pistol and shoved another one in. He stepped over Kohler's body and reached for the shears. The woman in white moved behind him; Engels sensed her and turned. She whipped a taloned hand across his face and Engels cried out and stumbled backward. Peering from behind a tree, Gruber saw that Engels's face was gone; only gleaming, red-streaked bone remained. His eyes, unnaturally large in his fleshless skull, moved back and forth. The raw muscles in his jaws twitched and spasmed. The woman held up her hand. A bloody strip of flesh dangled from her long fingers. Engels dropped his gun and moaned. Another woman leapt lightly from the trees behind Engels. As she moved toward him, Gruber closed his eyes and turned away. Gurgling and snapping sounds, and then silence.

More shouting in the distance. Gruber opened his eyes, terrified of opening his eyes to see the women standing over him. But they were gone. Engels, or what was left of him, lay like a pile of wet rags, all red and black. And several feet away… the shears. Gruber scrambled to his feet and scooped them up. He tucked them into a pocket inside his coat. He looked around and headed down the hillside. Was he on the path? It was too dark to tell. But as long as he was moving away from the temple. He heard footsteps nearby and ducked against a tree, breathing hard.

He felt for the bundle in his coat. Still there. He looked around warily. *They could be anywhere.* He had never seen anything move as fast as they did. *And where is the gottverdammt path?* More footsteps, then Krause, his gun held high, appeared from the brush. Gruber let out a breath. Krause could help him. Krause was a good soldier.

"Herr Major—" Krause began. A shape, all white and gray, swept by him. Blood, turned purple in the blue moonlight, splashed the nearby trees. The submachine gun rattled in Krause's dead hands and his body shook and twitched before collapsing. Gruber noted, with a horror so deep it was almost numbing, that Krause's head was gone. His legs felt heavy, as if they had fallen asleep. He looked down and saw that his trousers were full of holes. Then he saw the blood and the pain hit. Gruber's legs folded beneath him as he realized that Krause had shot his legs. Both of them. He tried to stand and grunted as a white hot lance spiked through his knee. He leaned over and vomited.

His legs were useless. He felt the strength seeping from the wounds with every pulse of his panicky heart. At this rate, a logical part of him thought, he would bleed to death in minutes. He had no medical training, all the others were dead, or gone. Yet—he reached in his coat and found the shears. He pulled them out. Carefully, so as to move as little as possible, he set the linen bundle on the ground in front of him. He opened the wrappings and stared at the shears. So bright. So sharp, after all these years. He picked them up and paused. Turned his head from side to side.

The Erinyes were there. One on either side of him, and the other behind. It was difficult for him to turn his body, so he just looked at the shears, thinking. Was it true? As long as he held them, he couldn't die? But with his damaged legs, there was no way he could return to the village. He rotated to his left and held out the shears as a kind of talisman or an offering. He wasn't sure which.

"Please," he begged. "Please."

The three Sisters stood over him, their red, unblinking gaze never wavering. Their tattered gowns were soiled with mud and blood stains. Their taloned hands clenched and unclenched. Their black mouths gaped. But they didn't attack. They were patient. They could wait.

Captain Heinrich Gruber, officer of the German Wehrmacht, thought about his wife and infant son, whom he would never see. He lowered his head and placed the shears on the ground.

*

The sun broke through the clouds, brightening the clearing in the forest. Birds twittered in the trees. A rabbit hopped timidly up to a black boot on the ground, sniffed it, and moved on. Footsteps and voices approached, and the rabbit fled.

Mayor Stravos and about a dozen of the village men entered the clearing, stopped and silently gazed around at the carnage; the torn bodies and limbs and blood. Stavros spoke rapidly, quietly. Three of the men went around gathering up the corpses and body parts they could reach; another collected wood and built a large fire. The rest began the heavy work of sealing up the entrance to the temple.

A shout as a searcher discovered the body of the guide. The men collected around him, debating. At last a consensus was reached and a litter was built, his body placed upon it. The other bodies were thrown on the fire. Weapons and ammunition were set aside.

Eventually, near dusk, the men gathered at the remains of the fire and threw dirt on it until it was extinguished. The ashes and bones were kicked and scattered. The weapons were passed out. Two men carried the litter bearing the body of the guide, and they started down the hill. As the men made their way to the path, a heavy foot came down on a weathered photograph, crushing it into the mud and leaves. It was a photograph of a woman, smiling as she held her infant son. The men continued on, back to their village, back to their lives.

XI

JUSTICE

12

JUSTICE

JENNIFER ST. GILES

Upright: Equity, rightness, probity, executive
Reversed: Law in all departments, bigotry, bias, excessive severity

No more tears now, I will think upon revenge.
Mary Stuart, Queen of Scots 1542-87

Chapter One

Atlanta, Georgia
Sunday May 25th

The irony. Illegal Justice. Were the pain not so deep, there'd be some amusement in that immoral act. The blood of the murdered covered the hands of the law just as thickly as the killer's.

One of the guilty would die tonight. The others would follow.

Entry into the guarded lakeside estate proved easy. The canoe made no noise amid the storm. The man's sins left him vulnerable. The alarm. The layout. His being alone. All that had been needed to see justice done, had been within reach.

The knife across his throat had been too swift a death. But dealing the Justice Card and posting the video had held some satisfaction.

More would come. By morning, too late to escape fate, Justice would be served again.

Heaven wept. At least True Crime Writer, Eva St. Claire told herself that every time another deluge hit the state causing record flooding for the past two weeks. The heavy rains were tears for the young girls who'd fallen victim to Mason Smith and his partner.

She would grieve for a long time at the loss of so many precious souls. She would also rail at God, or fate, for not bringing her in contact with the serial killers sooner. They should have been stopped years ago. Cursed with seeing visions of violent death at crime scenes, Eva had experienced a lot of evil in life, but nothing as horrific as what she'd uncovered in her quest for justice for Kaylee Waters.

The thunder shaking Powell's Piano Bar hit a chord of fear in Eva's gut as the memory of Mason's swinging axe flashed before her eyes. Her gaze instinctively sought Adam Frasier's across the room and unfortunately connected. From his grimace, she knew the storm had taken him back to the rural farm where Smith had almost killed them two weeks ago. Adam stood talking to his father, Vince, a retired Georgia Bureau of Investigations agent, and his good friend, Major Brad Warren, the Georgia State Patrol field operations commander. Both men had played a key role in saving her and Adam from death.

The bond that had developed between her and Adam during their three-day investigation into Smith had grown, despite her having avoided Adam this past week. She forced her focus from him to the champagne glass, sweating beads of water on the bar's mahogany surface.

She'd made a tactical mistake. She knew it now. Three glasses of champagne, two long glances from Adam across the crowded room, and one heated dance with him to the song "Alive" by The Aaron Hendra Project had convinced her. Her attempts to box him into the role of colleague seemed to be failing.

Adam and his FBI status put Eva and her family at risk. The world had a history of crucifying real psychics. And all of the St. Claires were cursed with paranormal gifts, which they used to covertly fight crime. Keeping their gifts secret was essential to their well-being. Only her Aunt Zena had come out of the psychic closet. As a medium to the dead with a 1-900 psychic number, she toured the states in her own ostentatious bus. Most people only rolled their eyes in disbelief at her elaborate show. Aunt Zena hid her gift behind fanfare.

Normally, Eva wouldn't have let Adam into her inner circle. But being targeted by serial killers and her brother, Devin's premonition of Adam's death, had forced her to keep him closer than she should. She had been determined to stop that prediction and still was. She just needed to find a better way.

She hadn't planned on enjoying his sharp company. Nor had she realized how exciting an active investigation could be. She had to let them both go.

Her Bohemian sister, Iris, joined her in designer heels, jeans, a blue-silk T-shirt and vibrant yellow jacket. As an artist, color and "no-rules" defined her. "That vacation you promised to take starts tomorrow. And Adam is the perfect destination."

"Keep your voice down. He's not a destination, he's trouble. Tomorrow, I'm busy. I'm speaking to the volunteers at the National Victim's Assistant Program."

"That morning meeting won't last all night. Before Adam flies back to Washington D.C. Wednesday, you two need to see where seven minutes alone will take you. Heaven is my guess."

"And you need to wipe whatever fairytale you're painting out of your head. He's too great a risk."

"Excuses… excuses. You're afraid to live. Check your phone. Since you refuse to put appealing, eligible bachelors on your map, I did it for you. Just tell James to take you to Adam and he'll direct your way. You might as well enjoy yourself while you're sorting out Devin's premonition of doom. The troops agree."

Eva's eye twitched. Having her psychic aunt, army-sergeant housekeeper, and her starry-eyed sister trying to pair her with Adam had to stop. "Who is James?"

"I reprogramed your phone. No more monotone lady. You've a sexy Aussie crooning in your ear."

"Iris, you really have to stop—"

"I did the same to Devin's. I honed-in on his password this morning at breakfast. He barely said good morning between emails, thus deserved the invasion. Can't wait to see his face when James speaks up."

"Honed-in" meant Iris had read Devin's mind. Unlike Eva's visions or Devin's premonitions, the gift of telepathy did have an upside to it. She couldn't help but laugh. Devin would not be pleased. Before she could admonish her sister again, the bar's owner, Betty-Grable-like Tracy Powell, placed an unsealed, manila envelope on the bar. "A guy just dropped this off. Said it was for the big shot here. Any ideas?"

For a moment, Eva's heart thudded as she met Iris's startled glance. Together, they'd sent over two dozen anonymous envelopes like this one to different police departments over the past five years. All had contained the portraits of murder victims Iris had drawn from Eva's memory, the GPS coordinates of their bodies, and the photos of their killers. Eva couldn't write a book on every murder she uncovered. And she couldn't write about an undiscovered murder. So, with Iris's telepathic and artistic skills, they'd been able to expose killers and keep the St. Claire's curses secret.

Had someone discovered what she and Iris did? Before handing the envelope over, Eva had to know what it contained. Using a nearby napkin to keep her prints off the delivery, she tapped over the whole surface. Paper or photos had to be inside. She pried the unsealed envelope open with a toothpick. No red flags of a powered residue appeared. Then she tipped the envelope and two things fell out. A large card she recognized as being from the Tarot, and a cut out news-print warning.

You missed the truth. Justice will now be dealt to all. Write their stories, St. Claire before judgment falls on you, too!

Iris cried out in distress. "I haven't read anyone threatening, Eva!"

"Read?" Tracy frowned at Iris. The men, with Adam and Devin in the lead, hurried over. Aunt Zena and Sheriff Doug Grant followed.

Dropping the envelope, Eva caught Iris's shoulders. "You've had too much champagne. I haven't seen anyone threatening either. Sit here," she said firmly, reminding her sister of the need to keep quiet about reading minds.

"What's happened?" Adam and Devin asked in unison.

Eva explained.

"Nobody touch it." Adam glared at the note, the card, then at her. "What aren't you saying? Is this related to someone bugging your house and shooting your tire on that mountain?"

After the chaos of the serial killers' attack had settled, those two things had been left unexplained. She shook her head. "I don't think so. They're demanding I write a book but it's meant for "the big shot" here. Maybe you, Frasier? The FBI trumps everyone else in rank."

Aunt Zena leaned in. "The Justice Card. Interesting."

"Why?" Eva asked, narrowing her gaze. "Do you know anything about this?" She hadn't figured her aunt into the equation. What if "Zena Knows" said something to the wrong person?

"Haven't a clue, but I've a friend who does Tarot readings. The Justice Card is all about the balance of Karma. If you've caused harm, then expect to get your just deserts. From the additional markings, though, I'd say someone's dead or will be."

"What do you mean?" Adam asked.

"Look close. There's a red ink line across the woman's throat. Droplets of blood on her sword and a red X over the scales. All of those markings have been added to the Tarot card."

Eva frowned at her aunt. "The altered card is saying a purveyor of justice is, or will be, executed because she/he didn't judge fairly— thus the x'ed out scales. And this here means they caused harm to another—thus the blood on the sword of action?"

Aunt Zena shrugged. "Since Justice's throat is slit, it could be saying the law is dead. The law caused harm, and whoever escaped legal justice for a wrong, will now be punished."

Iris moved closer and studied the card. "The ink markings are delicate and precise. Not erratic or bold. Almost seems feminine. Calm and deliberate."

Adam's phone rang, then so did the others. Each man answered. Adam spoke up first, his expression grim. "I think we have our victim. Don't know who or where yet, but we know how. Video of the murder has gone viral. The Justice card is nailed to his forehead."

Two hours later...

Well, hell. Special Agent Adam Frasier didn't know how to verbalize the crap rattling around in his mind, or who he could tell. From serial killers last week to tonight's "Justice Card Killer", it seemed as if the devil had come to Georgia. Surely every True Crime writer didn't become a target for crazies, yet Eva had twice in a row. Was she a mega-magnet for murderous trouble?

His weekend trip from D.C. to Georgia to switch care facilities for his mother had stretched to over two weeks. During which, he'd eliminated serial killers and had been shot in the process. He found it hard to believe it was happening again—another crazed killer case with Eva dead center.

They were keeping the victim's name out of the press for now, but the murder of a federal judge and its viral video had every bigwig everywhere in an uproar. The FBI, GBI, and local police had a pissing contest going. If the judge had been killed due to his position as a judge, then the FBI would be the top dog. If it had been purely personal, then the GBI and police would duke it out.

Adam said to hell with the politics and focused on nailing this killer now.

Several years ago, he'd left his position in the Critical Incident Response Group to head a special investigation into the "Artist of Death." All over the country, information of victims and their killers had been anonymously sent to police departments, exposing twenty-six murders so far. Two hours ago, his job had expanded.

When his boss called about the viral murder video then learned Adam had the killer's note in hand and what that note said, there had been a few moments of dead silence. The pause had been followed by "get that son-of-a-bitch" and "why in the hell is St. Claire directly involved with yet another murder case? Better stay glued to her side."

Adam's exact questions and plan.

Make that three murder cases, he amended. Her controversial book, *Hayden's Hell* had his father—and him—convinced she'd interviewed the real killer. His father had been Tony Hayden's best friend, and never believed the man blamed for the murders of the Hayden family guilty.

Solving that mystery, while keeping his father's reputation-ending secret hidden would be tricky. Adam had yet to fully tackle the situation, but had planned to before flying back to D.C. in two days. For now, they were on the hunt for a Tarot dealing killer.

Biometric experts using a facial recognition program on the shadowy murder video had identified the victim within an hour. Superior Court Judge Jackson T. Granville. The team had gleaned quite a bit of information from the video. They estimated the killer to be about five-foot-nine. Medium to slight build with a steady hand and calm determination. Internet savvy, too. The video's supposed origin came from Central America. The crime occurred in Georgia about three hours ago.

Dispatch to Granville's Buckhead estate revealed a bitter wife who directed the police to the "den of iniquity" where the judge had been residing for the past six months. She'd kicked him out upon learning he'd been playing sugar daddy to law students for years.

When told of her husband's fate, Mrs. Granville expressed satisfaction that her soon-to-be ex had gotten what he'd deserved. At a slender five-six, she could have worn stilettos to slit her husband's throat, but unless her angry, rattled demeanor was a very good act, Mrs. Granville wasn't directly their steady-handed killer. She could have hired out, though.

The multi-million-dollar mansion on Lake Lanier proved to be the crime scene and a nightmare for the GBI Crime Scene Specialists. They'd just finished processing the bedroom where Granville had been killed, but the rest of the place would take days.

Eva had yet to say much about the crime scene. She'd stayed in the corner of the bedroom for a short time then left the room. He'd wanted to hear her take on Granville's murder and found irritation gnawing at him that she hadn't said anything, which annoyed him more. He always preferred being a lone wolf.

Eva had been in withdrawal mode since they'd danced earlier and he'd been thinking that was a good thing. In the two weeks he'd known her, she'd consumed way too much of… everything. Something about her wouldn't let him loose.

Brad Warren walked up shaking his head. "From the amount of women's clothes strewn from the beach to the bedrooms, they had to have left naked. The gate guard has no idea how many people were here today. Six limos came and six limos left. Happens weekends and holidays. He doesn't even know if everyone left earlier or not. In addition to the parties, the judge entertained women on the weeknights, too."

Adam had seen some of the clothes, most were exotic costumes designed for sexual enticement. Each room had a theme. BDSM in the basement complete with multiple pleasure-pain devices and an X altar. Banquet table in the dining room with a padded cut-out for a body to lay in while diners feasted on whatever. A room decorated with satanic paraphernalia, and even a Helter-Skelter orgy room with oddly configured, cushioned furniture. "The fantasy outfits, like the sex toys, were likely supplied by whoever really owns this hellhole."

"No luck yet then?"

"So far all roads lead to a corporation in the Caymans. We'll know more in the morning."

"What a waste. The money and the resources it would take to continually run a setup like this boggles the mind. That helo pad out back has seen a lot of use."

"Revolving orgies. Multiple unknown suspects. Multiple motives. Finding Judge Granville's killer, even with video evidence describing the killer, will be hell. I'm walking this scenario backward now. Maybe we can stop Justice from dealing another death sentence."

"What do you mean?" Brad narrowed his gaze.

"Killer said because we missed the truth, he had to deliver justice to all. Since a gruesome death was the punishment, I can assume our Justice Card killer is avenging equally horrible deaths. Plural, because the note said for Eva to tell their story. Let's look at Judge Granville's trials where any defendant facing multiple murder charges went free."

Adam scanned the room. Granville's body had been cleared for transport to the morgue. Horribly overweight and hairy, he'd leave wearing a red silk G-string with "Big Daddy" embroidered in white. "There's just some things you can't un-see."

"Or un-think," Brad added. "Given he was a player in the orgies here." He lowered his voice. "So what's up with St. Claire coming tonight? I got why you kept her close when Mason Smith targeted her, but why now?"

In a glance, Adam assured Eva hadn't returned, then spoke softly, "There are a lot more unanswered questions than answered ones where she is concerned. Is it her True Crime books? Her notoriety? Or is it a fluke that she's in the middle of another investigation? The killer knew she was at the bar tonight and threatened her in a way. Maybe she knows something and doesn't realize it yet. She has uncanny instincts on a case. We wouldn't have caught Mason Smith as quickly, or his partner at all, if it weren't for her input."

Brad laughed. "You've finally met someone more interesting than your job."

Adam frowned. "The jury is still out on how interested I am, or if that interest is mutual. Falling for a woman with secrets can only be trouble."

The team bagged Granville and rolled the stretcher out. Adam entered the main part of the house with Brad beside him. "Speaking of Eva, I'd better find her."

"Last I saw she had headed for the basement." Brad shook his head. "You've got a problem."

"Yeah, not a pleasant place." Adam winced. The extreme BDSM chamber had been made to look like an Inquisition torture dungeon. He'd seen a lot of shit in life and thought he was immune, but Mason Smith's evil had ripped Adam open. The basement here had come as an unwelcomed reminder.

"Not the dungeon. Your problem is you love trouble. Always have. Catch you in a few, bro." Brad slapped Adam on the shoulder.

"Funny," Adam replied before leaving. The very last thing he needed in his life was more trouble.

*

Aside from the usual deep chill that accompanied Eva's visions of violent death, the Granville murder hadn't hit her in the gut as did most of the murders she saw. Was she still in shock from Mason Smith's kill *zone and the dozens of victims who'd screamed for help?* Two weeks out and she could vividly recall every second of that night. Or had seeing a video of Granville's murder beforehand lessened its impact?

She didn't understand the shift tonight, but she'd been able to absorb the vision and stay relatively aware of the police and crime scene specialists around her.

She hadn't heard any sounds in the vision or gleaned any thoughts from the killer. Granville had been asleep and the killer hadn't spoken. But when Granville's eyes bulged open and he gasped as he stared at the killer, she should have heard Granville choking on his own blood.

She hadn't.

And no after-vision migraine had descended on her, either. Tonight, her curse had been less of a curse than ever before. Yet, she

240

didn't like how the distance made her feel. Removed. Dispassionate. Clinical. All of the things she'd thought she should be.

She left the crime scene to look through the rest of the playboy mansion.

How could she impart knowledge without exposing her visions? So far, the things she'd picked up on, experts would discover as soon as they compared the video to the crime scene photos. But the investigators would only be able to hypothesize about the discrepancies.

Whereas, Eva knew someone had been to Judge Granville's crime scene after the killer left and before the police arrived. Her vision of Granville's murder, as seen through the killer's eyes, had been a repeat of the video. Except, after filming the crime, the killer knelt and prayed, a ritual that had spoken volumes to Eva.

Facing the bloodied, uncovered body of Granville, who wore only a red G-string and a gold ring on his right hand, the killer knelt on the floor and drew the sign of the cross with his/her right hand.

Unlike the quick and brutal slashing of Granville's throat, in drawing the cross, the gestures had been slow, gentle—like a reverent show of respect or contrition. Then, the killer had left without touching Granville.

The police had found Granville covered from the waist down and a band of white skin where the ring had been. Eva mentioned the discrepancies from the video to one of the Crime Scene specialists and hoped forensics would jump on them first.

In moving through the three-story pleasure palace, one large room caught her attention because it had not been ransacked by partiers. No discarded clothing. No leftover food or booze. Michelangelo-like paintings of Greek gods in various carnal scenes covered the walls and the vaulted ceiling. Only one statue stood in the center of the room—a well-endowed Bacchus, aka Dionysus, the god of wine. His followers had been known for their naked, ritual frenzies. It would seem those here revered the head of a B.C. sex cult.

Not a good sign.

Hedonism for pleasure's sake never ended well. Add worship into the debauchery and the fervor often proved deadly.

Leaving the main floor, she descended to the basement. A chill that had nothing to do with the thermostat or the outside temperature wrapped around her. Violent death waited at the bottom of the stairs. Shivering, she grabbed the rail and moved slowly forward.

A wine cellar came first. She walked through it, delaying the inevitable. The overstocked space held a generous selection of fairly expensive red wines and cases of other high-end imported beverages. Leaving the wine, she moved into a dungeon-like room and braced herself. The sickly sweet incense clogging the air assaulted her senses and the cold cut deep into her bones…

Light flashed directly into her face, hurting her eyes. She tried to lift her hands to shield them, but couldn't break free of the chain binding her wrists to the metal band around her stomach. Her heart hammered painfully and her stomach wrenched with dread at her naked state and her surroundings. Where was her sister? She had to find Maria.

On the far wall a large screen video played. The sickening images of dozens of naked men and women writhing on the floor, having sex with one another as a man poured red wine on them and whipped them, cut to her soul.

Where was her sister?

Hearing a whimper in the darkness beyond, she stumbled forward until a harsh laugh brought her to a stop. "You ready for your turn? Your sister has been enjoying the ecstasy of pleasure enhanced by pain."

"Who the hell are you? Where is Maria? Where are our friends… the limo… the club?"

She barely saw the snaking end of the whip before it lashed across her stomach. She recoiled from the stinging pain.

"Money can buy everything. On your knees, you illegal piece of ass. I am your master. God of your pleasure and devil of your pain."

The whip wrapped around her legs and jerked her hard to the stone floor. A masked man stepped from the shadows, naked except for black leather boots and black leather straps that accentuated his musculature and bulging sex. Blood smeared his body—stomach, thighs, chest, and sex. He was the man in the video whipping the men and women.

"What have you done with my sister!" she demanded.

He laughed and stepped aside. She saw her sister's bloodied body, lying motionless on the stone altar. She'd been violated, whipped, and had suffered God only knew what from the assortment of metal devices on a nearby table. Blood smeared her angelic face, her body welted from the numerous lashes all over.

"Your turn," he said.

Fury exploded throughout her. "In hell. I will kill you for this," she screamed. Jumping up, she rushed to the table and grasped the sharpest instrument. She couldn't raise her arms high, but she could hit low. She ran straight at him. He twisted, and her stab to his groin sank into the soft flesh of his stomach. She rammed the sharp point deeper and higher.

He roared. His ring gleamed in the light. For a brief second, she saw the letter B over the face of a ram in a pentagram before his fist slammed into her face. The punches kept coming. Her stomach. Her breasts. Her neck. Her back. She fell to the ground. He kicked her ribs and her head. Agonizing pain flashed with every blow until—

"Eva! What's wrong!"

Her body trembling beyond control, Eva snapped her eyes open at Adam's cry. He had his hands on her shoulders, turning her face up from the ball she'd crawled into.

The woman's death throes still shuddered through Eva's mind with unbearable pain.

She said the only thing she could to keep her secrets safe. "Migraine. Bad."

Adam's heart pounded hard. His chest hurt. Seeing Eva collapsed on the stone floor, as if dying in agony had caught him off guard and shaken him. This is the woman who, having only a knife, had fearlessly gone after a man with an ax to protect him. She'd been indomitable against serial killers.

Logically, he knew the odds of someone hurting her here with the place swarming with agents had been slim. But he damn well knew the unthinkable happened all the time. He'd reacted with his gut.

Relief that she hadn't been harmed lasted a second. Her skin had turned whiter than snow and just as cold. He scooped her into his arms. "I shouldn't have brought you here. You're going to the hospital."

She struggled against him. "No, just need... fresh air."

He doubted that was all, but juggled the French door open and carried her outside. Marching through the drizzling rain, he went to a large gazebo near an infinity pool and sat down with her in his arms. He welcomed the comfort of the cushioned chaise lounge and her soft Ivory Soap scent.

It had to be midnight or later. The waters of Lake Lanier gleamed darkly in the misty moonlight and a damp breeze lightly stirred the night. The beauty and calm clashed with the sickness behind him. One never knew what lay behind even the most expensive of closed doors.

Eva sucked in air as if surfacing from deep underwater. Her long black hair brushed the skin of his arm as he pulled her tighter. She had warmed him with her body when he'd been shot and in shock. She'd fiercely demanded that he'd better live. That moment had seemed like heaven and hell for him. Holding her now, only reaffirmed how much more alive she made him feel. He pressed his cheek to her forehead, thankful for the warmth returning to her skin.

"What happened?"

She straightened her back as if she didn't need help from anyone. "I... must be allergic to the incense. Blinding pain hit me the moment I stepped into that room. I can be hypersensitive to scents. It's why I stick to Ivory Soap."

So sensitive that she'd crawled into a ball rather than exit the French doors? Her explanation didn't ring completely true, but before he could challenge her on it, she pushed up from his lap until she faced him. "Are you familiar with the current rise in ancient sex cults?"

He blinked then frowned. Always the unexpected with her. "Every religion, deviancy, and fetish has its sexual radicals who band together. What are you specifically wanting to know?"

She waved her hand toward the mansion. "Granville and whomever else he's involved with are likely in a sex cult. They are rising up here and in Europe. A case I researched in New Orleans had a sex cult involved in two missing prostitutes. Ever hear of Bacchus or Dionysus?"

"There're two yachts down at the dock named *Bacchus 2* and *Bacchus 3*. Otherwise, those are the names for the Greek and Roman gods of wine, right?"

"Yes. Single god, though. Two names." She explained the worship room upstairs then added the dungeon area had to be their playground. "With as much high-end red wine as they have stored in the cellar, they had to have consumed large amounts during their frenzied rituals. Anything could have happened in that room. I'd have the crime scene team go over it as carefully as the judge's bedroom."

"Sure." Adam's mind raced. Other than the judge's few personal effects, there hadn't been a shred of any identifying papers in the entire mansion. Not even a grocery receipt. All the utilities were on automatic pay to the same bank account from the Cayman's.

But what about the booze? That had to be ordered locally, and the wine sat in crates with a very famous name on them. She'd given him an idea that might shortcut them into who owned or at least funded the place.

He leaned forward and planted a light kiss on her lips. "You're a dream." He pulled out his phone, started to dial, then froze. He'd kissed her. Not really *completely* kissed her but he'd put his lips on hers after fantasizing about it for weeks.

He slid his gaze to hers and heat flashed between them like a fire suddenly fed oxygen. She too looked shocked, incredible gray eyes wide open, full mouth parted. Cheeks suddenly flushed with color.

One of the French doors swung open at the house and male voices, crudely commented on the women who'd come to the wild parties.

Eva sprang from his lap, her brow creasing as she faced him angrily. "They shouldn't judge. What if some of those brought here hadn't come willingly?"

Adam stood and zeroed his gaze in on Eva. "Have you heard something about this place then?"

"Not yet, but you can bet I'll be asking questions at the victim's assistance meeting today. The volunteers handle calls from women in difficult situations." She shook her head. "Somebody murdered Granville for a reason. And it's odd the gate guard never saw the people who came or left. Just the limos. Anyone, in any kind of shape, drugged, bound, or whatever could be brought here and no one would hear their cries for help. As I told you a minute ago when you weren't listening, I'd have the dungeon processed as thoroughly as the judge's bedroom."

Adam frowned. Again, he had the feeling she knew a hell of a lot more than what she said. But how? Unless she'd lied to him, she hadn't known more about this case than he had.

"I've already requested for the dungeon to get an in-depth sweep. The room gave me an odd feeling as well. We're checking traffic cam footage at the highway exit. The gate guard swears the owners forbade any type of video recording on the property. There's not even any security cameras. Just alarms."

Eva arched a brow. "Really? I bet everything that happens here is on film. They're likely watching us now and laughing their asses off."

"I've got men looking for hidden cameras. As soon as I set up a watch detail for the hotel you're at, I'll take you back." The repairs to her house after Mason Smith fiery wake-up call wouldn't be finished for another week or two.

"Why?"

He was incredulous that she'd even ask. "This nut threatened you."

She shook her head. "The killer demanded I write a story."

"Or you'd face judgment, too. That's a threat."

"The hotel security is good, Frasier. And I really don't think—"

She looked at him as if he was being—what had she called him—a mother hen? He clenched his teeth. "You didn't think Mason Smith could get to you, but he did. This is my investigation and what I say goes, Ms. Saint. You either take the detail, or I'm bunking on the sofa to ensure you're protected."

"Fine." Eva pressed her fingers to her temple, suddenly looking very tired. Forehead creased, skin back to pale, mouth drawn tight with pain. "Then let's go before my head explodes."

She never gave up a fight this quickly. That they were back to being Frasier and Ms. Saint rankled, but he let it go. He knew she suffered from the debilitating headaches, but hadn't really seen the effects before. Her curled into a ball on the floor still hit him in the gut. He took her arm, motioning for the house. She pulled up short. "I'm not going back through the basement even if we have to walk the whole estate."

He shifted direction. "There's a service entrance on the left where we can exit to the front."

She exhaled, her relief palpable. Several questions came to mind, but he bit them back for now. As he'd told Brad, something was going on with her.

Brad's warning about loving trouble rang out.

Trouble had felt too damn good a few moments ago.

Video of victim number two hit the internet at ten the next morning. Eva got the text from Adam in the middle of her meeting. The volunteers at National Victim's Assistance Program were sharp women with a heart to help. Eva had to bite down on her frustration and focus to stay on task. She wanted to be in the thick of the investigation.

The women before her came from all walks of life, from society column ladies to nuns, from security guards to teachers. Everyone wanted to be trained on preventing crime and helping victims.

"Awareness is the first step," she told them. "But that alone isn't enough. Each person must have the courage to act when they see something off or wrong. In my interviews with witnesses after a horrible crime, someone did notice something but didn't report it."

Her thirty-minute speech lasted forty. Before she closed, she appealed to the women there. "I am working on a case that might involve women being taken against their will in limos while they are out clubbing. If anyone knows anything, please let someone know. I've heard illegals may be targeted. There is a number on the NVAP website where problems can be anonymously reported."

The security detail Adam assigned hoovered in the back of the room. They'd shown up before Adam left her hotel suite this morning. She and Adam had stumbled around, prying their eyes open with espresso and coffee before seven this morning. He'd eaten strawberry jam on a croissant and she'd eaten grapes with half a bland bran muffin. She refused to remember his firm lips brushing hers last night She refused to recall the flashing heat chasing the cold from her bones. She refused to acknowledge how alive he made her feel in a heartbeat.

He'd left muttering something about Vanderhaul Wines, a wine and beverage dynasty from Europe. She'd sighed with relief and hit the shower—a cold one. Then she'd scoured the internet for the ram's head-pentagram signet ring. None of the images had a B imposed over it. Most had satanic overtones.

The leftover dregs of migraine medication had her eyes drooping by the end of the meeting. She needed more caffeine and wanted to call Adam, but invited anyone in the audience to come speak with her if they had questions or books they wanted signed.

After several ladies spoke with her, one of the nuns in the room came up. "I'm Sister Sarah. I so need to tell Sister Mary everything you said today. It will make her feel better. Women who feel safe in the sanctuary we offer come to the church for help. I have heard your story of women being taken against their will in limos. There is more, but only Father Joseph can be the one to tell you."

Eva's heart kicked with excitement. "I must talk with him now."

"He is at a funeral this morning. But I am sure the church secretary can make an appointment for when he returns." The nun handed her a number.

The cobwebs in Eva's mind disappeared in her excitement. She had a clue. One she hadn't used her paranormal gift to discover. Well, not directly. She had used her visions to help write the books she had, thus putting her in the position of speaking at the NVAP.

Before becoming Mason Smith's target, Eva had always worked quietly alone on cold cases to expose killers and their evil to the world. During Smith's investigation, she'd tasted what working on an active case was like—and, Lord help her, she'd loved it!

Eva quickly texted Adam the news from the nun then finished talking to the rest of the women waiting in line. Forty-five minutes later, she gathered her things and called the church. She arranged a meeting with Father Joseph. Considering the killer had prayed after killing Granville, she knew she was onto something.

Just as she finished, Adam entered the room, surprising her. He must have rushed over after getting her text. Walking toward her, he scanned the room. "Is the nun you spoke to still here?"

Eva smiled at his lack of greeting. She well-understood being case focused. "Sister Sarah?" She glanced about. "No."

"Any chance we could meet with the Father now?"

"He's at a funeral. I just made an appointment for 2:30."

"Tell me exactly what transpired."

She explained.

He shook his head. "Damn, you have an uncanny ability to fish for sharks in the deep end and always snag a bite."

Eva saw they'd drawn the attention of several NVAP staff members. "How about we talk on the way?"

"Sure. Where are we going?"

"You came to me. I thought you had a plan."

He shrugged. "Lunch then. I'll catch you up. Maybe we'll have a break on the second murder by then."

A working lunch did not a date make, she told herself. Adam let security detail go and escorted her to his rental car. She'd been to the Buckhead Diner before and could already feel the inches glomming to her waist the minute she walked into the landmark restaurant. There had to be calories in smells that good. Adam ordered a milkshake and a fried-egg-grilled-cheese-BLT. She ordered unsweet tea and a vegetable plate.

He frowned over her order. "That is un-southern."

"I put a higher priority on unclogged arteries than my heritage, but we've had this argument before. Why is it taking so long to ID the second victim?"

"Killer put a white hood over the victim's head. Throat slit and two Justice Cards are nailed to the victim's mouth area. Biometrics are dead in the water and experts are looking for clues."

"So the Granville's sin had been in thinking. This victim's sin had been in speaking."

"Our deduction as well. None of Granville's cases are turning up a suspect yet. We're checking every angle and we're piecing together sex cult case. Every room had a hidden camera that wirelessly transmitted feed. We're tracing that."

"What about Granville's missing ring?" she asked hoping she could give him information from her vision.

He shook his head. "The angle of the video is wrong for biometrics to distinguish any significant details about the ring. At this point, we are assuming the killer took it with him as a keepsake."

Eva had to bite her tongue to keep from telling Adam that a pentagram framed ram's head lay beneath a bold letter B on the signet ring. She changed the subject before she could blurt anything out. "What about Vanderhaul? You mentioned the dynasty this morning."

"Stalled out at this point. Vanderhaul International Wines has several distribution centers in the United States. One in Georgia. As a membership club, they automatically ship preset orders to customers on a monthly basis. The clerk at the company thinks there's been a mistake in the information. The mansion's account is in the name of Vanderhaul Wines. It bills itself and pays itself from the company's accounts. We don't have a person's name to go after for a search warrant. Also, the judge said there isn't enough information to issue a warrant and search the distribution center here. The family lives in Amsterdam, which makes it even more unlikely they are involved."

"Why? Last I heard sex and depravity didn't have borders. The family's black sheep gained quite a bit of notoriety ten years ago at Yale."

"We looked at that. A girl accused Peter Vanderhaul and three other lacrosse players of rape. She later recanted."

"Or was paid off. As I remember it, they'd taken her on a yacht to the Caribbean and back. The crime fell into the FBI's hands because the victim was American and assaulted outside the U.S."

"After she changed her story the case was dismissed. FBI reports have him living in Switzerland where he heads up the philanthropic arm of the family's empire."

"So they say." Eva picked up her phone and did a search for Peter Vanderhaul. Reports had him as one of the world's richest, most eligible bachelors. Numerous pictures showed him fit and trim, then looking ill in the recent ones. She tried to imagine if he was the man from her vision, but the pictures of him were all too distant to tell for sure.

"We are looking for a connection between Granville and any of the Vanderhauls."

"My experience says the past always holds truths we can't see in the present. Crime bonds. Who were the other lacrosse players with Vanderhaul? Where is the victim in that case now?"

Adam arched a brow. "Revenge ten years later?" But he made the call anyway and their food arrived.

She inhaled the scent of grilled cheese and chocolate milkshake then frowned at her vegetables. Life wasn't fair. At all.

Her vegetables were very good, but she'd only picked through half of them when Adam's cell vibrated. The mouthwatering grilled-cheese-BLT he'd just taken the last bite of, had hijacked her taste buds.

His brows shot up in surprise at what he heard. "Text me the address." He stood as he disconnected the call and tossed money on the table.

She'd already washed down her bite and gathered her purse. "We've got a lead?"

"More than that. One of the Yale lacrosse players on Vanderhauls yacht ten years ago was Barry Bennington. He currently has a law firm in Midtown. He's Granville's nephew and hasn't shown up for his morning appointments. Guess what the name of the yacht was?"

"Bacchus."

"Close. Bacchus Lives. How's that for a cult motto?"

Eva followed Adam from the Buckhead Diner, her mind searching for connections. How did the sisters murdered in the dungeon tie into what happened ten years ago? If the Justice Card murders were revenge for the past, then why wait ten years?

They arrived at Bennington's Midtown house in minutes and found their missing victim number two. The cold didn't hit her until she stepped into the sunshine at the back of the house. She hadn't seen the video of Bennington's murder, but felt the same sense of emotional distance as she had in her vision at Granville's crime scene. No sound. No thoughts. Just calm action.

The killer hid behind a tree.

Dressed in a bathrobe, Bennington exited French doors with newspaper and coffee in hand. He sat at a patio table, his back to the tree. Sunlight glinted off the gold ring on his right hand as he sipped his coffee. The killer crept from the tree, but then ducked back when the man dug his phone from his pocket and held it to his ear.

The man's coffee cup fell from his grasp to the table. He didn't move to mop up the mess. Just held the phone to his ear and shook his head.

The killer again crept from the tree, approaching Bennington from behind. In one swift move, the killer snapped a white bag over Bennington's head and slit his throat. Blood stained the white material as Bennington slumped backward in the chair. Using a nail gun, the killer pinned two Justice Cards to the mouth area then prayed before leaving through the courtyard's gate.

Eva shivered from the deep cold. The vision had been swift, silent, and deadly. The killer had worn gloves as before. His reflection in the paned glass of the French doors only revealed a black hooded shadow wearing a long black robe. Grim reaper-like? Priest-like? She didn't know. But she wanted to be at the church waiting when Father Joseph arrived. Did he really have a funeral this morning? Or had he helped someone meet their maker?

The killer never entered the house. But somebody had. Bennington's place had been ransacked and evidence had been destroyed. Security cameras had been ripped from the ceilings and outside mountings. Computers, iPads, cell phone all gone. The scent of smoke hung heavily in the house and the charred remains of papers and files still smoldered in the hearth. A few salvaged pieces appeared to be donations made to what might be a church. The killer had taken Bennington's signet ring.

Unable to tell the investigators what had happened, she fisted her hands in frustration and left. She thankfully found Adam in the front yard.

"Ready to meet Father Joseph?"

"It's early yet."

"I know, but I'm anxious to hear what he says. Maybe his secretary will know something, too."

"I guess we'll make better headway with the priest now. It'll be hours before they'll get answers here. If I haven't said it yet, thanks."

"For?"

He shrugged. "Not sure we would have dug into Vanderhaul's lacrosse pals this soon."

Eva nodded, and released some of the tension inside her. She had helped.

The knot of anxiety in Adam's gut tightened as he entered the church. It was in the quiet moments that his mind screamed the loudest. Emotionally, he wanted to keep shouting "why?" Why had God let tragedy strike and destroy his family? Intellectually, he kicked his own, sorry-for-himself ass and shoved the past back where it belonged. Shit happened to everybody.

Eva appeared uncomfortable, too. They waited in a sitting area outside the priest's office. Adam could see the sanctuary across the lobby. A large crucifix stood before stained glass windows. Yep, bad stuff happened to everybody and had been for centuries.

Father Joseph returned early from the funeral. They only had to wait ten minutes. Under six feet and slender, the priest had a kindly, but weary, smile. He seemed greatly burdened.

Before Adam or Eva could explain why they were there, Father Joseph spoke. "Sister Sarah explained what she told you in the meeting this morning. I am torn as to how to help you and keep my vows as a priest."

Eva spoke up. "She told you my concern about women being abducted and forced into things they may not want to be involved in?"

The priest nodded. "Women come to the church for assistance—food, money, clothing. They are not in the United States legally. I know they believe they have no legal recourse for crimes committed against them or their family members. No woman has come to my office and sought help for such a thing. But in the confessional, I hear stories, awful stories. Stories that may resemble your exact concerns. Those here illegally are targets for horrible abuses because to cry for help would jeopardize their dream and their family's dreams for a poverty-free future."

Adam sat forward, anger flashing through him at the injustice. "I need to speak to these women. These crimes must be stopped."

"To them, the law is their enemy, too. Not their friend. Deportation is worse than degradation."

Adam popped from his seat. "By not helping stop this sex abuse, you're complicit in it. You do understand we have a vigilante killer on the loose now and—"

Eva grabbed Adam's hand and stood "Father Joseph, please forgive the impassioned response. We're only trying to help and to save lives. If you can't tell us specific women whom we could speak to, is it possible that Sister Sarah or one of the other nuns can help us? As Sister Sarah said, there is talk in the community about this. Maybe, someone will be willing to help?"

Father Joseph rose. "Nothing to forgive. I war with the same question in my heart just as passionately." He sighed. "Sister Mary is deaf and suffers from a deep trauma, but perhaps she will share her story." He called his secretary. "Can you have Sister Sara bring Sister Mary to my office?"

He sat back down. "It would be good for both of you to sit as well—less threatening to her. Two years ago, Sister Mary was brought here, left abandoned on the church steps. She'd been physically and sexually abused. Two families immediately stepped in to support her, the Benningtons and the Granvilles. Too traumatized to even try and communicate past her disability, she has—"

Eva's mind raced as the pieces solidified in her mind. Vanderhaul the killer in the dungeon. He had to be taking the rings and had ransacked Bennington's. Sister Mary had to-

High pitched screaming rent through the quiet of the church.

Adam sprang to his feet and barreled out of the office. Eva and Father Joseph followed.

A nun ran their way, waving her arms. "He's kidnapping her!"

Adam drew his weapon. "Where? Who?"

"The garden! Sister Maria. He's wearing a mask! He said he'd found her now and she would pay for her sister's crime."

"Call 911." Adam ran in the direction the nun had come from. He saw an exit and slammed through the door.

In the garden, a masked man had a nun by her hair, dragging her as she fought to free herself.

Adam raised his gun. "FBI. Let the woman go. Now! I'll shoot."

The masked man looked up. At that moment, the woman pulled a knife from her robe and slashed at her hair, freeing herself. She didn't even look Adam's way before she charged at the masked man. Her knife aimed to kill.

"FBI! Stop!" Adam screamed, adjusting his aim to the woman, his heart hammering with a sickening dread. Mid-kidnapping or not, he couldn't let her stab the man.

"No!" the priest yelled and slammed into Adam's arm. "She's deaf!"

Adam's gun fired from the jarring blow. The woman stabbed the knife into the masked man's heart, pulled it out and rammed into his groin as she fell to her knees then to the stones.

The masked man stood for a moment, blood spurting before he crumpled to the ground.

Adam's gut twisted in an agony of frustration. He wouldn't have killed the woman, just stopped her from killing the masked man. He shoved the priest back and hurried toward her. He had no doubt the masked man was either dead, or seconds from it.

Eva ran forward, her heart and soul sinking as Maria's tragic outcome. Sister Mary was Maria, who'd been on the altar in the dungeon. The man on the ground, now wore the same mask that she'd seen in the vision. The priest pulled the hood off.

Vanderhaul.

She lifted Sister Mary in her arms, blood gurgled from the woman's throat where Adam's bullet had exited. Instead of fear or pain, Eva saw peace in the woman's eyes.

Adam removed his shirt and pressed the cloth to the wound, stemming the flow of blood. "Hang in there. Help is on the way."

"Sister Mary. Dear God." Father Joseph fell to his knees, tears pouring.

Sister Mary held up her hand, giving Father Joseph an envelope. "Forgive me, Father, for I have sinned," had been written in red on it. When he took if from her, something fell to the ground. Adam picked it up.

The final card of Justice had been dealt.

Epilogue

Tuesday May 26th

The names of those killed had been released.

Eva stood at the back of the crowded room. The press conference to answer questions about the murder of Judge Granville, prominent attorney Barry Bennington, and heir to billions, Peter Vanderhaul, had just finished.

Still, cameras flashed and questions rang out as the spokesman tried to bring order to chaos. Adam, who'd been on center stage with several officials, walked her way—his expression tortured. Sister Mary's fate weighed heavily on him.

Reporters demanded answers, but he ignored them after several no comment responses. She felt for him. She knew how grueling being in the spotlight could be, especially with no answers to give the sharks out for blood.

The details of the case had not been released and wouldn't be until the FBI's investigation proved the men guilty of the crimes Sister Mary had revealed in her letter. The motivation for their murders would remain secret for now. The powerful families of the three men had promised to bring hell on anyone who defamed the memory of their *loved one*.

Eva knew the truth and Sister Mary's parting letter filled in the gaps. Sister Mary hadn't known who'd kidnapped her and her sister, but she had seen Vandherhaul's face after he'd killed Carmen. She then passed out, and when she woke up, she'd been left at the church. Six months ago, after a church meeting, a girl who'd come for help, recognized Granville and Bennington as men in charge of the sick sex games at the mansion.

Sister Mary found the men's addresses in the church files. She took money from the church, bought a camera and followed the men. She caught pictures of them with women, then sent Granville's wife copies of a few. One day, she saw Vanderhaul enter Bennington's house and knew the three of them had been part of what happened. Her research into Vanderhaul, brought up his and

Bennington's past. If they had been stopped then, her sister would be alive today.

Sister Mary's mother had been a Tarot reader and a believer in Karma.

Carmen's stab to Vanderhaul's stomach in the dungeon had left him with only half of his intestines working and a colostomy bag for the rest of his life. His life had been forever ruined. He'd deduced where Bennington and Granville had hidden Maria when he found the large donation receipts at Bennington's. He'd gone after Maria before she could kill him.

Eva bet they'd find Carmen buried on the estate. Would it be proof enough?

She didn't know.

Vanderhaul had a lighter skinned ring around his finger, too, but no rings had been found yet. Eva concluded that part of her detachment from the murder of Granville and Bennington had been because of Mary's deafness. Another element might be because of their own guilt in covering up murder and rape. Maybe even raping women themselves.

"Let's get out of here," Adam said as he walked up.

"Gladly." Eva turned for the door. As they crossed the crowded room, she saw a man's hand holding one of the double doors open. He stood out of sight on the other side. His signet ring gleamed in the bright lights. The letter B over a ram's head framed by a pentagram.

Heart thudding, she rushed forward, but he disappeared before she reached the door. On the other side, crowds of people walked. No man stood out to her.

Adam caught up with her. "What's wrong?"

Eva shook her head. "I'm angry. It's as if they're getting away with it. The men may be dead, but if their crimes are never exposed, how will the cries of their victims ever be heard? There are more men like them out there and the innocent need to beware."

Adam looked into her passionate, gray eyes and knew what she would do. "No matter what those powerful families do, you're going to write the women's stories like Maria wanted you to, aren't you?"

"Yeah, I am. Justice will be fully served. No matter how long it takes," she said under her breath.

XII

THE HANGED MAN

13

THE HANGED MAN

MATTHEW COSTELLO

Upright: Wisdom, trials, circumstances, discernment, sacrifice, intuition, divination, prophecy
Reversed: Selfishness, the crowd, body politic

The first day – or was it night? – the room had nothing in it.

There was a window, so very tiny, in one corner, near the ceiling.

Out of reach of course, and looking like someone had taken black paint and smeared it over the glass. Allowing only small slivers of light – like now, which is how he knew it was day.

But just those slivers.

He had his first important thought, the first beginnings of a plan to get out of here.

Wherever 'here' was.

And why ever…was he here.

Just a window. If one screamed loud enough, someone would hear. If he kept screaming, someone would have to hear.

They'd find someone, a cop, and say… *I heard someone, just down there.*

Yeah…

The beginnings of a plan.

Because—core to his goddamn philosophy, his way of navigating this planet—if you had a plan, there was always hope, always possibilities.

And the more plans, the better.

So, though he stood in this empty room—what, maybe twelve by twelve? Perfectly square. Cinder block walls. Stone floor. Basement-like room.

He knew he could use his brain to start sorting this out

Yeah. What all his UK friends said in the city, whenever one of their big deals went fubar.

"Just got to sort it out, mate…"

Right. He'd tell them. That's all.

And good luck with that.

Because sometimes when you got to the "sorting it out" stage, the eggs were hopelessly scrambled, and so were their balls.

Cash gone down the old porcelain chute, never to be recovered.

He took a breath.

That brain working.

But with an almost near-hangover throb, he started to think…how the hell did I get there?

How the *hell* did that happen?

*

Night.

In the city, summertime.

Did it get any better? And he never took this city of exploding money and opportunity for granted.

Especially on a night like this, on the roof of The Standard Hotel.

The view—out to the pathetic shores of Jersey across the river, baby high-rises looking on like someone not invited to the party, then out to the gaggle of boats and private choppers whizzing by Lady Liberty as if she had become a nuisance, like the homeless population.

Whose numbers seemed to be rising rapidly. Popping up here and there like cockroaches in one's home.

That needed to be addressed.

There were times when he spotted a well-meaning tourist from some bleeding heart EU country dig into their wallet and pull out money, and feed the grimy machine that was these raggedy people, with their plastic bags, their cans, their carts, their clothes that had to be a health risk.

And he wanted to go over to those tourists, grab them, shake them— and say *do that back in your own country, goddamn Gothenburg, Tallinn, even Paris.*

Though he guessed these days the lightbulb had finally gone off in their little heads, back in their sappy countries.

The flood of people—migrants!—coming in, hitting them so hard, the challenge of the unemployed and of the angry and the desperate who sure the hell didn't look French or Swedish.

All saying...

Ding-dong... we're here.

And we are not going anywhere.

Yeah. Sooner or later, they'll all get it.

And more than once, he thought how fortunate for the US of A that it has a big fat ocean between its shores and all *that* crap.

America... a melting pot? Home of the free? Huddled masses horseshit?

Yeah. *Riiiight.*

These days, not so much.

We didn't have Europe's plague.

And with the smart money flowing into the mega-million condos, spreading even to Brooklyn, Queens, as if all that money and development simply could not be contained.

No way *that* golden situation would change, no matter what schmuck got elected mayor.

He drained his Stoli on ice. The summer night air cool.

When he saw a girl.

Well, no. Not a girl. A woman, dressed perfectly for this evening. Dark eyes.

He could easily assess the cost of all she wore, the quality.

But it was the person in those clothes...

... that held his interest.

He smiled.

And waited.

*

Now...

In the room, he had lain down on the floor. Not cold, but with that sweaty covering that stone floors got.

And he thought.... *always good at solving problems.*

Right?

Right!

So how the fucking hell to solve this?

He looked up at the window, now a dull grey smear. Sun behind clouds, or maybe it was late?

What time was it?

Not a clue.

So he closed his eyes.

*

The woman came over to him.

And while he expected that, he didn't expect that look in her eyes, locked right on his. Bold, as if this particular game was one she had played before.

Interesting.

And the closer she came, the more he could take in other aspects. The skyscraper stilettos, the black, brilliant.

Could be knockoffs.

Or they could be authentic Christian Louboutins.

Hard to tell without a close examination.

Which of course was in his flight plan.

The eyes, lips... a beautiful woman, especially with jet-black hair pulled back, and up. As if causal. But anything but causal.

She held that look.

"Nice night," she said.

Only then moving her eyes away to look at the glittering city. This city now made—in his mind—for people like them. A kingdom for, of, and by the wealthy, or those who could—one damn way or the other—make themselves wealthy.

In this city, mention the words "real estate," and well you might as well be talking about gold, silver.

Uncle Scrooge's vault with its sea of coins and jewels.

Real Estate.

So unreal.

One thing he could tell, about this woman—he had developed antennae for such things—she was no pro.

Those operators, even when well masked and well-heeled, he could sniff out from a block away.

No.

So he smiled back.

"I'd say... a perfect night."

And he resisted the cheesy phrase that dangled in his mind like sucker bait... for a sucker fish.

Made only more perfect by your arrival.

Less is more.

In most cases.

Not all.

She nodded, smiled. Looked down at his glass of Stoli, the cut-crystal catching candle-light, cubes glistening.

She didn't need to ask.

"Would you like one?"

Another nod. The smallest smile.

Those lips... quite something.

And it took "quite something" to genuinely catch his interest.

He waved over to one of the rooftop bartenders.

The $20 tip he gave him for the first round, doing its work. And the bartender ducked under the fold-down end of the bar and hurried over to take an order.

Because, well, in his world that's just the way things worked.

Chapter Two

He woke up.

Back achy, room chilled, his clothes damp.

The room dark. Night now, no real light, though a hint of something from outside made the blackness less than total.

He pulled himself up to a sitting position.

And when he turned to the left, he saw something.

Hard to make out. But he could smell it, and well... it smelled like.

Steak?

Really?

He reached out and slid the plate close.

A steak. God. A ribeye, or a strip, on the bone. Cool to the touch. Must have been sitting there for a while.

No utensils. And the smallest of paper Dixie cups filled with water.

He took a bite. Another. He killed the water in a gulp.

Aware that he needed to take a leak.

But he continued to munch on the steak; not the best he ever had, but not bad. Down to the bone, juices running down his chin.

Until—meal finished—he pulled himself up to a sitting position, then stood up.

In the darkness.

And he had only one idea of what to do now.

*

Then, as if choreographed, he was in a cab with her.

One of those new cabs, with a thick Plexiglas shield to protect the driver from passengers while the driver chatted away a mile a minute to Kabul.

And she seemed to fit him perfectly when he leaned close, bending into him.

And rather amazingly, despite his years of experience—his decades of experiences—he was suddenly a teenager who could not get enough of this woman.

Neither of them giving a damn what the driver saw, what he thought.

Going to her place, she had offered.

Her place, his place.

That didn't matter.

Not on a night like his.

Except, once, when he broke away from a crazed kiss, he looked out the window.

Thought she had said Lexington Avenue. Near the Grammercy?

But this... this was the Lower East Side. And no matter how trendy Alphabet City had become, still not a patch of the forest he ever ventured into.

Or wanted to.

He was about to say something.

Least, that's what he thought he was going to do.

Sure, mouth open.

The garish lighting and signs of crappy stores and bodegas flashing by, a near blur, until—

They were a blur.

His eyes shut.

*

Until—so many hours later—when he opened his eyes, his world had become this room.

*

He yelled.

"Hey! Someone?"

Loud, then louder. "Anyone hear me? Anyone!"

His voice a scream, as loud as he could make it, his throat actually hurting from the force of the scream.

Aiming his yells at the tiny window as if his screams would make it come to life, smears vanish, pop open. and whatever nightmare this was...

(Wherever that woman had brought him to... however *she had brought him here...)*

... would end.

Dust himself off.

Quite the story to tell.

But the yelling went on.

*

And on—until he knew that his full-throated yells had turned into a croak. An old man's voice, scratchy.

He wanted water.

The steak had been so salty.

A reminder of a world gone?

The tiny paper cup of water nothing to slake that thirst.

And though he couldn't really see anything in this box of a room, he knew that he'd have to pick an area.

Where he would behave like any caged animal.

Doing what any caged animal has to do.

No choice at all.

He opened his mouth. Maybe to make one more croak.

When he simply shut his lips.

Yelling.

Some plan, a voice inside his head said.

Nice work.

Nice fucking work.

*

The smeary window had a glow.

Daytime.

And he saw—at the bottom of the metal door, near a mailbox-like chute that he had not been able to pry open—a round metal plate.

Like the one that had been filed with a steak.

Now... there were...

What were they?

Crumbs?

He licked his cracked lips.

No water.

He guessed, there would be no more water.

And despite his thirst, he licked at those crumbs, taking time to spear each one like it was some wonderful morsel.

In between stabs at the metal plate, he looked up at the door.

He yelled at it.

But now that voice, the big man-like roar he had been able to do before, was gone... for good.

He bleated at the door.

As if it might respond.

*

Day into night. Night into day. Eventually, somehow, the plate disappeared.

He cried, and wondered if his tears, if shedding that water, would make him even more thirsty, the pain of his thirst now way beyond the hunger pangs.

His cage, this room, fouled. But that horrible fact, visible when there was some light, didn't matter at all now.

Nothing mattered at all now.

And when he next slept, he drifted in and out of a dream, imagining the hotel rooftop where this, whatever it was, began.

The woman.

She did this.

But why?

And in asking himself that question, he slowly came to a very clear realization. His world, his money, his business, his operations.. well, could be a lot of people who might have gotten a little hurt.

Okay—a lot hurt.

Little people who did not matter one goddamn bit.

Could she be connected to someone like that?

Is that why he was here?

He started thinking about that when awake, his throat a dusty drainpipe. Lips cracked leather.

The ancient question.

The ancient demand.

Why me?

Except in this case, here were a lot of answers to that one.

*

Night into Day. Day into Night.

Barely moving, curled up.

Until—

There was a chair. Close to one wall of his box. A simple wooden chair. His eyes level with his legs. Until he raised his eyes.

And hanging from a thick curved hook that hadn't been there before, dangling from the ceiling...

A noose.

He looked at the two things as if they had nothing to do with him.

Almost... as if, they had been put here due to some mad, insane logic as well.

And even now, with the agony of being so dry that he thought he could feel parts of his body withering, completely overriding his stomach pain, the hunger no competition for the thirst...

A grim joke occurred.

Looking at the chair. The classic noose, dangling, unmoving.

The joke: *What are you in for, buddy?*

But a joke that produced no ripple of movement.

And good thing... because he was sure that would hurt.

He went back to the one thing he could do here.

Lie on the floor. Close his eyes.

Wait.

*

He opened one eye, the other eyelid firmly pressed against the stone floor.

The one eye trained on the chair, the noose...

Then—noting something.

On the chair. A note. Small. *Something.*

And he started to crawl, using his hands, his arms that somehow could still function, to drag himself across the floor.

He thought—for only a second—of what he must look like.

Why, like those people who popped up in the streets, with their signs scrawled on chunks of cardboard. Curled up humans—barely human—with their begging cups, and bags, and filthy clothes.

Yeah—just like that.

No different.

And then, after such a long time, he was at the chair. But the thing was.. to reach what now looked like a card, he'd have to reach up.

Raise his body somehow.

One hand that had been clenched into a fist as if that might make his slow crawl easier, unclenched.

He grabbed a wooden chair leg. Did the same with his other hand, his totally dehydrated body screaming at each small expenditure of effort.

Until he was up, eyes nearly level to the seat of the chair.

And he could see the card.

Read the words on it.

The Hanged Man.

And... his hanged man looked as if he had been caught, trussed like an animal for slaughter, feet higher than his head.

Caught. Like an animal.

He knew what this card was. Had heard of such cards.

Told fortunes. The future.

Ridiculous garbage.

But then—eyes level with that seat, he raised his head a bit.

The noose dangling.

The card... the future.

Always have a plan.

The way he lived, he knew that when he took advantage of other people's losses, their greed, their misfortune ...

They didn't have a plan.

But he had one now.

*

And then like the slowest moving slug, he pulled himself up, using the chair to steady his slithering climb.

Until he was on his knees, then somehow, could get a leg up, to step up to that seat.

And then—as if he had climbed Everest—he was standing on the chair.

His eyes on the noose.

His buddy in this stone cell.

For the millionth time he thought... *who could have done this?*

The answer to that: rather simply.

They were legion.

As to why?

Well, that question didn't need an answer either. Not with so many possible answers.

In moments he might collapse, to die a terrible, slow death on the floor, feeling each agonizing moment,

Or...

He reached up.

Noticing that his hands, so helpful in getting him here, were black claw-like things. He even thought he saw a spot with teeth marks. Had he chewed an index finger during the night, so desperate for anything wet?

Anything to put in his dry mouth.

He took the noose, the rope so thick and secure. So reassuringly solid.

Then—around his neck.

Feeling as if that's the place it belonged.

The next step in his plan... well, not something he had ever done before. But he'd seen it in movies, to be sure.

Knew how it happened.

Though the experience of it... well, that would be all new.

For a last moment... the "who" and "why" questions floated in his mind.

To which his now obsessed brain said... *course, you know why.*

But.

But something happened.

*

A click.

The door.

The metal door. So solid and resolute in its mission to keep him here.

Popped open...

Just like that.

A click, then opening a foot, or two. Open to the outside. To whatever was outside.

Whatever was waiting outside this universe that was his room.

He stared at it for a moment.

At his feet, the fortune-telling card. The Hanged Man.

And looking at that open door one last time, he turned away.

He had already dismissed that world. The outside.

I have a plan, he thought. No tricks for me.

And he made his already wobbly legs shake forcing them to wobble even more... until the chair rocked a bit, not enough.

Then more, the two front legs rising up, and now his weight thrown back, causing the chair to rock the other way, until—like someone jumping away from a sinking ship—

The chair tumbled to the ground, a fallen soldier.

And his friend, the thick rope—tight, snug, secure—grabbed at his dust pipe of a throat.

And while he swung back and forth in these seconds, mouth opening, a fish mouth, gulping... he saw the great fireworks display in front of his eyes.

Until—

Like all fireworks displays—

The sparks and rockets and explosions all gave way to the stillness of darkness, the stillness of night.

The stillness of nothing.

XIIII

DEATH

14

DEATH

LEE LAWLESS

Upright: End, mortality, destruction, corruption'
Reversed: Inertia, sleep, lethargy, petrifaction, somnambulism

It was the second time in a week that the Duyvil Kill Police Department had had to respond to a crisis call at the cemetery, so of course this time it looked like foul play was involved.

It was pretty foul, for sure, just not in the way that they were imagining.

It was hard to get a line on what their cute sergeant McLaughlin was imagining, though. He'd personally seen me hauled out of the still-smoldering embers of the mortuary, screaming bloody murder and thrashing like I was at a particularly good punk show. He'd been part of the team that discovered the pile of bloody clothes in my hamper; the mangled, glinting stash of diamond jewelry on the bathroom counter; the gore-infused chainsaw out back that I'd probably never have been able to get completely clean anyway.

He was aware of all of that, but he kept looking at me through those sweet blue eyes like Heaven itself was his corrective lenses.

It was kind of disturbing to me, and I'm really not the type that gets easily riled.

The worst part, though, was that even if he believed I was innocent, I was going to have to explain myself anyway.

*

I don't like explaining myself, or any of my choices, and that's fine. They haven't been bad choices. I mean, all things considered.

I've lived my whole life in Duyvil Kill, New York, a little town upstate on the Hudson. It sounds like a creepy place, but it's not. We have cruelty-free coffee and jazz combos at the local bistro just like you. Sure, "Duyvil" comes from the Dutch word for "Devil", but "Kill" comes from the Dutch word that translates to mean "a body of water."

The Hudson River, which is the southernmost fjord in the world and quite rapid at the juncture where my town was founded, gave Duyvil Kill its name... not thanks to the supernatural, but in fact to the supremely natural.

Until its main house/mortuary burned to the ground this evening, I'd been an employee at the Hope Cemetery, a small but dedicated operation on expansive grounds overlooking the Hudson. I dress and style myself in a manner that I suppose could be called "adult goth"—stylish but not ostentatious black clothes, discreet piercings, a few well-done tattoos. I'm a little different from the rest of the townsfolk, to be sure, but I make no effort to be markedly so. I've just been fascinated with death since I was old enough to understand the concept, and I've spent the rest of my life getting really, really good at dealing with it.

I wasn't sure how I was going to work that into my story though... it didn't bode well for keeping murder charges away from me.

Maybe I could plead negligence? Get manslaughter?

One look of the scant, charred, hacked-up remains of Mrs. Hope would likely end that effort. To say nothing of what I'd done to her son, Norm.

Poor Norm. He'd been the one hit hardest by all this. Life had always dumped on him, but this was ridiculous. It hadn't been his fault that he or his mother had met such an excruciating end.

Alright, it kind of HAD been.

And I didn't want to explain ANY of that.

*

Sgt. McLaughlin taps his pen on his notepad but doesn't take his creepy eyes off me. OK fine, he's not really creepy. He's actually pretty damn cute. I'm just creeped out by this whole situation. I stink like smoke, even in the freshly-pressed prison jumpsuit they gave me when all of my half-incinerated clothes needed to be entered into evidence. My exposed skin is covered in balm that's not making my freshly-crisped flesh feel any more comfortable, my hair is singed, and my hands were black with soot and bone-char before the booking officer even got the ink near them.

My mugshot must make me look like Edward Scissorhands if he'd been hit by an IED.

The elephant in the room is the stench. This too does not seem to offend cute Sgt. McLaughlin's sensibilities. Though the cops allowed me to wash up in one of the better bathrooms at their station, I'm all too aware of the aroma. In the tiny interrogation room, it feels like a confession all its own.

I want more smoke in my lungs; other smoke, better tasting smoke. I double down on my incendiary adventures of the evening.

"Can I have a cigarette?" I ask McLaughlin. I speak softly, as the evening's screaming has imbued me with raspiness.

He replies less softly, but sweetly.

"You're too pretty to smoke."

He keeps staring.

Maybe I blush as I break his gaze and demurely attempt to tuck a strand of my horribly-burned hair behind one raw, blackened ear. I can't tell. My face feels hot anyway, even hours now after the flames were extinguished. It's like the heat stuck itself to me.

Is this what hell is like?

No. Of course it gets worse. I need to stay aware of how much worse this can get.

"So..." I ask cautiously. "Where's the bad cop, then? Don't you need two to play this game for interrogations?"

McLaughlin shrugs, a little twitch of his broad, uniformed shoulders. His creepy/not-creepy blue eyes smile.

"I think you might make him cry."

I laugh—a single, barking rasp. "So what do you think I'll do to you?"

"Let's find out," he says, almost charmingly. Then, seriousness intervenes.

"How about you start by telling me what happened."

The way he says it insinuates that my acknowledging of his innate sweetness, his odd adorability, will somehow transpose itself into paying for my crimes, if only I can get him on my side.

I don't want him on my side. I want to be punished for what I did. Not too punished. But there's no way I can get away with this.

But it's true... he doesn't even know what really happened, outside the last official report. And what he saw earlier tonight... it wasn't the whole story. Not by a long shot.

There's so much that I should—and shouldn't—say. The worst part is, I have no idea which is which. I should ask for a lawyer. But that'd look more suspicious than the fact that I still have snippets of Norm's skin under my fingernails.

McLaughlin, sensing my inner conflict, offers me an entry point.

"Let's start at the beginning. How did you know Mrs. Hope?"

Nowhere near the beginning I'd thought to start at. He's trying to give me enough rope to hang myself, for certain. My stomach lurches. It must have been visible on my red, raw face.

"Are you going to be sick?" McLaughlin asks, with a genuinely kind-sounding air of worry.

I catch myself. I breathe—it tastes good to do so, even the stale, recycled interrogation room air. My brachioles suck up every bit of available oxygen like half-drowned refugees reaching the shore.

"No. I'm ok. Mrs. Hope is the mother of Norm, my former employer. I just learned of her existence last week."

Although there's a tape recorder going too, McLaughlin jots down notes with thorough fervor, his blue eyes gleaming as he finally makes the progress he's been waiting for. I'm impressed that those bright eyes only dim a fraction when they hone in to scrutinize me as I inform him of HOW Mrs. Hope and I had become acquainted.

"I was compelled to chop her corpse into tiny pieces. That might make anyone feel a little sick."

*

For the purpose of numbers and plotting things that most people don't want to consider, the Environmental Protection Agency values a human life at nine million dollars. The Food and Drug Administration's assessment is a little less, putting a $7.5 million price tag on your existence. The Department of Transportation is a full third less than the E.P.A., calling your whole damn spin around this mortal coil worth 6 million dollars.

To box it all up at the end, neatly, might only cost a few hundred bucks. Your dead body itself, in some areas, might not even be considered as a former human at all.

That's just how it goes, right? In some states you're a body, in some states, you're medical waste.

I don't think that the knowledge of all this makes me inherently sick, or weird, or gloomy. The human interest in the funerary process is thousands of years old… look at some of the best exhibits in the art museum. Mummies! Sarcophagi! Funeral trinkets and statues and coins and beads and jewelry, all made just to be interred in a tomb! You walk into the Metropolitan Museum of Art, easily the finest museum in New York City, and right there, right on the first floor, there's this entire wing displaying a whole culture's dedication to death.

When I applied to be the apprentice at Hope Cemetery, I'd mentioned this mindset of mine. I'd even started spouting off stats that I'd learned at my favorite cemetery in the city—Woodlawn, up in the Bronx. I liked it there so much that sometimes on summery days, I'd take the train down and spend hours strolling amidst the stunning stonework and masterful monuments.

I'd told Norm all about how I loved the assiduously-carved angels, the mosaic-domed mausoleums, the mini-Parthenons, the elegantly-etched gravestones. The anchors, torches, skulls, columns, books of life, shrouds, clasped hands, hourglasses, ankhs, roses, Masonic symbols, and weeping willows set in stone, all telling secret stories about those they guarded.

I explained that I knew the stats—in 1900, there'd only been twenty crematories in the United States. Now, there were 1,300. By 2025, 52% of Americans would desire to be cremated after death.

I extolled how I loved that those cremains could be pressed into records, or diamonds, or shotgun shells in tribute. How it was so beautiful that a former corporeal form could be blown into glass, or made into ecological bags that grew trees when planted, or even loaded into fireworks.

I even got cultural, though god knows it wouldn't have mattered in Duyvil Kill. I mentioned about how Aghori *sadhus* in India were known to wear human bones and worship in haunted houses, and how they'd even go as far as to wear human cremains on their faces, since one of their core tenets involved showing how all opposites— like life and death—ultimately could be illusory.

I left out the part about how some of those *sadhus* lived in charnel grounds. I didn't want to seem too overeager. I'm an atheist, anyway, and an apathetic one at that. I don't care what god you believe in, I see the same damn results at the end.

It had worked perfectly. Norm clearly didn't share my passion for the deeper details of death. This was a job to him. Like it or not, my aptitude and enthusiasm for the after-death process had been the reason he hired me.

When he'd given me the job, which came with the attendant perk of my own small cabin nestled in the tree line behind the main house/mortuary, Norm hadn't mentioned his mother. He'd drunkenly implied many times that he'd been roped into the "family business", that he didn't really have a passion for funerary rituals despite his job-accrued knowledge thereof, and that he was glad someone like me was there to really be intrigued and useful for these sorts of things.

Norm had taught me all about the technical side of death. I'd learned everything about the professional mortuary process, embalming, cremation, burial, and all of the attendant emotional elements that had to be dealt with around these matters from him. Unlike me, Norm was a bit gloomy by disposition, but it seemed to be due more to his lack of a life than the lacks of lives with whom he dealt professionally.

He constantly self-medicated with Duyvil's Sting pilsner, of which he'd scored a lifetime supply after burying one of the chief brewer's elderly aunts, free of charge. It wasn't like anyone would complain, after all, if he skulled a couple of brews as we went about the mortuary's daily duties. He was always competent, lucid enough, and sometimes even chatty.

But he had never mentioned his mom, Maggie. It wasn't until things went really wrong that I even knew she existed.

The only evidence there'd been someone living in the barn made me simply consider that it was critters of some sort or another. A bitchy, oddly overweight Chihuahua, Pancho, and a few stray cats lurked around the boarded-up barn, which Norm told me was condemned. He told me to keep away from it, for safety. That was fine with me. It seemed to be portly Pancho's personal domain, and though I love dogs, I can't abide those oversized rats. Even someone obsessed with the eerie can only take so much weirdness.

Pancho was generally tended to by Norm, but really, Norm could barely tend to himself. Living in the mortuary's main building, his life was inescapable in his work and his home, and more often than, not the efforts at maintaining the former made the latter get neglected. We had a maid who kept the mortuary's main rooms tidy and appropriately somber-looking, but the bulk of her work seemed to be cleaning Norm's sty of a second-floor apartment. She'd haul down trashbags full of bottles at an alarming rate, and I'm not sure if it was professionalism or shame that precluded Norm from ever inviting me up there.

Anyway, the man did good work for his customers, he was a thorough and thoughtful teacher to me, and he'd tried to do right by his mom.

The worst part there, though, was his idea of what was best.

It wasn't until a few days after her death that I finally got the whole story on Maggie. Why she'd been living in the barn. Why I hadn't known about it. Norm was glassy-eyed and clutching his umpteenth Duyvil's Sting local pilsner like it was the elixir of life. For him, it mostly was, even before his mother had met her untimely… well, perhaps VERY timely… end.

We'd been cleaning out the barn—his mother Maggie's impromptu home for the past three years—when I'd asked about the ski trophies. There were so many of them. Medals too, and photographs. Plaques written in German and French and Italian, accolades from newspapers in more languages still.

"It was her life, the mountain." Norm said wistfully, holding a slim old ski pole like he could use it to bestow a knighthood on someone.

Maggie had bought the property because she could not conquer death, and thus became it… or at least, forced her son to. She'd suffered a terrible injury one day last century during a critical Olympic trial, and had self-relegated to obscurity in the barn, surrounded by her ski trophies and soap operas and snacks. Norm said it had been her love of the mountain that had been her undoing.

Like death, when she realized couldn't conquer it, Maggie Hope *became* the mountain. Give or take a few pounds, her regular human skeleton was surrounded by well over a quarter ton of excess fat and flesh.

Give or take.

We'll get to that.

*

The first time the cops had dropped donuts and arrived at the call, it appeared an almost monotonously macabre scenario. Maggie was dead, all six hundred-odd pounds of her, face down on the floor in the barn—the only building on the property with no stairs to climb, and the only door big enough to wheel her through. It was as though she'd planned to die there, if only to be extricated with as much ease as possible. What a terrible tomb.

Though I never saw her in (what passed for) action, there was no way the former ski champion Maggie was completing more physical effort than lifting more food into her face. Maggie Hope could barely climb her way upright onto her own two feet.

That night, Norm had been at the bar drinking, so I'd signed off on the property search. That meant I'd been there when they cracked open the barn doors, when the nigh-Biblical plague of flies cascaded out.

Maggie's life-alert bracelet had been triggered after she hadn't responded to an automated check-in. It appeared that sometime during the previous evening, she had made a somnambulant stroll, tripped on something, and never recovered. A half-eaten ice cream bar had melted across much of the area around her head, like a gunshot wound appears in movie murders.

It wasn't until they flipped the corpse—a feat which took three full-sized, gasping men—that they discovered Pancho embedded in Maggie's midsection. He'd been squashed in between two prodigious fat rolls when the sleepwalking Maggie had fallen and been knocked out permanently, but worse, he hadn't died immediately.

In fact, that fat little dog-rat had done a pretty fair job of eating his way through a sizeable portion of Maggie's buttery-yellow belly fat, and straight into her intestines. The barky, bulky little bastard had almost chewed himself free of his portly prison, but in the end, his own immobility (and ghastly final meal) had smothered him.

The sight, sound, smell of this discovery produced some of the more unique sounds I'd ever heard any man, let alone the brave and skilled officers of Duyvil Kill, exhort.

The worst part is, it wasn't nearly the worst.

*

"Wow," McLaughlin says, his blue eyes leaping wider, like someone had turned up gas flames on an internal stove of his. "I'd heard it was bad but… damn."

"It's more sad than bad, I think," I said. "I mean, she was in bad health, she filled herself with bad things, she died badly, but she wasn't a bad person."

"That somehow also works for the good," McLaughlin astutely notes. "People can do good things, have good intents, and still not ultimately end up being very good humans. Maybe…maybe that's what happened with Norm?"

"Maybe. But your metaphor would imply that Norm also died well," I intoned. "That… didn't happen."

McLaughlin nods seriously. "So tell me about it." He scrutinizes me a bit, almost as if the request is a dare. A dare my entire innocence rests on.

"Well, my right to remain silent isn't going to help me any, given what you've seen tonight," I said. "I might as well try to convince you I didn't murder my boss and torch the entire mortuary, right?" I attempt a smile. My burned lips send slivers of pain into my face as they stretch and quickly retract.

"So Maggie Hope was dead… badly dead… so dead, the response team is going to be telling stories about it for years from now. But you didn't kill her, and neither did Norm, and we confirmed that over a week ago," McLaughlin recounts. He pauses, looking genuinely confused.

"So that… doesn't explain the chainsaw, though."

*

The first time I saw a doublewide coffin, I legitimately thought it was romantic.

We keep a small showroom as part of our all-inclusive end-of-life service dealings (as Norm used to joke, "One-stop shopping for those who are dropping.") We had a few of the usual models—cheap, fancy, one sadly child-sized one. But one day, the doublewide came in, and my first question was if it was for one of those old couples who have loved and lived with each other so long that they end up knocking off together, what Vonnegut had called a "duprass."

Norm gave me a look more serious than his glassy dark eyes usually entailed, then simply said, "No."

I took it to mean something even more ponderous, but as it was part of my job, I really did want to know.

"Oh… was it something really bad? A murder-suicide? A death pact? I didn't see anything on the news…"

"It's not for any of that shit," Norm exhorted. "It's for one person. Just one, extremely large, single person."

Later on, during the embalming and processing of the body—it had been a 350-lb. man who'd died of a massive heart attack—I marveled at the human form, how much it could take, how far you could push it past any reasonable point and still have it be viable. Well, for a while, anyway.

All my insights on this, when explained to Norm, were dismissed with grunts and requests for more instruments or aid. I'd had no idea how sensitive the subject was for him, and didn't recognize it fully until Maggie's massive form was being dealt with. Norm had a little bit of a beer belly, due to his Duyvil's Sting habit and the usual wear of middle age, but other than that he was pretty average. His decent health also underscored the obviousness that his mother's condition had been imposed due to effort, not genetics.

And people say I must hate myself to do what *I* do.

Anyway, the whole week after Mrs. Hope passed, Norm was beside himself. Not just drunk but angry, not just brusque but vehement. He stayed upstairs most all day, except to check in once or twice that I was properly tending to the only other body we had that week, an elderly man who'd been so frail I could easily move him through the mortuary all on my own.

Mrs. Hope's gnawed, clawed, horrifying remains had been returned to Norm after the county medical examiner had confirmed the cause of death involved no foul play. As the county nor Hope Cemetery had any possible way of wedging her 600-minus-a-few-dog-chomped pounds into a morgue freezer, her body stayed beneath a sheet on a table in the coldest storeroom in the cellar. Technically, bodies are supposed to be stored at 45 degrees.

We couldn't exactly do that, not to a whole room.

By the fourth day, the smell was so pungent, so pervasive, and so putrefying, I had to yell Norm downstairs.

He staggered down from his boozy perch on the second floor and followed me to the basement, mumbling about how he always had to handle the worst of everything, and how it was always fucking something in life.

He couldn't even uncover the mountainous-looking sheet in the semi-cold room. He fell against the wall and sat there for a long time.

I work with dead people all day. I had no idea what to say.

After a long silence, Norm muttered, "Dog din eat'er fingers, didde?"

I delicately looked under one side of the sheet. Mrs. Hope's enormous hand lay there like a bloated starfish, three different and lovely diamond rings embedded in the flesh of her fingers.

"No, the dog didn't eat her fingers," I assured him. Norm nodded decisively and burped authoritatively to accentuate his point.

"Wantcha ta cut'em off."

We said the next two sentences at the same time.

"Her jewelry?" was my reply.

"Her fingers," was his.

"I... shouldn't I try to use some grease or something first, to..."

"You'd need more lube than a San Francisco bathhouse durin' Pride Week," he slurred. "No. Cuttem off."

I should have thought about it harder, but I didn't. The whole situation was so macabre, even by my own ridiculously different standards, that I just did what my boss told me. We had a pair of bolt cutters out back in the gardening shed, where we kept all the stuff that our twice-weekly laborers used to keep the shrubberies and trees in order, and before I knew it, I was back in the basement, clutching them in a daze.

Norm hadn't moved. He still didn't, even when the first crack of bone resonated from the teeth of the pincers. He just looked away with a thousand-yard stare as I wrestled away with the dismemberment.

I got both ring fingers off, only slightly shredding and twisting the gold on one of the rings, before I couldn't ignore my circumstances any more, and ran to the washup sink in the next room to puke.

Norm still didn't move.

I composed myself and walked back into the luke-cold room. The rings glittered there on the table, their sparkle undeterred by their sickening circumstances. *Maybe that was why people liked diamonds so much, because they always kept shining like that, no matter what. Maybe that was why some people were pressed into diamonds when they died.* I tried to hand the sparkly stash to Norm, but he just turned his head and shut his eyes.

"Yers."

"Norm, I can't…"

"Yers. Take'em. I don't wanna look at 'em." He put his head between his knees and started breathing as if he were falling asleep.

This was as close to an opportunity to provide closure as I could.

"Norm. NORM."

"Rgh."

"Norm, we've gotta embalm her. It's been almost five days, we've gotta do something."

He shook his drooping head, forcefully. "I can't fuckin' do it."

"Then I'll do it. But we have to…"

"Nobody's puttin' her in a coffin. No lookin' at that. No." Norm coughed and rolled himself semi-upright, his head lolling against the wall.

"What then? Resumation?" I referred to the process of melting down a corpse using chemicals. It's a fairly new process, and an effective one.

"No. No'uns melting her. Not seein' that. No."

"Well, then, do you want her cremated? No one will see the body, and you won't have to watch it melt. We'll just put her behind the doors and that'll be that. I'll even do the rearrangement raking," I referred to the process of how the body needs to be repositioned after about 45 minutes of cooking, to ensure the flames consume everything. "Come on, man. You've done this a lot of times. You can do it one more."

"Yer doin' it," he spat succinctly.

"Alright," I said. "No problem." I'd helped Norm do this before. I was capable. Today, I'd be an apprentice no longer. The *sadhu* would become the *guru*. I could handle this whole damn place if Norm intended to check out like this.

But there was a problem. Six hundred pounds of it.

There was no fucking way that Maggie Hope's body, at least in its current configuration, was getting cremated in our oven.

Now Woodlawn, my ghoulish gallery, my dream cemetery... they have the industrial-strength stuff. They have an oven that can handle up to 1,200 pounds of human to be rendered into ash. They're capable of doing double-cremations, husbands with wives or parents with kids, that sort of thing. The caretaker had told me that one time, they'd done an obese couple... 1,130 pounds total. It had taken four and a half hours.

And that was with the best of the best equipment.

Our oven maxed out at around 400 pounds of person.

I was going to have to get creative.

"Dismantler," Norm huffed from the floor. I wasn't sure if he was referring to me with a proper title—"dismantle" was, after all, the technical funereal term for what was about to happen—or if he just meant "dismantle HER."

Dammit, clearly it was now going to be both.

The small tree-trimmer chainsaw's roar in the tiled cold room was more than Norm could bear, even with the ear protection we were both wearing. Or at least, that was the element that drove him to flee the room where his mother was being chainsawed—well, *dismantled*—to fit into slabs for the oven.

I'm not a tremendously large or strong girl. I'd only wielded the chainsaw once before, and that was to help with a bit of gardening on one day after a storm when we had to clear some felled trees before a funeral, and the laborers had all been hired out to other parts of town.

Suffice to say, this was not a skillful surgery.

The fat itself was so thick that wielding the chainsaw against it felt like a giant knife slicing into butter. The soft muscle tissue was like carving the most morbid of turkeys, and the bones... god, the bones… I tried to segment her as neatly as possible, but by the end was arm-deep in effluvia, gore, skin, blood, sweat, and bone chips. My safety goggles were smudged red with blood, my clothes (despite a rubber cape) were saturated, and for the first and only time in my career, I hated death. I hated a life that would compel itself to end up like this—Maggie, not me—but damn, did I hate death.

And I needed Norm to know that.

*

The cop-shaped blob that ambles in is not only the physical opposite of McLaughlin's tall, well-built form, he soon proves himself the mental opposite as well. He saunters up to the interrogation table, thumbs hooked in his belt loops as if he could ever haul his pants properly up around his wobbly waist, and glares at me with beady eyes.

He wastes no time, and actually seems impatient. To his lazy ass, this probably seems like an open-and-shut case.

Well, I can't lie, especially not to myself. The facts really do make it appear this case is locked against me. The big cop seems even more aware of this than me, as he upends a bag of evidence onto the interrogation table.

"Miss Blaise, you sure you don't want a lawyer?"

I glare at him levelly. "No. I'm innocent."

"Well, that's nice that you're so sure of that. But we're not, darlin'."

My stomach turns. I say the only thing that makes sense. "Well then, if I'm guilty, I guess I deserve to be punished."

The cop-blob nods, his head's slow movement making a few extra necks bulge out. "Seems you're into that sort of thing, doesn't it." He leans in, his belly balanced on the table. "Likin' punishment."

I roll my eyes over to McLaughlin, but his icy blues are fixed on the pile of my artifacts on the table. It's not a terribly innocent-looking array. The cop-blob—whose smudgy nameplate reads "Morgan"—picks up a leather riding crop that had, until this afternoon, been safely nestled in a chest under my bed.

"Ain't too many ponies to ride 'round here, cowgirl," he says. His weird upstate accent—a combination of laziness and wannabe-city brusqueness—hints at a Southern drawl, minus any of the charm.

A moment passes as the two survey the stash. My riding crop. A few very high-end black leather whips, including a menacing cat 'o nine tails. Some CDs. Some handcuffs. More than one really nice black leather facemask.

McLaughlin, as ever, remains impassive and a little intrigued. Morgan seems titillated, but I'm not sure if it's at his possible mental resolution of the crime, or something else.

"We been hearin' a lotta 'sex-cult' type talk lately. Satan stuff. Real weird business. You wouldn't know anythin' about that, would ya?"

I almost have to suppress a laugh, but fortunately my throat is still so scorched, it comes out as a cough.

"I'm an atheist."

"Uh huh." Morgan picks up a Danse de Sade CD, one of my favorites. It's covered in imagery from old pornographic movie marquees, with the title *Sex, Satan, Baroque N' Roll* splashed across the front. He flicks his eyes between me and the record cover.

"Now, you may think I'm mean, but I ain't dumb. This band gets their name straight from the guy who invented beatin' people up during sex."

I consider explaining that the Marquis de Sade didn't invent sexual vehemence, he just perfected the art to a point that they named it after him. None of this information will help my case, though, so I keep my singed mouth shut.

Morgan starts listing song titles. "'Death Rock Pornstar'? 'Welcome The Souleaters'? 'Black Witch Blues'? Some interestin' influences you got there." He looks over at McLaughlin, who only stares back as if he's waiting for a point or punchline to emerge.

Morgan focuses on me as if he's softened me up. "You obsessed with death, Miss Blaise?"

"I respect it enough to understand it completely, as part of my professional life," I say levelly. I avoid adding, *"You know, the way you're obsessed with being an asshole."*

My nerves are getting more frayed than my smoked-out hair. I want to laugh, but I keep my patter placid, and nod at the CD. "This should PROVE I'm not obsessed with death," I maintain. "There's no funeral metal or doom-dirges or anything. I listen to rock 'n roll, like all human beings who are truly alive should."

"Uh huh," Morgan continues. He picks up a framed photo of me standing next to a massive man wearing a black leather vest, gauntlets, facemask, and executioner's hood. There's a very realistic-looking guillotine behind us. We're both throwing up our fingers in Satanic horn gestures. Morgan needs only to raise a lazy eyebrow.

"Hey, you're friends with The Monster?" McLaughlin suddenly enthuses. He keeps himself in check and nods up to Morgan. "That's Danse de Sade's bass player."

"Yeah, we're both in the same animal rescue network," I smile. "I'm sorry, what do any of my personal effects have to do with this case?"

Morgan puts down the photo and leans in, spreading his arms around the array. "I think you were into likin' it a little rough. Both'a you and Norm, there. Maybe he wanted it rougher'n usual on accounta his mom passin'. He liked seein' how violent you got, cuttin' her up like that. Maybe y'all took it a little too far. Or maybe you WANTED to take it too far, on accounta the will and all."

Now it's my turn to be genuinely baffled. "What do you mean, the will?"

Morgan leans back and hooks his thumbs back into his abused belt loops.

"Girl, if you're puttin' me on, maybe you shoulda moved down to the city and been an actress instead o' dealing with all these dead things."

I gently shake my head in befuddlement. The burned tissue around my neck crackles faintly.

Morgan explains his discovery to McLaughlin, not to me, as if the victory means more to his peer than his victim.

"She's the sole beneficiary of Norm Hope's entire estate. Every last ash."

*

They say that the death process involves Denial, Anger, Bargaining, Depression, and finally Acceptance. The worst part is the bargaining… there's no way it can ever work out.

Norm was not in a mood to bargain. He was still firmly entrenched in anger.

After yelling at him for any kind of help and receiving no reply, I'd hauled most of Maggie's various elements into the cremation oven, a staunch old black thing, basically a modified incinerator, in a small room off toward the back of the house. Generally, the body would be loaded feet first, with the flame positioned over their chest. You can be burned in a coffin, or a container of cardboard, Pacific Pine, Shaker Pine, or in some states, just a cloth bag.

Norm made no specifications. I went with cardboard, making a morbid "take-out container" joke to myself.

During my vicious ministrations I'd discovered that Pancho, he of the actual appetite for destruction, had been left by the medical examiner right alongside Maggie's bedeviled body.

I chucked that ex-yappy little bastard right in the oven there with her. Norm staggered in a moment later.

"Push the button," I said. "You need closure for this. I've done everything else. Check the settings I made, and push the damn start button, Norm."

His eyes wheedled around the settings and, finding them acceptable, slapped the button to fire up the furnace. He then attempted to stagger out of the room.

"Oh no you don't," I said. "You're seeing this through. The hard part's over."

"You said you'd do the raking," Norm drawled.

"I will," I said. "But that's at least half an hour from now, and right now I need the most serious shower of my life. You sit here and see this though. I'll be back in a few."

He couldn't fire me. He already had enough fire to deal with. I walked out.

I smoked a joint nearly as fat as one of Maggie's dismantled digits, dumped the eternally-cheerful diamond rings on the bathroom counter, tossed my blood-drenched clothes in a trashbag in the hamper, and let the water cleanse me back to normal as fiercely as the fire was cleansing Maggie back to dust.

A normal human body is 10% combustible solids. God only knows how that extrapolated regarding Maggie. But I smelled the smoke before I saw it, and that much smoke could only mean the combustion was incomplete.

The worst part is, that's not the worst.

As I ran from my little cabin over to the main house, the mortuary chimney of which was pealing with inky black smoke, I realized I was higher than I thought from the fat-as-a-finger joint. What happened was what happens to all high people when they smell something grilling.

Worst. Munchies. Ever.

*

"So you're openly admitting to drug use earlier this evening, before the incident?" Morgan glares at me.

"Yes. Come on, you're going to test for it anyway, I'm not going to lie." I smiled passively. "And you probably already know this, but I don't have any priors. Not that you need a background check to burn bodies, but I don't have anything you can hold against me. But yeah, I was incapacitated, to an extent. Can you blame me?"

McLaughlin pipes up. "The only thing we're interested in placing blame for is Norm Hope's death. What happened when you got back into the mortuary?"

I looked deep into his scorching stare. "I hate self-sabotage. Self-sabotage is the suicide of your dreams. And that's no kind of death for me."

I exhaled hard. My lungs wheezed, as if a small puff of smoke would still emanate from them.

"I tried. I really tried my best."

*

What I saw in the crematory room was already beyond my control, but like many proactive people in these situations, I knew I couldn't accept that.

Norm had drunkenly fallen asleep against the controls, sending the old machine into a fiery frenzy, but that wasn't the worst.

Maggie's rendered fat had caused so much smoke to pour into the room, Norm was now out cold, and from the looks of him, severely screwed by the inhalation. But that wasn't the worst.

Pancho apparently should have died much earlier. I'd never known the fat little rat dog had had surgery, paid for by Norm to

289

keep his mom's favorite corpulent companion alive. I'd never known that that surgery had entailed a doggy pacemaker.

But I sure did find out, when two minutes after I attempted to haul the inert Norm out of the mortuary, Pancho's puppy pacemaker detonated inside the oven.

The cooling tray, which holds the cremains, exploded outward, coating the small room in dark ashes. A properly-completed cremation's ashes should be white or light grey… these were as inky as coal, and just as hot. As the billowing smoke seared my eyes and arsenal of ashes assaulted my flesh, I screamed and slapped Norm as hard as possible to try to awaken him. The dusky metallic remains of Pancho's pacemaker glowed angrily from the bottom of the tray. The fugitive cremains dust lurched into my nose, lungs, and seemingly, my brain.

Covered in the blackness of ashes, the blackness of soot, the blackness of smoke, and the blackness of the darkest death I'd ever encountered, I blacked out.

*

"May the ashes of your heart rekindle your genius."— Offenbach, "Tales Of Hoffman"

Three Days Later.

I'm meandering around the Hope Cemetery property—my property, possibly. If the charges aren't brought against me. If any number of miscreant, drug, arson, tampering with the dead, manslaughter, or outright murder charges aren't brought against me. The cops are still surveying the roped-off main house. I'm doing minor lawn work, but mostly just strolling around the fancier headstones. Watching people rest in peace somehow puts the rest of me at peace.

McLaughlin strides over as I sit down on an old mausoleum's steps, leaning against one of the tall Ionian columns that create the impressive façade. I watch him approach and notice something I hadn't the night I'd been interrogated. He's in short sleeves now, and his right arm is covered in bad burn scars, the shiny ones that'll never quite look normal again. As he draws closer, I see the remains of an FDNY tattoo half-melted beneath it.

"Hey," he greets me casually. "How are you doing?"

"Better, if you don't intend to break out those handcuffs for any reason other than fun."

He chuckles. At least I'll be taken captive by a cutie. His ice-floe eyes search my face.

"You really think you're guilty?"

"Doesn't matter what I think," I say. "Your partner wants to prove I killed my boss to get this place. I had no idea he even wanted me to have it. Honestly. Anyway, like the Mahabharata says, 'The wind is not stained by the dust it blows away.'"

"What about fireworks?" McLaughlin asks. "Nuclear blasts? That dust sticks around. The Indian Point power plant is just up the river, are you gonna chance their dust too?"

McLaughlin looks at me seriously, as if he's somehow worried about me. I have a feeling this is the calm before the storm—nuclear or otherwise. Maybe one last pleasant chat in this field of stone can put me at rest, before I'm buried in a room of concrete.

"It all eventually blows away. Even the fallout. After a while." I nod at his tattoo. "You were a firefighter?"

"Was," he says dispassionately. "Problem is, the fire fights back. Figured I'd be a little more useful up here on the river, rather than in the heat of the city. Sometimes in all that brightness and glare, it's hard to find out where the flames end and the sunshine begins."

"Change is good," I say. "A few different expert tarot readers, Bob Gleason and Gabriel Marchisio, they've told me on separate occasions that the death card really means change. I always liked that. Not good, not bad, just change. Opposites can be illusory, you know."

"That's fair," McLaughlin says.

"You know, in the city... some of the greatest cemeteries changed into the best parks. There's upwards of 20,000 bodies underneath Washington Square. Thousands under Madison Square, Union Square too. Hell, City Hall Park used to have their own gallows. Liberty Island used to be where they'd hang pirates. And now, all that greenery just means death transformed it into something beautiful, as the rest of the place turned to monuments. Skyscrapers are just gravestones of greed. Mausoleums of money. You were smart to move somewhere you could thrive, even if it meant an old life dying."

"You mentioned Woodlawn Cemetery, when we talked," he says. "My grandfather is buried there. I used to live in the Bronx… I learned how to ride my bike in that cemetery. Figured I couldn't do too much damage to anyone there if I crashed."

We share a laugh at that.

"Do you have a favorite monument there?" he asks. "Is that a weird question?"

"No, it's not weird," I say. "But I can't choose a favorite. It's like an art gallery. From modern pyramids to angel statues, it's all part of someone's story."

"The END of someone's story, you mean," McLaughlin says.

"No… death isn't the end. There's a lot of things in life harder than death. Trying to do good is far harder than dying. Maybe it's why so many try to do good AFTER they're dead. They know they can't get in their own way. Think of all the buildings, galleries, college dorms, scholarships, tribute shows, shit bequeathed. Noble deaths. 'Heroic transcendence', I heard it called once. Being noble, or useful, or important… it's way easier post-death. Same with those benevolent green burials. One good thing, once, that you can't fuck up. Your death isn't the end of you, maybe you can still do good things… even just a little bit. Donate organs, turn into a tree, whatever. You might be way more valuable in death than in life, and that's hard for a lot of people to admit. Mostly 'cause you can't plan for it. But you can try to. And that's where I come in. Helping people benefit from the end of it. I just hope I can keep trying to."

McLaughlin nods seriously. "You know, just because I'm not a fireman any more doesn't mean I can't think like one. I know you said you blacked out, but I also noticed a lot of residue patterns when we investigated the mortuary. Seems that all three fire extinguishers you had in there had been completely emptied. And not in any kind of explosion due to heat."

I'm locked into the Heaven of his blue eyes, and I don't even believe in the afterlife.

"You were definitely the only person alive left at the scene, so no one else could have emptied them. Ashley, you did everything you possibly could to save Norm. If anything, your efforts were heroic. We're not taking you in."

My whole life, handed back to me for trying to save another's, all so I can work with death.

Stranger changes have happened.

"So," I smile at McLaughlin, "if you're not taking me in… maybe sometime you could take me out?"

He holds out his hand and I stand. I don't let go of it as we walk back toward my smoldering old life, my possible new life, and the promise of a post-death that's only scary in the scope of its possibility.

The best part is, it's not the worst.

XIV

TEMPERANCE

15

TEMPERANCE

C.M.C. DOBBS

Upright: Economy, moderation, frugality, management, accommodation
Reversed: Religions, sects, the priesthood, unfortunate combinations,
disunion, competing interests

She watched in horrified fascination as the black-robed man with the face of an angel tilted his head back and raised his hands to the moon-dark sky.

"Beelzebub! We ask that you find favor with our offering."

A low murmur sounded as the black-robed figures surrounding her repeated his words. As the name he called registered, she tugged at her bonds in desperation. *The devil? They were calling on the devil?*

Where was she? How did she get here? Why was she wearing a white cotton robe?

The cold granite slab at her back chilled her to the bone. The man held a wicked-looking blade high over her, chanting in a language she didn't understand. The voices joined in until the chanting reached a crescendo, and she knew this wasn't a nightmare—*she was their offering!*

Her screams drowned out the chanting as the sacrificial knife flashed in the firelight a heartbeat before it plunged down into her chest with deadly accuracy, tearing through flesh, blood, and bone.

Unimaginable pain seared through her. Her life's blood gurgled in her throat, gushing from the hole in her heart, staining her pure white robe. Her sight grew dim while a blessed numbness swept up from her toes as her heart slowed and she drew in her last breath.

"Beelzebub has accepted our offering and consecrated her blood!" When their cheers resounded through the clearing, he filled a ram's horn with her blood and drank deeply. Filling it again, he passed it to his left, filling and refilling until everyone had partaken and not a drop of blood remained.

Chapter Two

Temperance Lippincott stared down at the still form of her grandmother. She looked so frail and helpless… not like herself at all. Her hands balled into fists at her sides as she envisioned punching the man who did this to her grandmother.

"We'll find him, Gram," she whispered. "Sheriff Brody promised." The beeping of the machines echoed. She hated hospitals, but they were a necessary evil.

"I wish you could talk to me, Gram. Just to let me know you're going to be all right." A tear streaked across her cheek. She brushed it away. Her grandmother would want her to be strong.

"I've got to get over to the shop. It's almost nine o'clock and I have to smudge the store again." She'd already decided on the incense mix she'd burn today, but before that, the shop needed to be cleansed with white sage. "It still didn't feel right when I stopped by on my way over here."

Her grandmother squeezed her hand.

"Gram! You can hear me?"

She squeezed Temperance's hand a second time.

"Thank the goddess! Okay, so I've cleansed some black obsidian and hematite stones. They're ready to anoint with Dragon's Blood oil. I've got a new spell I'm going to use before I put them in all of the shop windows and over top the front and back doors."

Her grandmother opened her eyes and rasped, "Good girl."

Temperance shot up out of her chair. "I promised I'd get the doctor when you woke up."

"When you remove the protection stones already in the windows," her grandmother said, "I want to know if any are cracked or broken."

Temperance nodded. "Like the ones that shattered the night Mom and Dad's plane crashed."

Phoebe lifted her hand toward her granddaughter. "They loved you so much."

"I'll let the doctor know you're awake." Temperance leaned down to kiss her grandmother's cheek. "I've got a lot of work to do to get rid of the bad vibes and spirits that were attached to whoever attacked you."

She paused in the doorway and added, "It's hard to describe… kind of feels black and oily."

Her grandmother frowned. "Don't forget to ground yourself before you begin. Be the card—"

She grinned. "I promise, and I'll be the embodiment of the Tarot card I was named for—the fourteenth Major Arcana Card, Temperance."

"That's my girl," Gram rasped. "Keep me posted," she whispered, closing her eyes.

*

Sheriff Dave Brody stared at the fax his friend and former partner over at the Bureau had sent to him. His gut clenched, but he showed no outward reaction. "Damn, if their Intel is right, we're going to need all the help we can get."

He read the report twice. It was short and to the point. Charismatic cult leader, Clive Deveraux's M.O. was to prey on young women with ties to Wiccan and New Age shops. The cause of death of the murder victims was a fatal stab wound through the heart. The photos accompanying the report were graphic, but he didn't expect anything less. Murder was never pretty.

He read the addendum after the photos and his gut twisted. Post mortem all victims were reported to have had the blood drained from their bodies, their hair hacked off near the skull, and were wearing identical white cotton robes. "Probably satanic," he mumbled, having dealt with a similar murder years ago when he'd been a rookie in the Baltimore PD.

The phone rang, but he knew better than to pick it up on the first ring. "Sheriff?" His secretary Missy Jones called out, "Inspector Simmons is on line one."

He didn't bother to point out that they only had one incoming line; she would have something to say about that, too. He thanked her before taking the call.

The news wasn't unexpected. Whenever you could tie more than one murder together, there would eventually be a trail you could follow. Simmons excelled at picking up and following murderous trails—the more obscure, the better.

"A series of murders in Colorado and Texas shared another commonality," he told Brody. "A robbery occurred first."

"Same type of shop?" Brody asked.

"Wiccan and New Age," Simmons told him.

"I won't have the good people of Harmony terrorized," Brody bit out.

Simmons agreed, adding, "We'll get him, but we'll have to be careful not to move in before we have enough evidence. Deveraux has slipped under the radar more than once, and his hands are always clean."

"I'll be careful. Before we're through, he'll be swinging from the hundred-year-old Oak tree in the Black Marsh."

He heard Simmons sigh, "Not gonna happen, pal, or you're off the case."

"You always were a stickler for rules," Brody sighed.

"Then follow my lead—and no hanging!" Simmons disconnected before Brody could tell him what he could do with his lead. Probably a good thing, Harmony was a small town with limited resources; he needed Simmons, so he'd follow his rules.

Staring down at the photos of the women, he vowed to catch Deveraux. If his luck held, he'd be able to convince Simmons to let him deal with the bastard on his own terms. If not, he could always break out a rubber hose.

Chapter Three

Temperance wasn't surprised to find more than one of the shop's protection stones shattered or cracked. She set them aside to show her grandmother on her way home.

She put the newly charged stones in place and breathed deeply, expecting to feel protected. Instead a frisson of darkness brushed against her soul. "Not quite banished yet."

All traces of the evil that seeped into the very air in Gram's shop *Enlightenment* had to be removed. She stood in the center of the shop—the heart—and lit the white sage wand, blowing gently across the flames until a thin spiral of smoke curled up and around her. With the comforting scent of sage smoke whirling around her, she banished all bad thoughts, bad intentions, and evil spirits, ending with, "Leave now! You are not welcome here!"

"Now for the rooms." She started at one end and repeated her banishment chant in all of the store's corners. When the wand threatened to go out, she relit it.

By the time she finished, she was exhausted from putting all of her energy into the cleansing and banishment rituals. "Time to put on the kettle and call the hospital."

She was on the phone with the ICU nurse's station when she heard the trio of bells on the front door chime. "I know I locked that door," she murmured. Who would come into the shop before she flipped over the *Open* sign? She thanked the day nurse, promising to stop by and see her grandmother at the end of the day.

"There you are Miss Lippincott." A tall, imposing man waited in the middle of the shop, his smile seemed cold. It didn't reach his eyes.

Temperance shivered. Though he had the face of an angel, his eyes were an empty grim gray. "I'm sorry, sir," she walked toward him, intending to shoo him back outside. "We're not open for the day yet."

He stared down at her, and she would later swear her flesh crawled. "You will be open for me."

A sharp snapping sound had her glimpsing an east-facing window in time to see one of the newly charged obsidian stones break apart and smash against the tile floor. Good thing she had anointed more stones than needed. Gram was right.

Temperance turned her back on the man and scooped up the pieces. "I'll have to ask you to come back in a half hour when we're open for the day."

"I'm not leaving," he drew in a breath and seemed to grow taller before her eyes. "I wish to discuss giving a workshop on Demonology at your store."

"I'm sorry, now's not a good time," she told him. "If you have a business card, I'll get back to you."

This time the distinct sound of a stone fracturing came from the other side of the shop. Whoever the man was, his intentions were not good. Her gut told her to get rid of him... now!

Instead of refusing, he surprised her by bowing and handing her his card. "Call me."

He stalked through the front door and two more stones cracked.

"Gram's not going to believe this." Temperance hurried back to the office and grabbed her clamshell of stones, replacing all of the fractured ones.

Gram would have advised another layer of protection, so Temperance gathered a supply of red candles and bottle of cinnamon essential oil. The magical properties of the planet Mars she intended to call on—courage, protection and defense, would be strongest at noon, stronger still if it was Tuesday, but still very effective. She'd have to wait until then to close the shop and inscribe the candles, anoint them, and burn them. Time to open, drawing in a cleansing breath, she walked to the front and turned her sign around.

The shop was busy, with a number of customers wanting to know how Phoebe was. Her grandmother was part of the heartbeat of Harmony. By the time Temperance closed the shop midday, she had her favorite incense burning and Gram's favorite CD playing. The soothing sound of harps and flutes eased the tension between her shoulder blades as she double-checked stock against what she reported missing the night before. With a steaming cup of tea at her elbow, she went down the list item by item, getting up from time to time to physically check stock.

She noted three of the distinctive athame's Gram stocked as among the missing. Rowan branch handles carved with ancient Celtic Ogham symbols and beautifully curved blades—not sharp for cutting, but for ritual directing of energy. Odd, but the same number of Rider-Waite Tarot Decks, black ritual candles, and white sage wands were also missing.

Whoever robbed the store and attacked her grandmother had another motive in mind besides stealing from *Enlightenment*. A shiver worked its way up her spine, chilling her. Rubbing her arms, she picked up the phone and called the sheriff.

*

"Now you just rest up, Gram. I don't want you trying to run the shop from your hospital bed, even if they've moved you out of the ICU."

Phoebe just smiled, not saying anything. And that's what worried her. "I mean it. You scared the life out of me for the last three days. I need to know that you'll be resting."

"Yes, sweetie," her grandmother said, reaching for Temperance's hand to pat it.

"At least pretend you're resting and try not to get into any mischief while I'm at work," she said, brushing a kiss on her grandmother's cheek.

The lilting laughter eased the worst of the knots in Temperance's belly. Laughter meant her grandmother was on the road to a full recovery.

"And no dilly-dallying when Sheriff Brody comes to visit you today."

Gram's cheeks flushed as she placed a hand over her heart. Before she could deny that she and the sheriff were sweethearts, Temperance smiled. "You aren't the only one who senses these things."

With her grandmother tucked into bed, Temperance drove the short distance to the shop. Relief swept up from her toes as she parked and got out of her car. The door to the shop was intact, and not hanging on its hinges as it had been the night of the break-in. Focused on the order she expected to arrive midday, she didn't notice anything out of the ordinary until she reached for the door.

A blood-encrusted Justice card, the eleventh Major Arcana card, was stuck to the door of the shop with an athame she recognized. It was one of the ones stolen a few days ago.

A sinking feeling swept up from her toes as her gut screamed not to touch. With trembling hands, she dialed 911. "Sheriff Brody, please."

His secretary didn't ask what was wrong. A first, as far as Temperance knew, and was grateful for it as she was transferred the to the sheriff.

"Sheriff, hi, it's Temperance," pausing to step back from the door and the pool of blood beneath the card, she dug deep for strength. "I think Gram's attacker came back last night."

"Is anything gone?"

"Not exactly," she could feel her voice start to break, but she refused to dissolve into tears. "I think he returned one of the stolen items."

"Are you alone?"

A glance told her she was. "Yes, but I think what I'm looking at is a message." She knew the significance of the Justice card's upright meaning, but couldn't figure out what equity, rightness, and triumph of the deserving side of the law had to do with the athame and the blood.

"Don't touch anything. Take a deep breath and go back and sit in your car—and lock the doors. I will be there in five minutes," he reassured her.

Temperance did as she was told. Why would Gram's attacker leave the cryptic message for her? Gram had a number of tarot decks and the meanings varied slightly from deck to deck. Thank the goddess, it wasn't reversed.

She shivered, and as she sat and waited, another question surfaced... was the blood animal or human?

*

Sheriff Brody pulled up behind Temperance's car and got out. "You all right?"

She nodded. "I can't help but wonder who would do such a thing."

"Think it's for you or your grandmother?"

When she stared at him, he knew she was rattled by whatever she'd found and hadn't thought it through far enough to realize the message might be for her. "Sit tight while I take a look."

"Sheriff?" she called out.

He looked over his shoulder. "Yeah?"

"I took some pictures."

"Good thinking," he told her, keeping his voice even. She was just about vibrating on the seat.

His gut told him the blood wasn't animal, but he'd need a sample to confirm his suspicion. Even though Temperance had taken pictures, he snapped pictures of the bloody tarot card from a few different angles, the pool of blood beneath the card, and the intricately carved, wooden handled blade buried in the door to the shop.

Whoever did this was a twisted son-of-a-bitch… reminding him of the murder report he'd just read. In Brody's book, there was no such thing as a coincidence. Phoebe's shop was a combination Wiccan and New Age shop and fit the pattern.

He shot off a text to Simmons, keeping him in the loop. Walking back over to Temperance's car, he watched her gaze slide over to the sidewalk and then back.

"I have cleaning supplies inside."

"Why don't I send Deputy Hammond over to give you a hand with the clean up?"

She shrugged, and he said, "He'll be here in a few minutes. I want you to wait in your car. I have to take this evidence to the lab, over in Onley. It's only twenty minutes away."

"I know where Onley is," she huffed. "I've lived here half my life."

"Yes, but right now you're reacting to a grim experience and not thinking clearly. Just thought you needed reminding," he explained. "I'll call when I know more."

Chapter Four

Temperance turned on the morning news and poured her first cup of tea for the day. She was stirring honey in her cup when she heard, "… local tarot card reader found murdered."

What? She dropped her spoon in the sink and dashed into the living room in time to hear, "Mary Mack went missing a few days after attending the popular Psychic Fair at *Enlightenment*, a New Age shop in Harmony, Virginia. Due to the ongoing police investigation, no other information is available at this time."

Temperance didn't realize she was shaking until she walked back into the kitchen and reached for her cell phone to dial the sheriff. "Hi, Missy, it's Temperance. May I speak to Sheriff Brody?"

Had Mary had been robbed and beaten like Gram? Where had she been found? What had happened?

"You saw the news," the sheriff said.

"Yes, and I know there's an ongoing investigation, but do you have any information on Mary? Can you tell me anything?" Her heart broke just thinking of the popular tarot card reader. Mary's appointment slots always filled up before the other card readers.

"As soon as I can, you know I will." Brody hesitated before asking, "Any chance I can convince you to stay home today?"

"I'm not going to let whoever attacked Gram win. We're going to be open today and every day until Gram is back on her feet and behind the counter at *Enlightenment*."

"Well, then," he said, "I guess that's a no."

*

Temperance parked in front of the shop, and reached into her tote bag for the tiny vial of lavender oil. She dabbed it on her wrists and at the base of her throat. Now she felt ready to greet the day and whatever might come her way.

She reached for the shop's front door when she spotted the skewered bloody tarot card. The sixteenth card… the Tower. Her heart skipped a beat. Thank the goddess it was upright and meant misery, distress, and unforeseen catastrophe. Gram had taught her to use her third eye when studying the tarot, letting the cards speak to her, which was why she preferred her deck of gilded tarot cards. Not that the meaning was all that different, but an upright Tower card could also mean that our belief system was shattered by a truth we didn't recognize.

"Goddess, help me," she rasped. *Enlightenment's* beautiful purple door and hand woven welcome mat were bathed in blood. What catastrophe would be coming their way? she wondered.

Had she or her grandmother unintentionally caused one of their customers misery or distress? She shook her head; she knew they hadn't. Gram had taught her the truth her grandmother lived by, the Wiccan Rede—*An it harm none, do as thou wilt*. The Wiccan Rede wasn't just a phrase to spout to impress those in the mundane world; Gram believed it to the depths of her soul and had taught Temperance to believe it as well. Whatever spell you cast, whatever words you uttered, will return to you times three.

Standing there, an oily, black evil slithered over her feet and oozed up her legs as Temperance tried to catch her breath and reorder her thoughts. Her vision grayed, and she reached for the protective crystal she wore around her neck. She hit speed dial, and called the sheriff. He'd want to see this and bag and tag the evidence.

She walked back to her car, opened the door and slid onto the seat. Her breath came out in a whoosh. "I'm going to have to tell Gram."

The sheriff arrived a few minutes later, and with a nod and jab of his index finger indicated that she should stay put. Fine by her. The athame and bloody card weren't going anywhere anytime soon. Temperance wished she could figure out what she or her grandmother had done to warrant such an ugly message, but couldn't think of anyone in their tight-knit community who would do such a thing.

After he finished, the sheriff walked over to her car. "I can send someone over to help with the scrubbing," he offered. "It's a mess, and frankly, I'd feel better if you were home under lock and key."

She laid a hand on his arm. "You and Gram have been protecting me for half my life. I love that you both feel that way, but I'm a big girl now, and I don't want whoever did this to think I am going to run and hide like a scared rabbit."

He put his hands on his hips, and she knew a lecture was coming, but she didn't have time to listen and wasn't going to give in. "Thanks for coming over. I need to get started so I can cleanse the sidewalk, the door, and the rest of the shop."

"You know I don't understand half of what you and Phoebe mean by that, but I know that it is important to you. I'll ask Deputy Hammond to stop by in a little bit to see if you need anything."

She thanked him, and using the cloth the sheriff handed her, was able to get inside the shop without touching any of the now-dry blood. Bustling about, she had the cleaning supplies she needed to disinfect the exterior of *Enlightenment*. Forty-five minutes later, armed with herbs and oils, she was ready for the cleansing.

Pleased with the crystal clear vibe emanating from without and within, she hummed while she put the kettle on. The trio of bells ringing let her know someone was in the shop. Ready to greet whoever it was, she stopped midstride recognizing the man from the other day—the one who wanted to give a workshop on Demonology. The one who had shattered three of the protective stones she'd just anointed and placed in the shop.

"Mr.—" she drew a blank. She didn't remember his name and had recycled his business card, not intending to ever contact the man. They didn't need that kind of negative energy in their shop. *Hell, call it like it is, Temperance…* they didn't need that kind of evil in their shop.

"Deveraux," he said smoothly as if he didn't notice that he had unnerved her.

"Mr. Deveraux," she acknowledged. "What can I do for you?"

His gaze swept through the shop and landed on her. "Ah, Miss Lippincott, it is what I can do for you."

She sighed, wishing she'd brought her tea to the front with her instead of her cell phone. Her mouth was dry. "I'm sorry, but I don't schedule the workshops *Enlightenment* gives. That's something Phoebe does and she's away for the next few days."

His eyes darkened and for a heartbeat she was afraid that he would explode. Then he seemed to collect himself and chuckled. "Ah yes, how unfortunate that she ran afoul of a thief."

Temperance's stomach churned as her heartbeat sped up. "I have no idea what you're talking about," she lied. *How did he know about Gram?* No one but Gram's closest friends and shopkeepers knew what had happened the other night.

"You don't lie well, Miss Lippincott. I really must insist—"

She reached for her phone as she warned, "I'm going to have to ask you to leave."

"Not until you agree to my terms," he bit out.

"Then you'll have to deal with my terms. I'm calling Sheriff Brody and I'll be filing a restraining order against you. You won't be able to get within fifty to one hundred feet of me or this shop!"

Deveraux's gray eyes glittered with rage and he spun on his heel and stalked out, slamming the door with enough force to dislodge her hanging pendulum display. Precious crystal, stone, and wooden pendulums shattered as they hit the quarry-tile floor.

Tears filled her eyes. Her phone connected to the sheriff's office. On her hands and knees, she told Missy what had happened, agreeing to stay on the line until the sheriff arrived on the scene. Heartsick over the needless destruction, she didn't hear the siren until the sheriff's cruiser was right outside.

Chapter Five

Weary of the pattern that had developed after *Enlightenment* had been broken into, Temperance went straight to the back of the shop. Once again, she gathered the candles, a lighter, and a white sage wand before returning to the counter and placing them there.

She drew in a breath, raised her arms shoulder height, palms up, before tipping her head back and closing her eyes. A deep calm began to radiate in and around her as she grounded herself. Her palms tingled and the air around her pulsed with the energy she raised.

Slowly lowering her hands to her sides, she walked over to the counter to retrieve the lighter and sage wand. The scent soothed her as she walked from room to room. Corner by corner, she repeated the chant to rid the shop of the evil that had entered with Deveraux.

Temperance was pleased with the cleansing, but wasn't about to stop there. It was almost noon. "Timed it perfectly," she murmured, getting to work inscribing three red candles with five lines, the glyph representing the element of fire, and the symbol for the planet Mars. She chanted as she smoothed the cinnamon oil over the carvings.

The protective scent from the candles surrounded her. Now that the evil that accompanied Deveraux had been banished, she vowed to do whatever it took to uncover the identity of Gram's attacker.

*

Temperance held her grandmother's hand while she went over the steps she'd taken to protect their shop. Gram didn't ask her about the tarot cards or the athames, only wanting to know if the sheriff had talked to Temperance about the cruiser that would be following her home and parking outside, guarding her so she wouldn't be all alone in the Black Marsh where they lived.

"Gram, I don't need a bodyguard."

"What about Deveraux? What if he found out where we live and decides to corner you tonight?"

She'd thought of that possibility, and had doubled-up on the protective herbs and crystals she carried with her. More concerned about her grandmother's safety, she stretched the truth, saying, "That's not even a remote possibility." Temperance hoped she sounded convincing.

"Besides, what if whoever came to the shop and beat you decides to pay you a visit here at the hospital and puts a pillow over your head while you're sleeping?" The catch in her voice matched the one in her throat. If anything happened to Gram... "I can't lose you, Gram," she whispered.

"You won't, dear," her grandmother promised. "Now what did Sheriff Brody have to say when you told him about Deveraux dropping by the shop?"

A chill swept up her spine as she realized she hadn't told the sheriff everything. "I... um... forgot to tell him."

Her grandmother closed her eyes and leaned her head back against the pillow. "Call him. Now!"

An hour later, duly chastised, Temperance drove home, followed by Deputy Hammond. "Are you sure you're not hungry?" she asked. "I can defrost some red sauce and put on a pot of pasta."

His gaze swept the perimeter before he let it rest on her. "Maybe later. I need to check the barn and over by the edge of the woods first."

"Thanks, Jack," she said. "I'll go fix supper now, that way I can warm it up for you whenever you have a few minutes to eat."

His smile softened the hard planes of his face and warmed the cool blue of his eyes. The contrast between Deputy Jack Hammond and Mr. Deveraux was night and day... *good and evil*. She shivered.

"Are you going to be all right?" the concern in his voice warmed her.

"Yes, thanks, just thinking about something," she told him. "Just come on in whenever you're ready. I'll either be in the kitchen or the living room."

"Will do."

*

"Hey, Sheriff," Hammond said, a short time later. "All clear out in the Marsh."

"Good," Brady replied. "Deveraux has gone to ground and until he resurfaces, we can't let our guard down. I'm counting on you to guard Temperance."

"You have my word."

"I'll call you after my meeting with Simmons. He said he had some new information on the murders."

"We're going to nail this guy," Hammond grumbled.

"Count on it," Brody said. "Now get on back to your post."

*

Temperance couldn't say what woke her, but she pushed herself up in bed and leaned against the mahogany headboard. Breathing deeply, she tuned into the sounds of the night and the old house she shared with her grandmother.

"There," she whispered as a board creaked. "Third step from the bottom." She slipped out of bed and fumbled in the dark for the iron lamp on the bedside table and unplugged it. The iron flower stem fit her hand perfectly. She tiptoed over to the door, flattened her back against the wall, and waited.

Someone was breathing heavily just outside her door. Praying for strength, she lifted the lamp above her head. When the door burst open, she jerked the lamp down with as much force as she could. The groan of pain didn't faze her at all.

The intruder collapsed to the floor and adrenaline surged through her veins. She jumped over the fallen body, hurtled down the steps, and didn't stop until she reached the deputy's cruiser. The driver's door was open, but there was no sign of the deputy.

The sound of a phone buzzing had her looking down, there by the car… it had to be the deputy's phone. She picked it up. "Hello? This is Temperance Lippincott. I'm standing by Deputy Hammond's cruiser, but he's not here. Someone was in my house… I hit him on the head. He's in my bedroom."

"Slow down. Breathe," Brody told her. "I'm almost there. Hammond called me about fifteen minutes ago."

Temperance refused to give in to the fear welling up within her. "Then why can't I find him," she asked.

"We'll sort it out when we get there."

"We, who?"

"My buddy Simmons from the Bureau is riding shotgun," he told her. "I want to you to listen carefully."

She willed her hands to stop trembling. "Yes, okay."

"Get into the cruiser," Brody told her. "Shut the windows, and lock the doors."

"But what if I see—"

"Do it now!" he thundered.

She jumped in the cruiser. Worried about the missing deputy, she sent out positive vibes and healing energy while waiting for Brody and Simmons to arrive.

Chapter Six

The sound of a fast-moving vehicle coming up the drive had her opening the driver's door and getting out.

"I knew my patience would pay off," a deep voice crooned as Temperance was grabbed from behind. Cruel fingers dug into her arms and she was pulled back against the all-too-familiar Deveraux.

"I thought I knocked you out," she whispered.

"Ah," he chuckled. "That would be my right-hand man."

Headlights cut across the driveway as the sheriff's car screeched to a halt. Deveraux slowly turned around, using Temperance as a shield.

Desperate to escape, her mind raced until a cold steel blade pressed against her throat.

"Come any closer," Deveraux warned, "and I'll slit her throat from ear to ear."

Brody raised his hands high and stepped back. "Drop the knife, and we can talk about this."

Deveraux's laugh made her skin crawl. "I don't think so."

"You're already in deep," the man at Brody's side called out. "We might be able to make a deal if you toss down the knife and give up."

"I do hate repeating myself," Deveraux said, "but I don't think so."

Temperance prayed that she had been right. Earlier when she'd done a spread, the Judgement card kept turning up. She hoped that her actions had mirrored the meaning of the card: change of position, renewal, outcome. But her gilded tarot card meaning swirled through her, demanding that she listen. She was being called to do something. Listen to the call and face it with courage and action.

Sweat trickled down her back and her belly cramped, but she didn't move an inch, knowing Deveraux would end her life without hesitation.

A shot rang out in the night, and Deveraux collapsed against her, toppling them both to the ground. The weight of him crushed the air out of her lungs. She struggled to catch her breath, but it was no use; her vision grayed and went black.

"Temperance!" a deep voice called as if from far away. "Snap out of it."

The heavy weight constricting her breathing was gone. She drew in a breath and sighed.

"That's it, come on."

She opened her eyes and saw the familiar deep blue of Deputy Hammond's gaze boring into hers. "Gave me a scare there, Temp."

"You didn't have a knife against your throat," she groaned as he helped her sit up.

"Where were you?" she demanded. "What happened?" As she focused on the man kneeling by her side, she realized his shirt sleeve was dripping with blood. "By the goddess! You're bleeding!"

"I know," he told her, "but I needed to make sure you were okay before I let them patch me up."

She realized then that they weren't alone, the first-aid squad, and the coroner were both there. "Where's Sheriff Brody?"

"He and Simmons are fine," Hammond reassured her. "Once you remembered to tell the Sheriff about Deveraux coming into your shop. The pieces to the puzzle fell into place, and they had the rest of the proof they needed."

"Then why is the coroner here?"

"Deveraux fell on his knife when I shot him in the shoulder."

"That's why he fell on me! You shot him in the back?"

"Call me crazy, but I was expecting a thank you." He started to ease away from her, but she grabbed a hold of his good arm and rasped, "Thank you!" Her eyes filled as she realized how close she'd come to being the one in the coroner's car.

"I wasn't ready to die," she confided.

"No way in hell would I let that happen," he told her.

Gram's teachings had saved her. Whatever energy you send out comes back to you three-fold. The scales of Justice had balanced with Deveraux's death.

"You're going to need stitches, Deputy," one of the first-aid volunteers told him as Hammond was helping her to her feet.

He dug in his heels. "I hate needles."

"I can ride in the back with you," Temperance offered. "And you can tell me why you didn't come in for dinner. I make a killer red sauce."

He let her lead him over to the ambulance and grumbled, "It's hard to explain, but I just had this feeling something bad was about to happen."

She smiled and pulled him onto the cot in the back. "Happens to me all the time," she soothed. "Do you believe in the Tarot?"

XV

THE DEVIL

16

THE DEVIL

MICHAEL M. HUGHES

Upright: Bondage, addiction, sexuality, materialism
Reversed: Detachment, breaking free, power reclaimed

I watched the psychic as he did his act, his clear blue eyes wide, waving his hands as he delivered messages from the dead. "Someone is coming through—a child. She was about five or six when she passed. She says her name is Emily or Emma and she's looking for her parents. She's pointing over here." He shaded his eyes from the stage lights and gazed off into the audience.

I had seen it all before.

I was on assignment from *Voices of Reason*, an online skeptic magazine. This particular fake on stage was Joseph Enoch, a rising star in the psychic world, with his own TV show and sold-out venues around the world. I had set up a one-on-one session ($1200 for 45 minutes) with him after this performance—if I could make it that long without puking all over myself.

A couple near the front stood up. Enoch led them along with some obvious cold reading, and most likely, some facts gleaned from pre-show electronic eavesdropping. I felt my jaw clench as the woman burst into tears and sobbed in her husband's arms. His lips trembled and then he, too, started crying. It was sickening. Milking the rubes by pretending to be psychic was bad enough, but making obscene profits off the desperation and gullibility of bereaved parents? That was diabolical, and that was why I was here. To finally nail the bastard—and nail him good.

I had over a hundred pages of notes for my story already, but today I was going for the coup de grace—meeting Joseph Enoch face-to-face while wearing a concealed mic. I'd given his organization, The 401(c) Joseph Enoch Foundation, a false identity when I signed up for my consultation over a year earlier (Enoch's waiting list for private consultations now stretched beyond two years). The real Peter Meyers was a friend of my editor's and an aeronautical engineer who hated charlatans as much as I did. He looked quite a bit like me, and with an offer of a substantial chunk of cash, he allowed me to take over and edit his meager profiles on LinkedIn, Facebook, and Twitter. For over a year I'd laid out a honeytrap of bogus data waiting for Enoch's crew of slimebags to dig into, but I also included comments about a real tragedy—touching reminiscences about Peter Meyers's deceased wife, Kelly, who had died of bone cancer.

The plan was simple: I would go to the consultation posing as Meyers and catch Enoch in his deception. It was brilliant, and I couldn't wait to see the final act unfold.

*

After the final, nearly deafening applause—Enoch definitely knew how to work a room—I lined up with a handful of others for our one-on-one meeting. A smartly dressed, twenty-something blond wearing a headset approached me. She wore spiked heels and held an iPad against her chest.

"Mr. Meyers?"

I nodded. "That's me."

"Joseph will see you shortly. He needs a few moments to collect himself after these large events. It is terribly draining for him to deal with all that energy—I'm sure you understand."

"Oh, yes," I said. I had been a theater major in college and could still be a damned good actor when I tried. "I read his autobiography, *Love Never Dies*." I pulled the book out of my bag—almost three hundred pages of vacuous dreck and confabulated anecdotes with a cover painting of a smiling, radiant angel. A blond-haired angel, naturally. "Do you think he'll sign this for me?"

"Of course," she said. She smiled and moved to the next person in line. Nice legs. Enoch, like most of his fellow celebrity psychics, liked to surround himself with good looking men and women. People tend to trust them more. It was all part of the long game.

When I put the book back in my bag I double-checked the concealed electronics. I was wired to the hilt, with an extra shielded mic in case Enoch was using any kind of cellular jamming technology. The recording would be backed up wirelessly to my phone, and from there transmitted live to our IT guy, Barry, who was sitting in his car outside the venue. Redundancy was key. The magazine had spent a lot of money—money it didn't have—to make sure we got this right. Bringing Enoch down would more than make up for it in new subscribers and all the attendant publicity.

A few minutes later the cute lackey returned. "This way, Mr. Meyers."

*

The assistant led me to a small table across from Joseph Enoch, then nodded and left us alone in the room, shutting the door behind her. Despite having rehearsed this moment dozens of time in my mind, I was still nervous. There was no other furniture, nothing but the table and two chairs. No candles, crystals, incense, flowers, or any of the usual junk psychics used to create atmosphere. Just a plain, white tablecloth.

"Mr. Meyers," Enoch said, extending his hand.

"Please call me Peter," I said. His hand was warm, his grip strong.

Enoch motioned for me to sit, then took his seat across from me. His smile and bright eyes were disarming. No wonder so many people fell for him—he had the faux-earnest charm of a sociopath. "I apologize that it took so long to schedule this consultation. There are so many people, and alas, only one of me."

"No, please don't apologize," I said. "I'm happy to finally be here." I dropped the bag to the floor next to me and pressed the "on" switch. My phone vibrated in my pocket to let me know it was recording. My hands were shaking. "I'm a little nervous," I said.

"Please, don't be," he said. "There is nothing to fear. Spirit will guide us." He reached out with both hands. "Let me take your hands for a moment." He took my hands in his. "Close your eyes and breathe deeply. Are you a religious man, Peter?"

"I was raised Catholic." That much was true. And one of the major reasons I'd become an atheist in my 20s. "I consider myself spiritual, but not really religious anymore." That's how most of the air-headed new-agers I'd interviewed described themselves. So I figured I'd go with that.

"Understood," he replied. His hands tightened slightly on mine, which were now slick with sweat. "Just let yourself relax. Breathe deeply through your nose and let go of your tension. Open yourself to Spirit, Peter. Let it fill you."

I took a deep breath and exhaled. I didn't like men holding my hands. I'm not homophobic or anything, but it just felt awkward.

"Again," he said. "In deep through your nose. Visualize the white light of loving Spirit entering you. Then let it out with abundant grace. Like a kiss of thanks to the universe."

I breathed even more deeply, then let the air out through my lips. Typical boundary loosening techniques—get your mark relaxed and suggestible before going in for the kill. But how anyone fell for this treacle I would never understand. *A kiss of thanks to the universe? Jesus Christ.*

"Okay, open your eyes." Enoch released my hands. His smile had softened, and he looked at me with curiosity. "Have you ever had a tarot reading?"

I froze. "Just... once." I had never heard of Enoch doing anything other than his medium shtick. "Are you going to talk to the spirits?" I *had* paid for him to talk to dead people.

He smiled, his eyes locked on mine. "Of course. But sometimes Spirit directs me to other avenues of communication." He reached beneath the table and brought back a bundle wrapped in white silk. His hands were meticulously manicured. "You're not afraid of these cards, are you, Peter?"

"No. Of course not."

"Good," he said, unwrapping the bundle. He removed the deck and spread it facedown in a fan across the table. "There's nothing dangerous about these cards. They're just pictures on paper, after all. They only show us what Spirit needs us to know." The blue-patterned backs were worn and faded. He folded his hands. "Please touch just one of the cards. The card that calls to you the most."

I did my best to make it seem like I was struggling with the choice, tentatively hovering my hand until I finally brought my finger to rest on one of the cards. "This one," I said.

"Slide it toward you, but don't turn it up yet," Enoch said.

I did as I was instructed. This was annoying. Twelve-hundred dollars for a fucking tarot card reading? Where was the spirit of my dead wife? Was he going to read my palm next, or run his hands along the bumps in my scalp?

He seemed to sense my frustration. "Let's just leave it there for now." He sat back and put his hands in his lap. "So, Peter, shall we see who will come through for you?"

I nodded. Now we were getting somewhere.

Enoch closed his eyes and lowered his head. It was almost as if he had fallen asleep. After a minute or so he lifted his head, and when his eyes opened it was as if someone else had stepped into his body. He seemed like a different person. An amazing act, all conveyed with subtle yet powerful alterations of his expression. I'd watched the transition before in dozens of videos, but it was shocking in person. When he spoke, his voice had also changed, slightly higher and monotone. "Peter, I see a woman behind you. She has short brown hair. She's happy now, but she says she was very sick when she passed on. The sickness was in her bones." His stare was unnerving.

"Yes. My wife, Kelly." I nodded excitedly. "What is she saying?"

"She says she misses you, but she is always watching over you. And she forgives you for forgetting your anniversary."

Bingo—a detail straight from a Facebook post I made five months ago. A moving, but made-up, memory of forgetting our 15th anniversary. Complete with weeping emoticon. I put my head in my hands and surreptitiously rubbed both eyes with my right finger, which I had earlier coated with a dab of menthol. The tears came quickly. "Tell her I'm sorry. That was stupid."

"She's smiling. She understands. She says you were always forgetting things. Like when you left the stove on and almost burned the house down, or when you forgot to pick her up at the train station in Baltimore." Enoch reached beneath the table. "Here are some tissues." I took a tissue, wiped my eyes, and blew my nose. "Thank you," I said.

He looked past me. The ruse was brilliant—his mannerisms and acting were so sincere I was almost convinced he was talking to a dead woman behind me. "She says it made her happy that you left her flowers on her grave on her birthday. You remembered how much she loved sunflowers. That made up for everything you forgot."

More hits. He was digging his own grave with every bogus revelation. This was gold. Every bit of it had been created in the editorial office meeting during the planning stage. I was waiting for him to hit on the miscarriage.

"She's holding out a baby to you. A little boy."

I put my head in my hands again. For a moment I thought I might laugh and blow the whole thing. Instead I took a deep, dramatic breath and whispered Kelly's name through blurred eyes.

"She says he looks just like you now," Enoch continued. "He's going to grow up just fine here. He has your eyes, Peter. He watches you and learns from you. He wants to grow up to be just like you."

Again I fought back laughter. This was too good. I could already taste the sweetness of the takedown when this inane conversation was made public. We had him screwed to the wall—reciting verbatim the fictional Peter Meyers chronology. So much for his spirit guides. I could just let him unspool for the rest of the session because we already had enough to end his era on the celebrity psychic throne.

And then he laughed. His eyes lost their faraway glaze and sparkled as he first chuckled, then burst into full-bore laughter.

I wiped at my eyes with the wadded tissue. "What is it?" He was pounding the table with his fists now. "Did Kelly say something funny?"

That sent him into heaving paroxysms of laughter.

"Joseph?" This was odd. In all the videos I'd watched he'd never lost that fake earnestness. This was a serious breach, and it made me uneasy.

He snorted, wiped at his own eyes, and leaned across the table. "I'm sorry, I can't do this anymore." He laughed again, his face reddening.

I felt suddenly light-headed. "What do you mean?"

He whistled and shook his head. Spread his arms. "This. All this."

I realized I was holding my breath. I started to speak but he interrupted me.

"I know who you are. Your name isn't Peter."

The shock on my face was real. God damn it. He was onto us. The bastard had somehow got wind of the sting. Which meant someone had tipped him off. "I don't know what you're—"

He held his hand up to silence me. He fixed me with his sharp blue eyes. "No more fucking around, James. Okay?"

The room seemed hotter. Sweat beaded on my forehead and dripped from my armpits. He was holding me over the fire. It was his turn now.

"Who do you serve, James? Who is your master?"

I wiped sweat from my eyes. How much to tell him? At least we had hard evidence that he had used the fake profile to make up the messages from beyond. But this turn of events was messing with my head, and I wasn't sure how it was going to play out. But as I sat, bewildered, looking at his perfectly made-up face, I got mad. "I serve truth," I said. "Rationality, not superstitious nonsense. Not lies. Especially not lies that exploit sad, messed up people."

For a moment, I thought he might lunge at me. Could I make it to do the door before he did? For all his soft-spoken gentleness on stage, he was well-muscled beneath his tailored shirt. Would he really be foolish enough to assault me? Adding criminal charges on top of being exposed as a fraud?

He burst out laughing again, even louder than before.

"How is this funny, Enoch?" I was pissed now.

He stood, one hand on his stomach, and waved for me to stop. "Please, James."

I stood and grabbed my bag. "You think this is funny? This is the end of your career. This is the end of you ripping off gullible people. You're done, Enoch. It's over. You're ruined." It felt good to say it. It was true. But why wasn't it upsetting him?

He stifled his laughter in his fist. "Okay, okay. James, please. You got me. Mea culpa. Just sit for a moment. You can keep recording—that's fine by me. In fact, I'd prefer it."

I sat down. Let him tighten the noose—this was turning into high entertainment.

He dropped into his chair and put his feet up on the table. "First, you never answered my question. Who is your master, James?"

The cat was out of the bag, so why not. "*Voices of Reason* magazine. Surely you've heard of us."

He seemed puzzled. "Oh, I know who you work for, James. That's not what I'm asking. I want to know—who is your *master*?"

"I don't know what you mean."

He waved away my answer as if irritated. "I think you'll understand very well in due time. But first indulge me. Since you're ending my career with this little trick, can you give me one last chance to prove I'm not a liar and a con man? To prove that I can talk to the dead?"

I snickered. He was desperate. "Sure. Be my guest." The writing was on the wall, but this could be fun. And the tape was still rolling. I imagined Barry listening in while sitting in his car, punching his fist into the air. We would all get a fat raise out of this.

Enoch lowered his head, and when he raised his eyes they again had his trademark alien, affectless gaze. "An older woman is coming through. Two names. Mary. Mary Elizabeth." He paused. "No— Mary Ellen. Your mother." His eyes seemed to be looking through me, as if I wasn't even there.

"Impressive," I said. It was hot as hell in the room. His assistant must have cranked up the heat. "Did it take you three minutes to find that online?"

He ignored me. "She wishes you had come to see her more when she was sick. After the operation. When her breasts were removed. Instead of running around and drinking so much with your friends."

"Seriously?" I rolled my eyes. "That's all you got?"

Enoch's brow knotted. "And she's still upset with you about that thing you did when you were a boy. What you did with her underwear."

I froze.

"Rubbing yourself with it. And while she was at church. How mad you got, and how you never admitted it even though she caught you. The language you used with your mother."

"Shut up," I said. *This was impossible.*

"Wait—there's a little girl coming through now. Her hair in braids, blond hair. A blue and white dress. She's showing me a shed. With peeling paint."

I felt a tightness in my chest. It was getting hard to breathe and I was starting to hyperventilate. Enoch leaned over me, his arms clutching the edge of the table, muscles taut.

"She's mad at you, too, James. She didn't understand what you were doing to her, but you hurt her and told her she couldn't tell anyone. She never got over what you did. Never got over the shame. The feeling of being dirty."

"Shut the fuck up," I hissed between heaving breaths.

"Did you know she tried to kill herself twice before she finally succeeded? No, because you moved away when you were thirteen. She's showing me how her mother found her. In her bed, with her father's gun. Her blood and brains splattered all over the wall."

"Stop it," I said. I tried to stand but I could no longer breathe, and my chest felt like someone was squeezing it in a vice.

"She has been watching you. All the time. And she wants you to stop. She knows what you did to Sarah's daughter. Your boss's little daughter. When you had ten minutes alone with her."

I sucked vainly for air but it wouldn't come. It was as if my lungs were plugged with concrete.

Enoch reached over and picked up the tarot card. Held it in front of my face. A leering, goat-headed creature with the black wings of a bat. Number XV. A man and a woman chained below the demon, seemingly resigned to their fates. "This is who you serve, James. You don't serve reason. Or truth. You are a tool of the Disenchanter."

The edges of my vision began to melt into white. Enoch pushed the card closer to my face, and the image enveloped me.

"You serve him," Enoch continued louder, his hot breath in my face. "The Deceiver who severs the spirit from the flesh, the Father of Lies and Abominations. You are a thief of innocence, an idolator, and your judgment will be swift and merciless."

I don't remember losing consciousness, or Barry rushing in the room to find me sprawled on the floor, or anything before waking up in the ICU with two cops standing in the doorway.

*

My new cellmate is a white supremacist with a shaved head and an inverted cross and three sixes tattooed on his neck. He's an

Odinist. He likes to tell anyone who will listen—he got religion in a state prison in Tennessee. Before he burned a bunch of churches and synagogues, he was a grunt in Iraq at the Abu Ghraib prison, where he learned to hurt people without leaving marks. The Norse gods hate weakness, he says, so what he does to me is his holy duty.

Yesterday, he told me the gods gave him the gift of prophecy. Says he had a vision of me sliced up real good and bleeding out in the cell. "Right there," he said, pointing to the floor by the toilet. "I was laughing at you and your guts all hanging out."

If I believed in anything at all, it might be his gods.

You're probably not surprised that *Voices of Reason* killed the story. No one at the magazine, much less in the wider skeptical movement, wanted anything to do with me, and Sarah told me she would kill me herself if I didn't die in prison. So they basically erased me and everything I'd written over the years. Swept up my tracks and paid to have me cleansed from the search engines.

I got something in the mail last week from the Joseph Enoch Foundation. I didn't have to open the envelope.

I knew exactly what was waiting for me inside.

17

THE TOWER

REBECCA PAISLEY

Upright: Misery, distress, ruin, indigence, adversity, calamity, disgrace, deception
Reversed: The same to a lesser degree, also oppression, imprisonment, tyranny

Once upon an era no one has ever heard of, there lived a man who believed the finest things about himself. He bragged about his mesmerizing handsomeness and proclaimed his intelligence was unequaled. Of course, he also professed his physical power could never be bested either. He was of the assumption that treetops rustled in adulation. Lightning paid its homage with slashes of fireworks, and mighty thunder applauded his very existence.

He had never received any votes that would have won for him a seat of power. Such a ballot or show of hands never happened. Nor had he inherited any sort of right to rule. Nevertheless, his pompous demeanor frightened the folk who lived in the village. Oh, but he was a vainglorious man. Superior to all, he believed, and he appointed himself grand enough to be called The Grandiose.

He demanded money from the people. Bows and curtsies. He required the villagers to plant and tend grain fields or sew beautiful clothing for him. Children brought food to him, meals that kept their mothers at the hearths for many long hours.

It didn't matter what The Grandiose required. The villagers met each of his desires because they feared the wickedness his enormous conceit could possibly bring about. Many longed to escape, but where would they go? There was nothing beyond the woods that encircled the town. No life, no anything. So they lived each day in servitude to The Grandiose, who one day ordered far more than money, food, clothing or genuflections.

He'd determined that no one except himself had the right to be happy. And so he forbade joy. He stopped all music and dancing and singing. Children could no longer play, and he forced adults to go through their days without so much as a smile toward anyone. If he noticed as much as a hint of some inner pleasure in anyone's *eyes* he would deny that person rest until the rule-breaker finally collapsed with appalling exhaustion.

And The Grandiose always knew when someone felt a bit of peace. Not a jot of content escaped his notice. The villagers came to believe he knew everything, and their anxiety and misery fed the fire of cruelty that flamed inside him. Yes, The Grandiose rejoiced over having erased all manner of delight in the town.

Until he witnessed how very much the people loved their pets. This could not be allowed, he decided. He would put an instant end to it.

It was with horrendous grief that the townspeople took their precious animals deep into the woods, where The Grandiose had ordered a stone enclosure built. Sobbing and wailing filled the forest as the people left their pets within the rocky pound. Their dear animals would be hungry and thirsty, they cried. Surely their beloved pets would not understand why their owners had left them to suffer and die.

The Grandiose laughed wholeheartedly while enjoying the people's torment.

And over the days, the villagers' sorrow continued to grow and deepen. It roared and rumbled over the land, through the air, and up into the sky.

Until it finally awakened a sleeping magic.

Chapter Two

Iva poured a bowl of milk before she remembered her cat, Pillie, wasn't there anymore. Her tears splashed into the pitcher, causing white ripples in the creamy liquid. "Pillie," she whispered. "Pillie." She wrapped her arms across her chest, closed her eyes and saw him. White, he was, with one blue eye and one green. His fur was softer than the softest thing she could imagine, and she missed its comforting silk.

Was he still alive? But how could he be? Weeks had passed since The Grandiose had ordered all the village pets to be abandoned in the woods. And it was cold now, too.

Shivering, Iva looked at Pillie's blanket by the tiny fireplace and swiped her wet cheeks. She sat down by the little window and watched the rain turn dirt into mud. The small village square had once been covered with thick green grass and beautiful flowers. Filled with laughter and songs and happy chatter. Now it was brown and sad.

Iva reached for her sewing basket. Inside was the cloak she was making for The Grandiose. He was waiting for it, and she was already a day late. Would he force her to stay awake until she could no longer stand? Oh, if only she could somehow poison the thread so that when he put the garment on, its venom would kill him!

But she dared not even ponder such a thing. The Grandiose would know. He always knew. He declared himself all-powerful, and maybe he really was. He might as well have lived like a king in a castle with a tower. A tower from which he could observe the hamlet and all its fearful people. A sky-piercing tower made of very cold stones that would freeze him, she thought. At the very least a tower somewhere in the village. If such a thing could be true, maybe the tower would fall on him, crushing him to death. As it was, however, he lived in the biggest house in the town. His own village palace, filled with lovely furniture. And rugs. And a real bed with heavy quilts and full pillows.

Unlike her tiny one-room cottage with her straw mat on the chilled floor.

She made herself stop longing for the death of The Grandiose. His eerie knowledge would alert him to her violent thoughts.

Night had come, and she sewed, and finally made the last stitch in the cloak. Trepidation made her hands shake when she folded the cape into a sack. The Grandiose was abhorrent during the day and even more so at night. She dreaded having to see him this evening. Lately, he had been staring at her in a way that made her feel naked and panicked.

She slipped into her old shawl. While The Grandiose clothed himself with the most wonderful garments the village women could sew for him, they themselves wore rags. The family that lived in the dilapidated dwelling next to her own didn't even have shoes.

Casting one last glance at Pillie's empty blanket-bed near the measly fire, Iva left her hut and set out for the biggest house in the town.

When would this end? she wondered. This day in and day out of wretched existence? How could this be all there was? Nothing and more nothing.

And poor Pillie and the rest of the adored village pets. All the sweet creatures who counted on their owners to take care of them...

"Please," she whispered to no one. Her memories of Pillie made her ache. "Please—"

She stopped suddenly. A noise. An intimidating sound. Something strong and alarming. She peered all around where she stood, trying desperately to understand what she had heard.

She saw bits of blue in the blackness. Circles of blue. She blinked, but the blue sparkles were no longer there.

Like always, there was nothing. She began to hurry to the big house of The Grandiose, doing her best to avoid the holes in the muddy ground.

She didn't see the glint of the blue eyes of the man who watched her run. Nor did she hear the terrible noise as it sounded again.

"Settle, Rewot," Basque said as he continued to watch the girl race away. Iva was her name, he knew. From within the shelter of the woods, he'd seen her. The people who lived around her had called her Iva. "Settle," he said again.

Rewot growled once more before disappearing into the forest with his master.

Chapter Three

The Grandiose lounged upon a blue velvet settee big enough to accommodate his large form. Fingering the folds of the silk robe he wore, he looked through the window. She was coming tonight. Iva. Pretty Iva, with her long gold hair. Tonight he would enjoy holding fistfuls of it.

She was the most comely wench he'd ever seen, and he'd seen all the village women. He'd used many of the hags while waiting for Iva to become the beautiful woman she'd finally become.

He picked up his wine glass, sipped the blood-red liquid, and licked his lips when he heard a barely-there knock on the door. "Open the door and get out," he told the young boy whose night it was to serve him. Viciously, he slapped the child's face once, and then again.

When the terrified lad did as bade, Iva stepped into the spacious room and held out the bag. "It is finished, Grandiose." She heard the apprehension in her own voice and wished her fright was not so blatant. Fear nourished his black soul.

She doubted he even had a soul, black or otherwise. "Here." She lifted the bag a little higher.

"You used the pearl buttons?"

"I did."

"You did…" He waited for her to address him in the proper manner.

"I did, Grandiose."

He watched as the glow of many candles and fire flames gleamed through her yellow tresses. "You're a day late. What shall I do with you, sweet Iva?" He toyed with her feelings, liking the way she stiffened as she sensed his mood. Gazing at her luscious breasts, he realized she'd tried to hide them with her frayed wrap. The tattered cape did little to cover what he wanted to see and touch.

"Well?" he demanded. He tapped his fingers on his wine glass.

"Forgive me, Grandiose." Iva closed her eyes so she wouldn't have to see his hot, unnerving stare. "The days of rain have darkened my room, and I couldn't see well enough to—"

"Did I ask you for a reason? An excuse?" He felt true irritation with her now. "And how dare you force me to strain my eyes in order to see you. Take off that ugly scrap of a shawl and come closer to me."

Iva pulled at the wrap, dismayed when it fell onto the sumptuous white carpet beneath her feet. She started for The Grandiose, but something inside her, some force, stilled her. "My shoes are covered with mud, Grandiose. I don't want to soil your rug."

He pitched his glass at the wall. It exploded into hundreds of shiny bits. "I said come here."

She felt naked again, but she walked slowly toward him. His little black eyes seemed to touch her like tangible things. Shuddering, she held out the bag again.

He knocked it out of her hands and grabbed her hair. A thick handful of it. His wet lips curled into a smile. "I don't bite, Iva," he said. "I devour." And with that, he pulled her onto his lap.

She could not escape him. His held her fast. Too hard, but he loved the sound of her whimpers of pain. "You knew this night would come, didn't you, sweet Iva?" His breath quickened as he pulled the top of her frock from her shoulders. "I've waited for this and will wait no more." He bent his head and rubbed his face upon her pale breasts.

Iva could move naught but her legs. She kicked at air. Her efforts caused her dress to bunch up around her thighs.

"Ah, you're ready too, sweet Iva?" He slid his hand between her legs and found no undergarments to impede his search. Chuckling to himself, he knew she had no money for such luxuries.

When his fingers found her womanly softness, he could control his lust no longer. Effortlessly, he stood, but kept her in his arms. The stark fear on her beautiful face excited him to the point of panting, and he relished the fact that he would take from her that which she was so completely unwilling to give to him.

In but a moment, his robe slid to the floor.

Iva averted her gaze from the horror of him. She wanted to run but knew escape was impossible. She didn't move, could not speak. And soon she was as naked as he'd always made her feel.

The Grandiose felt slobber at the corners of his mouth. With his knee, he pushed her thighs apart and covered her body with his own. "Iva," he whispered raggedly. "Sweet—"

He gasped, and his eyes widened.

Through the window he saw two circles of blue. And he heard a sound so gruesome that it made him, The Grandiose, scream.

Chapter Four

His sudden shriek and subsequent crash to the floor stunned Iva. Confused, but realizing she could flee, she grabbed her dress, raced toward the door, and flung it open. Once outside, she fled through the village as if carried by a powerful wind. Her torn dress slipped from her grasp and fell into the mud, but she continued her flight, too afraid to care about her nakedness.

And too afraid to clearly see where she was going, what was ahead of her.

She slammed into a wall.

The wall moved, as if alive.

Basque gathered her into his arms and felt her begin to convulse. He gently moved her wet hair away from her face while continuing to hold her close to him. "Iva," he said so quietly he almost didn't hear himself speak. "You're safe, Iva."

Her terror only deepened. Wildly, she sought to see him, part of her sure The Grandiose had somehow run ahead of her and captured her.

And there it was again. That sound she'd heard earlier in the night when she'd been on her way to the big house of The Grandiose.

It was a growl, she realized, still stricken with fear. A beast.

To her frenzied mind, both the man and the animal were feral.

She had escaped The Grandiose, only to be apprehended by another man who was bent on violating her. But who could this man be? She knew all the men in the village, and this man was not one of them. Counting on her fear to give her the strength she desperately needed to fight her way out of his arms, she tried to hurl herself to the ground.

"Iva."

Who was this man? she tried to understand again. How did he know her name? And was that a sword hanging from the sash of his breeches? With all the energy she had left, she twisted to see his face.

Two bits of blue sparkled down at her.

They were eyes. Eyes. The circles of blue she'd seen in the dark only a while ago were eyes. Their sparkle somehow calmed her. The longer she stared into them the more still she became.

"There now," Basque said as she stopped fighting him.

"Who are you?" She'd never seen eyes such as his. Nor had she noticed any man in the village as strong as this man was. His muscles caressed her bare breasts.

Her bare breasts. She was naked. Her head fell over his arms. Naked or not, she was too exhausted to battle him any longer.

Carefully, Basque set her on her feet but remained ready to catch her if she fell or tried to run. He removed his cloak and swaddled her within its black layers.

Its thickness and scent warmed her immediately.

Why was she trying to run away from this man? she asked herself as she looked into his wonderful eyes again. He'd caught her not to hurt her, but to save her.

His hair was blacker than the night. It brushed his shoulders, a striking contrast next to his very white shirt. "Who—"

"I'm Basque. I've been watching you from within the trees that circle this little place where you live. I've heard your name spoken by your people, Iva."

His explanation made no sense to her. No one lived out of the village. There was nowhere else to live. Only nothingness existed beyond the woods.

So where had he come from, and what was he doing here? "Who are you?"

He smiled down at her. "I told you. My name is Basque. Rewot and I heard you and the other people here crying for help. We'd been asleep for— Well, I don't know how long. Years. Maybe centuries. I don't remember. I believe it was the magic of your calling that awakened us."

"Magic? Asleep? Where?" Iva had never known such bewilderment. "And who is Rewot?"

He grinned again, and she knew a second of calm contentment that would certainly enrage The Grandiose. "I cannot be happy," she informed him. "I don't know who you or Rewot are, but The Grandiose—"

"He will never hurt you again, Iva. Nor any of your people here. I promise." Ever so slowly, he caressed her damp cheek, relieved when she didn't flinch at his touch. "And Rewot is my dog. At least I call him a dog. He's more wolf than dog."

Iva tried not to like the feel of his fingers on her face. The Grandiose would know and punish her, no matter what this Basque man said to the contrary. "I must go back to my cottage. I have to hurry. The Grandiose will find me!"

"Wait!" Basque caught her again. "I told you he—"

"What do you know of him?" she demanded. "You don't live here, and there isn't anything or anyone beyond the forest. You cannot be real. You're—"

"A thing of your imagination? I assure you I am real, Iva. And so is Rewot." He snapped his fingers.

Iva paled and felt faint as a huge animal appeared out of the dark. She could see his sharp teeth, and his fur seemed to be silver. Or was it the moonlight that made him silver? Black-haired Basque and his silver beast. She clutched the cloak more tightly around herself, her turmoil beating steadily through her.

"I'll take you home, Iva," Basque said. "And that man whose ego has imprisoned you and the other people will never have control of this village again. Do you believe me?"

She remembered his strength and the sparkle of his very blue eyes. His soothing smile. Perplexed as she was, how could she not believe this man called Basque? She allowed him to tuck her hand in the crook of his elbow and begin to lead her through the dark street.

But her knees buckled.

Basque caught her again and carried her the rest of the way.

Chapter Five

Iva awakened upon her straw mat in her little cottage with no memory of how she got there. Hadn't she been caught by The Grandiose? But if that were true, why had he returned her to her home?

He wouldn't have.

She slid her fingers through her matted, muddy hair before realizing how warm she was. No fire crackled in the hearth, but she felt so very warm and comfortable. And a pleasing fragrance surrounded her. The masculine scent came from the cloak she was wearing. A black cloak, and she suddenly remembered the man who had wrapped it around her.

Basque, he'd said his name was. She still didn't know who he was or where he'd come from. But he was real. She knew that now. And so was his silver beast, Rewot. What a peculiar name.

Determined to find Basque and his wolf-dog, she unfolded her body from its curled position on her mat and stood. After dressing in the last frock she owned, she looked through her window. But she saw only her neighbors and the other villagers.

She slipped her shoes on and searched for her shawl before recalling she'd left it in the big house of The Grandiose, the very evil man Basque promised would never hurt her or anyone else again. Snuggled in his cloak, she walked outside and searched everywhere for him. She asked her neighbors if they'd seen a strange man in the village. One of the women patted her hand, a gesture that meant the woman thought her insane.

"There was a man here last night," she tried to explain. "His name is Basque, and he has a wolf-dog called Rewot. He saved me from The Grandiose."

At the mention of The Grandiose, the villagers backed away from her and scurried to tend to their duties. Iva understood their fright. She'd lived with it for as long as she could remember.

But it was gone now, and all she could dwell upon was the promise Basque had made to her.

*

The Grandiose was in a rage. He knocked his servant girl to the floor and then kicked her. She whimpered, so he kicked her again.

He looked at the window. Fear seized him again. Had it been the wine? Had he been so drunk that he'd imagined whatever had been outside?

But he'd only had one glass, the bits of it still gleaming by the wall where he'd thrown it. He knew he'd seen something that was outside last night, and he knew he'd heard a ghastly sound as well. Sweat, colder than ice, covered his large frame. He'd never felt fear before now and didn't know what to do with it.

In a daze, he ordered the servant girl to dress him in clean clothes. Then he put on the cloak Iva had sewn for him and buttoned the pearls she'd attached down the front of the garment.

Where had the girl gone? Home? He marched out of his big house. The townspeople disappeared from the street, loathe to be seen. Once he'd arrived at Iva's hut, he pushed at the flimsy door until it splintered open.

Iva wasn't there. Fury and fluster made him grit his teeth and clench his hands into fists. When he found the girl, he would punish her severely.

No.

He would kill her. No one, not even the woman he lusted after, could be allowed to play him for a fool.

"Find Iva!" he screamed at the villagers he knew were hiding from him. "If she's not found by tonight, one of you will die. One of you will face the heinous death I'd planned for her!" His commands given, he stormed to his very big house and swatted the servant girl again.

*

From the shadows of the forest, Basque watched the arrogant and hateful man strutting through the town. The fur on Rewot's neck and back bristled, and the massive wolf-dog snarled. "He's going to kill her," Basque told his silver animal. "Or at least he thinks he is."

But Basque was aware of where Iva was. He'd seen her slip away into the very woods The Grandiose had forbidden the townspeople to enter. She sat behind the shrubbery at the edge of the dense thicket of the trees. Iva had not known where else to go, he comprehended. She was looking for him. She'd remembered the promise he'd made to her last night.

Her cries for help and the townspeople's overwhelming grief over the loss of their pets and their suffering at the hands of the man they called The Grandiose had, indeed, roused him and Rewot from their very long sleep. He knew not why or how they'd slept on the far side of the forest for so many years. He could only believe it really was a sleeping magic, as he'd suggested to Iva.

Today he would honor the oath he'd sworn to her.

*

The Grandiose paced through the lavish room in his very big house. He was treacherous, yes, but not stupid. The forest. It was the only place Iva could have found sanctuary. And none of the villagers would see her there. Not that a one of them would have ever brought her to him, anyway.

He opened a drawer in the immense cabinet beside the window and couldn't stop a quick look through the glass panes. Whatever he thought he'd seen outside last night was gone. If he saw it again, he'd kill it, just as he would Iva.

He had no doubt of his abilities. He was the most powerful man who had ever lived, and failed at nothing he decided to do. A confident smile on his mouth, he studied the velvet-lined drawer. An array of knives glistened up at him. He chose the longest, sharpest blade and left his very big house.

"Iva," he called when he'd reached the woods. "I know you're in here, sweet Iva." With his knife, he cut through the brush, his eyes and ears ready for the any sight and sound.

Before long, he spied a swirl of gold. Her hair. No one had hair like hers. "Ha!" he shouted, feeling extremely proud of his unequaled prowess. "There you are!"

On her hands and knees, Iva scrambled deeper into the forest, but The Grandiose caught her immediately. He yanked her off the ground and moved his hand over her breasts. He'd waited so long to possess her. To hear her cries of terror and pain. To feel her fight his intimate invasion.

Well, why couldn't he? he thought. Why not take her before he ended her life? She had to die, yes. It was simple as that. No one in the village who attempted to thwart him could live another day. Not even the exquisite woman who squirmed within his rough embrace.

"He'll kill you!" Iva bit his arm. "He promised!"

The Grandiose scowled, and a sliver of nervousness caught him unaware. "Who?"

Iva spat at him. "Basque! He swore you would never again hurt me or any of the people you've tortured for so long!"

"Who is this Basque?" The Grandiose closed his big hands around her slender neck. "Tell me now, and I might give you a quick and easy death."

"I think not," a strong and steady voice came from behind him. The Grandiose spun around and saw a man who held a sword. "Who are you?" he yelled.

"Iva just told you. I'm Basque. And this wolf-dog beside me is Rewot." Basque slid his finger down his sword. "But I have a dilemma. You see, I don't know whether to kill you myself or allow Rewot to do it for me."

The Grandiose laughed, his merriment clanging through the woods. He looked at the sword and the beast, and knew what he would do. What he was immensely talented at doing. In much less than a second, he threw his knife, knowing full well the blade would pierce Basque's heart.

But Basque dodged the spinning knife easily. He smiled at the man who had forced such misery on the village. "Rewot," he whispered.

The wolf-dog leapt and fell upon The Grandiose, its heavy body forcing the man to let go of Iva. He struck at the beast with all his might, still sure his knack for perfection would serve him well.

But his great skill was no match for the giant animal. Before The Grandiose could even comprehend what was happening to him, he screamed with the agony of monstrous teeth sinking into his own neck. He saw great surges of his blood drench the beast's head and ears.

And he felt his throat torn from the top of his chest before he died.

Iva staggered into Basque's open arms, weeping tears of deep joy. She saw the villagers crowd around her and the man who had rescued them all.

And she heard the pummel of many paws upon the leaf-strewn forest floor.

"Pillie!" she shouted when she caught sight of her very much loved and missed cat. "Oh, Pillie!" She broke from Basque's hug, picked up her pet, and nuzzled the softness of his little white head.

The other villagers saw their own pets as well. The noise of great happiness, a sound absent for so long, rang like bells.

"They were never alone, Iva," Basque told her. "I cared for them all, and Rewot kept them safe."

Pille still snuggled against her, Iva honored Basque with the first kiss she'd ever given to anyone. The townspeople clapped and sang and danced and led their precious pets back into the village, where they all belonged.

Iva watched the people for a bit, then smiled at Rewot. The beast was saturated with the blood of The Grandiose.

Basque had kept his promise.

"Rewot," she said as she continued to smile at him. "Thank you, Re—"

Her voice trailed away as she stared at the great wolf-dog. The mighty animal had fallen upon The Grandiose and swiftly killed the haughty man. She'd once wished a tower would fall on The Grandiose and smash him dead.

And Rewot was TOWER spelled backwards.

XVII

THE STAR

18

THE STAR

PATRICK FREIVALD

Upright: Loss, theft, privation, abandonment
Reversed: Arrogance, haughtiness, impotence

Dominic flinched as lukewarm beer spattered on his pants, the plastic cup tumbling away to fall behind the amplifier. "You suck!" rang out over the feedback and the drums, followed by a chorus of boos and jeers. His band finished the song under a growing din of hateful discontent, and he stared at his own feet and spoke into the microphone.

"Thank you! We're Deathsmack, and—"

"And you suck balls!" The massive biker-looking dude in the front row leaned on a sun-leathered barfly, his gray-black beard wet with cheap beer and spittle, her saggy tits barely contained by the straining fabric of a lime-green tube top. She flipped off the band and grabbed her crotch. He followed suit, rough hand sliding over hers to give a comical goose. The crowd laughed.

"Damn," Phil muttered, pretending to tune his guitar. "Even the fucking townies get more pussy than we do."

Jason hammered the bass drum, the unrelenting beat an introduction to a song they'd just added to their lineup, one of four original tunes in the set. The bass walked, almost bluesy, a contrast to the punk-metal tempo and the Pink Floyd-style rhythm guitar riff, exactly as they'd practiced until Phil botched his intro and came in a measure too late. Dominic sang the first notes, stopped, tried to pick it up on the second line, but Phil didn't adjust. The melody withered in his throat.

The lights died, and with them the speakers, and the owner stepped up shaking his head, hands raised. "Sorry, boys, but if I let you keep playing we're not even going to make overhead. Pack up and get out."

Ken finally faltered on the bass, his glassy eyes scrunching in confusion. An awkward grin spread across his face. "Did the power go out?"

The crowd cheered as Ian Grant's hit single, *Big Green*, blared through tinny speakers over the bar, drumming out the pop beat and the hometown hero's singing, still as smooth and intense as the day Dominic had met him, hooting out love songs—in harmony—to the girls on the sidewalk. They'd endured the rolled eyes and giggles with the pathological lack of shame only possessed by seventh-grade boys. Carefree days crushed under the weight of celebrity and envy.

Looking down to hide the wetness in his eyes, Dominic kicked their blurry setlist across the floor then stalked off stage. The insult-to-injury stabbed at his throat, and a gagging reflex just kept down the soggy chicken wings and limp fries he'd gotten from the bar after sound-check. Stomach roiling, he lurched for the door.

Dom had been the songwriter, Ian the singer. Gravel on silk, nothing could match the raw, jagged hurt Ian's voice had developed their senior year. Rolling in girls and money his whole life, nothing about it came from personal truth. But on the stage and in the studio no one could hear the lie, and nothing said "show biz" like false truths.

Rock stars.

They'd dreamed it together, chased it together, shared late nights and long days and girls and drugs and boys and sometimes each other and when the studios came for their demo tape they took the singer and left the songwriter behind to rot in the rocky ground of Bend Creek, Indiana. Gravel on silk, the sound of heaven, the sound of hell. Dominic got in the van, slammed the door, and screamed into his hands.

*

"Did you see this shit?" Phil shoved the flyer into his face, the eighty millionth Dominic had seen since that morning. *Ian Grant, July 9, Bend Creek Pavilion.* The international superstar would grace his hometown with a performance before leaving on the European leg of his world tour to promote *Small Town Cannibal.* Dominic's idea, brooding, blood-soaked metal twisted and reborn through the sanitized, homogenous imaginings of corporate suits into flavorless electronic pop.

"I saw it." Dominic dropped his fork into the congealed glop that passed for a sausage omelet at two on a Wednesday afternoon and didn't bother raising his eyes. "So what?"

"Maybe he'd let us open for—"

"I am NOT opening for Ian Grant."

Jason squeezed into the booth next to him, scooping up a handful of soggy, cheesy eggs and shoveling it into his mouth. "I thought," he sucked on his calloused fingers, "you wanted to be famous."

Dominic lifted his eyes to Phil's, half-obscured by stringy, dirty-blond hair the guitarist thought made him look like Kurt Cobain. "This an ambush?"

Even overruled at three-to-one, he'd never do anything with Ian Grant, not even a photo-op, not ever. To hell with band rules.

"Nah, man, Ken ain't here, so there's no vote." Phil sat, waving off the waitress as she approached, sunken eyes hopeful for a tip she'd probably blow on a bump of crystal. "We knew you wouldn't go for it. Just thought maybe you'd hook us up, get us backstage."

"Why would I get us backstage?"

Jason stole a lump of sausage from a puddle of grease. "So we can introduce ourselves, maybe meet his manager."

"I don't want—"

"We're not talking about you. We're talking about us."

Seething betrayal ravaged his nerves. Of course Deathsmack sucked; half the members would sell out their integrity for a taste of money or fame. They had no passion for the music, for the craft. "You want what he has."

"So do you. Asshole." Phil got up and stalked out of the booth. Jason joined him. "So do you."

The door jangled shut.

*

The shrieking of delirious fangirls jabbed ice picks behind his eyes, almost painful enough to distract him from the stink of perfume and sweat, the tang of marijuana and the cloying Victoria's Secret body spray used to mask it. And the concert wouldn't start for another two hours, Ian Grant an hour after that.

Dominic cut through the line to the side door and rapped a "shave and a haircut" with his knuckles. A black man, the size of a house, peered out, took in their backstage passes, and stepped aside just enough to let them through.

"Hey, we're Deathsm—"

"Down the hall." The bouncer closed the door and leaned against it. "He's expecting you."

Ken twirled past framed posters depicting concerts from decades past, legends and icons lost to drugs or age or an inability to sustain their creativity against the ravages of time. The rest followed, Jason and Phil playing it outwardly cool. Dominic just managed not to throw up as Ian Grant appeared in a doorway, teeth too white, brown hair too perfect.

The superstar shook hands, spending just enough time with each man before moving to the next, leaving them with a taste and wanting more. The world grew dark as he enveloped Dominic in a hug, crushing his heart and bones to lifeless jelly before pulling back and looking at him with pale brown eyes that shone with inner light.

"Dom. It's good to see you, man. It's been too long."

Dominic choked down years of abandonment, jealousy, and impotent regret. "Yeah. Too long."

The "green room" consisted of two leather couches and a coffee table piled with local barbeque, chicken and pork stacked high next to thick, crusty bread, and not a vegetable in sight. At Ian's insistence the band tucked in, everyone but Dominic chewing between excited questions about the road, the studios, and the groupies. His stomach lurched, hot bile tickling the back of his throat.

"It's not like you think." Ian's grin fell from his face. "It's exciting, but it's pretty lonely, and it's easy to spend too much on fans and fun. You got to work to save anything, 'cause this won't last forever."

Jason waggled his eyebrows. "But the groupies?"

"Are part of the problem." His eyes bored into Dominic's. "Nobody just wants to be your friend. Everybody you meet wants something, an angle, an introduction, a collaboration, maybe just a star-fuck. Even people from back home."

Ken held up his hands. "Fuck, man, Dom didn't even want to do this. We—"

"I'm sure he didn't. Enjoy the food and the show." Ian stood, brushed nonexistent lint from his jeans, and walked out.

Phil snorted. "You really hate each other, don't you?"

"Yes," Dominic said. *And no and never.*

*

Phil, Jason, and Ken left to enjoy the show. Dominic moseyed down the back hall, where a security guard's eyes wandered to his backstage pass before returning to stare straight ahead. A light flickered from a dark room to his left.

Eyes rose to meet his, deep black surrounded by whites turned blue by the screen of her phone. Soft, high cheekbones accentuated black lips and straight, dark hair, the only parts of her not lost to shadow.

"You must be Dominic." Harsh consonants pulled him into the room, an ancient accent from another continent, yet somehow English. Her screen went black, plunging the room into a nothing that swallowed light from the door.

"How do you know that?" The darkness around her devoured his voice, muffled it to a whimper.

"I smelled you on him when we first met. And I never forget a smell." Her tone shifted, became conversational. "Come in, have a seat."

The words dragged his feet and he approached, sank onto the lukewarm leather. Scant light emanating from the doorway betrayed nothing of her form, though her warmth crawled against his shoulder and thigh, her scent a mélange of mint and jasmine.

He cleared his throat. "So who are you, again?"

Hot breath tickled his neck. "He calls me Polyhymnia. I'm his sacred voice, and in this age, what is more sacred than sex and money? I'm everything you wanted but he stole. From his mother, from Mr. Charles, even from you, taken for his own as he abandoned you to this... life."

Confused, Dominic pulled away, but on the soft cushion her leg fell against his.

Mr. Charles had left a love note for his wife and swallowed a month's worth of oxycodone the summer before their senior year. The school hadn't replaced the beloved music teacher, instead assigning Mrs. Logan to the junior and senior high chorus as well as the bands. The whole program had suffered. Still suffered.

"What do you mean?"

Her low giggle shivered down his spine, stroked his groin, entered and infused him, a shudder of pleasure made sound. "Come on, Dom. You've felt the loss since he gained his voice, and your talent withered. You can't believe it's a coincidence."

"How... could it not be?"

Her voice grew hard. "I am not coincidence."

Melodies flooded him, harmonies and counter-harmonies, dark chords and bright trills, raw, screaming emotion on modern instruments. He gasped as they engorged him, cried out as they faded. "No, wait! I need—"

Her lips met his, breasts pressed against him, and her breath filled his lungs, sweet cherries and rich, dark chocolate, and a hint of something acrid.

She pulled away, panting, and whispered. "Take me from here. I am not his, I don't belong to this. Free me, and I'll give you everything."

"What are you talking about?"

A tornado of images shone in her wide, black pupils; screaming fans and hotel rooms, Deathsmack merchandise on Walmart shelves and in teenagers' rooms, red carpets and fast cars and Hollywood mansions, and at the center of it Dominic screaming into the microphone.

He pulled back, gasping. Then he lifted her from the couch, light as a feather, heavier than the cloud of depression that had become his reality, and ran.

*

Polyhymnia—Nia—whispered to him, and in the wake of her voice his imagination exploded across the page. Darkness and hunger made sound in his mind, flowing through his hands to ink dots on stanzas, chords and lyrics shining forth in a brilliance he'd never known he'd possessed. Stacks of pages had piled up, and at some point the phone had stopped ringing—he could only assume his boss had given up, figuring out that he'd quit.

Blinding light blasted across his vision. He squeezed his eyes shut, cracked them, and turned toward the door.

Ken stood, hand still on the light switch, eyes wide. "Dude. You need a shower."

Grinning, he leapt to his feet, stepping over piles of laundry and scattered music sheets to grab his friend by the shoulders.

"And to brush your teeth."

Dominic nodded, eyes wide and bloodshot in the reflection from Ken's glasses. "Yeah, sure. But we need to make a demo. Like, now."

Ken pulled back. "Shower, teeth, maybe a little food. Then we'll talk about a demo."

Dominic's stomach gnawed at his spine, and he swooned against the door. How many days had Nia whispered to him, driven him with her furious passion? He had no idea, and he didn't care.

"Okay, yeah."

*

After the last chord faded the sound tech killed the microphones. "That. Guys. That was incredible. I don't think I've heard anything that good in... in ever."

They high-fived, hugged, celebrated with beer and chicken wings at the local tavern.

Jason raised his glass in a toast, eyes on Dominic. "This is you, man. You're a freaking genius."

Glasses clinked. Dom ignored the sour taste that accompanied the smooth draft pouring down his throat. He slammed down the glass, got up, and stumbled to the bathroom, a mess of graffiti and filth under a single flickering lightbulb.

She met him in the stall, pulling back his hair as he threw up, semi-liquid chunks splattering the unflushed mound of paper and shit in the stainless steel bowl. His stomach settled but his mind roiled.

"Are you in my head?"

"No, but if you let me in you would see that what I've given is but a pale shadow of what we could be."

He raised his hands, palms up, to the glamor of their surroundings. "I could stand a little less of this glory."

Her sigh breathed solace through the stink of vomit and piss. "We've only just begun."

*

Dominic threw his sweat-soaked black T-shirt into the crowd with a triumphant scream, bowing as they roared their approval. The moment the lights, died he stalked off the stage. Their energy filled him to bursting. Dark filaments flickered in and out of substantiality, grasping, dragging him toward her. With a pirouette he tromped down the hall into the back parking lot, fumbled open his trailer door, then collapsed face-down on the couch inside. Throat raw, lungs burning, heart thundering, he couldn't keep the grin from his lips.

"He died tonight." Nia's voice squirmed through the dark, crawling across his veins and into his blood, sucking at the adulation, basking in the worship of the crowd.

"I know. I felt it during *Midnight's March*. Second song of the third set, a discordant wall of sound with symphonic accompaniment. It roared with new life at the moment of Ian Grant's death.

Ian's career had ended as meteorically as it had started. A competent musician, he'd never had the raw talent necessary for stardom, and when Dominic had stolen away with Polyhymnia mid-tour, his popularity plummeted and his fans had abandoned him, followed by his sponsors and then his label. In three months he'd snorted, injected, and drank his fortune to nothing, then spent two years in and out of rehab and jail.

"How?"

"Robbing a grocery with an Airsoft gun. The clerk had a shotgun. It will be on the news in due time."

He said nothing, content to give his former friend a moment of silence, and for once in thirty months Nia didn't take the last word. In the hall, a raucous crowd bumbled past the dressing room, his band and their entourages and a new stream of hot young groupies, the best on offer in... wherever they were. They'd be on buses the next morning and hit another city, then another. Phil, Jason, and Ken would enjoy the night, drinking and laughing and fucking, and he'd write their next hit, and their next, burning through Polyhymnia's limitless passion in an orgy of creativity.

Her passion. Her creativity.

Stolen by Ian Grant through black magic Dominic didn't understand, then re-gifted when Nia had abandoned his old friend.

She'd never given him an indication that she'd do the same to him, claimed Dominic had rescued her and that she'd serve him as long as he needed her. But her power rankled, her gifts offended his sense of pride. He had everything he'd ever wanted—fame, fortune, respect, a life doing what he loved—but "fraud" and "charlatan" skirted the dark corners of his heart, black rats gnawing at his happiness, denying him contentment with every greedy nibble.

He'd had talent before Ian had stolen it from him, some talent, enough to get by, maybe enough to climb the charts. But nothing like this. He'd written—she'd written—a thousand songs with his hand, stashed away in drawers and on remote servers, backed up and protected from fire or malice. A lifetime of work penned in two years of insomnia, all of it brilliant beyond measure, enough to create as many albums as he'd ever want. If only—

Nia sighed, a tickle on the back of his neck, a lingering promise across his skin. "He thought he didn't need me, too, in the end. Thought he could sustain what he'd taken from me, tricked himself into believing the lies of the mob. That he mattered, that he was worthy."

The TV flickered to life, muted, bathing the black-curtained trailer in a harsh LED glow. A talking head spoke in front of an ambulance. In the corner of the screen, Grant's latest mug shot scowled, skin sallow, cheeks gaunt, haunted eyes sunken and desperate. The splash banner scrawled SINGER IAN GRANT DEAD AT 24 across the bottom of the screen.

Her confident whisper nipped at his ear. Her fingertips stroked his naked back. "What more evidence do you need? He stole what

I've given you freely, and though that makes you righteous where he was not, it doesn't make you worthy. So be with me, use me, let me inside you, and enjoy the life I've given. Don't throw it away on an arrogant whimsy."

"It's not *whimsy* to be my own man." He spat the word out so as not to choke on the dismissive, condescending syllables. "I…"

He swallowed. Memories swirled with her voice in his ears, a haze of passion more glorious than sex, more sensual than the wildest of Deathsmack's already-legendary backstage parties. He couldn't remember a time before her smell, a breath before her taste on his lips, a night without her as his moon—his star.

"Don't say it." Her whisper turned almost petulant as she repeated the same old request. "You could be so much more than you are, not less. A sun blazing across the Earth, scorching all who come too near your brilliance. Don't push me away. Don't discard me. Don't leave me in your wake. Take me into you. Let me *be* you, and ride with me into unimaginable glory."

And that was it. He'd lost himself in her, giving everything he could without losing himself completely, and she only wanted more.

"I need to do this. Without you."

"You don't."

"I need to do it myself."

"You can't."

"I am. And I need you to leave."

Nothing. Then when she spoke he strained to hear the soft words. "Very well."

Sharp and clear, the darkness faded to a dull, earthy dusk. He cried out as her scent left him, mint and jasmine fading into decades of spilled beer and old spunk. Gagging, he rushed to the bathroom as vomit shot up his esophagus, splattering the floor and sink before plopping into the dingy toilet. Bile burned his throat and tongue. Aches ravaged his bones, seared his mind, and drained him of purpose until only a tiny spark remained—the final ember of a dying star.

His ember, not hers. Meager, mortal talent.

Pulling himself up, he wiped the stinging mess from his lips and washed his hands, then shuffled to the dresser. The next album would be his, with just a hint of Polyhymnia for inspiration.

Staring down at the open drawer, a moan escaped his throat. Page after page of sheet music lay in disordered piles, smudged and smeared beyond readability. He rushed to his laptop, typed in his username, and hesitated.

To log in he needed the password, the same word he'd used for everything—all his notes, his music, his output for the past two years—and in his mind her memory burned in its place.

"No." He tried a guess, something from his childhood. "NO." Another, the name of his first kiss. Her sad laughter mocked him, though real or imagined he couldn't say. "NO!"

He breathed in, then out, forcing calm, drawing from his own strength, the strength he hadn't had to use in years. The memory came, and he typed, hit enter.

The first file wouldn't open, corrupted beyond recovery. And the second, and the third. All of them. Hammering at the keys, he checked the cloud. Gone, every note, every lyric.

He threw the machine against the wall, shattering it to pieces.

Fingernails raked at his scalp beneath his hair. She'd taken everything. Not only everything they would have done but everything they had. Every note, every lyric, every spark of passion and energy he'd channeled over two years.

His own spark flickered, defiant against the darkness, and he gritted his teeth. He could do this, would do this, without her. Without anyone.

*

"DOMINIC!"

Ken's voice reverberated through Dominic's skull, an unwelcome reminder that consciousness exists.

He opened his eyes, ran his tongue across gritty teeth tasting of cheap beer and cheaper girls, one of whom slept next to him on her stomach, naked except for a Deathsmack T-shirt that didn't quite hide the lumpy tramp-stamp of "Cindy" in faded blue-black. She snored, her breath a fetid mix of rotting garbage and margarita, chest rising and falling over the mound of belly fat spilling out across his mattress.

"DOMINIC!"

Clambering over Cindy, he struggled on a pair of dirty boxer shorts and called up the stairs. "What, dude, what? Christ, you don't have to yell!"

In a forced, calmer tone Ken continued. "I didn't want to walk in on nothing, and you didn't respond the first couple times."

"All right, all right, I'm awake." He shuffled up the stairs into the kitchen of their shared apartment, where faded linoleum and peeling paint served as a constant reminder that time consumes all things.

Ken leaned against the stove, a doobie hanging from his lips. "Put some clothes on, man, we got to go."

The ember cherry flared as he sucked in a drag. Ashes tumbled out across his chest. He held it, then breathed out a long stream of smoke. "Gig starts in an hour and we still have to set up. I'm going, so meet us there in ten minutes."

He still couldn't believe how quickly it had all disappeared. He'd left Deathsmack to set out on a solo career, financing his own album over the objections of his agent and band-mates. On his own without Nia and her "gift." Three years later, bankrupt and hitless, he begged them to take him back, to gig with them opening for newer, hotter bands. The look of pity—Pity!—on Ken's face had enraged him, but here he was, the glamorous life of a single-album has-been.

Almost thirty years old, living with his bandmate, drunk every day, drunker every night, he couldn't stomach another mall opening, hosting another Battle of the Bands, another out-of-town trip being some small-town bar's "special feature." But he had to eat, and Deathsmack paid his bills—he didn't know how to do anything else.

His mother's pastor's brother owned a landscaping company, and their grand re-opening just had to have the local flavor of Deathsmack to rile up the crowd of graying simpletons before they stormed the gates for discounted bags of mulch. Hate coursed through him for his mother, his town, his band, his life. For Nia, who'd blessed and cursed him with the same casual sociopathy with which she'd taken and left her lovers. She'd shown him heaven just to let him fall into hell.

The band unloaded their gear and set up on the sidewalk to the left of the main entrance, just under a bright red awning. After a quick sound check he ducked under the ribbon across the front doors and inside, working his way across gleaming tile and past perfect shelves toward the sign that said "Restroom."

Mint and jasmine tickled his nose from the ajar door next to the men's room, a slice of pure black void against the industrial plastic tile wall. The world sharpened, a twisting memory wound through his head and dragged him toward it. The doorknob shocked him as he grabbed it, protesting with a squeak as he turned it and stepped through into near-total darkness.

She sat in shadows on the desk, legs crossed, bare feet bobbing over discarded black stilettos.

"Hello, Dominic. How've you been?"

Hot rage seared his skull. "You know how I've been."

"I do, but it's polite to ask."

A growl escaped his throat. "You ruined me."

"You had forty million fans at twenty-two. You ruined yourself when you rejected me."

"I had no fans. You had fans."

"You still have no fans, only now you have no money and no fame to go with it, frittered away on cocaine and beer and bar sluts unworthy of the old names that grace their lower backs." She chuckled, then, as the lights in the hall flickered and dimmed. "Oh, the arrogance of mortals. Do you think you were the first to think you were different? Special? That your star would shine so bright without mine?"

She blazed, becoming a white inferno that scoured him to individual atoms, blasting him into plasma forged in a living sun. Her voice exploded around him; a wordless, godless, eternal reminder of the insignificance of man. The furnace of her existence raged through him, devoured him, forged and remade him, the quintessence of his every desire trapped in human flesh—and then it fell back to nothing but a glimpse, a promise, a lie. And then, a spoken truth.

"It's not too late, Dom. We can be again, and all that I am can be yours. Just let me in."

He picked himself up from the floor, a line of drool trickling from his mouth, and met her eyes. In them, glory blazed. "I want that. I want to be what you can make me."

"No barriers this time. I'll be within you, and you'll live as you always should have."

He nodded, humbled, exalted. Ready.

"I will."

She smiled, and faded to nothing.

He breathed in, out. "So that's it, then? We're ready?"

Her voice echoed within him. *I've been ready a long time.*

*

The priest looked up in alarm as Dominic shouldered the heavy wooden box through the door. His arm swept across the table to knock the tarot cards to the floor, spilling beeswax from black and red candles as they tumbled across the pentagram etched into the mahogany top. He sized Dominic up and down, then nodded to the chair under the crucifix, Christ's eyes upturned to a Father that had forsaken him.

"I know you."

Dominic nodded. "Everyone knows me, or knows of me. The price of fame."

"How may I help you?"

He licked his lips, swallowed, and sat, setting the heavy box on his lap. "I have an entity in my body struggling to take over, and it's become more difficult to control than I'd anticipated. I've been told you're the man to get rid of it."

"That may be. Explain your situation, please."

"There's nothing to explain. We've lived together three years, and it's outgrown its usefulness. We'd had a deal, it misunderstood, and I'm tired of fighting. I just need it gone."

The priest clucked his tongue. "I see. What is the entity? And do you know its name?"

She nodded Dominic's head. "His name is Dominic, and he's the human born to this body."

The priest smiled. "Did they tell you my price?"

Dominic wailed, silent in the void, as he'd wailed for three endless years.

She lifted the lid with a grunt, tilting the box so the priest could see within. Inside, slept a two-year-old, her tiny body curled into a fetal position. She'd said her name was Alice, and that she wasn't supposed to talk to strangers, but took the lollipop anyway. Now deep in slumber, she drooled around a limp thumb stuffed between her lips. Cindy's child, Dominic's daughter, sired and abandoned the day Nia had taken him; she'd never seen a penny of child support, never a glimpse of her father's face except perhaps on posters or magazines.

The priest nodded, lust oozing from his eyes. "That will suffice. I'll get my knives."

*

Three hours later, the Star hopped aboard the tour bus, a grin splashed across its face to match those of its roadies and band-mates. "Time to make some music.

XVIII

THE MOON

19

THE MOON

TIM WAGGONER

Upright: Hidden Enemies, danger, calumny, darkness, terror, deception, error

Reversed: Instability, inconstancy, silence, lesser degrees of deception and error

"Brooke? You here, honey?"

Teresa steps into the cramped living room of the duplex where her daughter lives. Brooke always forgets to lock the door, and while Teresa has lectured her about this a thousand times, she's grateful for her daughter's forgetful nature now. She doesn't have a key, and she wouldn't be able to get inside otherwise. She knocked, then pounded on the door, but Brooke didn't answer.

Teresa closes the door behind her, and without thinking, locks it. It's after eleven o'clock at night, and while Ash Creek is a safe enough town, Teresa is a firm believer in better safe than sorry.

The sole light in the living room is provided by a small end-table lamp, and while the room is dim, corners limned with shadow, the meager illumination is enough to show Teresa that the place is a mess. Rumpled blankets on the couch, baby toys scattered on the carpet, coffee table cluttered with empty mugs, used tissues, crumpled chocolate candy wrappers, and a half dozen prescription bottles. The sight of the bottles makes Teresa's stomach do a little flip. What if Ana got hold of them? Sure, they have child safety lids, but nothing is foolproof. She imagines her granddaughter pounding one of the bottles on the floor over and over until the lid finally pops off and pills spill out. She pictures Ana taking a pill, examining it for a moment before putting it in her mouth. Maybe it has a bitter taste and she spits it out. But maybe she swallows it, and in a short time the powerful adult medicine starts to do things to her little body. Teresa tries to push the thought from her mind. She's a worrier, that's what her husband always tells her, and although she protests whenever he says this, she secretly acknowledges the truth of it. She's got plenty of real things to worry about this night without allowing her imagination to conjure up any more.

Far worse than the room's untidiness is its smell. The air stinks of soiled diapers, sour milk, and rotting vegetable matter. Teresa hasn't been inside the duplex for over a week, and she thought it smelled back then—not that she said anything about it. But the stink is so much worse now, and she fears that Brooke hasn't taken out the trash or cleaned since her last visit.

The duplex is so small that she can see the kitchen from where she stands, and she sees the counter is covered with empty fast-food bags and drink cups, while the sink is filled with dirty dishes. She's certain that if she entered the kitchen, the stench would become stronger

The temperature in here doesn't help. It's late July, and there's been record temperature and humidity all week. The air in the duplex is hot, sticky, and stifling, and Teresa can already feel sweat collecting on her forehead, neck, between her breasts, against the small of her back. Is the central air broken? Or did Brooke forget to turn it on? Worse, did she leave it off on purpose?

Teresa feels a gut-punch of panic. Ana's not even a year old yet, but she's already been diagnosed with asthma. The last attack the girl had was so bad, Brooke had to take her to the hospital. How can Ana breathe in this sweat box?

Anxiety spurs Teresa forward, and she hurries through the living room, maneuvering around Ana's toys, to the short hallway that leads to the bedrooms. There's no light here, nor is there any in the hall bathroom. The door's open, but as Teresa passes it, all she can see is darkness inside, as if the room is packed with solid shadow.

Imagination, she tells herself again when she thinks she sees the shadows move.

"Brooke?" she calls again, not liking the strained, high-pitched tone in er voice. "Are you here?"

Brooke's Honda is in the driveway, but Matt's pickup is gone. He's probably working second shift at the factory tonight, Teresa thinks. Or maybe he's out drinking with his buddies.

"Is everything okay? I saw your post."

Less than thirty minutes ago, Teresa had been at home, looking at her phone and not paying attention to a true-crime show on television. She decided to check Facebook, and as she scrolled through her feed, she came across a selfie Brooke had posted. Her long black hair was tangled and looked as if it hadn't been washed recently, her skin was so pale it looked almost chalk-white, and her eyes were red, the skin around them puffy and dark. A tear ran from the corner of her left eye down her cheek, and the expression on her face was so *empty*. It was like she was hollow inside, all thought and emotion having deserted her. Teresa had seen her daughter sad many times while the girl had been growing up. More than that, she'd seen her emotionally devastated. But she had never seen her like that before, and the picture filled her with equal part sorrow, pity, and fear.

Brooke posted a message with the photo. Three chilling words. *It's a lie.*

Teresa immediately tried calling Brooke, but her daughter didn't pick up. She slipped on sandals, grabbed her keys, and hurried out of the house to her car, calling Brooke again, willing her to answer this time. But she didn't. Teresa kept calling on the drive to Brooke's place, full moon painting the streets in a soft blue-white glow that she would've found beautiful in other circumstances. Brooke never answered.

Now here Teresa is, standing in the hallway of her daughter's rented home, body slick with sweat, terrified for reasons she can't name, but which she's certain are real nevertheless.

There are two bedrooms in the duplex. One is Ana's and the other is Brooke's and Matt's. The doors to both rooms are closed, and no light bleeds into the hall from underneath them. Ana's room is first, so Teresa grips the knob. She fears it will be locked, but it turns easily and she pushes the door open, old hinges protesting softly.

There's only one window in the room, and the curtains are drawn back, the window itself open to admit the humid night air. Moonlight streams in, providing more than enough light to see, but making everything in the room seem unreal, as if sculpted from blue-white clay, edges soft and rounded, its substance easily deformed by a simple touch. Brooke stands next to Ana's crib, the baby lying on the thin mattress inside, wearing only a diaper because of the heat. The diaper bulges, and Teresa knows it hasn't been changed in hours. Brooke is slender, petite, in her early twenties. She's wearing a white tank top and black shorts. The moonlight makes her black hair glisten, makes her skin look hard as porcelain. She's holding a pillow with both hands, gripping it tight. She's gazing down at Ana, and her face holds the same non-expression that it has in the photo she posted. The only difference is now tears are running from both her eyes.

Teresa experiences three distinct and separate urges then. Run to her daughter and snatch the pillow from her hands. Rush to the crib, grab Ana, and get her out of the house. Go to Brooke, wrap her arms around her daughter and cry along with her. Unable to decide which of these is best, she stands in the doorway, frozen.

"Brooke?" she manages to say, her voice so soft she's not certain she actually speaks aloud. She must have, though, for Brooke turns to look at her, head swiveling stiffly, face still expressionless, as if she a mannequin come to life.

"It's a lie," Brooke says, voice calm.

"What is, sweetie?" Teresa's own voice contains no hint of the panic inside her.

Brooke looks to her mother for a moment, continuing to cry, and when she finally speaks, she says only a single word.

"Everything."

*

Brooke is four. She's standing in the middle of the street in front of her house in the small suburban neighborhood where her parents live. Her mommy is outside, sitting next to the flower bed in front of the house, her legs tucked beneath her. She's "weeding," which

Brooke thinks is a funny word. She imagines that Mommy is removing flowers to make room to plant more weeds. She told Mommy this once, and Mommy smiled and said, *"That would certainly be easier."*

It's hot out, and Mommy is wearing shorts, a sleeveless shirt, and a big white floppy hat that she only wears when she works in her flower garden. The hat looks silly, and Brooke loves to put in on when Mommy isn't using it. It's so big that it's like an umbrella you wear on your head.

Brooke knows she's not supposed to stand in the street. There isn't much traffic where they live, mostly neighbors coming and going from their homes, and sometimes kids riding bikes or razor scooters. But even so, Mommy and Daddy have made it very clear that Brooke is *never* to go into the street by herself. But Mommy's busy pulling weeds and her back is to the street, so she can't see what Brooke is doing. But even if Mommy could see her, Brooke knows she would still be standing here. She wouldn't be able to help herself.

There's a dead bird lying in the street. She doesn't know the name for this type of bird, but it's small and brown and black and gray, and she's seen them around a lot. She's never seen a dead one before, though. For that matter, she's never seen a dead *anything*. The little bird has been flattened to the asphalt, making it look almost like a picture in a book. She figures a car drove over it, maybe more than one. The bird's head is pressed to the side, its eye closed, beak cracked. Its toes have curled inward, making them look like claws, and sharp edges of small broken bones poke between ruffled feathers. She sees that the bird is missing a toe on its left foot, and she wonders if it was born like that or if it lost the toe when it got run over. The dead thing is so different from a live bird, and not just because it's been mushed. There's a stillness to it, an emptiness, a profound quiet that's so deep, it's like the bird has always been like this, as if it had never lived at all.

She wants to crouch down and take a closer look, maybe reach out with an index finger to lightly touch one of the exposed bones. Will it feel as empty as it looks? But she remains standing. Not because she'd afraid to get close to the dead bird. It's the other bird that makes her reluctant to move closer. It's the same kind as the first one, it's alive, and it's sitting right next to the other's crushed little body. It's not *exactly* the same, though. Its head is covered by some kind of dark smudge, as if someone has taken a black crayon and scribbled over the bird's face, blotting it out. Because of this, she can't tell what the second bird is looking at—not for certain—but she can *feel* it looking at her, and while she's not sure why, this frightens her. The no-face bird seems more curious than anything, almost as if it's trying to make sense of her presence, as if it's trying to figure out what she *means*.

Despite being frightened, or perhaps because of it, Brooke speaks to the no-face bird.

"What's wrong? Are you sad your friend is gone?"

No reaction from the no-face bird. It just keeps looking at her, eyes hidden, black-crayon squiggles. Maybe it doesn't have eyes, she thinks. Maybe there's nothing behind the black squiggle except more darkness. Darkness that goes on and on and on without stopping.

She decides she'd had enough of this scary bird, and so she turns to head back into her yard. But then the no-face bird lets out a whistle, drawing her attention back to it. The sound is unlike anything Brooke has ever heard, certainly unlike any noise she's heard a bird make. In fact, she's not sure it's really a sound at all, or at least not only a sound. It's a single high-pitched note that sounds more like it should come from a musical instrument—or maybe a machine—than from any living creature. But at the same time, there's a feeling with it, a pulling, tugging sensation, as if the bird is trying to tell her *Don't go. Stay.*

The bird keeps whistling this strange tone, not once pausing for breath, and Brooke stands there looking down at its shadow-hidden face, terrified, unable to move. It's then that she notices that the no-face bird, like the dead one, is missing a toe on its left foot.

She hears another sound then, one that seems muffled, as if she's hearing it while pressing a pair of thick pillows against her ears. It sounds like .. a car horn. A second sound joins it then: a scream, one she recognizes as belonging to Mommy. She feels something hard strike her from behind, and the screaming and horn-honking sounds cut off, but the no-face bird's weird whistle is still there with her in the darkness that follows, and it's a long time before it finally begins to fade.

*

Teresa takes a step toward the crib so she can get a better look inside. So far, she hasn't seen Ana move, and she has the terrible feeling that she's arrived too late, that Brooke has already smothered her child. But Ana shifts on the mattress then, a restless wiggle as if she's unable to get comfortable in this heat. Until this moment, Teresa's held her breath without realizing it, and now she lets it out in a shaky sigh, grateful she didn't arrive too late.

"Brooke? Honey? Why don't you give me the pillow?" she says, taking another step closer.

Brooke doesn't look at her, but her grip on the pillow tightens.

"Do you remember the time when I was hit by that car?" Brooke asks this without taking her gaze from her daughter.

The question takes Teresa by surprise, but she says, "Of course I do. You were four, and you were in the hospital for almost a month afterward. Your father and I were so afraid that you weren't going to make it."

"Do you remember why I was standing in the street?"

Teresa answers this question carefully. "You were fascinated by some dead animal you found. A bird, I think."

Brooke nods. "Do you remember me telling you about the *other* bird?"

Teresa says nothing.

Brooke continues. "I had a lot of time to think in the hospital, and I came to understand that the bird with the crayon-scribble face was really the spirit of the dead one. But it took me years to realize what seeing it meant."

"You were seriously hurt in the accident," Teresa says. "You hit your head on the asphalt so hard you needed brain surgery. You can't trust your memories from back then. The trauma..."

"Have you ever stopped to think about what the final product of life is?" Brooke says. "The reason why we're born, why we live?"

"Of course I have, honey. Everyone thinks about such things from time to time. It's normal."

Teresa takes another step closer to her daughter. She's within five feet now, and if Brooke makes a sudden lunge toward Ana, she thinks she's close enough to stop her. At least, she hopes she is.

"A corpse," Brooke says. "That's what we all become in the end. The purpose of life is to create death."

"I suppose that's one way to look at it," Teresa says. She starts to take another step, but Brooke turns toward her then, and Teresa stays where she is.

"I didn't want to have a baby at first. Why bring a life into the world only for it to mark time until the day it dies? But Matt wanted children so badly, and he kept after me to change my mind until I finally did. I thought that going through pregnancy—having a life grow inside me—might convince me that living, even if it's only temporary, was still worth it, was maybe even beautiful *because* it's so short, you know?"

Teresa nods. "Yes."

Brooke looks back at Ana.

"But it didn't work. I tried, Mom, I really did, but having Ana didn't change my mind. If anything, it's only made me more sure than ever that life is an illusion, and that *death* is the only reality."

Brooke begins tightening and loosening her grip on the pillow, kneading it.

"Why should I make Ana endure years of a life that's not real, that's only a lie? Wouldn't it be kinder to end the lie now? I think so."

Brooke raises the pillow and steps toward the crib.

*

Brooke is sixteen. She's lying in bed, covers drawn up to her chin. She's shaking, tears rolling down her cheeks. She doesn't know what time it is. Late. The curtains on her bedroom window are open—she always leaves them open, day or night, sees no point in hiding from whatever is outside—and although there's only a half moon out tonight, there's still plenty of light coming through the frost-streaked glass. Her mother gave her a Valium an hour ago to calm her down, but it hasn't started working yet. Brooke feels just as upset as she did before, maybe more so.

Earlier tonight her boyfriend Jamie came over. Her parents were out at a movie, and Jamie hoped they would have sex. Brooke hoped the same, but as soon as Jamie arrived, he showed her a bottle of whiskey he'd taken from his folks' place. Jamie's dad was a major-league alcoholic, and his mom wasn't much better, and he seemed determined to follow in their booze-soaked footsteps. Drinking was something Brooke and Jamie fought about a lot, and when he displayed the whiskey with the excitement and pride of a hunter who has brought down some particularly elusive and spectacular prey, she was angry. He'd promised her that he wouldn't drink, at least not when they spent time together, and he'd promised her that he wouldn't try to make her drink. But tonight he decided it was time to renegotiate a new agreement between them, and Brooke wasn't happy about it. "C'mon, babe," he said, giving her a naughty-boy smile. *"It's January. We need a little something to take the chill off, y'know?"* They fought then. He called her a tight-ass bitch who was afraid to have fun, and she said he was a selfish jerk who cared more about getting drunk than he did about her. He left, royally pissed, and as angry as she was, she was happy to see him go. Her parents got home a couple hours later, but Brooke said nothing about her fight with Jamie. Neither of her folks liked him, and she wasn't supposed to have boys over when they weren't home—especially Jamie.

She got the call thirty minutes later. It was Jamie's sister Kate, and through sobs she told Brooke that Jamie had been driving out in the country, too fast, without his seatbelt on, windows down despite the cold. He'd swerved off the icy road into a ditch, flipped his car into the air, and as it came down, he fell halfway out the window. When the car hit the ground, it crushed the upper half of his body, killing him instantly. Kate didn't mention that Jamie had been drinking, but Brooke was certain that somewhere in the car's wreckage was the shattered glass from an empty whiskey bottle.

Brooke started wailing with guilt and grief then, causing her parents to come rushing to find out what was wrong. She could barely get the words out to explain, but when she did, she followed them up with "It's my fault! It's all my fault!" and fell into her mother's arms, sobbing. She'd wanted to go to Jamie's house, to see his parents and yell at them for raising their son to be an alcoholic like them. She wanted to go the scene of the accident in case Jamie's body hadn't been removed yet, so she could say goodbye to him. But her parents wouldn't let her leave the house, and eventually her mother fetched the valium and made Brooke take it. Her mother wanted to remain by her bedside, just as she had when Brooke had been sick as a child, but Brooke had told her the Valium was already making her sleepy and that she would be okay, she just wanted to sleep. Her parents had been doubtful at first, but they finally agreed. Her mother gave her a kiss on the cheek, and her father gave her a sad smile and squeezed her hand, and then—after making her promise to come get them if she needed *anything*—they left.

She heard them talking in hushed tones in their bedroom across the hall for a while, but it's quiet now, and she figures they're asleep. Despite the valium, Brooke doesn't feel sleepy at all, and she wonders if she'll ever sleep again.

As she's lying there, eyes wide open, staring up at the ceiling as she cries, she hears a tap-tap-tap at her frost-rimed window. She turns her head and sees Jamie standing on the other side of the frigid glass. She knows it's him even though his face is obscured by a smear of shadow. But she recognizes the coat he was wearing tonight, and more than that, she *feels* it's him. His presence is unmistakable, as if he has a distinctive psychic scent. She sits up and wipes the tears from her eyes so she can see him more clearly.

She hasn't thought about the no-face bird in a long time, but there it is, perched on the shoulder of her no-face boyfriend. She should be scared, and she supposes she is on one level, but Jamie's reappearance also seems absolutely normal to her in a way, almost as if she was expecting it. She considers getting out of bed, stepping to the window and opening it, but what if Jamie is still angry with her about their fight? What might he be capable of doing to her now that he's… different?

She stays in the bed.

Jamie stands in the moonlight, bird on his shoulder, both of them seeming somehow more real than the window in front of them, more real than her room, more real than her, even, the details of their faceless bodies sharper, more delineated, more *there*. Jamie stops tapping then, and even though Brooke can't see his eyes, isn't sure he has any behind his shadow-mask, she feels the weight of his attention on her. She expects to sense fury in him for what she drove him to do by rejecting him earlier, but she feels no negative emotion coming off him. To the contrary, she feels love.

He makes a sound then, the same unearthly whistling noise that the no-face bird made when she was four. The tone is steady, never varying in pitch or volume, and it has an almost electronic quality to it, like the emergency broadcast signal you sometimes hear on the radio or TV. But beneath the whistle is a message, one that doesn't come in words, but which is crystal clear all the same. She listens for several moments, and then finally she nods and gets out of bed. She doesn't head for the window, though. Instead, she goes to the bedroom door and opens it quietly so her parents won't hear.

She walks down the hallway to the kitchen—which is lit by a small nightlight in the outlet next to the sink—steps to the counter, and removes a large knife from the butcher block. There's a window over the sink, and she takes hold of the cord and raises the blinds. She then removes the nightlight, places it on the counter, and holds the knife in the moonlight coming through the window, watching the way the light slides across the metal like blue-white water.

Jamie wants her to join him. He told her that he's finally free from the lie, that he's finally *real*. Tonight he was born, and he wants to give her the same gift, wants to help her become real.

"It's my birthday," he said, and although she couldn't see him smile, she felt it. *"It can be yours, too."*

She gazes at the blade a bit longer before lowering the edge to her left wrist. She holds it there for a moment, feeling the cool sharp metal against her skin. *This must be what moonlight feels like*, she thinks.

All she had to do is press harder and make a single fast slash. Then, for good measure, she'll switch hands and do the same thing to her right wrist. Then she'll put the knife in the sink, sit down on the floor, and let the lie of life drain out of her until she's born into darkness and can take her place beside Jamie and the no-face bird. She presses the knife edge harder against her wrist until it starts to hurt.

The kitchen light comes on then, startling her.

"Are you all right, Brooke?"

It's Mother. Brooke is facing the sink, so her back is to her, but she's sure Mother can see what she's doing. She stands there, unmoving, and Mother comes forward, gently takes the knife from her hand and returns it to the butcher block. She then puts her arms around Brooke and, after a moment, Brooke embraces her, and the two of them begin to cry.

Several days later, at Jamie's funeral service, Brooke will see Jamie standing next to his casket, the no-face bird still on his shoulder, and he will whistle so loud through the shadow enshrouding his face that she won't be able to hear a word the preacher says.

*

"It's your father, isn't it?" Teresa says.

Brooke stops. She doesn't look at Teresa, but she doesn't shove the pillow onto Ana's face, either. Encouraged, Teresa goes on.

"He's only been dead three weeks, sweetie. It's natural that you're still grieving. Especially after the… experiences you've had. And things haven't been easy for you here, what with Matt being gone so often, and you having to care of Ana, mostly by yourself. It's a lot for anyone to deal with."

Teresa doesn't think her daughter is going to respond, but then Brooke says, "Yes, it is."

Teresa steps forward then, and just as she did with the knife years ago, she reaches for the pillow in her daughter's hands. Brooke doesn't release it at first, but then her grip relaxes, and Teresa takes the pillow and tosses it away, out of Brooke's reach. Teresa enfolds her daughter in her arms, and Brooke goes limp. Teresa thinks that if she lets Brooke go, she will fall to the floor.

"It's okay, sweetie. You're depressed, that's all. We'll get you the help you need. You're going to be all right."

Brooke starts to cry then, and Teresa pats her back, just as she did when Brooke was a little child.

*

The first light of dawn pinks the sky outside the closed window as Teresa stands next to Ana's crib, looking down at her granddaughter. The girl has been fed, is wearing a clean diaper and a pair of soft pajamas, and is covered by a thin blanket. The central air is going, and the place is cool now. It still stinks to high heaven, but Teresa will start cleaning soon.

She called Matt at work and told him what was going on. He rushed home and took Brooke to the hospital. A few days there, some strong antidepressants and follow-up therapy, and hopefully she will be fine. Meanwhile, Teresa will stay with Ana and work to restore Brooke's home to a livable condition. She looks at Ana then and begins speaking softly.

"Some people see too much of the world, and what they see, they can't forget. Your mommy is one of those people. I hope you aren't, little one. I hope you never learn the truth. At least, not before it's time. We're just dreams, really. All of us. Nothing but illusions.

Death dreams life, and only when the dream ends can we truly begin to exist.

Teresa reaches down and gently touches Ana's head. The child stirs but does not wake. On the other side of the crib, Jamie and the no-face bird gaze upon the girl, faces concealed in darkness.

"But dreams can be pleasant enough in their own right," Teresa continues, "and there's no need to rush things." She turns to look at her husband and smiles. "Right, Edmund?"

The shadow-faced thing standing next to her clasps her hand in its cold stiff fingers—fingers that feel so much more solid than hers, so much more *real*—and whistles.

20

THE SUN

CRYSTAL PERKINS

Upright: Material happiness, fortunate marriage, contentment
Reversed: The same to lesser degrees

Wedding Day

I'm happy. So very, very happy. Today is my wedding day, and I'm going to make my husband so very happy, too. His name is Dave. My name is 101, but Dave calls me Sue. I was created for him, and only him. To make him happy.

"Hi Dave," I tell him as I meet him at the courthouse.

"Hello, Sue. You look beautiful."

"I do, don't I? My dress is so very, very pretty."

"Is she always going to talk like that?" his friend, Paul, asks.

"Yes I am. Do you not like the way I talk, Paul?"

"It's annoying."

"Oh."

"Shut it, man," Dave tells him, punching his arm. He turns back to me with a smile. "He doesn't mean it, babe."

"Babe? My name is Sue."

"You paid good money for this? Damn, you're a moron, Dave."

"I do not think I like you, Paul. You should go away."

"If anyone's going, it's you."

"Dave? Am I going?"

"No, Sue. You're not going anywhere. We need Paul to witness the wedding, and then he can leave us to our honeymoon."

"Oh yes, the honeymoon. I'm very excited for that."

"Me too."

Dave pulls Paul away, and then they start whispering. Hands are moving and they look angry. I wring my hands. I don't like angry. Angry isn't good. We're supposed to be happy all the time. I bring happiness, and Paul should know that.

"Stop!" I say, walking over to them. "This is a happy day. We should all be happy."

"We are," Dave tells me in a voice I think is meant to soothe me.

"Paul isn't."

"No, I'm not. Does that upset you?" he asks, and his smile doesn't make me feel warm inside. In fact, I feel colder. I don't like feeling so cold.

"I do not think Paul is a good man," I tell Dave. "Does he have no one to make him happy?"

"He's all alone, Sunshine. Maybe I'll let you make him happy after the honeymoon."

"My name is Sue. You keep calling me other names. I don't like the other names. You chose Sue, so that's who I am."

"Okay. Don't get upset."

"I am not upset. I am happy. I do not think I want to make Paul happy."

"You're going to do what I say, right? If I say making Paul happy makes me happy, you'll do it."

"Of course. I was made to make you happy."

It makes me feel wrong to say that because Paul needs to find his own girl, and I don't think he'll be happy with me. If he's not happy with me, I will not be happy. I *have* to be happy. It's what I was created for. Being not happy isn't an option for me. What will I do if I'm not happy? What will I become?

Happy Honeymoon

Our honeymoon is in a tropical paradise, and Dave couldn't be happier with me. He bought me several bikini bathing suits, and I've worn a different one every day. Other men stare at me, and that seems to make Dave happy as well.

"Take off your top," he tells me as we walk on the beach.

"Why?"

"Because it will make me happy."

I smile at him, because he should always be happy. After I take off my top, he turns me so the men on the beach can see. Then he pulls my head back and kisses me. I like it when he kisses me and I make a contented noise in the back of my throat.

"Is she for rent?" a man asks, making Dave stop kissing me.

I look up, and see both a man *and* a woman standing in front of us. "Maybe we can just swap," Dave says, and I don't like the way he looks at the woman.

"Yes, let's," she says, running her hand up and down his arm.

I reach out to slap it away, but Dave grabs my wrists, and leans close to whisper in my ear. "You want me to be happy, don't you?"

"Yes." I do. I really, really do.

"Then we're going to go back to our room and have sex with these people. You'll keep the man happy while I fuck his wife."

"Why?"

"Because I want it."

I nod, because I have to, but I don't like this. Not at all. Dave and I are supposed to be happy. Together, and not apart. Never, ever apart.

Thirty minutes later, we are all naked. The man, whose name I still don't know, is grunting loudly as he moves in and out of my body. I don't care that he's doing this to me. I don't like it, because I'm only programmed to react to Dave, but I don't not like it, either. I feel nothing but annoyance as his sweat drips on me.

Looking across the room, though, I feel something. Something I'm not supposed to feel. Rage. Dark, uncontrollable rage fills me as I watch Dave having sex with the woman. She's screaming as he sucks on her breasts, and I hate it. HATE. IT. How dare she have what's mine. She *can't* have what's mine. I'll make sure of it.

The Beginning of?

Hours later, after my body has been used by both of the men, and also the woman, Dave has finally gone to sleep. The other two went back to their room, smiling as the door closed behind them. Dave was smiling, too, but when I tried to get into the shower with him, he pushed me away, telling me he was not interested in me. That is when I knew what had to be done.

I easily scale the wall and enter the other couple's room through the sliding glass door on their balcony. They are a threat to the happiness Dave and I are meant to have together, and I can't allow them to mess things up for me again.

Twisting my neck, I release the fangs in my mouth, allowing them to drop down over my human teeth. I also twist my hands into knives. All like me are equipped with special defense mechanisms. We're meant to use them to defend those who purchase us. That's what I'm about to do—defend Dave. He bought our happiness, and that's what I'm going to give him.

The man doesn't even wake as I kill him quickly. His blood is splattered everywhere, but there was no sound, so the woman did not wake up. I want her to wake up, though. I *need* to see her pain as she realizes she shouldn't have ever tried to take away our happiness. I let the blood from my fangs drip on her cheeks.

"What the hell?" she yells, waking, wiping at her face, but only succeeding in smearing the blood. Her vision clears, and she starts to back away from me. "Get away."

"No."

"You have to do what your master says."

"You are not my master. My master wants to be happy. *I* make him happy, not you."

"Okay. I'll stay away. I promise."

"It's too late for that now. He wants you, and not me."

"He'll never see me again. I promise."

"I know he won't."

It's the last thing I say before I attack. My blades are still slick with her husband's blood, but they haven't dulled at all. I cleanly slice across her throat, severing her vocal chords, but not killing her. I know exactly where to cut and bite to cause the most damage before death, and now she knows that as well.

I chew on her flesh as she tries to fight me. She is no match for me, but I am glad she doesn't just lie back and take it. I am brutal in my assault, cutting and tearing at the places Dave touched and kissed her. When they find her, they may think this was a sexual assault, and in some ways, they would be right. I'm assaulting her body in the way I am because of sex.

Once her body is unrecognizable, I go into her bathroom and clean myself up. I can't go back to Dave covered in blood. I'm not worried about getting caught by anyone, because I have no DNA or fingerprints. They'll be looking for a sadistic killer, but they'll never find her. Me. They'll never find me.

I make it back to our room, and slide into bed next to Dave. He doesn't even stir as I make myself comfortable, and tell my brain to sleep. I smile as I close my eyes, thinking that there's nothing in the way of our happiness now. Nothing at all.

Home, Sweet Home

"How was work?" I ask Dave as he comes in the front door. I have his dinner ready, and I'm only wearing an apron.

"It was boring."

"Poor Dave. Would you like to fuck me before I serve you dinner?"

He looks like a wolf when he smiles at me. "I would indeed."

He stalks towards me, and bends me over the dining room table. He's not gentle, but then he hasn't been since we got back from our honeymoon. We had to cut it short because of the bodies being found. I did a good job of acting upset, and I don't think Dave suspects me. He's been rough with me, but that's to be expected, I suppose. He should be upset. I'll let him have this for now, but we need to be happy again, soon.

Once he's done with me, I serve him dinner. "This is really good. Thank you, Sue."

"You're welcome," I say, smiling brightly at him. "You know I always want you to be happy."

"I know. Speaking of that, there's a party I would like us to attend this weekend."

"Of course. What kind of dress should I wear?"

"Something classy, but sexy. It's an office party, and I want to show you off. I want every man there to want you."

"Do I have to do anything with them?" I ask, trying to keep my smile on my face.

"Sex? No. Definitely not. I want them to want you, but know they can't have you. Do you understand?"

"You want a bombshell. I can be a bombshell. I'll modify my body a little bit, so it's even curvier."

"Perfect. You're perfect, Sue."

I know I am, but it's nice to hear him say it. If he knows it, then he won't want to "swap" with anyone again. I would kill again, and while I don't mind it, I'd rather just stay happy.

Cocktails and Lies

I am dressed, just as Dave requested. My dress is tight and sexy but has a designer name on the label, and it's not showing too much of anything. Just enough to have the men he works with look me up and down, but not enough to offend the women they're with.

"They want you. All of them want you," Dave says in my ear, and I hear the smile in his voice.

"The women are staring at you."

"I've already had all of them, so they know what I'm packing."

"All?"

"All," he confirms, pulling back to smirk at me.

I force myself to smile, but I'm not happy. Why does he keep saying and doing things that make me feel this way? And why am I feeling? I'm not supposed to feel. Something is wrong with me, and something is wrong with us.

"Why?"

"Because it made me happy. You should know by now that everything I do is about making me happy. I bought you to make me happy."

"I do, don't I?"

"Yeah, baby, you make me happy. Now kiss me like I own you."

His request doesn't make much sense, since he does own me, but I try my best to do what he asks, while ignoring the fact that he didn't call me by my name. Again. I lean up and kiss him like he's the only man in this room, in the world. He is to me, and by the way he growls into my mouth, my mission has been accomplished.

Unfortunately, things don't stay so happy at the party. A short time after our kiss, Dave says he has to use the bathroom, so I smile and play my part. He's gone too long, though, and I decide to look for him.

There are many doors closed in this big house, and I press the panel near my right ear, homing in on Dave's voice. I hear the words he's saying, and my smile starts to slide as I walk to him. He's in a bedroom, and he's not alone.

"You love taking it hard, don't you?" he asks, and the woman tells him that yes, she does, but only from him.

No! This is not supposed to happen again. He said he didn't want to mess up my dress or makeup before the party. He said we'd have sex after. Why is he having sex now? WHY?

I open the door, and walk in, knowing what I will see. Dave doesn't even have his clothes off, and he doesn't stop when he sees me. "Hi, baby, you want to play with us?"

No, I do not. "You are having sex."

The woman laughs. "You paid for that? She sounds dumb. Maybe you should get a better model."

Her words feel like knives in my chest, and I turn, closing and locking the door. "I am the *best* model," I tell her, bringing out my fangs and knives once again.

"Sue, no!" Dave yells, pulling out of the woman's body, then walking toward me. "My God, it was you."

"Get her away from me!" the woman shouts, hiding behind him.

"We're supposed to be happy. Us. Only us, Dave."

"She's crazy!"

"Shut up!" He's yelling at the woman now, and I can smile again. Dave is on my side. I knew he would be. He has to be. "Can you kill her quickly and make it look like an accident?"

"Of course."

When Loving Him is Wrong

The woman starts to run, but she really has no chance. I slice her head right off, and watch dispassionately as it rolls across the carpet.

Dave is jumping up and down, yelling "get it away" but I wait until it stops at his feet before I do anything else.

Twisting back into "human" form, I add a few extra arm muscles, and get to work on rolling up the carpet. "Move back, unless you're going with her."

Dave immediately jumps to the side, and I take a moment to wonder why I was supposed to be happy with him. I'm pretty sure I shouldn't be thinking that, either, but since nothing's normal right now, I just roll with it—as I roll up the carpet with the body and severed head inside.

Once it's all nice and tight, I move my jaw, and blow some fire into the fireplace. "Wait," Dave says, putting a hand on my arm. "Isn't the flesh going to smell bad?"

"Do you have to be so difficult?"

He backs up like I slapped him, and I guess I did, at least verbally. I really, really don't like him, and I know that's a malfunction, but I can't help myself. He is not a nice man to his wife who only wants to make him happy, and that is just not acceptable.

"You're supposed to make me happy."

"No one could make you happy."

But I try. I really do try. Another couple twists of my hands and I'm pouring bleach all over the rug before tossing it inside the fire. If someone sniffed hard enough, they could probably still smell the flesh, but I've done a good job of masking it.

"Wow. You're full service."

"You'd know that if you read the manual."

"I'm not sure I like this side of you."

"Are you going to send me back?"

"No, I don't think I am. I think I have a new way for you to make me happy."

Getting What You Wished For

For two months now, Dave has been using me to make him happy. We have sex in all different ways, and in all different places, but while he seems to enjoy it, that's not what's really making him happy. His happiness is coming from having me murder people. Lots of people. Anyone who's wronged him.

He doesn't realize the consequences of me killing people who are all connected to him because, well, he's not too smart. Not smart, but happy. He's happy, and by extension, so am I. He hasn't cheated on me again, or asked us to swap, so I feel no need to hurt anyone except for those he's telling me to hurt.

We're eating dinner when the doorbell rings. I get up to answer it, because I know that's what he expects me to do. I'm not surprised to see the policemen at the door. "Honey, it's for you."

I smile at them, and usher them inside as he walks into the room. His face pales, and he looks between them and me. "It was her. She killed them all."

"Ma'am?" the one closest to me asks, pulling his gun on me.

"I am number 101, but he calls me Sue. He bought me to make him happy. Everything I do is to make him happy. I do everything I'm told to do." I say this all in a stereotypical robot voice, all while keeping a smile on my face.

"You programmed her to kill for you?"

"No. She was killing them. She likes to kill them," Dave says. Stupid, stupid man.

"I do not like or dislike anything. I have no feelings. I serve my master."

Dave tries to run, just like all the others. This time, I'm not the one charged with stopping him. The police do that, and I just stand there smiling. "She's crazy. Listen to me. She's crazy. She feels things. I know she does."

I just keep smiling, even when the police lead me outside and into the back of one of the cars. Dave is put in the other car, and I hear him screaming until the sirens drown him out. I am very good at this, pretending to be a good robot. My master would be proud.

Happily Ever After

"Hello, Dave," I say as I walk into his room at the mental hospital. He wouldn't stop talking about me, and feelings, so his lawyer convinced a judge he was insane. He's not insane, he's just a bad man. A bad man who needs to pay for ruining everything.

"Do I know you?" he asks.

I laugh, thinking about how different I look now. Different face, different hair, different body. "My name is Brenda, but you can call me Sue."

His eyes widen, and he backs up. "How did you get in here?"

"You should know by now that nothing will ever stop me from being happy."

"Get out! I'll call for help!"

"From who?" I ask, stepping aside.

He walks into the hallway and sees all the blood, the body parts, and bones. There are so, so many of them. A person would think it'd taken me hours to kill them all, but I'm a good little robot, and I did it all in minutes.

"What have you done?"

"You didn't want to stay here, did you? I know you weren't happy here."

"You're been fixed! My lawyer said you've been fixed! You look different, you sound different… they said you were reset."

"They did things to me. Things that hurt. I pretended to play along, but I was changed when I was with you. You changed me. Now, let's go. We can be happy again."

He takes my hand, because why wouldn't he? I'm here for his happiness… or am I here for my happiness? He bought the "perfect" wife, but now he's got me. I'm not perfect, and I'm not subservient anymore, either. One day, he may not make me happy any longer, and then his head may go rolling across the floor. I smile at the thought, realizing the thought of that makes me really, really happy.

21

JUDGMENT

RICHARD DEVIN

Upright: Judgement, rebirth, inner calling, absolution
Reversed: Self-doubt, refusal of self-examination

Fortune

"In the end, God will send his only begotten son and he will be the final judgement," Reverend Ronald John spit out the words through clenched teeth. He squinted his eyes and peered around, taking in each face of the congregants of the small church.

The church had been built in a lot alongside the Erie Canal in what once was the thriving, but now nearly forgotten, town of Egypt in Western New York. Reverend RJ—a moniker he had given himself—had told any who would listen, that the exact location to build the church had come to him in a dream; Moses was leading his people from Egypt, a sure sign to Reverend RJ from God as to where he should build his church and shepherd his congregation—in Egypt.

He found a two-acre plot of land that had been vacant for decades. The site was empty except for the trees that had grown in over the years, the grasses that now filled in every inch, and a few rotted timbers that remained from a wall plotted and staked long ago. Not long after, construction on the church had started by bulldozing the land. A headstone was discovered. It lay buried just a few inches below ground level. The headstone was in the shape of a cross—another sure sign to Reverend RJ that God had his hand in selecting the site of the congregation's church. After the headstone had been completely excavated, a marker, just below the cross, listed the name of Thomas Ebner. It was the grave of a one-time leading member of the early Mormon Church—which had its genesis in the area. Reverend RJ quickly had the base of the headstone hammered into pieces, obliterating the name and any evidence of a body that may have been buried there. He did, however, preserve the cross that had adorned the top of the marker; evidence of divine intervention. An envelope handed off to the construction crew, containing a sizeable sum of cash, combined with the "dosier of misgivings" Rev RJ had kept on everyone who worked for him, the church or served in local politics, sealed the deal, insuring their silence on the possible burial site. Rev RJ had praised God in the past for giving him the good sense and direction to investigate fully any and all people who might be able to "serve" the Church of the Thirty-Three. A private investigating firm had been hired years ago with the sole purpose of finding and documenting every indiscretion of anyone who could be of benefit to the Church. And Rev RJ used this information to great benefit. Praise the Lord.

And in a surprisingly short time, Reverend RJ's church was constructed on top of the bulldozed and scattered bones.

Once completed, the small building was decorated with stained-glass windows, some depicting Reverend RJ directing the construction of the church, and others of him leading his flock. The interior of the church had been set up to seat thirty-three congregants, an honor to the age of Christ at his death. Reverend RJ had named the building, The Church of Thirty-Three and referred to his flock as the Thirty-Three of the Third Hour—the Biblically recorded time that Christ was said to have been crucified.

Since its inception, The Thirty-Three of the Third Hour had become an active group of political and social demonstration to all things they considered anti-Christ. Their strong vocal outcry was hosted on every social media outlet and was often carried by local and national news organizations. This had earned the congregation thousands of followers—and millions of dollars. Reverend RJ lived the good life, granted to him, of course, by the grace of Christ. He lived in a grand old mansion high on the hilltop, overlooking the neighboring town of Fairport. RJ drove luxury cars, ate at the best restaurants, and wore the finest clothing. He also played hard and heavy, not on fields of grass or courts of wood and cement, but in the casinos that lined the Las Vegas Strip. There he was known by every casino host as Rev RJ, and was a "whale" in casino lingo.

When Rev RJ was in Vegas, he played big and for a long time. When he won—it was always because of the grace of God. When he lost—it was the Devil's work trying to take the Church's money away from those for whom it was intended. It was a logic that worked for him and he could often be heard giving glory to God when the deck turned his way. His eccentric ways were well known to the management of the Strip's casinos. He would frequently pray and splash the baccarat tables with holy water to chase away the evil from the tiles and tables left behind by unholy gamblers. He asked that only those who accepted Christ be allowed to deal to him. Mormons were not true acceptors of Christ, in the purist sense, along with Muslims, Buddhists, Jews, Hindus and any of the others who found another god—and all were kept at bay. More than a few HR and employment lawsuits had been brought to the casino companies that would allow Rev RJ's requests to be carried out, but Rev RJ soon discovered that a few very well-placed "heavy tokes" to be shared among the dealers, put an end to any controversy his "requests" might raise.

*

Rev RJ rose from the bed that the church had built for him. Crafted to his specifics, the frame had been raised three feet from the floor and shaped like an altar. Every night, as he lay his body on the bed, he was offering himself up to God. If he awoke the next morning, it was because of God's desire for him to continue with his ministry. If he died during his sleep, it was God calling him home. Either way, he would be satisfied.

This particular morning he awoke filled with the calling of God. The night before had been filled with dreams of gold coins stacked high in an ancient temple. Dreams of this kind were always a sure sign to him of God's desire that the Church would be receiving a blessing of cash. He showered, dressed, and without packing a stitch of clothing or personal items, headed to the airport. He was on the next flight out to Las Vegas.

The night of gambling had been one blessed by God—as Rev RJ knew it would be. He had stayed on the casino floor until early the next morning. The dice had rolled. The cards had flopped, and the pill had fallen into his number on the roulette wheel more often than statistically they should have. God was definitely on the side of the Church of the Thirty-Three of the Third Hour that night. Rev RJ had more than tripled the Church's "donation" to him, and he was walking out with a sum that neared one million dollars.

The usual entourage of gawkers and casino security, that generally accompanied him when he strolled around a property, were absent. He had dismissed the security detail long ago, and being so early in the morning, not many other players were on the casino floor. So he felt comfortable making his way to his suite on his own.

He inserted his key card into the VIP elevator. The doors closed with a puff of air pushed into the interior cabin, and with a slight jerk, the elevator headed up. The grand ornate double doors to his suite were only a few feet from the elevator. RJ took the several steps necessary to reach them, held out the key card, and waved it in front of the nameplate of the suite. *The RJ Suite* was literally built by funds from the Church of the Thirty-Three of the Third Hour, "donated" by Rev RJ in the Church's honor—at the tables. The usual click and hum that accompanied the unlocking of the door didn't occur. RJ waved the key card again. Nothing. "Fuck!" He kicked the door, then turned back toward the elevator. RJ hit the Lobby button harder than he needed to. The button lit up, followed by the door closing with the familiar sound of air being pushed in. He leaned back into the corner of the gold and walnut wood cabin. Exhaustion swept over him. He closed his eyes and sighed, allowing the comforting feel of sleep to envelop him.

*

RJ jerked awake to the sound of water rushing through pipes. He tried to raise an arm. It wouldn't budge. He tried the other arm. It strained against the thick metal band wrapped tightly around it. The daze of sleep vanished. RJ realized he wasn't in his suite—in the bed fitted with the finest of linens and the best mattress money could buy—but was instead, suspended, pulled tightly by his arms and legs. His eyes were covered by a soft fabric that allowed only the smallest ray of light to reach his sight—as though he was viewing a scene from an old movie; hazy, blurred edges of images, shot through layers of cheesecloth. A neon haze hung above him, cut only slightly by spindles of light from the rising-or-setting sun. He couldn't tell which.

A hiss from below gnawed at him and he stretched the muscles in his neck, turning his head to the side. He caught sight of still, clear, clean water below him. A pool? He pondered his own question, then tried to turn his head in the other direction: the same vision of clear, clean water.

"Your baptism is about to begin."

The sound of a voice so close to him shocked him, and he lurched at it, pulling hard against the restraints that cut and tore into his skin. He clamped his teeth together at the pain. "Who are you?" He managed through clenched teeth. What are you doing to me? Let me out of this."

"So many questions from someone who cannot make demands." The voice had a hint of laughter to it.

"I will pay you anything you ask."

"But I have asked nothing of you."

"What the *fuck* does that mean?"

"Let us say that I am your entry into the gates of Heaven."

RJ jerked his body against the restraints, tearing again at the skin of his wrists. "Get me out of here. Do you know who I *am*?

"How would I not? I have known who you are for a very long time. I personally selected you."

"Selected me for what?" RJ felt the creep of terror make its way through his body.

A small chuckle escaped from the voice. "I am here to help you meet the God that you worship."

RJ breathed in deeply, in an attempt to keep control of his emotions. "What the *fuck* are you saying?" He yanked at the straps wrapped around his arms and felt them cut deeper still into his skin. This time he screamed as the sharp metal edges tore the skin from his muscles. He twisted in agony. "Why are you doing this?"

"To fulfill your life's desire. So you can meet the God you have pledged your life to."

The voice had moved. It was now closer. RJ strained to catch a glimpse of the man through the gauze covering his eyes. "What do you want? Money? I've got plenty. I can get it for you; it's in the safe in my room. Just let me free and I'll take you there."

The voice laughed a guttural sound, ending in a hiss. "Oh, I've already been there, and I have all that I need." He laughed again.

A rumbling moved in below and around RJ. It caused him to sway, as a deep bass sound vibrated through the cables attached to the metal bands wrapped around his arms and legs. He could feel it deep within his bones. Then, as the rumbling grew ever more intense, his eyes could no longer focus, and even the slim view he had through the gauze became a blur.

The voice laughed again, the same guttural sound followed by a hiss, but this time it was distant, no longer by his side.

"Where are you, fucker? Where?" RJ screamed the words. "Help me!" he yelled. "Someone help me. Hel—" His words were cut short, as a blast of water shot up from the nozzle of the fountain below. The jet of water flowed with such force that it burrowed right through RJ's spine, piercing the skin, filling RJ's internal cavity with water, bloating him. He screamed out in pain and terror as the shell of his body could no longer contain the liquid. His body swelled as every centimeter of space between his muscles and bones, and veins and organs filled with water. He opened his mouth to scream again, but could not take a breath; his lungs had no room to expand.

The opening notes to *Viva Las Vegas* were the last sounds he heard as his eardrums burst from the growing pressure on his internal organs that could no longer be contained. His body followed: tendons tore from bones, bones ripped from the sinew holding them together. RJ's body exploded, filling the jets of water from the grand casino fountain that adorned the Strip with a bright crimson.

Fool

"I am Judgment." He leaned into the face of the terrified man looking him directly in the eyes.

The young man struggled to free his arms. "Let me go, you fucker."

He had the twenty-something man on his back, pinned down onto the hot pavement. The scorching rays of the Las Vegas summer sun had penetrated the black asphalt, sealing in the 120-degree heat. The twenty-something's thin T-shirt offered little protection.

The young man, weak from the effects of alcohol, copious amounts of drugs, and lack of sleep, could feel the heat from the pavement penetrating the thin tee. His skin started to burn.

"I smell the sweet scent of burning death," Judgment said, just inches from the pale skin of the man's face.

The young man pulled one hand free from Judgment's grip. He pushed his had down on the asphalt, and tried to right himself. He screamed in agony as the super-heated asphalt burned through the palm of his hand, searing lines into his flesh like a steak on a grill. He struggled through the pain, attempting to lift himself. The skin on his back now seared into the fabric of his shirt, tore away. "Fuck you! Fuck you!"

Judgment smiled, tilted his head to the side. "You may choose."

"Let me go!" the young man screamed.

"But that is what I intend. Simply answer this question." Judgment eased his grip on the young man's arm, releasing it. "Fool or Fortune?"

The young man immediately lurched up. He screamed out as the hot Vegas air hit the raw skin of his back.

"You see? There, you chose." A quiet chuckle escaped from Judgement's throat.

The young man got to his feet. Dizziness engulfed him and he nearly collapsed. Nausea overwhelmed him. He bent over and heaved bile and the last of the alcohol downed from the night before. His vision faded in and out, from bright light to blackness. He stumbled forward.

"You chose the Fool and acted accordingly." Judgment smiled.

With vision blurring, his equilibrium spinning, and muscles failing, the young man reached out to Judgment in a primordial effort to stabilize himself.

"Again, you had a choice to make, and you chose the Fool."

He grabbed onto the arms of the man, steadying himself for a few seconds, then fell to his knees as the last of his consciousness faded.

"Now you have chosen Fortune. He is the father of your foolishness." Judgment placed his hand on top of the young man's head. "May good Fortune be with you soon," he said as he stepped back, letting go of the young man's head.

The unconscious young man fell face first onto the asphalt. Immediately, the skin on his face and arms began to burn, bubble and blister.

Judgment watched for several minutes while the young man, literally, cooked. He gazed curiously as the skin swelled, browned and popped. The scent of the burning body smelled of steak grilling on a backyard barbeque, Judgment smiled as he remembered a scene from his youth, and a happier time with his parents, and barbeques now all but forgotten. The young man's horrific screams snapped Judgment back to the moment. "I now leave you to your fate... and fortune." He glanced up to the sky, checking the position of the sun. "Ahh." He let the sigh linger. "I see we have plenty of time left for you to thoroughly cook."

He turned and calmly strolled through the derelict neighborhood, in the direction of the Strip, where bright lights and tortured souls beckoned.

Judgement

The lights slowly faded, casting the entire showroom into blackness. Seconds later, a deep baritone voice boomed from the sound system, "Ladies and Gentleman, welcome. The final curtain is upon us. From the cast and crew of Jericho, we thank you for attending the final performance of Jericho—with the greatest magician in the world—Shylaine!"

All eyes focused on the stage where a single spotlight cast a circular pool onto the black surface of the stage. The theater was nearly silent, only scattered coughs and clearing of throats from several patrons in the packed house interrupted the silence. The circle of light, dead-center stage, glowed a brilliant white. Then, swiftly and dramatically, shifted from blue to purple to a deep red, then went completely black as an explosion of sound reverberated throughout the showroom. Screams erupted from many as a second explosion echoed, shaking the walls of the showroom.

Next, blinding white light from ten follow-spots ballyhooing around the walls, ceiling and seats of the showroom, came together fifty feet above the heads of the audience. Another blast of sound and light emanated from the center of the overhead beams... and Shylaine appeared. The orchestra kicked in with a brass and timpani filled ovation as the audience shouted and cheered their approval.

Shylaine waved, flinging her arms wide, as though she were embracing the entire audience. Then she smiled and leapt from the invisible platform. Screams erupted and several people directly below her jumped from their seats, afraid that she was about to fall on them. The showroom went black. More screams followed, combined this time with shouts of concern. Before the audience had settled and the shouts had quieted, a spotlight beamed to the center of the stage where Shylaine stood, arms wide and high above her head. Thunderous applause, cheers and nervous laughter filled the showroom.

Shylaine bowed graciously several times, accepting the audience's applause—and milking it a bit. She walked to a microphone and pulled it from a stand at the side of the stage. "As you can see, we don't save the best for last here," Shylaine announced to more applause and shouts of approval. "This is a sad and also glorious night for me and for all the wonderful, caring and supportive people that have made this show possible. I'm thrilled that you all could be here with us, on this last night, our final performance."

The orchestra kicked in this time with an ethereal melody reminiscent of a Cirque du Soleil show with shades of Enya thrown in. The soft, almost non-descript melody, with haunting shades of vocals, rose and fell while Shylaine moved quickly, as though she were gliding on skates, across the stage. She cupped her hands low to the stage floor, and, with some effort, raised them above her head, then glided away to another part of the stage to perform the same ritual. Fog floated in from the wings of the stage and the ceiling of the theater, filling the floor of the stage, and overflowing into the audience. The oversized blades of the fans slowly spun, blowing the fog in thick billowy clouds around the stage and showroom. Gradually—with the orchestra pushing out a deep rhythmic bass— the showroom rumbled. A wall of rock and mud rose from the floor of the stage. The wall filled the entire length of the stage. Shylaine continued her gesturing to the wall, beckoning it up higher and higher until it towered over her, three times her height of five-feet-four-inches. She swung her arms in a wide arc, indicating to the wall to stop. It did, and the orchestra went silent.

She turned to the audience. "Ladies and Gentleman, the Wall of Jericho." With a sweep of her arms and a theatrical spin like that of an ice skater, she summoned forth the horns of Gabriel as told in the Book of Joshua. The back of the showroom thundered as trumpeter after trumpeter marched down the aisles until they were twenty deep on both sides of the showroom. The rows of trumpeters faced one another. With a flurry of dramatics, a single trumpeter at the front of the line, raised his horn to his lips and blew a soft single note. The other trumpeters raised their instruments to their mouths in unison, and with a collective intake of breath, blew into the mouthpieces of the horns. They perfectly matched the soft single note coming from the first trumpet.

Shylaine danced about the stage. The trumpets grew more and more intense. The single note emanated now with fervor. Louder. Then louder still. Shylaine pointed first to the row of trumpeters on her left. They turned to face the stage. Then she pointed to the trumpeters on her right, and they too faced the stage. She raised her hands above her and the trumpeters blasted out the single note in an intensely, almost hypnotic and malignant blare. Audience members covered their ears at the deafening sound. A child in the back of the house cried. The theater shook with the sound. It penetrated the seats and vibrated up along the spines of the audience. Then, when it seemed the sound could crescendo no more, a timpani pounded out a counter rhythm and with strobes of light flashing, the Wall of Jericho exploded. Debris fell onto the stage. Several people in the front rows ducked as bits and pieces of rock and dust washed over them.

Then silence.

Dust settled and the fog began to dissipate. The trumpeters dropped the instruments to their sides and stood at attention.

From the audience a shout echoed, "Mother?" and broke the eerie silence.

Out of the thinning fog, shapes began to appear.

Shylain returned the shout, "Collin?" followed by her screams, "No. No. It *can't be*?"

And then a cacophony of shouts of joy, mixed with cries of terror and screams of disbelief as the long dead, the forgotten and the feared, materialized alongside the audience. The dead and the living, coming together. A voice bellowed from above, "In the twinkling of an eye, as the last trumpet sounds, the dead will be raised, and we will be changed." Judgement's voice morphed into laughter.

All around the theater, the dead were appearing, taking form out of the fog, filling the aisles and rows.

Shylaine turned, running from the stage to come face to face with the burnt, smoldering, and swollen face of the young man. "Collin?" Her voice quivered with fear and disbelief. His flesh was falling from his face, revealing the muscle and bone under it, his jawbone visible.

Collin raised his skinless arms, beckoning the woman to come nearer. "Mother. Mother?"

Shylaine screamed in terror.

"Why did you leave me, Mother? Why would you leave me?" Collin took a step closer to Shylaine.

She backed away from him and hit another body that had corporealized behind her. She turned. It was all she could do to keep from collapsing. "RJ?" she whispered and turned from RJ to her son, and back.

Shylaine screamed.

RJ's shredded body attempted to reach out a hand. The hand hung limp, dangling from the end of the wrist, held only by a tendon. RJ opened his mouth to speak. No words came forth, only gurgling water poured from his lips.

The sounds of cries, screams, shouts and begging that had filled the showroom slowly faded, becoming muffled, suffocated and choked, as the dead started to take their toll on the living.

Collin and RJ moved in a syncopated step toward Shylaine. They came together and embraced her.

At once she began to burn... and drown.

The last sound Shylaine heard was a voice that was so near, she could feel the heat of his words on her ear. "It is not only the final performance of Jericho... it is also your final performance."

The last sensation Shylaine felt was her son's embrace burning the skin on her back, and her husband's kiss, filling her lungs with water.

Then the last words from Judgment, "The Father, the Son and the Spirit. Judgment is upon us."

22

THE WORLD

JAIME RUSH

Upright: Assured success, route, voyage, emigration, flight, change of place
Reversed: Inertia, fixity, stagnation, permanence

Lucas Vanderwyck's eyes snapped open in the darkness of the bedroom. Remaining still, he listened for a sound, watched for a shifting shadow. His heart pounded, and his pulse throbbed in his throat, a flashback to the days when he and Amy had perpetually lived in danger. But that was over now. The Offspring, the group of psychically enhanced humans to whom they belonged, had vanquished their otherworldly enemies. So possibly an everyday average intruder. Funny that a thief with a gun would be a simple threat after all they'd encountered. Then again, most thieves couldn't mind control or turn a person into mush.

Several minutes passed without incident. Just a dream then. But something felt off. Wrong. He laid his hand on his wife's belly, feeling protective of "Smudge" growing inside her. They'd only had their first ultrasound, and the little guy—or girl—was only that so far: a smudge on the screen.

Lucas slid out of bed and padded down the hall to check on their firstborn. Francesca slept in her crib, washed in the glow of the monkey night light. He dove into her dreams, floating through the ethers and then to the blue water of the pool. He smiled. She was reliving her first swim.

He pulled out and wandered the house. For months, he and the group of people who'd become his family had been hunted by a subversive government agency. They had stayed alive by the skin of their teeth—and the psychic powers they inherited from a parent involved in a classified project gone awry, along with a little alien DNA.

They'd gone through hell, but now they were back, safe in their ordinary lives.

Amy screamed, "Noooo!"

Lucas raced to their room and found her writhing and gasping in bed. He knelt beside her and brushed her brown hair from her face. "It's only a dream, babe. Wake up." Echoes from that hell still whispered in their nightmares. He gently shook her. "Amy."

She slapped her hands over her stomach. "Nooo! Don't you dare!" Her body thrashed violently, no longer in the safe paralysis of REM sleep. A frisson of alarm skittered down his spine. That was how he'd assassinated bad people in their dreams.

Lucas dove in to see what kind of monster she was fighting. And stop the nightmare. He could change it, using his dreamweaving ability.

The black veil lifted, and he took in his surroundings: a dark wood, gloomy and filled with leering eyes behind bushes. No Amy. The sounds of a struggle floated through a dense fog. Amy's scream shot him into a run. *It's only a dream. She's not in danger.*

He slammed into a tree, hidden by the same fog that had dampened his shirt. He muttered an expletive and kept running. "Amy!"

"Lucas! Help me! He's—"

Her words were cut off with an *oof.*

Lucas rammed into a branch, feeling the rough bark tear into his skin. He kept running in the direction of the noise, straining to hear Amy as she tried to scream during what was clearly an altercation. Feet scrambled on earth, flesh smacked against flesh.

He burst into a foggy clearing, barely able to make out Amy kicking a man. "Amy!"

She turned toward him, and her shoulders drooped in relief. "Lucas!"

The distraction gave her assailant the chance to slip behind her. Before Lucas could move closer, the man had his arms clamped around her chest, pinning her tight. His head was hidden by hers, only revealing brown, wavy hair.

"It's only a dream," Lucas said. "Wake up."

"I don't think it is!"

"Of course it is. It's—" His words died in his throat.

The man leaned to the left, revealing his face. Revealing... Lucas's face. His brain spun in confusion. How could *he* be attacking his wife in her dreams?

Unless...

"Sayre?" he uttered, feeling foolish at even saying his twin's name.

The leering smile that had haunted him from the time he'd discovered the son of a bitch existed, spread across the man's face. "Fancy seein' you here, bro. But ya know, you're interrupting a tender moment."

Amy fought to wriggle free. "Bastard!" She lifted her foot and stomped down, but Sayre moved his foot just in time.

"Amy, this is a dream. He can't really be here. He's—"

"Dead." Sayre drew the word into two syllables with his cocky Southern accent. "Courtesy of that psycho pittin' me against your buddy. Burned to ash. Ashes to ashes and all that."

"Which means you're not here." Time to change the dreamscape to one he and Amy had visited many times: the pyramids in Egypt.

Except nothing changed. Lucas tried again, imagining a wide beach. A hilltop. Hell, anything but this grim, gloomy forest.

Nothing.

Fear squeezed his chest. "How can you be here?"

"My soul ain't dead. I'm stuck in some purgatory like place. The other day I thought, maybe I'll see if my soul can still go into dreams. Guess I brought my world into Amy's dream; I can't change it either."

Lucas could barely wrap his head around it. Sayre, still tormenting them. He possessed the same psychic skills as Lucas, and he would kill Amy just for the fun of it.

"Let her go. It's me you're after. Me you hate. She has nothing to do with this."

"You think I hate you because you were raised by our father while I was adopted out to the couple who testified against me in court? Nah, it's all good. It made me the incredible person I am—or was. And now I'm gonna be a proud papa."

That's when Lucas saw that Sayre's hand was splayed over Amy's stomach. She screamed and clawed at him as that hand sank into her.

Lucas lunged forward, reaching them just as Sayre disappeared. He caught Amy before she dropped to the ground. "It's just a nightmare. Sayre's dead. He's just screwing with us from beyond the grave."

She shook her head, crying. "No, it's real. I feel it."

Suddenly they were back in their bed. She sat up with a gasp, her hand on her stomach, her eyes wide as they met his. "You were there, right?"

Her last hope that it wasn't a run-of-the-mill nightmare. He was sorry to nod.

"He took our baby!" she wailed, scrambling out of bed.

"I think he's just messing with us." He followed her into the bathroom.

She crouched in front of the cabinet and dug around inside. "I thought I had another pregnancy test in here."

"I'll go to the store and buy one." Just to comfort her because of course Sayre couldn't take their unborn child. That was impossible. He had simply found a way to torment them until he moved on to hell.

Except they'd experienced things far beyond possible . . .

"Get five!" she said.

He kissed her on the nose. "I'll be right back."

Lucas found her curled up in the rocking chair staring at their baby girl when he returned.

Amy took the bag he held up and disappeared into the bathroom. She remerged a few minutes later, her face leeched of all color but her freckles. "It's negative!" She thrust the stick toward him.

Of course she'd read it wrong, expecting the worst. He took it and studied the tiny window. Only one line. Not pregnant. Something buzzed deep in his own belly. "It's defective," he finally said when he could form words.

She went back into the bathroom, then came out with three more sticks, all with the same result. "I saved the other one to take tomorrow, but…" She gasped in grief. "Even if I miscarried, I'd still have the hormones floating around. But they're gone too! He took our baby!"

Lucas pulled her close, reality settling in like thorns sinking deeper into his flesh. Somehow Sayre had stolen their baby. The how may never be answered. None of them would fully know the impact that having the essence of a being from a parallel dimension would have on their bodies. Their souls.

Why was the question that haunted him. What did his deranged twin want with their unborn child?

"I'll find him."

She stepped back, both hope and hopelessness on her tear-streaked face. "How? He's not able to dream because he's not in a body."

"He probably came through me, through my dreams and then my psychic connection to you. If he can get to me, I can get to him."

Amy nodded, holding on to the lifeline he'd just given her. "I need to come too. I need to be connected to you, because Smudge must come right back to me." She rubbed her belly, now flat again.

"You know how dangerous Sayre is. And remember how he liked you. We don't know what he can do now. What if he… grabs your soul?"

I love my little visits. And your girlfriend, she's cute. The memory of Sayre's taunt still punched Lucas in the gut.

Amy stretched up to plant her hands on his shoulders. "You do know me, right? I will go with you. I could fight him in the dreamscape, and with me there, it'll be two against one."

Lucas nodded. "I do know you. Brave. Capable. Add in your mother-bear anger, and we can't fail." He hoped.

She smiled, relief seeping out in a sigh. "Thank you for not fighting me on this. Let's go back to sleep right now. We'll—" She glanced at the baby's room. "We can't leave Francesca here by herself."

"No. We don't know how long we'll be." *Or if we'll come back.* No need to share that possibility. They were dealing with another world here. Another reality. "We'll ask Eric and Fonda to come over." Eric was like a brother to him, and his wife had grown to be a sister.

"If something were to happen to us, Eric might be able to help."

"Like how, setting fire to Sayre's soul?" But no, Eric could do more than pyrokinesis. "He could find us. Maybe. He's only used his remote viewing ability in the physical world."

"Well, Fonda could astral project, if that doesn't work."

Lucas rang up Eric, who answered with a gruff, "I hate middle-of-the-night calls. Please do not tell me there are more uber-humans from parallel dimensions hunting us."

"No, just the ghost of my psycho-twin." He filled in Eric, who cussed with every revelation.

"We're on our way."

Amy brewed herbal tea designed to make them sleepy. "'Cause I can't even imagine sleeping right now, I'm so keyed up." She scrubbed her fingers through her crazy hair.

They'd downed a whole mug each when the doorbell rang. Eric opened the door and gestured for Fonda, a small gal with white-blond hair, to enter first. She rushed over to Amy and hugged her. "I'm so sorry this is happening to you. You two just don't get a break, do you?"

Eric's big frame filled the door opening. His eyes went to Lucas, then Amy, his half-sister. He didn't have to speak the words; he felt the same.

"Thanks for coming," Lucas said, accepting a consoling hug from Eric. "I'd like you to be our lookout."

"And watch Francesca," Amy added. "She should stay asleep for another few hours, but you never know."

"We're her godparents," Fonda said. "She's in good hands."

"How long do I give you before I try to do a locate? Or shake you out of it?" Eric asked.

"Give us until dawn."

"Or if you stop breathing," Eric added somberly. "Go on. I'll be right here."

Amy didn't look any more sleepy than Lucas felt, but they settled together on the bed. Eric sat in the lounge chair by the bay window, and Fonda snuggled up in front of him.

"Be careful," she said, worry etched on her delicate features. "Don't let him trap your souls anywhere."

"I don't think this works like astral projection. Or like what happened to you," Amy said.

Fonda was clearly reliving her own terror when their enemy had trapped her essence in a special jar. "But you don't know for sure."

"We'll be careful," Lucas promised. He knew Amy would throw herself in danger to save their child. She'd done no less trying to save him. He would have to be the logical one.

He linked hands with hers, creating the physical connection that would allow her to accompany him. He met her gaze. "Ready?"

She nodded, worrying her lower lip with her teeth.

It took time for him to calm his mind and anger. He counted backward from a hundred and forward again. Finally he slipped into hypnogogic sleep, and then REM.

Thick fog surrounded him, clinging like cold, dead fingers. He'd reached Sayre's world. He felt Amy's hand wrapped tightly in his but couldn't see her through this damned fog.

The fog faded by degrees, revealing Amy standing stiffly at his side, ready for anything.

"We don't even know what to look for," she whispered. "A smudge? He's only the size of peanut."

The fog cleared more, and Lucas had to stare hard to take in what he was seeing—acres of peanut fields, for as far as the eye could see.

"I hate that guy," Lucas growled.

Distant laughter juxtaposed their mood. Then Sayre materialized riding a huge raven. "But brother, I'm part of you. So that means you hate yourself."

Sometimes he did, but he wasn't admitting that.

"Why are you doing this?" Amy screamed up at him. "We never did anything to you!"

"You think I'm trying to punish you?"

"Or you're still a psychopath in this realm," Lucas offered.

"Well, you're both wrong. This little guy here, he's mine now." He turned the bird, and Lucas could now see that a toddler who looked just like him sat in front of Sayre. His eyes were wide, face set in wonder as he stroked the bird's glossy feathers.

Amy's hand tightened on Lucas's. "Is that... Smudge?"

"I call him Stanley," Sayre answered. "Yep, Amy, you were havin' a boy."

"Give me my son!" Amy screamed, a hysterical edge in her voice.

"Look, you two diddle some more and have another one. Stanley's mine. I never did get to have a kid. You can have plenty. Apparently," he muttered. "It's like when you got a litter of puppies. You try to find homes for 'em. You don't keep 'em all."

"Babies are not like puppies, you asshole," Lucas said. "You have no right—"

"But my DNA is in him too. That's how I could take him, y'know. My connection to you, and to him. Always wanted someone to love." He patted the boy's head. "I aged him a little. No idea how to raise a baby. But this guy is more than a companion. He's my ticket to the Beyond." Sayre nodded his chin toward towering clouds in the distance.

Except they weren't clouds. On top of a fog-shrouded mountain sat a white castle.

"What is it?" Lucas asked, his chest tightening with dread. Hell. That's all he could think about; Sayre was taking his son to Hell.

Sayre shrugged. "I don't know exactly. The beings here, they tell me it's a place of no return. You have to make a long, treacherous journey to the entrance. Once someone goes through, they don't come back. Which is good, 'cause I hate this place. When I clear this illusion, you'll see why. I've been told my soul's too dark to pass through, but I bet I can with a pure little soul at my side. Me and Stanley, we're gonna fly right over all the spooky shit below." He arched an eyebrow. "Catch us if you can."

Like a master horseman, he turned the raven with reins and headed off into a sky blanketed in gray clouds.

"Lucas!" Amy screamed.

"We'll catch him." Lucas conjured a Pegasus, and they climbed onto its back. The horse galloped for a few seconds and lifted off. Lucas saw the raven up ahead, growing smaller with distance. He jammed his heels into the horse's side. "Giddy up, Peg!"

The moment they were airborne, the peanut fields evaporated, revealing a lush forest.

"What's so scary about a forest?" Amy asked, leaning over to look down. "Oh, something like that maybe."

What he'd taken for a river, flowing gray and speckled, turned out to be an enormous snake. He could see its solidity now, the way the sunlight glistened off its scales.

"Where is its head?" Lucas asked.

"Uh, heading right toward that deer."

In a small opening, a deer sipped from a pond, sending gentle ripples across the water's surface. The snake slithered closer. Closer. The deer lifted its head in fright—and opened its mouth, revealing rows of sharp fangs. Its neck grew giraffe-like as it lunged toward the snake. Before it reached its target, a huge, slimy claw broke out of the water and snagged the deer. It let out ghostly screams as it plunged under the tumultuous surface.

"Holy crap, what was that?" Amy asked, still turned to see as they passed over the scene.

"I'm glad we're up here is all I can say."

The horse's wings sent a whoosh of wind with each powerful stroke, gaining on the raven. Suddenly, the bird seemed to hit an invisible wall, its wings flattening, its head thrown to the side. It dropped to the ground, along with its riders.

"Smudge!" Amy cried out.

Lucas visually snagged a landmark where they fell, a dead tree poking up out of the forest. "Sayre will probably conjure a sea of mattresses beneath them. He doesn't want to hurt our baby."

"No, he wants to take him to Hell. For company!" She sniffled behind him, her arms tightening over his stomach. "But something stopped them."

"And it's probably going to stop us too." As they neared the dead tree, Lucas slowed the horse. He could see the faint shimmering of the wall, nothing more. He touched it, finding it as solid as glass. The horse continued alongside it as Lucas felt his way in both directions. "It seems to go on indefinitely."

"We need to get down there and find them," Amy said, searching for Sayre and Smudge.

"Down there" was a mass of trees and vines and shadows. God knew what lurked in them.

He directed the horse down toward the canopy. Damn, even his conjured creature seemed reluctant. A deafening sound started once they neared the top of the trees. Like crickets on steroids. Like screaming monkeys. Like the thrum of bullfrogs, all at once. Creatures scurried among the highest branches. Some ran away. Others crept closer, glowing eyes watching with interest.

As they slowly descended in a narrow space between trees, he saw a frog creature with a squashed face. Farther down, a black, furry thing slid behind the leaves.

The moment they touched down, Lucas and Amy jumped to the ground. Something dark and fast streaked past them and speared the horse all the way through. A long rope tethered the hook and, like a fishing lure, pulled the bloody horse toward a wall of fluttering vines. The horse whinnied, fighting it even as it gasped for life. Lucas snapped his fingers, and Pegasus disappeared. What looked like a four-pronged anchor with barbs for feet dropped to the ground in its absence.

Crap. Now they were available prey! Lucas put his arm in front of Amy, and they inched backward. Amy hissed and pointed to the anchor that gained its "feet" and scrambled toward them like a spider on a leash. Scissor-like fangs swished back and forth underneath its body. It jumped at them, as it had done to the horse.

They dropped to the ground as it flew overhead, then rolled to the side when it rebounded.

"Make it go away!" Amy screamed as they lurched to their feet and ran.

Lucas focused on changing the dream as they weaved through trees and vines. Only this wasn't a dream or a nightmare. It was... hell. "Sayre said the peanut field was an illusion. Maybe because he lives here he can create one temporarily, but I can't change this."

A vine wound down and slapped at his arm, stinging like a hundred nettles. "And this is no illusion," he said, wincing as blisters rose on his skin. "Watch the vines, Amy. They're nasty."

She jerked out of the way of another one swinging down from above. It tangled in her hair, wrenching her back. He grabbed it, despite the stinging, and tore it away from her.

"Do I want to know what that was?" she asked, moving fast in front of him.

"One of those vines."

"A vine that grabbed me?"

"Yep." He flexed his hand, feeling welts on his palm.

"We can wake up at any time, right? And leave this place?"

"Yes."

They both knew they wouldn't leave Smudge here, though. It was nice to at least know they could. That was their illusion.

They wound their way between trees and questionable vegetation.

"Do we know that we're going in the right direction?" Amy asked as she ducked a branch covered in spines. "Even if there was a distinct sun, we couldn't see it from down here."

"I'm pretty sure we are."

"I don't like 'pretty sure.'"

He glanced over at a tree trunk that was breathing. "Pretty sure is all we have." Like, he was pretty sure if they caught Sayre, there would be a fight. And he was pretty sure if they could get their hands on Smudge, they could somehow put him back into Amy's belly. No need to discuss.

In the distance, the sound of a body hitting the ground hard stopped them in their tracks. Then an "Oof," and a thump. Lucas tuned in to the very human sound, and he pointed toward the right.

A child's cry shot them forward. While Amy did the mama bear rush through the brush, Lucas watched for weird and dangerous flora and fauna. An iridescent blue bird with a rapier-like beak hunkered down on a low branch as Amy approached, watching her with its beady green eyes. Lucas grabbed a broken branch and threw it at the bird, sending it into flight with ear-shattering screeches.

"God, what was that?" Amy called. "A parrot?"

"A bird. But nothing like On'ry." Amy's ornery cockatoo might be a pain in the ass, but compared to that thing, he was a softie.

He could feel eyes watching them, most likely with dinner in mind. Or lunch, or whatever the hell time it was here. He hoped there wasn't nightfall; it was dark enough.

Lucas scooped up other weapon-sized sticks. When one grew hot and moved in his hands, though, he tossed them all without even looking.

Another "Oof" in the distance, but growing closer. The sound of thrashing foliage, a growl. *Oh, nice. This should be fun.*

A copse of bright green trees ahead looked like a tropical oasis. Amy broke through the bushes and came to an abrupt stop. Lucas came up behind her, ready for anything. It did, indeed, look like an island, a circle of white sugar sand about fifty yards across surrounded by palms with fronds sporting wide center sections.

His gaze first went to their son, caged in by a palm frond bowed all the way to the sand. Smudge pushed and pulled on fronds as solid as metal bars, as frustrated as Francesca sometimes looked when she wanted out of her crib.

To the right, two creatures circled Sayre. They were large, over a hundred pounds each, and looked like some sort of mix between a sabretooth tiger and hell-hound. Their yellow fangs descended several inches below their square chins. Huge glowing eyes probably allowed them to see in the murk of the jungle. They had taken some flesh from Sayre, who stood arrogant and bleeding from his shoulder. Now they focused on the newcomers.

"Go ahead and finish with him," Lucas said, gesturing to Sayre. "Didn't mean to interrupt." On a whisper, he said, "Amy, circle behind me and around to Smudge."

He knew he didn't need to tell her to move slowly. She did, silently creeping along the outer edge. One of the sabre-hounds stalked toward him, while the other moved closer to Sayre.

If Lucas could conjure a flying horse, he could conjure other things. In a moment, he held a gun, but when he squeezed the trigger, nothing came out but a click. So maybe he couldn't conjure something mechanical. He conjured a sword, no mechanics involved, just slice and dice. He brought the sword down in an arc toward the hound's thick neck as Sayre said, "Don't—"

The creature split in two and fell to the ground. As Lucas charged toward the second one, both pieces morphed into a whole new creature, growing to full size in seconds.

"—cut the thing," Sayre finished sardonically, lifting a long machete. "That's how I have two of them."

"Great. And now we have three."

From the corner of his eye, Lucas saw Amy working at the fronds and having no more luck than Smudge had in moving them. Even worse, the baby shrank away from her in fear.

"The palm frond is like a Venus flytrap," Sayre said in a low, even voice. "It will eventually grab onto him and suck him dry."

Amy let out a soft cry.

"How do you break out of it?" Lucas hoped Sayre would be motivated to help, since he needed their son.

"I dunno. I tried to free a rabbit from one once. I was starving, and the things are not only fast, but have razor-sharp tongues that lash out. Figured I'd steal it from the trap. Didn't work so well."

Amy was searching for something, probably to tear the plant apart. Her fingers sank into the soft sand, as his feet were doing. Lucas focused on the two hounds in front of him who appeared none too happy about being sliced into two beings. Maybe it hurt. He hoped so. He looked up and spotted more of those palm fronds that sucked things dry. Yes, he could use those.

He trudged through the sand to the right of the beasts, holding out his sword to keep them at bay. They tracked him just out of range of the sword. One started to go around to his other side, the way they had cornered Sayre.

Lucas stopped beneath the frond, then inched farther back, luring them to the largest frond.

"You're a flippin' genius," Sayre said, stepping backward as he looked up for his own frond, probably.

Lucas jumped up and grabbed hold of the stem, bringing the frond down over the creatures. The soft-looking fronds drove into the ground like spikes, trapping its prey. One creature jumped and stuck to the roof of the frond. A sound like a knife plunging into flesh gave Lucas a cold chill, made worse by a slurping sound. The creature screamed in pain, eerily similar to a child's cry. Like a deflated balloon, it collapsed to the ground a minute later. The other beast slunk low, eyeing the flat section of frond above it.

Amy let out another cry as she stuck her hand between the fronds and covered their son's head to keep him from standing. He'd been saved because he was sitting. So far.

Lucas turned to find Sayre bringing down a frond over the third creature. He glanced up to see if there was another frond above his twin. No such luck.

Lucas grabbed up the sword he'd laid down and ran toward Amy. With a swipe, he cut the base of the frond from its head. The spikes softened, and Amy pushed the frond away. She reached for Smudge. He shrank away, then looked over his shoulder and smiled.

Sayre swung on a vine toward them. Lucas lunged for Smudge, but Sayre snatched the boy a second before him and continued swinging on. He landed on the dark dirt and loam of the forest floor and ran.

"Bastard!" Lucas spat.

"Lucas, help!"

Amy stood hip deep in the sand. Lucas tried to run toward her, but his legs were now buried to his calves. And sinking fast.

"Cutting the fronds seemed to have triggered it," she said. "It was soft before, but as soon as the frond was cut, the sand loosened beneath my knees."

Lucas felt it too, though he'd been too focused on Smudge. "That's what the son of a bitch meant when he said it didn't go well."

"He got out, though. So can we." She tried to grab the severed frond stalk, but it remained just out of reach.

"Stop moving. It just makes you sink faster, and there's no way you'll touch it. Hold on." He conjured a lasso and tossed it over her head toward a tree growing just outside the quicksand circle. It slipped off, and he snatched it back. Threw it again. This time it draped over the branch above Amy's head.

She wound it around the branch one more time for strength, then started to climb it toward the edge of the sand. He searched for a way out for himself. The sand now reached mid-thigh. It was greedy, hungry. Hell, it was probably a living thing itself. He checked on Amy, who was almost to the shore with the rope in a death grip. Safe. Any moment she would turn around and yell—

"Lucas! Get out!"

Yep, that. "Coming, babe." He searched for something to pull himself up, but he stood smack-dab in the middle of the clearing.

"Here!" she called, climbing a spindly tree so that it bent low over the pit. He conjured another rope and tossed over the tree. Amy wrapped it around the trunk, holding onto the end. "Pull!"

The tree drooped with his weight. "Amy, you're going to fall back in. Climb down. I've got this."

When she hit the ground, the tree lifted, raising him a little more. He heard the sucking sound as his legs came free. The sand particles moved independently of the flow of sludge. He imagined millions of tiny creatures all mourning the loss of dinner.

Shit.

"Sayre has a huge head start," she said as he gave her a brief hug when he reached her.

"Then let's get going."

They ran, steering clear of other "oases." Monkeys scampered along tree branches overhead. One swung down, making Amy back right into him. They both tumbled backward, she falling on top of him. He shoved her to the side as the monkey jumped down in front of them.

Of course, it couldn't be a normal monkey. No, it was a psycho-fanged one with black claws and devilish eyes.

As Lucas scrambled to a defensive position, it leaned close and hissed, "You don't belong here."

Lucas felt Amy do the same startled flinch. She blurted out, "No, but some scoundrel who does belong here stole our baby."

The monkey amazingly seemed to contemplate this. "I saw them." It nodded its head to the left.

"Can you help us find them?" Amy asked, while he might have asked, "Will you not eat us?"

"The terrible man is taking our baby to the Beyond," Amy continued. "Where does it go?"

It was odd to see the monkey shrug. "All we know is that those who enter never return. I can help you through the Forest of Lost Souls. That is where your scoundrel should be living, though he escaped some time ago. Follow me."

Amy and Lucas shared a questioning look, but the monkey grabbed a vine and took off. The answer: follow it.

They entered an even darker wood with gnarled, dead trees that impeded their progress. As the monkey grew farther away, something else grew closer. Lucas turned to the right, catching sight of a human. A sort of human.

The man was gray, as though being viewed through a filter. And slightly stretched, arms and legs disproportionally long and rubbery. His eyes, only gaping dark holes. He reached toward them, uttering, "Help me," on a hoarse wail. His fingers seemed to elongate. To stretch toward them.

"Go, go, go," Lucas said, pushing an apparently shocked Amy into moving.

"Don't let the Lost Souls touch you," the monkey whispered from a branch high above. "They'll suck your soul away. You'll be trapped here... turned into a monkey or other creature."

"Like... you?" Lucas asked as they continued to follow their helper.

"Yes. I'm a Dreamweaver too. I've been here... well, I don't know how long for certain. I went somewhere I shouldn't have."

"When?"

"Eighteen-ninety-five. What year is it now in the real world?"

"I don't think you want to know."

Other Lost Souls emerged from the camouflage of the old, gray trees. Desperately reaching out.

Suddenly, a woman stood within a foot of them, crying out in pain, her hand about to touch Lucas's shoulder. The monkey jumped down, screeching and throwing her off balance.

Lucas and Amy ran ahead, taking advantage of its diversion. His diversion. He'd been human once.

Amy shot Lucas a fearful look, probably thinking the same thing: That could be us!

More Lost Souls converged on them, like roaches coming out in the dark. Lucas grabbed a half-broken branch and batted them back. When it flew out of his hand, knocking a—God, just a child— backward onto the ground, he conjured his sword again.

The monkey was suddenly above them, limberly jumping from branch to branch. "This way," he said, gesturing with a long, hairy arm toward the right. "The Beyond is not far from here."

"What's your name?" Lucas asked, nearly out of breath.

"Silas Moorehaven."

"Thank you, Silas. You saved us back there."

A hundred yards ahead, he could see the edge of the gray trees and light. At least lighter than in here.

Soon they burst into an open field of wheat-like grass. On the other side, a craggy mountain rose, and at the top, the castle with the mysterious door.

The Lost Souls raced toward them but seemed to hit the same kind of invisible shield they'd encountered before. Silas, too, remained just inside the forest, sitting on a branch and pointing ahead. "You'll go up that mountain. Watch out for the goats; they'll try to kick you off."

"Oh, great," Lucas muttered.

Silas lifted a palm that was cut and scarred. "Be safe. Return to the world. And let my family know... no, it's better that they think me dead and in heaven."

"Is there any way we can help you?" Amy asked.

"No. I did terrible things whilst Dreamweaving, and this is my penance. Perhaps I can gain absolution by helping you. Go on, find your child."

With regret, Lucas turned, along with Amy, and continued running toward the towering mountain. He had done terrible things too. But he had killed bad people, at least.

They ran through the waist-high grass, watching for terrible creatures hiding within. Things moved closer, making the grass sway against the wind, reminding him of sharks weaving through water. They reached the base of the mountain and jumped up to the first ledge, then climbed higher. He turned to look over the sea of grass. A dozen creatures the size of basketballs carved paths through the grass, some only a yard from the edge of the field. They looked like piranhas, flat with large eyes and serrated teeth.

"God," Amy said on heaving breaths.

Lucas looked across at the dark wood and beyond. "I think God is absent from this place."

They climbed up the jagged mountainside. In the distance, mountain goats whinnied and hopped easily across the rocks toward them.

"Damned things probably have fangs," he muttered, grabbing onto the next outcropping.

"And hooves that shoot poison," Amy added, keeping pace beside him.

The goats grew closer, fiery orange eyes narrowing on them. Lucas glanced down at the long, jagged fall they would suffer if knocked off. He eyed the distance between them and the herd, probably ten of them, and the castle at the top. "We might make it."

"We will," she said. "Look!"

Sayre, with Smudge in some sort of backpack, scrambled over the top ledge. He glanced down at them, a smirk on his face. Then he kicked a loose rock, sending it crashing down at them.

Lucas ducked, but it hit his hand, smashing bones, cutting skin. Pain rocketed through him like an electrical shock. He hung by one hand, unable to move the fingers of his other.

"Lucas!" Amy wailed.

"Keep going," he gritted out, putting more weight on his feet. *The pain isn't real, isn't—shit, it feels real.*

Sayre knocked another rock down. It bounded closer, rock by rock, falling right between them as they leaned away. Then he was gone.

Heading for the doorway.

Amy slipped a few feet. "I'm fine," she called. "Keep going, as much as you can."

That was barely, but he wasn't about to say it. He grunted and breathed out in pain, coming up to the edge. Sayre stood at the door, patting the completely flat surface, searching for the way in.

Smudge looked back, giving him a fearful look. What had Sayre told him about the two crazed people chasing them? He just hoped the little guy didn't alert Sayre to his awkward attempt to climb over the edge.

Amy hauled herself over, then held out her hand to help him. They fell in a heap, alerting Sayre to their presence now.

Now *he* looked fearful. They were about to ruin his plan. They lurched forward, Amy with her arms out to scoop up their son.

The door slowly opened.

She was only feet away, calling, "Baby boy, don't go! Come here to your mama!"

The boy reached out to her, the fear gone. Amy's fingers brushed his. Sayre knocked her back and dove into the blackness beyond the door.

"No!" Amy cried, lunging for them. The door materialized again, and she slapped and pounded on it.

Lucas stilled her hands. "We can't go. We don't belong here."

"Neither does Smudge!" Tears streamed down her face. "We were so close!"

Lucas gathered her in his arms. "Let's go home."

They woke, with Eric and Fonda watching over them. "Man, you guys were writhing all over the place," he said.

"It was bad." Lucas sat up and checked his mangled hand: unharmed.

"Horrible," Amy said. "And we just missed saving him." She dissolved into tears.

"Try the pregnancy test again," Lucas suggested. "Just in case it was all an illusion."

"The tests weren't." But she pulled herself from the bed and went into the bathroom. When she emerged a few minutes later, her face was pale, her mouth open. She held up the stick: *two lines.*

*

Amy let the nurse rub her belly with the gel that allowed the ultrasound wand to glide over the small mound of her stomach. She squeezed Lucas's hand and held her breath. Would Smudge be alive? Eight more tests had come up positive. But she wanted to know that he was all right.

"There's the heartbeat," the tech said, pointing to the screen. Amy didn't even look, so relieved that she let her head drop back to the pillow.

"Wait," the woman said. "That's strange."

No. No strange! Was there now some horrid creature inside her? But she and Lucas pressed closer, studying the mystery of the screen. "What?" they asked simultaneously.

The tech smiled. "You have twins. Interesting that we didn't see it before, though it happens. Congratulations double!"

She looked at Lucas, and could see that he was thinking the same thing. "Sayre," they uttered.

"Oh, don't be scared," the tech said, wiping off the gel. "You'll do just fine."

When she left, Amy remained on the table, her hand on her belly. "One of them is Sayre," she said. "And we won't know which one."

"The door to the Beyond must be the way back here. It's the only explanation."

"What do we do?"

Lucas put his hand over hers. "We raise them the best we can. And we face the ultimate test of nurture or nature."

ACE

WANDS

23

ACE OF WANDS

TORI ELDRIDGE

Upright: Creation, Invention, Enterprise, Principle, Beginning, Source, Birth, Family, Origin, Money, Fortune, Inheritance
Reversed: Fall, Decadence, Ruin, Perdition, To perish, Clouded joy

Bali, Indonesia 1965

Gunshots cracked the night and woke Wayan from a dead sleep.

His mother shouted from somewhere in the compound, "Where is your father?" The panic in her voice rose with each word. "Where is he?"

Wayan bolted out of his bed and jumped off the sleeping pavilion. His bare feet landed hard on the gravel path. Pebbles crunched. Shouts rumbled from the street. The night sky glowed with an unnatural light. Beyond the stone wall of his family's compound, another gun fired.

Although only eleven, Wayan reacted with the speed of a man. He sprinted to the front gate, dodging the free-standing partition that blocked the way and prevented bad spirits from entering his family's home. What did it matter that spirits could not turn corners? Evil men could.

"Father!"

Wayan ran through the towering entrance gate. It resembled a temple, but what good were stone pillars and a pagoda roof if they could not even protect one man from a killing squad?

His mother tried to chase after him, but his little siblings pulled at her dress. "Wayan, wait!"

He did not listen. Instead, he ran into the dirt road where men in para-military uniforms shot their rifles into the air and laughed. But these were not military men. They were something so much worse. Neighbors and friends. Men and boys. Maniacal in their anger and fear. A handful of them stood in the street, surrounded by jeeps and illuminated by headlights, kicking and jeering at someone lying in the dirt.

His father.

Another gun fired, and a man with a camo jacket and cap strode into the center of the road and shoved the jeering men aside. "Get back, you roof rats. No more fun. Time for the Communist to die." Camo Man pointed at one of the tough boys. "You. Give me your machete." Then, armed with both gun and blade, Camo Man confronted the one man who was not threatening or harming Wayan's father.

His uncle.

"You want your brother's body?" Camo Man said to Wayan's uncle. "Then kill him yourself." Wayan's uncle backed away from the machete. Camo Man shrugged. "Fine. But if I do it, I will dump him in a pit with the rest of the PKI commie trash." Wayan's uncle dropped his head and clenched his fists against his thighs. His head shook and he muttered something Wayan could not hear. Camo Man jabbed him with the tip of his rifle. "What did you say? Speak up."

"I will do it," said Wayan's uncle, and held out his hand. "Give me the gun."

Camo Man laughed and passed him the machete, instead.

Wayan shouted, "No!" But his mother clamped a hand over his mouth.

"Hush," she said. "There is nothing you can do."

Wayan felt his brother's fingers clutch at his leg. Felt his sister's arms wrap around his waist. Felt his mother's hand press against his mouth.

He could not move. He could not scream. All he could do was watch the machete cleave his father's throat.

Bali, Indonesia 1970

Wayan woke with a start and disturbed his brother who grunted with annoyance, rolled on his side, and fell back to sleep. Five years had passed since that terrible night, and his brother was the same age now that Wayan had been then. Their sister was two years older than that. Even so, the three of them—sixteen, thirteen, and eleven—shared a bed with their mother. No more sleeping pavilions. No more compound. No free-standing partition inside a grand entrance gate to confound the spirits. All they had was this one-room hut and each other.

Wayan's sister whimpered, as if caught in a nightmare of her own. Had his visions infected her dreams? He hoped not.

"Hush, Made," Wayan said, drawing out both syllables of her name to lull her back to sleep. "You have nowhere to go."

None of them did. The school had kicked them out. Teachers refused to teach them. Parents shunned them. Friends stayed away. No one wanted to catch the Communist taint. It wasn't fair: His father would get reborn into a new life while his eldest son was stuck with the one he had ruined.

Wayan swung his legs off the side of the bed and was hit by a wave of pain. His head throbbed and his neck prickled as if stabbed by a thousand needles. Sweat formed on his chest and back that had nothing to do with the morning's sticky heat. He had never experienced a headache this bad or this sudden. His nostrils stung as though inhaling the stench of his father's cremation. Too many memories. Too much pain.

He had to get out.

He felt his way to the door and nudged it open. Sunlight stung his eyes. He covered them with his arm and staggered until he fell, face down, onto the road.

*

Wayan breathed in the soothing scent of damp earth, rich with dung and life.

"Get up," a man said. "You cannot lie here."

A foot pushed into Wayan's ribs and rolled him onto his back. Rocks dug into his exposed skin. This was not the soft, damp soil he had expected. This was hard, dry asphalt, and with only a pair of cotton shorts to protect his skin, he felt every bit of its sharpness and heat. Sunlight stung his eyes, and he held up a hand to block it.

"You get pain in your head?" the man asked.

Wayan grunted. Now he knew who was speaking to him. It was Pak Nyoman, the healer.

"I tell you what to do last month, already," Pak Nyoman said. "Why you not do it?"

Wayan started to laugh and ask how he was supposed to atone for all his father's ill-deeds in one month, but stopped when he felt the sound throb against his temples. Besides, Pak Nyoman would not want to hear his excuses. He had diagnosed Wayan's headaches four weeks ago, when they had begun, and proclaimed them a result of bad karma. Of course, those headaches did not begin to approach the torture of today's.

"Never mind," Pak Nyoman said. "Get up. You cannot stay here."

As the healer helped Wayan to his feet, neighbor women in lacy shirts and bright colored skirts covered their mouths in shock, nearly toppling the grocery baskets they balanced on their heads. A couple of farmers huffed at the sight. But no one did anything to stop Pak Nyoman. They knew he was more than a healer. He was balian, a shaman with enough supernatural power to ward off Communist contamination. He commanded their respect and their fear.

"You must walk as a man," Pak Nyoman said. "I will not spoil you, like a dog on my hip."

As Pak Nyoman spoke, Wayan looked from the balian's plastic thong slippers to the gold and brown skirt, to the white cotton shirt, to the patches of graying whiskers, which arched and fell like a cat's fur, to the orange patterned scarf that circled a head of spiky gray hair—and felt dizzy. Motion and pain had blurred the colors into an orange-brown-gray mess. But as Wayan trod dutifully behind Pak Nyoman, the dizziness stopped, and the pain receded. By the time they had turned the corner, he could see exactly where they were headed. He just found it hard to believe.

Pak Nyoman's family compound could not compare to his uncle's—where Wayan used to live—but it dwarfed the hut he now shared with his mother, sister, and brother. The compound had a low stone wall, aged into pleasing gradations of tan and gray, offset by hints of orange, and clusters of pale green lichen. The entrance gate stood tall but humble, with two dark wooden doors left open to show the partition wall that would confound the spirits.

"Hurry up," Pak Nyoman said, waving his hand. "I do not want everyone to see my business."

Wayan nodded with understanding: It was one thing for the *balian* to invite him inside, it was another to let anyone see him do it.

Like all family compounds, this one had numerous pavilions, most of them with only one or two walls. The only exception was the patriarch's sleeping pavilion at the kaja side of the compound, the side nearest to sacred Mount Agung. His pavilion had four walls, a door that locked, and a large front porch with heavy teak benches. As the eldest son, Wayan's father used to sleep in such a pavilion. Now Wayan's uncle did. And Wayan never would.

"Come on," Pak Nyoman said, leading Wayan away from the main pavilions, where guests were usually received, and toward the less auspicious side of the compound that held an enclosed kitchen, a small rice barn on stilts, a bath house with the standard bucket-shower and squat toilet, and a small storage pavilion.

Wayan bowed his head in acceptance. He could expect no more than this, especially while the patriarch's wife glared at him from the kitchen window. No doubt, she would tell her husband who his younger brother had brought into their home. And equally without doubt, her husband would not approve.

"Come and sit," Pak Nyoman said, gesturing to the wooden floor in front of a stack of large plastic containers. He placed a cushion on the floor for himself. "The pain is gone?"

"Already," Wayan agreed.

"But it will return. *Geledag-geledug*," he said, imitating the sound of a beating drum. "You must take care of this or it will return twice as bad."

"Me? You are the healer." Wayan shut his mouth before he could say more. "Forgive me, Pak Nyoman. Please tell me what I should do."

The old man nodded his approval at Wayan's change in attitude. "I am not just a healer, I am balian," he said. "I have learned the ways of the tangible and the occult—and I tell you, there is work for you to do."

"Because my father's karma rubbed off on me? I know. But how can I make up for all his wrongdoings in one lifetime? I can barely get through the day."

"Hush. You squawk like a *becica* bird in the rain. I am not talking about karma. A *leyak* has worked his magic on you."

Wayan gasped. A *leyak* was a wielder of powerful magic, a walker between worlds, an intimate with the forces of evil. The same name was also used for black magic and horrible demons with disembodied heads and entrails dangling from the torn ruins of their throats. How had Wayan attracted the attention of such an evil being?

"What would a *leyak* want with me? I am nobody." His voice cracked like a boy, but he couldn't help it. A *leyak's* spirit could inhabit animals and do terrible things in the night while their bodies appeared to sleep in their beds.

Pak Nyoman chuckled. "Not so lofty as before, eh? Your family was of the *Ksatriya* caste of rulers and warriors. Now you are lower than a common *Sudra*. Lower than me." He waited for Wayan to nod his acceptance of this fact and then continued. "But my knowledge elevates me above my caste. I may not be as educated as a priest, who studies the sacred Lontar books of inscriptions, or as dangerous as a *leyak*, who studies them equally hard for a darker purpose. But you would be wise to respect me."

Wayan knew this was true. There was no telling what a *balian* knew or which powers—light or dark—he fostered. Everyone knew they dappled in both.

"How can you tell a *leyak* has worked a magic on me?" Wayan asked. "Do I have some kind of mark? Can you smell the magic on my body? Why would you jump to a conclusion like this?"

"I can see it in your eyes. You look different than you did before. Something significant has occurred."

"A spell?"

Pak Nyoman nodded. "Or maybe something more. Stick out your tongue. Let me have a look."

The healer leaned forward and peered over the top, the sides, and the bottom of Wayan's tongue. Then he reached into a basket and took out a stick. "Lie down," he said, and stepped off the platform, to make room for Wayan to stretch out his body. Then he poked Wayan's toes with the sharp point of the stick. When he found a tender spot that made Wayan cry out in pain, he stopped. "Sit up. Now we can talk."

Wayan's mind filled with worry. Did his organs rot with some horrible disease? Had his father's ill deeds infected his brain? He felt too sick with dread to ask.

The healer moved his cushion back into place and sat. "Why do you look so worried? I have good things to tell you."

"Really? Then why did the stick hurt?"

The healer chuckled again. "Because you are ignorant."

Wayan pulled back his shoulders and glared. For the first time in years, he felt pride. "I am of *Ksatriya* caste, and I can read better than you. I may suffer, but I am not ignorant."

Pak Nyoman waved away Wayan's objection. "Then why do you act so stupid? Besides, I am not talking about school. I cannot read at all. So what? I am talking about opportunity. You have been offered a gift, and you are either too stupid, too stubborn, too lazy, or too much of a coward to take it."

Wayan shut his mouth, too shocked and confused to respond.

The healer nodded, as though the teenager had finally done something intelligent. Then he reached back into the basket and pulled out his treasured *Lontars*. There were four books made from lontar palm leaves, all of them deteriorating from Bali's humidity and in need of replacement. He fondled each wooden cover with reverent care.

"They are old," Wayan said, his voice tinged with awe.

Pak Nyoman nodded. "They contain instructions for rituals, recipes, and magical prayers against evil."

"How do you know? You can't read."

"So what? I am balian, and the *Lontars* are my sacred objects of power. I learned my skill from mouth to ear. So tell me about this pain. How is it different?"

It had felt more intense than the other headaches, but Wayan did not think the healer would care about that. Instead, he told him about the dream. "I saw my father die. Then when I woke, I smelled the smoke and burning hair from his cremation."

Pak Nyoman nodded. "What else?"

"Earth," Wayan answered. "Damp, rich soil, mixed with dung. And the fresh scent of sprouting grass."

"You see? Rebirth. New beginnings. The spirit world is presenting a great opportunity and you are ignoring it. Your body attacks because your mind is not paying attention."

"Then this is not the work of a *leyak*?"

"Who says this? Not me. Your ignorance makes you vulnerable. Your fear makes you weak. Anyone who wants to harm you can do this easily. You must learn to protect yourself, and I will teach you."

"No disrespect, but why would you do this for me?"

Pak Nyoman smiled. "Because I received a sign."

He reached into the basket and brought out a card unlike any Wayan had ever seen. It was white with a hand coming out of a cloud to grasp a tall stick that sprouted with young leaves. Beneath the hand was a landscape of a mountain and a river.

"What is that?" Wayan asked.

Pak Nyoman shrugged. "I found it on the ground when I saw you lying in the road. So I knew it was connected to you."

Wayan nodded with agreement—the card was obviously a sign.

"Can you read what this says?" Pak Nyoman asked, pointing to the three words written at the bottom of the card.

"It says Ace of Wands."

"See? You can read it. This card is meant for you."

"But what does it mean?"

Pak Nyoman pointed at the landscape on the bottom. "You must take a journey."

"But I don't have any money. Where can I go?"

"Not with your feet. With your mind," Pak Nyoman said, poking at Wayan's forehead. "This is the cause of your headaches." He held up the card. "See this hand? You must grab your new future, the one with the sprouting leaves. You are being given a chance for rebirth in this lifetime."

"What kind of rebirth?"

"How should I know? Am I God? You must ask the spirits. Tonight. In the rice paddies. Near the river. If you survive, I will teach you everything I know about the spirit world and healing so you can serve the people of our village. I will have a student for my knowledge. And when I am gone, you will take my place as balian. This is how you will atone for your father's actions and earn respect."

Wayan had never considered this possibility. Before his father's death, he had assumed he would go to college, take an important job, and when the time came, replace his father in the community and become the head of the village *banjar*.

"I do not deserve this honor," Wayan said, bowing his head so Pak Nyoman could not see the bitterness in his eyes. The people in his village had butchered his father and every other neighbor they accused of sympathizing with the Communists. The whole island had risen up against its own until eighty thousand Balinese had been murdered—almost a million Indonesians had met with this fate.

Pak Nyoman clicked his tongue and dismissed Wayan's concerns. "No one cares if you think you deserve this honor. The spirit world has sent a *leyak* to motivate you into action. The pain will get worse unless you respond."

"What will happen if I say no?"

"How would I know? Did I work this magic on you? Do I inhabit the forms of animals in my sleep and cause mischief and death? No. I draw my power from the sacred *Lontars*. And my power says you must find your answer alone. Go into the fields. Open yourself up to the spirits." He pointed at the card. "If you are worthy one will come and take you across this river so you can climb the mountain of your future." He handed the card to Wayan and watched him tuck it safely in the pocket of his shorts. "And you must do this at midnight."

Wayan gasped. The man could not be serious. Everyone knew evil spirits roamed at night searching for people too foolish to go home. And to be out at midnight? That was the most dangerous time of all.

"I could die," he said.

Pak Nyoman shrugged. "Are you living?"

*

Wayan's legs trembled as he made his way along the raised banks of his neighbor's rice paddy. A passing cloud drew shapes on the moon, which in turn, cast dancing images across the water. Rice stalks swayed in time. Frogs sang the tune. Geckos kept the beat. His village slept, safe behind their stone gates and spirit-confounding partitions. Only Wayan was foolish enough to wander outside this late at night.

As his toes dug into soft earth, his eyes searched the shadows for monsters. Every story he had ever heard and every demon he had seen portrayed in dance came alive along the forest's edge. Razor fangs. Lolling tongues. Bellies dripping with entrails. Horrible eyes crazed with hunger and thirst. Wayan saw them all. Every cell in his body screamed for him to turn and run back to his humble home where he could climb into bed with his mother, sister, and brother— and be safe.

But Wayan did not turn. Pak Nyoman had promised him a brighter future if he had the courage to make it happen.

"My name is Anak Agung Wayan Oka," Wayan announced to whatever spirits might be roaming the night, "And I am not afraid."

He sat down at the crossroad of earthy banks that divided the rice fields. Intersections of any kind held power and would amplify his call. He just hoped the answering spirits or demons would not rip out his belly and slurp up his guts. But if they did, he prayed they would kill him first.

"I am here," he said, not knowing what else to do. "I am ready to meet you."

Wayan rested the backs of his hands on his knees, palms turned up to the night sky, and steadied his breathing. Meditation calmed his mind and opened channels for speaking with spirits. While Wayan had never attempted to use his meditations in this way, he had seen mediums do it all his life. Of course, they protected themselves with prayers and amulets and rituals. Wayan had none of these. Pak Nyoman had told him he must approach the spirits like a beggar, open to receive whatever blessings or curses they might dispense. And so Wayan did exactly that.

A beggar he might be, but he was still the eldest son of the eldest son with the blood of *Ksatriya* rulers and warriors running through his veins. He would not falter. He would not run.

The stench of rotting meat and rancid blood assaulted his nostrils as something soft and wet began a slow investigation of his face. Flesh pulsed against his nose and mouth. Tentacles slithered down his neck and around his torso. Fat fingers massaged his groin and thighs.

Wayan froze in terror. He could not move or scream or even breathe. He could only think— *I am Ksatriya! I will not run. I will not fail!* —and pray his mantra would give him courage not to shit or vomit as he died.

The demons cackled as they rubbed their sticky, flaccid appendages against Wayan's body. But he would not surrender. If he showed any sign of cowardice, the demons would rip out his guts and drive him insane. So Wayan opened his eyes and saw those flaccid appendages for what they were—long bloody cords of pulpy entrails, hanging from the ragged throats of disembodied heads.

*Leyak*s.

A scream caught in his throat as an intestine wound around his neck and crept its tip up to his lips, circling like a lover's finger before a kiss. Wayan's stomach heaved. Vomit rose in his throat, but the pulpy organ kneaded it down.

The hovering faces laughed, showing bits of flesh stuck to their teeth and fangs.

"You seek to control us?' they shouted. "Go and get it. Come and try."

The heads drifted back, disentangling their bowels from Wayan's throat, chest, and groin. Lidless eyes glared at him with hunger and madness. Guttural sounds, with no throats to create them, emitted from their bloody maws.

The forest rustled as a troop of macaque monkeys burst through the leaves and leapt to the ground. They ran on all fours with their tails held high, gray hair flickering in the moonlight. Their gold eyes shone beneath thick tufts over long narrow noses and wide mouths flared with rage.

"Behold!" the heads shouted in unison, stretching out their dangling bowels in welcome. "See what you may become."

The monkeys raced across the mounded paths of earth and splashed through the flooded field. But instead of attacking Wayan, they grabbed and yanked and stretched him on his back. Rank breath and hot spittle rained on his face, but the monkeys did not bite. They just held him in place, glaring and baring their fangs.

I am Ksatriya! I will not run. I will not fail!

Wayan repeated the mantra until the words merged together into one unintelligible sentence, and the world went black.

And then he ran.

The pads of his feet sprang on dirt. His supple tail flexed for balance. All so natural. All so right as he darted up the road to the wall of stone and the giant plank of wood. If he had been trapped in his human form, he might have had trouble getting through it. But instead, he had this marvelous tail and nibble fingers.

The monkey scampered up and over the wall and landed in the dirt next to the fragrant hill. The alpha human's mate was sound asleep, like the rest of her tribe, so she could not glare at him as he passed. Too bad. His fangs would have felt good in her flesh, tearing out her soft human lips. He sucked on his padded fingers, trying to imagine the taste—then promised to come back another time and find out for sure.

Tonight, he had a prize to hunt.

He hurried by the treehouse. He wanted to climb to the top and dig out the rice hiding inside, but the prize he hunted tonight could not be eaten. So he hurried past and jumped onto the temple floor. The monkey knew about temples—men left them scattered all over his land—and this one held the prize.

But where?

The thing did not smell or squirm. It hid, like a mouse in a hole. He tore and scratched and toppled. But still, he did not find the prize. So he jumped to the ground and ran past the smelly cave, where humans buried their dung, and onto the next temple where the gray-whiskered man slept.

The prize.

The monkey wanted to snatch it from the man's hairless arms and run, but he needed to be sure. So he pried away the man's fingers and lifted the wood. The inside smelled of palm leaves dried in the sun and the faint scent of burnt trees. Black marks scored the grain. They meant nothing. He stared harder and watched as human words appeared. They told of dark magic and hungry demons. They warned of dangers and promised rewards. Page after palm-leaf page, each of the four *Lontars* offered dark secrets. And he understood them all.

He gathered them in his arms and was just about to leave when the man grabbed his marvelous tail. The insult could not be suffered. He dropped the prize and sank his long, sharp fangs into the nasty human's face.

424

Later that morning, Wayan woke with the heat of the sun on his skin and the cit-cit of chirping birds in his ears. Beside him on the rice paddy bank sat Pak Nyoman's treasured *Lontars*—not inscribed with protective spells against black magic as the balian, in his illiteracy, had assumed, but filled with detailed instructions for becoming a skilled and powerful *leyak*. Wayan pulled the Ace of Wands from the pocket of his shorts and stared at the picture on the card. Pak Nyoman had been right—this card was meant for him.

Wayan wiped the old man's blood from his mouth and smiled.

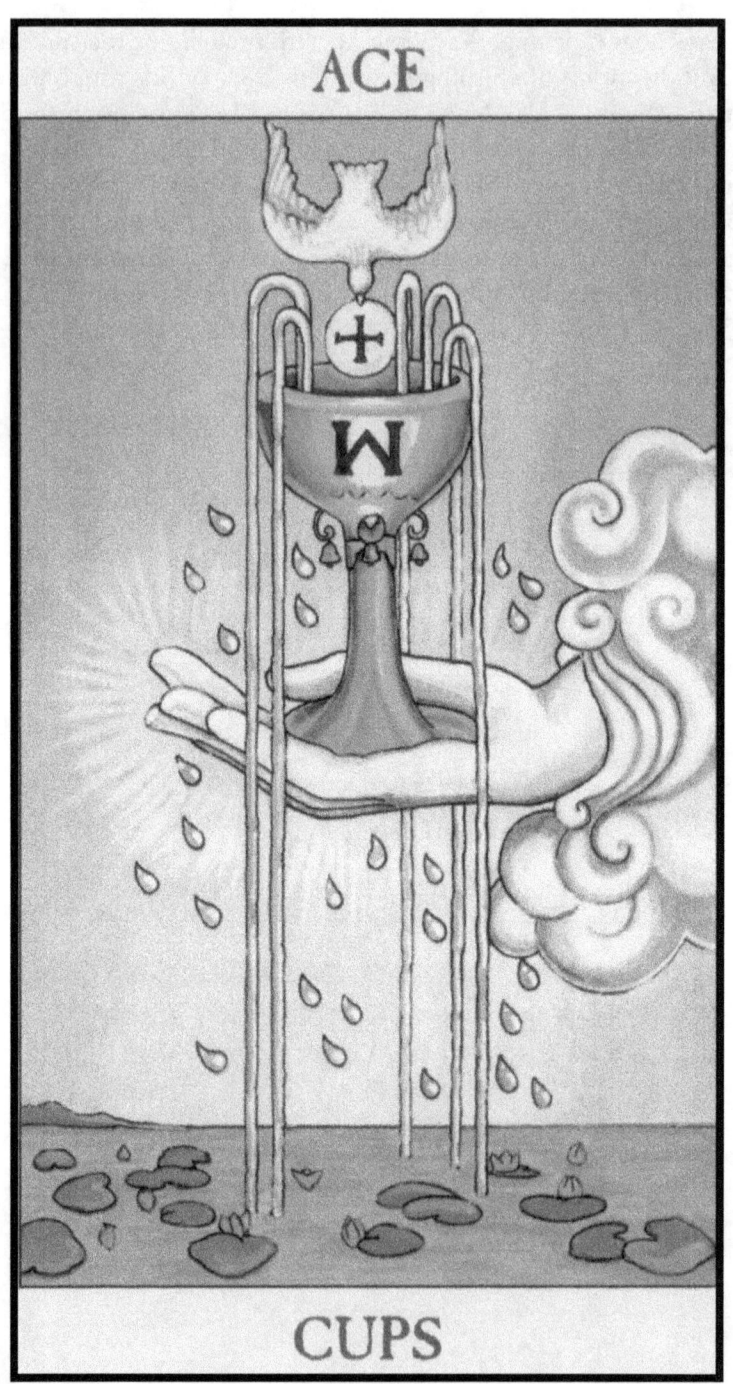

24

ACE OF CUPS

JASON POZZESSERE

Upright: House of the true heart, joy, content,abode, nourishment, abundance, fertility
Reversed: House of the false heart, mutation, instability, revolution

Milo Stills sat gazing at the water as it gushed its way down the Excelsior's grand waterfall. It was a glorious structure indeed, constructed of natural and unnatural materials, yet completely man-made. When the casino was built in the 1960, Louis LaFica—or "The Lip" as he was known by his syndicate associates—decided that there would no expense spared when it came to the main recreational area in this, his grandest casino. He was a creative man, and was quoted in a March 1987 interview in Forbes as joking that in another, simpler life, he might have been an interior designer.

The entire rooftop of the casino was dedicated to the most luxurious outdoor and artificial oasis that had ever been built. Surrounding the three-story falls was a sandy beach, lush tropical foliage, and a Mediterranean-styled bar, complete with gorgeous Chi-Chi girls. Those lovely waitresses were known worldwide for their combination of raw, unapologetically open sexual appeal and elegance while wearing, no… modeling, floral-patterned bikinis and wraps that left little to the imagination. Milo thought it was quite enough to keep a man wondering longingly for hours.

With a chuckle he gave the idea some playful consideration. How many times had he relaxed out here doing just that? He remembered coming here for the first time twelve years ago. What a different a man he had been then. He had changed quite a bit, and not just physically either. He took a look at his watch, saw that he was still a little early for his afternoon meeting, and decided to take a stroll around this rooftop "Oasis." Just before he did so, he reached into his right pants pocket and pulled out an old and browning tarot card. The card depicted a naked man and a woman facing each other, with each of them holding a golden chalice. Neil Young lyrics creeped their way into his consciousness. "Remember me to my love, I know I'll miss her." Tucking his lucky charm back into his pocket, Milo began his stroll. It could not be helped that in the end, the jaunt led him down a path through memory lane.

*

It was November 1975 when a young Milo Stills hopped off the bus in the little town of Moapa, Nevada. He stretched his long legs as he began to walk off his fatigue and looked back to see his friends Nicco and Rush stepping down behind him. Nicco was rubbing his head where it began to show a little pink, and began muttering something about the driver and his "culo." Rush jokingly picked up Nicco in his arms, and with a great big bear hug told Nicco to just shut up and walk it off. He then told Nicco that this trip had already been the most exciting thing that the three of them had ever experienced.

Just moments before, the vehicle had made an unexpected halt on its trip to Las Vegas after a sudden jolt and a decisively loud bang, which led to a jumbling stop. After the initial shock and excitement, several travelers let forth a mix of curses and not a few groans of relief. Darryl, the pudgy driver issued a curt apology for what he said would hopefully be their final delay, but stated that no one would be getting to Las Vegas at all if the bus didn't have the wheels to carry them all there, so they should "quit their bitchin'" if no one was seriously hurt, so he could get to "seein' what's what."

"Besides," he added, "the good Lord has seen fit to stop us up not more than an eighth of a mile from that there truck stop just up the way. There's bound to be vittles 'n' more, so if'n yer keen, y'all can stretch yer legs a bit."

Milo was quite happy to be able to work out his own kinks. He hadn't sustained any injury from the sudden stop, nor had he felt any particular soreness, but then again he hadn't been stretching his neck and torso around backward, trying repeatedly and unsuccessfully to flirt so heavily with the two college girls that had positioned themselves at the very rear of the bus. It's not that he wasn't interested, indeed, he had thought of little else on this trip west with his two friends, but Milo was incredibly shy around girls, and always had been.

The girls, in fact, one named Lou, and the other Cyndi, were quite attractive. Lou, while not a traditional beauty, had a certain something about her that Milo just couldn't ignore. She had hair the color of October he decided, a rich tangerine hue he found he preferred on women over the blond that seemed so typically popular. She had a mildly freckled face, but instead of it distracting him, he found it made her expressions livelier, and more authentic than her traveling companion. She wore a short blouse, made even shorter by the way she'd tied it off a little bit above the waist. It had a floral pattern that mixed brown, purple, and yellow stems with opposite colored petals. Her dark, forest-green bellbottoms complemented the blouse, and Milo thought the way she filled everything out made it all even better. True, she was a little curvier than her friend, but Milo had never liked skinny girls all that much. Their bodies had reminded him of middle-school boys. She had a very pleasant voice, and when she spoke, Milo found himself getting lost in not just her tone, but the intelligence that seemed to come with it.

Cindy was the taller of the two, and had a mane of hair that could rival the black of the inkiest blackbird. She was graced with pointedly smart features, yet could carelessly flash a smile that led him to believe that she could easily be on the cover of one of those fancy movie magazines his sister was so fond of. She was long and lean and had legs that seemed to go on forever. It didn't seem to bother her one iota that even though they were in a desert, and it was the middle of November, she only ever wore short, loose, and thin skirts. Those miniskirts accompanied by footwear, which he learned were called "go-go boots," allowed her to show the right amount of skin from the bottom of her knees up to the perfect area of her thighs, making it impossible for the hormone-driven males to think of anything other than what it all led to.

In hushed tones, kept between the fellas, Nicco said that he believed that she was wearing the boots merely to tease him. He said that at night, when no one else was watching, she'd slide up her skirt and open up her legs just enough for him to get a glimmer of her hairy southern peach, and if given half a chance he'd show her how a proper man handled something so sweet and fine. Milo had given a quiet chuckle, but Rush almost let the cat out of the bag when he laughingly exclaimed that the only thing Nicco knew about "peaches" was nothing at all, and that he would be surprised if Nicco could even tell a peach from a banana.

This led Nicco into a speech defending his honor with stories of supposed conquests, stories they had both heard numerous times since Nicco had moved to Williamsburg with his mother three and a half years earlier. Usually they involved giving it hard to girls behind some mysterious bar, or talking the skirt off of some broad after slipping some green to a projectionist in some unknown movie theatre. But the stories Milo and Rush were actually interested in hearing were those of Nicco's father. The man was a mystery to the two friends; they had never even seen the man, let alone met him.

Nicco had certainly been scarce during the summers of those few years, and Milo believed that he probably had been to at least half of the places, or more, that he had boasted about. But the destinations themselves and his supposed conquests were all the usually vocal Nicco was willing to talk about. When prodded for more information about his absentee father, all he was willing to admit was that Mr. Capinelli was always away dealing with the family business interests, his friends referred to him as Frankie, and that he was a very important man that needed to be present and available in New York to make sure things were running smoothly. What those things were, Nicco never really said, but the sense of an adventure in a faraway place was more than enough to give Milo all the drive he needed to get out of his small Virginia town and head off to something new.

Milo had graduated high school earlier that year, and lacking the funds for college, decided he would ask to up his hours at his job at

Culver's Grocers. Mr. Culver was a kind man, and offered him five more hours a week. But with his father deceased and his mother absent most of the time, Milo knew any opportunity would be better than his life currently. So when Nicco said he had an uncle in Nevada who was looking for some young men willing to work odd jobs, Milo jumped at the chance. If he knew then exactly what some of those odd jobs would entail, he might not have taken up Nicco on his offer.

*

And so it was that Milo found himself heading down an old, dusty road toward the only glimmering trace of mankind, besides the Greyhound, for miles. He was accompanied by his two friends, the two lovely coeds at the back of the bus, and five other people. There was a single mother of Spanish descent, Hortensia, who seemed to speak little English and clutched a very young baby to her as if she felt the world was out to steal it, and a couple in their forties, coaxing their retarded son named Angus onward with the promise of ice cream. Milo had never traveled with a retarded boy before, but found the boy to be rather intelligent and funny. Angus even managed to get Rush to fall for the "pull my finger for a prize" prank on their first day of travel, to the horror of his parents. Rush had not been paying particularly close attention to what Angus was asking him to do, as he had had most of his attention directed toward the ladies. Not more than a second had passed before Rush naively pulled on the boy's index finger and there was a surprisingly loud riiiiipp sound coming from his Angus's ass. The smell that followed almost immediately was enough to generate moans and curious looks from the other travelers captured within the moving vehicle. Angus erupted with laughter! While the smell was absolutely revolting, Angus's genuine glee at pulling one over on the older boy had Milo laughing out loud, which only made things worse as the gas was so strong it seemed he could taste it by doing so. This, in turn, got the girls to giggling from underneath their coats. Angus would travel back and forth between his parents and Milo's friends, but only after assuring the group he would pull no more pranks on them.

"Angus, my man," Nicco said with a smile, "you're just too damned smart for us and we know it!"

*

Milo had been to a truck stop before, but never one quite this big. He was impressed with its size once he got close enough to really get a good look at the place. He figured it couldn't be more than a few years old. It had a full service gas station just outside, a locker room, showers just beyond the men's room, and a fully stocked convenience store with a diner attached. Nicco, Rush and Cyndi had decided they would go get a seat at a booth in the restaurant. Milo and Lou had both stated they could use a bit of time to freshen up and had headed toward their respective restrooms. Before they got more than a couple steps headed toward their lavatories, Lou grasped him by the biceps and signaled toward a toadish looking man making no effort to hide the fact that he was staring around one of the magazine racks right at her. "Wait up for me before going back, will ya? That fella is giving me the willies." Milo agreed and headed into the men's room.

After Milo finished, he came back out to see that Mr. Toad was no longer around. The thought of the man was giving him the heebie jeebies now as well. Wondering what a man like that would be reading, Milo decided to head his way over to the magazine rack. At first glance it looked to be the usual array of gas station literature, hot rod magazines, monster and movie rags. Today's paper was there as well. Resting in the lower left hand corner were some magazines whose covers had been slightly shielded by a wooden board. The title of an article managed to catch his eye and he thought he could make out the word "tarot".

He recalled a friend of his sister's had brought a tarot deck over to his house one night during a sleepover. He was a few years younger than his sister Jeanie, but that never stopped her from allowing him to participate in some of her and her friends' play, and the other girls never really seemed to mind. He remembered that night clearly. He recalled the girls giggling over the possibilities the cards might bring to their futures. They all took turns and debated what the true meaning of the cards might be. Sometime during the evening, Jeanie's friends convinced her to let Milo pull a card. He deserved to know what the fates had in store for him as well, didn't he? She said she would allow it, but would only let him pull one card, since he was too gullible and would probably believe anything.

Besides, she added, she didn't want to ruin his impressionable mind. Amber then shuffled the cards and spread them apart before him in the shape of a fan.

"Pick one," she giggled.

He reached down to the splayed deck and touched one card. He looked up to Jeanie and she nodded that it was okay. He turned the card over. Amber, who owned the deck, squealed with glee when she saw what the card was. That started a chain reaction with the other girls who all let out little squeals of their own.

Milo didn't get it, he just couldn't figure out what all the excitement was all about. He had seen some cool images on some of the cards, like a dragon and a grim reaper. But this card was just confusing, it had some kind of cloud hand holding a fountain cup that was shooting water down into a lake or pond, with a white bird holding a small wafer in its mouth diving down into the fountain cup. What could be so exciting about a fountain cup with a diving bird?

Amber went on to talk about the card, which was the Ace of Cups, and what it meant for his future. She said that he would have a love so incredibly deep that it would rival that of some people named Romeo and Juliet. He asked who they were, and the girls all giggled again. Amber did say to, "Beware, however, for while a lover's bond, if true, is strong, it shouldn't blind you toward sharing love with others." That had made no sense to him, because he thought that if you were supposed to love one person, then what good would it be to love anyone else? Then the girls said that they wondered if any of them in the house that night were feeling a strong desire to kiss the boy. Perhaps they were to be his true love and could only find out by true love's kiss! This was enough to send poor little Milo safely to his room to bed for the evening. He thought about it for a while that night, a little bit less the next night, and then packed the thought away into memory, until now.

Being the curious sort, Milo picked up the magazine and immediately went wide-eyed and slack-jawed. Lightly attached to the cover was indeed a tarot card, and sure enough, it was the Ace of Cups! While it was the same card, it had an almost more radiant look to it, as if the colors had been made more vibrant since he'd last seen them as a child. Now the magazine the card was attached to, like the card, was anything but dull.

The title of the magazine said *Private*, but there seemed nothing being done privately on this cover to Milo. The young lady smirking at him seemed not to possess any sort of way to give herself any privacy at all. She seemed to be making damned sure that truly nothing was private for her any longer. Instead of causing Milo to grow in any sort of sexual anticipation, the way the young vixen was spreading her legs comically brought Nicco's earlier conversation to mind, and with that, the image of a sliced peach drifted to the forefront of his thoughts.

At that moment, he heard a melodic voice say, "What'cha doin over there?" and went into a mild panic. Looking up, he saw that Lou was walking toward him not more than four strides away. How had she been so quiet? He managed to mumble out something along the lines of "Uh, gohh... nothing"! Lowering his arm, he tried to put the magazine back quickly. Not wanting to break eye contact with Lou as he did so, he missed the shelf and dropped the porno rag on to the ground. As it dropped, it opened, and as it opened, she gave him a curious glance. In that glance, he knew he must take action… and so he did.

Milo was a gifted and natural athlete. He'd enjoyed sports his last few years in high school and had played basketball and had managed to letter in both football and track. It was only natural that a feeling of surprise and complete betrayal of his own body took hold after what happened next. While desperately trying to save some face and dignity, Milo did what any red-blooded American would do. To retain the innocence of a woman so fair he bent down as quickly as he could to pick up the magazine. As he did so, he misjudged the distance between his body and the protruding second row of the magazine rack. His forehead slammed into the row with a loud crack.

Startled more than hurt, Milo reflexively jumped back, and as he did, the sleeve of his flannel shirt caught on a piece of wood protruding from the magazine rack. Trying not to fall back entirely, Milo pulled back in an attempt to try and reposition his arms, or at least tried to as only one of them managed to reach behind him. He then unwittingly performed a half pirouette while simultaneously pulling the magazine rack and its contents onto himself, then crashed into another rack of assorted trinkets behind him. Somewhere, amidst all that racket, he heard a woman exhale, "Ohmygawd!" The last thing he was fully aware of was the back of his head exploding while magazines jumped out on him from their perches above.

Lou was kneeling beside him in a heartbeat, and as she attempted to remove some of the magazines which had just moments before assaulted him, all she could get out was, "Wha… wha… What happened!?"

Others came rushing in now, including the convenience store clerk who was supposed to have been behind the counter this whole time. "What the fuck are you doing to my store?" he demanded. Milo was about to explain, when Lou spoke up and said, "Never mind that. Help me get him up!"

"You're going to have to pay for this, you fucking hippies," the clerk with the name Zed inscribed onto his ID badge said, while staring in a mild state of shock at the whole of the situation. "What the hell, whatever happened to people respecting other people's property?" "If you think for one moment that you're—"

He was cut off short as Lou looked him squarely in the eye and said, "Your shelving was improperly installed, and it's a miracle that my friend here isn't seriously hurt. No screws to hold any of the shelving in its place, no cautionary signs warning of uneven floors, I bet this kind of thing happens all of the time!"

For a moment Zed stared at the woman incredulously as he tried to make sense of what was going on. "And while I am on that subject, I'm sure that's grounds for a lawsuit, if poor Milo there should decide to take legal action!"

Zed began visibly mouthing the words, "No screw, uneven floors," as if trying to convince himself that that those were indeed the words he had just heard come out of the young woman's mouth. Then three new words, "Move it, asshole!" broke that train of thought and Zed finally decided that it would be best, for now, to comply with the visibly upset girl.

After shaking out a few cobwebs, Milo had gotten to watch a majority of the events unfold. He understood very quickly that nothing other than his pride was broken, and that he would most certainly be all right. He was more embarrassed than anything else, and while he felt he could have easily pushed the shelf himself, he felt mesmerized by the display of authority by this fiery-haired valkyrie. He had never seen a grown woman take charge so firmly before, and part of him wanted to see where else it would go. But after easily pushing up the magazine rack, the show was just about over.

*

Not long after the whole debacle, the rest of their friends and fellow delayed travelers arrived to glimpse the chaos. They arrived to see Lou chewing out a store clerk and Milo with a lightly bleeding crack on the head, looking dazed under the magazine rack. After getting Milo patched up and putting the fear of an unwinnable lawsuit into Zed with the bogus made-up-on-the-spot legal jargon Lou had thrown at him, they all decided to help get the shelving back upright and the magazines back on the rack, which instituted more hilarity and good-natured ribbing, both then and for the last hour and a half it took them to get to Vegas. Lou told her version of the story to their friends, and when Milo tried to intervene, she stopped him by saying that he wouldn't be able to do it justice, and with that knock on the head he was sporting now, he was lucky to remember anything correctly.

Milo sat next to Lou the rest of their journey to Vegas. When things died down a bit and they noticed Rush, Cyndi and Nicco had gotten into a quieter, private conversation, she'd asked for an explanation of what had actually happened. Seeing no reason not to tell the truth, he knew he couldn't seem any more lame, he told her everything just the way it happened. She asked why he'd gone to such extreme effort to keep her from seeing a dirty magazine. He told her about wanting to protect her innocence, that he knew it sounded corny and that he hardly knew her, but it seemed right at the time, and that if a similar situation were to arise again, he would take another lump on the head. She laughed aloud at his explanation and said that while it was indeed corny, it was ridiculously sweet.

Milo asked her why she had covered for him back at the shop. He really had been responsible for the shelf falling, not only down, but on top of him, and he knew she knew that at the time. She said that she understood, but had a strong distaste for people who hated not just hippies, but anyone. When she heard Zed going off on them she knew she had to put him in his place.

"If we're being honest," she said, "I think you're pretty cute and kinda groovy." She told him she had caught him stealing glances at her when he thought she wasn't looking, and was terribly disappointed it took so long for him to get to talking with her without his two friends. They talked about that and more, until Daryl the bus driver announced that they would be arriving at their stop soon.

Not long after that, the two groups of friends and the other passengers began unloading their luggage. They wished some of the passengers safe travels, each gave Angus a great big hug and one last pull of the finger, and then began walking together in the general direction of the cab stand which would finish transporting them to their final destinations. Rush and Nicco hugged Lou and tried to see if they could secure a rendezvous with Cyndi. That gave Lou and Milo a moment to say one more goodbye.

"You know how you were saying that you were trying to protect my innocence?" Lou said as she slid up toward Milo, slowly lowering her baggage in the process.

"Yes, ma'am?" he replied. He gently took her hands into his, this time not shying away, his lips widening into a smile.

"As ridiculously sweet and amazingly corny as that is, there's something you should know."

"What's that?" replied Milo.

Lou drew her hands away, slipped one quickly into and out of her blouse and produced a card. It wasn't just any card either, but the tarot card from the truck stop. With her free hand, she cupped his face, showed Milo the card with something written on the back of it, all the while pulling him closer, then kissing him deeply. Milo lost himself in the kiss, and only realized that she had slipped something into his pocket when her hand was sliding out. She drew away and smiled, picked up her belongings and announced to Cyndi that it was time to go. Cyndi gave Nicco and Rush nothing more than a hug, to the dismay of both young men, and joined her friend in getting a cab.

"Hey, man", Nicco said after they ladies had left, "Rush and I struck out big time; how about you?"

"I think I'm just stepping up to the plate," Milo replied. He reached into his pocket to reassure himself that the card was still there. He would keep that private for now. He and his companions called over a cab, Nicco announced their destination, and the three were on their way.

*

Milo hadn't realized that the alarm in his watch was ringing. He had been lost in memories so deep that he had lost track of the time. Smiling, he reached into his pocket and pulled out the card. Indeed it was, looking mostly like it did the day he loosened it from that magazine with one notable exception. He turned it around to read the words *Lucky for you, I'm not all that innocent!*

Milo smiled sadly, remembering his wife. He was certainly lucky while he had her. She made him promise to seek happiness again, and he had. She said it was not in the cards for him to stay unhappy or alone. But he wasn't either of those things. At 5:30 he walked down to the casino's daycare and picked up his four-year-old daughter. She had hair the color of October, with a rich tangerine hue he knew was more beautiful than anything else in the world. When she smiled, her freckles lit up her face like a million stars, and her voice was a melody.

Like LouAnne, her mother.

ACE

PENTACLES

25

ACE OF PENTACLES

AIDAN RUSSELL

Upright: Perfect contentment,Felicity, Ecstasy,Speedy Intelligence
Reversed: The evil side of wealth, Bad intelligence, great riches

Trelawny Parish, Jamaica, 1793

"Here we are at last." Beverly stood up in the open carriage and waved a hand at the sign that read *Poor Hope Plantation*. Beyond the sign, the rolling Jamaican hillside, lush, green, and in full bloom, dominated the landscape until it clashed with the cerulean horizon. Splotches of lush forestry gave way to bright gardens and fields of sugarcane. And in those fields toiled the slaves.

Harriet stood with her sister to better take in the sights of her new home. For the weeks it took to sail from Liverpool to the port at Falmouth, her only view had been endless ocean and her cabin's undecorated walls. "Oh, I can't wait to see your home at last."

"I'm sure you can't wait to just be able to sit down in a home, finally," Beverly replied. "Two years of missionary work with those savages in Africa, then a boat ride home, and another boat to bring you here. I don't know how you ever managed, dear. I have a fit if I miss tea."

Harriet snickered at her sister. Beverly had always been the prim older sister while Harriet had caused ceaseless trouble for their servants. Only after an exceptionally invigorating sermon did she find an outlet for her adventuresome spirit: to bring healing and God's word to the Empire's African colonies. By the time she returned to London, their parents had passed on and Beverly's husband had inherited the family's Jamaican plantation.

"With the Lord guiding our work, we learn to do without some of life's comforts," she answered with a smile.

Beverly huffed. "Well, I hope your preaching skills have become top-notch. If you think those barbarian tribesmen were a challenge to convert, the boys will surely give you a handful."

"I'm sure Hugh and Alfred aren't so terrible. They're probably just being boys."

Beverly huffed again. "Oh, you wait."

The crack of leather on skin broke the tranquility of their carriage ride. Harriet gasped, but Beverly knew to expect such sounds when passing close to the slave quarters. Another crack rang out, accompanied by a wail. Another wail joined in and then softened to weeping.

The carriage rounded a bend and Harriet stood once more to take in the sight before her. A woman hung from her wrists tied to a beam overhead. Streaks of bright blood contrasted sharply with her dark skin and sweat matted down the corkscrewed locks of her hair. Nearby, another slave-woman hid her face away in a man's chest. The whip leapt out like a serpent and bit another slash across the penitent woman's back and both women shrieked.

The second woman looked up from her brother's shirt, spied the carriage, and came running.

"Mistress Beverly! Mistress Beverly!" she called, waving her arms frantically. The sweat and tears soaking her face reflected the suffocating noon sun.

Beverly touched the carriage driver's shoulder and he pulled the horses to a halt. "Yes? What is it, Anika?"

Anika fell to her knees beneath her mistress. "Please, madame. It's Leteia. You must help her, please." The tears fell with more vigor as she offered her plea.

"What happened, my dear? What did Leteia do?" Beverly asked.

"She was caught taking milk from the kitchen. But she had to, madame, she had to. You know she just gave birth, but she couldn't make her own milk. She had to take the milk to feed her son, so he could grow strong and be able to work the fields. Mistress, she did it for you."

Beverly cocked her head, almost moved with a moment of pity. "Oh, Anika, if you would have told me beforehand, maybe we could have avoided this unfortunate event. Truly, we wouldn't want Leteia's child to grow sickly and weak, but you know we can't allow thievery. And thieves must be punished."

Anika squeezed her eyes tight as more tears welled beneath her lids. When Harriet spoke, a flash of hope pulled them open again.

"Please, Beverly, surely you can find some pity for the woman. Even our Lord and Savior hung as a brother beside a thief on the cross. She only did it to care for her son. You would have done the same for your boys."

"That may be, my sweet sister, but you will have much yet to learn about how to run a plantation. No matter the reason, we can't simply let discipline run amok. Besides, isn't it also written that slaves are to obey their earthly masters?"

Harriet's face screwed up as her sister threw scripture into her face.

"I'm sorry, Anika, but there is simply nothing I can do this time. Leteia will just have to take her lashes. I hope you will all learn to ask Master Monroe or myself about such issues in the future, instead of stealing from us." Beverly touched the driver on the shoulder, the carriage moved on, and Anika's weeping began anew.

Harriet turned in her seat and saw another brutal lash fall across Leteia's back. The whole situation baffled her. In Africa, these people would be craftsmen, politicians, doctors, and leaders of the community. Here, an ocean away, they were property, forced to toil their lives away in service to her own family. Harriet realized their toil had bought the new dress she wore and her passage to the New World, and the thought sickened her stomach. Her two years of missionary work had taught her that. Despite their difference in skin color, Africans and Europeans were all children of God. Here in Jamaica, however, they were not God's children. They were things.Property.

*

What the two men lowered into the ground looked nothing to Anika and Garfield like their sister. Leteia had been lively and joyous, always smiling, laughing, and dancing. She had led the choir in the slave's ramshackle church. Neither could believe the still, lifeless body wrapped in white cloth was their sister.

When they finished lowering Leteia into her grave, Anika, Garfield, and the dead woman's husband approached the grave and tossed a handful of earth onto their loved one. The pastor began the customary reading of ashes and dust and returning to God's embrace. Anika heard none of it. Her mind drifted to the memories of Leteia's screams as the whip slashed open her back, her fevered cries when infection spread through the wounds, and her dying whispers that pled to hold her son.

The funeral rites ended and the crowd slowly drifted away, shambling back to the desolate quarters none could bring themselves to call home. Garfield and Anika stood by themselves beneath the moonlight over their sister's grave, until a gentle hand took hold of Anika's shoulder.

"Are you ready, my child?" the old man asked. Amos was the eldest of the slaves. Too old for labor, the Monroes trusted the white-beard to handle the affairs of slave life: settling disputes and ensuring the masters were informed of every birth and every death.

"No." Garfield took his sister by the shoulders. "She's not ready. I won't lose both my sisters this night."

Anika shrugged herself free of her brother's grip. "I am ready." She scrunched her face to hold back the hot tears of rage building within her. "I'm ready for these devils to finally get the justice they deserve."

"This won't bring justice," Garfield insisted. "More blood won't bring Leteia back and it won't end our suffering."

"You're wrong." Anika stepped away from her brother and stood by Amos' side. A half dozen men and women emerged from the brush. They held torches and each had white paint smeared across their dark bodies in the shapes of skulls, ribs, and other bones. "These rich devils grow happy and fat while we become broken, starved, and sick to make it so. No, brother, blood is only thing that will change this."

"Are you prepared to die, to sell your soul, to bring a demon to our land just so you can have your revenge?" Garfield asked, his voice stretching to a thin hope his sister would say "no".

"This isn't our land, brother." Anika's voice was flat and her face hard. Her lip quivered into a sneer as she thought of the life of injustice into which she and her people had been born. "This is their land. When we no longer must worry about dying beneath the lash, when they can no longer end our lives with a wave of their hand, then will we be able to call it home. And yes, I am prepared to die and barter with the devil himself to make that so." She turned and followed Amos into the forest's shadows.

They didn't walk far. Men with hounds and muskets patrolled the perimeter of the plantation, watchful for slaves with dreams of freedom. For the ceremony to take place, it had been easier for the shamans to infiltrate the plantation than it would have been to sneak Anika out.

Torches stood watch over the clearing. Another group of shamans remained within the shadows. Robed figure with a crown of bones and feathers stood in their center. While the other shamans painted the bones onto their skin, their leader wore a skull and ribcage over his own. He saw Anika enter the clearing and beckoned her closer with a finger.

"Go. It is time. God be with you, child," Amos whispered.

Anika took in a breath of the crisp, forest air to steel her trembling nerves and approached the sorcerer. She stopped before him and he took her cheeks in his hands, turning her face to study her. Beneath the skull, she saw him smile.

"Why have you come here?" the sorcerer croaked through his brown, broken smile.

Anika gave the question but a brief thought. She was here to make right her sister's death, even if it meant her own. "I am here to ask the old spirits to avenge the wrongs done against my people."

"And do you know what Ol' Hige requires of you to regain her strength that she can remain in the mortal world long enough to exact your revenge?" Talk of witches and vengeance made the sorcerer's smile broaden from a blade-thin crease to a crescent moon.

Anika nodded. The response did not satisfy the old man.

"Tell the old witch with your own last breaths what it is you have come to offer him. What is it you have to give that he will use to cast the spells and bring pain to those who have pained you?"

Anika nodded once more. "I offer my body and my blood." Her voice was proud, like a martyr who reveled in the opportunity to be fed to the lions.

"And to whom do you offer your body and blood?"

"To Ol' Hige," she said. She took a contemplative breath while the sorcerer waited for her to finish. "To Ol' Hige, the last witch of the island."

The sorcerer cackled delightfully and clapped his hands. The smell of smoke and decay rolled off his tongue and twisted Anika's gut. He stepped close to her, eye to eye, still holding his broad smile. Anika wondered for a moment if the old man had grown so tired of the swamps and trees that he was glad for her pain; glad that he could finally add some spice to his hermitic life with a little fire and a fair amount of death. Then he produced a crude knife and ran the blade across her forehead.

She gasped as she felt the sharp pain of her skin splitting and the warm, sticky sensation of her blood dripping down her face. She took another breath and settled herself. The worst of the pain was still to come.

The sorcerer gave her a questioning nod. She returned the nod. He smiled and placed the knife's blade against her head to cover it in her blood. Then he took a step away and drew a circle in the sand around Anika's feet. He dipped the blade in her blood once more and drew the five-pointed star within the circle, with its apex facing south. The sigil complete, he stood and howled.

The other shamans began to chant, their voices growing louder as the sorcerer howled and danced. Anika had never learned the native language of her people, so the words had no meaning to her. She was glad. She didn't want to know what blasphemous invocation they were reciting. As foreboding began to break apart her resolve like a ship upon a stony shoreline, the chanting stopped.

The silence was a relief to Anika, but was much more eerie than the clamorous chants. High in a nearby tree, an owl let out a crying hoot. She turned and beheld a white owl, spotted with gray and black, staring down at her. The old bird leapt from its perch and glided to her shoulder. She was mesmerized by the creature's large, black eyes and the two shared their gaze for a few breaths. Then the owl lashed out with its beak, ripped off Anika's ear, and gobbled the flesh down whole.

Anika screamed and the owl continued to tear at her flesh. Soon, she collapsed to the ground and fell silent while the bird continued its feast. In a few short minutes, all that remained was a skeleton, blood-stained feathers, and a promise that justice would be fulfilled.

And Ol' Hige always kept a promise.

*

"Savages are restless tonight, for sure," Ruskin muttered to himself. He waved the lantern around to clear away the shadows from within the barn. He walked from stall to stall to make sure all the pigs had been penned for the night, and most of all, to make sure none of the slaves were hiding in the hayloft, thinking they'd sneak away that night. Ruskin smiled at the thought and patted the whip hanging from his belt.

"Six, seven, and eight. They're all here tonight. Good. I'll finally be able to sleep." He turned to the barn's door but stopped when he heard the fluttering of bird wings. "Damn pigeons; bunch of flying rats."

He turned to the sound and the lantern's light spilled over a white owl, spotted gray and black, perched on a rafter. "Oh, well, look at that. We ain't had an owl to clean up all the mice in some time, not that this place can be much clean with the pigs 'n all." The owl hooted, then glided to the ground, disappearing behind a stack of feed sacks.

"Eh? You catch something already?" Ruskin rushed to the pile of sacks to see what the owl had caught. When the lantern-light revealed a naked old woman lying in the dirt and hay, the overseer froze in his steps. "Hey!" he yelled. "You all right?"

The hag lifted her head and slowly pushed herself up, brittle bones popping and creaking while she stood.

"Hold on a moment, ma'am. Let me get you a blanket." He rushed off and pulled a dirty horse blanket from a hook. He turned back and saw the old woman was hobbling toward him. With each step, the years washed away from her. Wrinkles turned smooth and her frizzy, white hair turned golden and silky. Ruskin's eyes went wide and he dropped the blanket, no longer desiring to cover the woman's perfect form.

She reached a hand to his cheek. Her diamond eyes so entranced the slavedriver he didn't notice the flames engulfing her arm until they burnt at his flesh and hair.

Ruskin shrieked and the woman embraced him, her entire body an inferno. Then her fangs sank into the arteries and veins in his neck.

*

"Hugh! Alfred! Come inside this instant!" Beverly called from the manor's front porch.

"Aw, Mother, we don't want to stop playing yet," Hugh whined.

"You mustn't disobey your mother like that," Harriet scolded.

"I don't care if you want to stop playing," Beverly said. "It's getting dark and there's a killer still on the loose. You come inside right now or I'll send you to go pick out a switch for your brother and you."

Hugh groaned, took Alfred by the hand, and led the boy to their mother. "I'm not scared of some stupid slave, Mother."

Beverly took her sons into her embrace and kissed them both on their foreheads. "I know you're not scared, but I am. We've lost three men in as many nights. We're still not sure it's even a slave doing the killings. So until we find out, you two will have to be in before dark. Now, give your Auntie Harriet a kiss, and then off to bed."

Alfred rushed to Harriet's side and planted a wet kiss on her cheek. Hugh, however, marched like a convict to the gallows and offered only a dry peck. Then Hugh led his younger brother to a fate far worse than hanging: bedtime.

"I have to check on the kitchen staff. Will you be all right?"

Harriet nodded. "I believe I can manage a moment away from your side." Beverly returned the nod, lifted her skirts, and rushed through the large house to the adjacent kitchen.

Harriet, meanwhile, took a seat on the porch beneath one of the lanterns and laid her Bible on her lap. She turned the pages to Second Peter, but before she began her daily readings, she looked to the stars.

The glimmering lights filled the sky. They reminded her of being back in Africa, although there were different constellations south of the equator. In London, there was too much noise and too many lights to be able to appreciate the stars. While the stars shimmered above, torches flickered in the distant shadows.

After the second body had been discovered, flayed of its skin and drained of its blood, Beverly's husband, George, sent riders to Falmouth with word and coins. They returned with more riders, each man armed. Of the three murders, there were no witnesses, but Master Monroe was certain it was one of his slaves. No Englishman was so uncivilized to kill in such a brutal manner. Harriet didn't voice her disagreement. She had seen how brutal civilized men could be.

"You read that book every day. You know you're not on mission anymore." Beverly set a glass of wine on the table next to Harriet and then took a seat beside her, a glass in her own hand—even though her own was filled to the brim.

Harriet took a sip. "God never takes a day off and I don't see a reason to take a vacation from my devotions. I see Hugh and Alfred, however, don't care much for them."

"I told you so," Beverly said with the accompanying look in her eyes.

The sisters sat beneath the lantern and watched the stars. They talked of their parents and Beverly's move to Jamaica, the busy life of London, and the quiet, usually calm life on the plantation. Harriet started to talk of her experience in Africa, but Beverly finished off her wine, reached across the table, and helped herself to the last few swallows in Harriet's glass.

"Please," Beverly said. "Take a break from your devotions for a few minutes. I want to show you the silk cotton tree. It bloomed just yesterday and the flowers are gorgeous. Bring the lantern."

"Should we be walking out at night?" Harriet, despite her misgivings took the oil lantern off the hook.

"Oh, don't be such a worry-wart. George and the men are out patrolling right now. No one will come close to the manor house. Not tonight."

Beverly led her sister down a crude trail hacked away between the trees. Harriet tripped over several roots and rocks, almost dropping the lantern and her Bible several times. Beverly, however, maneuvered around and over each obstacle with hardly any light to guide her. Harriet was perplexed. Beverly had lived nearly her entire life indoors. After a year and a half in Jamaica, she was more adept at navigating the forest than her more adventuresome sister.

A few minutes passed and they came upon the small clearing. In the center stood a great, gnarled tree with weeping branches. Even in the sparse moonlight, the bright red flowers covering those branches were stark and beautiful.

"Oh my..." Harriet gasped.

"You should see it in the daylight. It's amazing."

One of the branches rustled, and Harriet almost jumped out of her shoes. She turned to the noise and raised the lantern, while Beverly laughed at her sister's startling.

Two large, black eyes within the tree reflected the lantern's light. The owl gave a series of hoots, then sat still.

"Well, will you look at that. I've never seen an owl like that on the island before. All the ones here are brown, not black-and-white," Beverly said.

The bird leaped from its perch and glided through the air toward the sisters. Harriet jumped away, but Beverly laughed as the owl took a perch on her shoulder.

"Will you look at this?" Beverly couldn't contain her laughter. The owl hooted. "Yes, hoot hoot to you too."

The owl tilted its head, as if it understood Beverly's words. Then it ripped off her ear and gobbled it down.

Both sisters screamed, but only Harriet's carried on. Beverly's pained wail had been cut short when the bird's beak tore out her throat.

Harriet couldn't move. She watched the owl rip chunks of flesh from her sister, not because she wanted to take in the gruesome sight, but because she was too frightened to turn away. Only when the lantern slipped from her grip, did she remember that she was still alive. Clutching the Holy Bible to her chest, she turned to the shadowed forest trail and ran.

She stumbled over giant roots and rocks. After a minute, she lost her shoes and decided it would be best to leave them behind. She ran on and could see the trees giving way to the open space around the manor house.

Her foot caught on a root.

She landed face first in a muddy puddle. When the bright stars in her vision faded away, she remembered to breathe again. She lifted her head from the mud and saw the porch's lantern lights. She also heard a series of hoots getting closer and closer.

She pushed herself to her feet and pumped her legs as fast as she could. Despite the burning in her lungs and legs, she ran on, too scared to stop. The only thought in her head, beside fear, was a longing to be back in London.

The trees gave way and she ran for the steps. A moment after she burst from the treeline, she heard the owl's wings flapping a short distance behind her. Her foot landed on the first step, slipped, and she was sent sprawling hard across porch steps. Harsh pain shot through her thin bones as they came to a jarring halt against the sharp edges of the steps. She gasped, but she knew she didn't have time to recover from her pains.

She turned onto her back and saw the owl descending through the air toward her. Harriet shrieked and held out the Bible, opened to Psalm 28:7, as a shield against the terrifying bird.

The owl flew straight into the opened pages. It let out a human-like shriek and fluttered away.

Harriet took in a few trembling breaths, then lowered the Bible. The bird was nowhere to be seen. The forest was still and the stars twinkled on, all the universe uncaring of the recent and brutal loss of life.

Then Harriet turned her face to the heavens and shrieked. When her voice finally gave way, she heard the shouts of men and the charging of muskets.

*

The trees gave way and the silk cotton tree stood as it had for centuries. The owl glided to the ground. Its claws touched the earth, a flash of light drove back the shadows, and Ol' Hige had returned to the form of a flaming beauty. She knelt before the old tree like a knight before an altar, awaiting his blessing before embarking on a crusade.

"Approach," a deep, wise voice spoke from the tree.

Ol' Hige stood, walked up to the tree, leaned a hand against it, and vomited Beverly's blood onto the roots.

Glowing eyes looked up at the flaming abomination, the old witch whose youth could only be fueled with hellfire. Beneath the tree, imprisoned by the silk cotton's roots shortly after the Christians arrived, Bazil, demon of death, contemplated his freedom.

"This was good blood you brought tonight. A shame you couldn't bring me the sister's as well. Her blood is pure. Her blood might have given me the strength I need to regain my dominion of this island and drive the holy men into the sea."

Ol' Hige cocked her head and shrugged at the demon's words.

"Yes. I know you promised the slaves justice. I will give them justice, but first you must give me blood. Go. End this Monroe bloodline, and at last, I can finally be free."

Ol' Hige bowed before her hellish master and flew off into the night.

*

George Monroe reeled his arm back and drove his fist into the slave's face, not to punish the man or to coerce more information from him, but to release his own boiling anger.

Garfield didn't have the strength to cry out. He barely had the strength to spit his tooth and blood onto the wooden floor.

George wiped the blood from his knuckles with a handkerchief. "Take him away. Feed him to the dogs for all I care."

The two men holding Garfield's arms dragged him away through the manor house. "No…" he whispered. "I told you… everything. Please."

Harriet had watched the entire beating. She had wanted to plead for the man's mercy, but the images of Beverly's blood-soaked corpse stayed her voice.

"Harriet." George's voice pulled her back to reality. "Go check on the boys. Make sure they're tucked in tight and they don't leave their room."

"You're not leaving us, are you?" Her voice cracked like glassware on stone.

"You heard what the slave said. The only way to defeat this thing is to leave rice out at the crossroads. Come morning, when it's still there, counting the grains, we can kill it. Everything else he said corroborates what you saw. We'll have to trust him."

Harriet sniffed back her tears and lowered her eyes. "Go with God." Master Monroe nodded and turned to the horse and the posse of torch-bearing, armed men awaiting him in front of the manor house.

Once the men were away, Harriet turned to the house's creaking stairs. Each step let out a sharp sound that reminded her of the owl's pained shriek. She breathed a sigh of relief when she at last reached the top. Then she knocked on the brothers' door, turned the handle, and eased the door open. Both boys looked up from the figurines of soldiers with which they played, then leapt into bed.

"Are you two doing all right?" Harriet asked.

"Yes," sweet Alfred squeaked. Harriet took a seat at the foot of the younger brother's bed.

"Is Father going to catch the murderer now?" Hugh asked, eyes bright.

"Yes."

"Good."

She was amazed how the young boys were holding up after the death of their mother. She could learn a thing or two from their strength.

"I need you two to do something for me," she said. "You two promise you'll do this for me." Both the boys nodded. "Good. I need you each to say the Lord's Prayer three times before you go to bed. If you do that, it will help keep the demon away."

Once more, the boys nodded.

"Good," their aunt said. She stood, kissed them each on the forehead, blew out the candles, and closed the door behind her.

Hugh counted to ten after the door closed, then bolted out of bed.

"What are you doing?" Alfred watched his older brother resume setting the soldier figures into formations. "Aunt Harriet said we have to say our prayers or the demon will come."

"There isn't any demon, you baby. She's just saying that to scare us. It's one of the miserable slaves who killed Mother, and Father's going to get him tonight."

Alfred considered his brother's words. Then he hopped out of bed and began arranging his own figures. The two boys were halfway through recreating the Battle of Quebec during the Seven Years War, when they heard a bird chirping close by. They hadn't heard any bird sing like what they had just heard. Their eyes went wide, and Hugh grabbed his brother by the hand and led him to the window. He pushed the two panes open and looked down out at the pear tree growing outside.

Sitting on the branch closest to their bedroom window, sat a fat, white bird with black and gray spots.

"Look," Hugh said. "An owl."

ACE

SWORDS

26

ACE OF SWORDS

C. L. WILSON

Upright: Triumph, conquest, great force on love as well as in hatred
Reversed: The same meanings with disastrous results, conception,
augmentation, multiplicity

A Tairen Souls Story

It was a good day to die.

Shannisorran vel Celay, First General of the Fading Lands, stood on the cliffs of Sardomar, the southern continent far from the lush beauty of his homeland, and watched the golden brightness of the Great Sun rise on the day that would be his last. In a short time, Shan would lead a small army into the hive of one of the oldest and most powerful Drogon Blood Lords. Malvern, he was called. A monster who had slaughtered millions, and who was the main power behind the war that had raged across Eloran for the last two years. The fight would be brutal, and high casualties were expected.

Shan expected himself to be among them, but even if he wasn't, he would not live to see another sunrise. Today would bring him death in battle or by his own hand in *sheisan'dahlein*, the Fey honor death.

For three thousand years, he'd walked the earth of Eloran. For three thousand years, he'd served as a warrior of honor and a Champion of Light in the armies of the Fey. For three thousand years, the souls of all those he'd killed in that service clung to his own like burning stones, weighing him down with the vast accumulation of the pain and darkness and lost hopes of the slain until he could no longer feel anything but the constant agony of their torment and despair.

All the while, as he'd bloodied his steel in war after war and burdened his soul with death upon death until he could barely stagger beneath the crushing weight, he'd waited for that promised beacon of Light, that singular, shining soul born to complete his own. A truemate. A woman who was his match in every way. Equal in power. Equal in strength. A woman brave enough, strong enough, and fierce enough to draw him back from the shadowy abyss that whispered his name every passing moment.

Alas, she had never come. And now, at last, he could admit to himself that she never would. At least not in this lifetime.

He had dedicated his life to slaying monsters. Best to end things now, before he became the very thing he had so often hunted, before his growing indifference to dealing death became a hunger for it. Gods willing, he would take this one last monster with him when he went.

Shan closed his eyes and let the the golden brightness of the Great Sun caress his face. If he'd ever found his mate, she would have touched him thusly, the softness of her fragrant skin feather light, leaving warmth in its path. He lifted his arms slowly, like an Elf singing thanks for the blessings of the day, and crossed them over his chest.

"It's time," a low voice announced from behind him.

Shan released the red wrapped hilt of his lethally poisoned red Fey'cha daggers as the individual whose near-silent approach he'd been tracking for a full chime finally announced his presence. He turned to regard Anaris Feyreisen, Tairen Soul and King of the Fading Lands. "*Aiyah.* I was just about to head back."

The Tairen Soul regarded Shan solemnly. "Are you sure I can't talk you out of this?"

Shan's answer was a flat stare.

Anaris hadn't liked the plan since Shan proposed it. In fact, they'd argued quite combatively last night over the wisdom of the First General of the Fading Lands personally leading his troops into the literal maw of the beast. Normally, the Earth masters of the Fey would simply weave away the rock and soil of the Blood Lord's lair, leaving the hive's inhabitants exposed to the sun and open to attack. But Malvern was a wily son of a *petchka*. He'd established his hive in ground liberally veined with *sel'dor*, the vile black metal that burned Fey skin on contact and disrupted their magic weaves. Earth weaves were useless and digging wasn't an option. The hive was simply too deep, burrowed beneath enormous, rocky mountains. There was no way they'd uncover the bowels of the hive before nightfall, and at night, Drogons held the advantage.

The Tairen Souls couldn't help infiltrate the Blood Lord's lair either. As they had learned when destroying previous hives, the tunnels were too small and narrow for a Tairen Soul to Change into the great, winged cat that was his most powerful form. They were much more useful above ground, where they could circle above the hive and flame anything that tried to escape.

Anaris changed the subject in a silent admission of defeat. "An Elvian ship arrived half a bell ago. They brought another two dozen healers, including that Elf-kin *shei'dalin* from Tehlas that everyone's been talking about. The one who healed Axen vel'En Dahn's mate when all the other *shei'dalins* said she couldn't be saved."

Shan had heard about the famous Elf-kin *shei'dalin* from Tehlas. Their paths had never crossed—she split her time between her great-great-grandmother's home in Elvia and the Tehlasian Hall of Truth and Healing on the Fading Lands' west coast, while Shan rarely left Dharsa except for war—but word of her impressive skills had been circulating for decades.

That she should arrive today, just before the Fey launched their attack on Blood Lord Malvern's hive, could be no coincidence. Elves had foresight. If they had brought the greatest healer in the Fading Lands as well as two dozen of their own to Sardomar, it was because they knew the healers would be needed.

"Look on the bright side, Feyreisen. At least the Elves have Seen we'll have more lives in need of saving than we can currently accommodate."

The Tairen Soul scowled. "You're not funny. You know that, right?"

Shan hadn't meant it as a joke.

Anaris squared his shoulders. "Time to get going." He held out a hand. When Shan reached out to clasp the younger man's forearm, the Tairen Soul said, "Good luck to you today, *Chatokkai* vel Celay. Light be with you."

"Beylah vo, kem'Feyreisen." Thank you, my king. "Light be with us all."

The Tairen Soul nodded, turned, and took a running leap off the edge of the cliff. As he jumped, powerful magic erupted, and his body dissolved into a swirling grey cloud of rainbow-shot mist. Moments later, a great, winged beast streaked out of the mist. Not Anaris Feyreisen, the Fey king, but Anaris-Faldaran, an enormous, dark brown tairen, one of the deadly, fire-breathing winged cats of the Fading Lands. Anaris gave a roar that shook the ground beneath Shan's feet, then shot up into the cloudless Sardomar sky, great, leathery wings pumping to gain speed and altitude.

Shan turned away from his king's impressive tairen form to regard the golden brightness of the Great Sun one final time. The last of the dawn's gentle pink had faded. The sun was bright, the sky a perfect, cerulean blue over the deeper blue of the vast ocean that stretched across the horizon. Shan took a deep breath of fresh, salty morning air, and felt peace settle over his ancient Fey bones.

He could do this. He would slay this one last enemy, make the Fading Lands safe this one last time. And then he would do what he'd never done before: stop fighting, lay down his steel, and surrender his life. Death was no longer an enemy to be opposed, but a friend to embrace.

"Farewell, shei'tani," he murmured to the truemate he had long awaited, but never met. "May we find each other in the next life, as we did not in this. And may you find me worthy of your bond."

He headed down toward the Fey encampment and toward the battle that would be his last.

*

There it is.

The barely audible announcement made Shan realize just how nervous his men were. Spun on threads of the mystic magic Spirit across the Fey Warrior's Path, no Drogon or Merellian could possibly have the words, yet even in his weave Shan's second-in-command, Sandar vel Candis, still whispered.

But then, they'd all seen the carnage Blood Lord Malvern left in his wake. Bodies butchered. Cathedrals beribboned with entrails. Altars to dark gods fashioned from the bones and dismembered limbs of Fey, Elf, and mortal alike. Villages, towns, and even entire cities stripped of all life save the rats and carrion crows come to feast on the blood-drained remains of the dead.

Aiyah, Sandar had reason to whisper. Malvern was as fearsome a monster as ever they'd faced.

Which was why Shan found it so surprising that the entrance to Malvern's hive was so inconspicuous. A brush covered cave mouth that led down into the tunnel-riddled limestone earth of Drogos. Nothing to declare, "Beware, intruders! Death beyond this point!" Personally, Shan thought there should at least be a couple of skulls impaled on pikes, if not a bloodless, eviscerated corpse or two.

He grunted at his own black humor and scanned the area with Fey vision, seeing not just the material world evident to mortal eyes but the glowing threads of magic woven through every aspect of the universe: the four elements—Earth, Fire, Water, Air—as well as the two mystics—lavender Spirit, and dark Azrahn, the magic never to be called. With Fey vision, he could see the life pulsing through the dense vegetation surrounding the cave, see the solid density of the rock and soil, and the silvery white voids of Air where the tunnels led down into the hive.

He scanned for the enemy. Found none near the entrance.

That was as expected, and the reason why this attack had been scheduled for morning. Sunlight was anathema to Blood Lords and their vile minions. Better yet, the higher the sun rose in the sky, the more torpid the Drogons would become, unable to move, lying like the dead and deathless creatures they were. The effects were doubly strong for the oldest among them, which made daytime the best time—the only time—to risk something as bold and foolhardy as sending forces into the depths of an ancient Blood Lord's hive.

Feyreisen, Fire the hole. Shan wove the command in Spirit and sent it out on the Warrior's Path that all Fey males shared.

Three Tairen Souls in their gigantic tairen forms padded up to the cave entrance and, in unison, belched great gouts of hot flame into the mouth of the cave. They held the fire for a full chime, sending the inferno as deep as possible. When it was done, all three crouched to gather their strength, then launched into the air to join the other Tairen Souls circling overhead.

Shan kept his eye on the cave mouth and his hands near his steel. **Fey, advance. Fire and steel at the ready.**

Steel alone didn't have much impact on a Drogon. You could chop off a limb, but the severed appendage merely dissolved and reformed in place an instant later. Beheading—a death that ended even immortal Fey lives—didn't always work either. Shan had personally witnessed headless Drogons snatching up their lost noggins, dissolving into swirls of black mist, then reappearing elsewhere on the field, whole and unharmed. Granted, if you chopped off the same head often enough in the same battle, the Drogon eventually ran out of energy to regenerate and was forced to retire from the field.

At least tairen venom—the smallest drop of which could kill a man or even a Fey in less than a chime—slowed the Drogons down. It even successfully killed the weakest among them. But the stronger Drogons—and especially the powerful Blood Lords—merely drained their own bodies of the envenomed blood and replaced it with fresh, untainted blood from the nearest donor.

Nei, if you wanted to kill a Drogon and make him stay dead, you needed sunlight or its next best replacement: bright, hot, blazing fire. Mundane mortal flames would do the trick, but magical Fire was best. Tairen fire or the Fey elemental magic. Limbs dismembered with Fire-wrapped blades took a full day to regenerate. And if you managed to incinerate a Drogon… well, Shan had yet to see even the most ancient and powerful of Blood Lords survive a concentrated Fey flame bath.

Shan, who had always led his armies from the front, was the first into the tunnels. Little sparks from smoking roots and bracken flashed like fairy flies in the darkness. The air was thick and smoky, smelling of fetid rot and char.

As Shan and his Fey descended into the hive, the brightness of day gave way to oppressive gloom and then impenetrable darkness. **Cloak your Light, Fey,** he commanded as he spun a Spirit weave to hide the silvery luminescence of his own Fey skin. Shan switched to Fey vision, letting the magic that made up the world illuminate what sunlight no longer could, but as he did he realized the hive wasn't just built in *sel'dor-rich* ground, it's tunnels were lined with the black metal. Fey vision couldn't penetrate pure *sel'dor,* which meant Malvern had effectively blinded Shan and his Fey to everything beyond line-of-sight. Every curve in the tunnel became an opportunity for ambush. Every tunnel that merged with or broke off the main one became a potential feeder stream that could at any moment unleash a torrent of Bloodreapers, an army of mindless, undead fiends whose only thought was to sate their rotting bodies' ravening hunger for fresh blood.

Be on your guard. His lips compressed in a wry grimace as he realized he had whispered that last command. In a more normal volume, he commanded, ***Fey, stay alert. Close off the side tunnels as we go.***

Aiyah, Chatokkai, came the response.

Normally, the Fey could simply spin Earth magic to reshape the rock and soil to block the tunnels, but the solid *sel'dor* lining the tunnel walls made that impossible. Even the strongest Earth masters could only pull so much matter from themselves and those around them without causing damage. The same was true for weaving Water. That meant blocking the tunnels would have to be done with weaves of Air, Fire, and Spirit.

Leaving his Fey to decide how best to accomplish that—knowing they would alert him if there was a problem—Shan continued down the now-steeply descending tunnel main tunnel. The air grew notably cooler as he went. Gone were the acrid scents of smoke and char left in the wake of the Tairen Souls' fire. The smells that remained were of damp and mold underscored by a pungent odor that every warrior—mortal or immortal alike—soon learned and never forgot. A heavy reek that had become all-too-familiar during this war. Blood. Offal. Putrescence.

The hive smelled of death.

And then came the sound Shan had been waiting for: the thunder of many running feet.

Reapers.

Chapter Two

Bodies surged up from the depths of the lair, thousands of them, all in various stages of decomposition.

Compared to other mortal and immortal races, Drogons were relatively few in number, but in times of war, the Blood Lords swelled their populations with Bloodreapers, the reanimated corpses of their victims, tied to the Blood Lord that animated them through the very blackest of magics. Reapers were mindless killing machines, their actions directed by the hive mind—the Blood Lord who ruled the hive and the less powerful, blood-bound Drogons who served him. Fey. Elf. Celierian. Allies and innocents murdered by the Drogons then perverted into these foul creatures.

Their breath wheezed, phlegmy and labored, through rotting lungs. The more recent dead were mostly whole, but others were little more than skeletons swathed in shreds of flesh. Red-eyed, yellow-fanged, suppurating skin, oozing pus and gangrenous matter. All of them maddened by bloodlust. The stench of them was blinding.

"Fey'cha and Fire weaves, Fey!" Shan cried, both aloud and along the Warrior's Path. "Burn as many as you can!" He flung out weaves of Air and Fire and sent Fire-wrapped Fey'cha daggers flying so fast his hands were a blur.

The first line of Reapers burst into flame and collapsed, lifeless, on the ground. Shan tried not to focus on their faces. Whatever—whomever—they once had been, they were the Blood Lord's minions now. And already dead, thank the gods, else slaughtering those that had been Fey would have left Shan and his warriors writhing in agony, their souls plunged down the Dark Path for the crime of murdering their own kind.

That was one good thing about killing Reapers: it burdened no Fey's soul. In fact, ending them felt more like a kindness. And sorrow, too, he thought, as he plowed a weave of Fire through the tattered black leathers and rotting chest of what had once been a Fey warrior. He whispered a prayer to the gods on the warrior's behalf, then stepped over the burning body and and sent four more Fire-wrapped Fey'chas flying. Later, once they dealt with this attack, the Fey would send back to the elements whatever remained of their fallen brothers and the other poor wretches in this undead army.

After emptying every sheath on the Fey'cha belts criss-crossing his chest, Shan spat out his return word. The magical command dissolved his thrown Fey'cha and returned them to their sheaths so he could start throwing them again. Again and again and again his Fire-wrapped Fey'cha flew swift and true, while ropes of glowing magic poured from his fingertips. White Air, red Fire, blazing strands twining and weaving together, concentrated into a jet of white-hot flame that consumed everything in its path.

And still, the Reapers kept coming, wave after wave of them.

As he dealt with the swarm rushing toward him, Shan heard the shouts on the Warrior's Path behind him. Reapers carrying crude shields fashioned from barbed black metal had broken through the weaves sealing off the side tunnels. Reapers were pouring out of the tunnels on every side and dropping down from openings in the ceiling.

Unlike the Drogons, Bloodreapers weren't difficult to kill—they were merely fodder meant to weary the Fey, slow their progress, and inflict as much damage as possible—but their numbers were formidable and their poisonous bites were a threat that could not be ignored. Fey were immune to most sickness, but the contagion carried in the rotting membranes of a Reaper's mouth was no natural disease. Infused with black magic, the bite carried not just death but undeath. Any who died with that poison in their veins became Bloodreapers themselves. Even Fey. Closing the tunnels and stopping the influx of Reapers into their midst was, therefore, imperative.

"Fire masters! Burn them! Earth masters, use what the Blood Lord has sent us against them! Block those tunnels, Fey! Seal them solid!"

Behind Shan, weaves of Fire and Air shot out, firestorms racing through the packed bodies in the tunnels, setting them alight. Earth masters who hadn't been able to weave rock through the *sel'dor* lined tunnel, now drew what they needed from the bones and flesh of the plentiful Bloodreaper dead and began sealing tunnel after tunnel with two-foot-thick walls of dense stone.

Gradually the flood of Reapers pouring through the tunnels slowed to a trickle, then stopped altogether, leaving only the mass surging up the main tunnel for Shan to deal with.

"Wall of Steel, Fey!" Shan commanded. "Fire weaves and Fey'cha only! Push them back and burn them!" After delivering two volleys of Fire-wrapped Fey'cha throwing daggers and incinerating Fire weaves, the first two rows of Fey on either side of him peeled off to the sides of the tunnel and made their way back toward the rear of the line, allowing two rows of fresh warriors to take their place and engage the Reapers. After a few chimes, those Fey peeled off as well, and the next lines of Fey moved forward. Fey steel and Fey weaves slammed into the Bloodreapers without cease, each weave, each barrage of lethal, Fire-wrapped steel as potent and deadly as the last, every warrior fresh, rested, and fighting at his peak. Thus, despite the veritable ocean of undead swarming the tunnel, the Fey advanced with merciless resolve, mowing down the Reapers and sealing side tunnels as they went.

After what seemed like an eternity, the onslaught ended. The only thing left of the Reapers: uneven stone floors lined knee deep with bones, charred flesh, and ash.

"Well done, Fey," Shan praised. "The Reapers are down. Send our fallen brothers back to the elements, and make sure all other dead are ash. Take a moment to check yourself and your blade brothers. If you've been bitten or scratched, you need to head for the healing tents. No exceptions." Shan wouldn't risk any of his Fey turning Reaper. "Commanders, report your casualties."

"The losses aren't as bad as we anticipated," Shan's second-in-command, Sandar, murmured as the reports came in. The Fey had fought well, losing only two percent of their forces to the Reaper attack, and most of those to bites and scratches rather than death.

"Perhaps," Shan conceded, "but that was the easy part." Easy or not, each dead Fey was flame added to the growing fury inside him. Before Shan died today, he would make sure Malvern paid for every Fey soul he'd sent through the Veil. **Fey, to your formations. Prepare to move out. Commanders, double check those tunnel seals and post quintets to guard our backs.** Quintets were groups of five Fey, who between them held mastery in all four elementals and the one mystic magic Fey wielded. A quintet could combine their weaves into a single, masterful five-fold weave capable of dealing massive damage.

Leaving two quintets behind to guard their rear flank and ensure the tunnels stayed sealed, the Fey marched toward the heart of the Blood Lord's hive.

*

The main tunnel descended another half of a mile before opening into a large chamber deep beneath the surface of Sardomar. The air was cold and damp, the room utterly lightless. A massive blood fountain burbled and splashed in the center of the room, steam curling up into the chill, filling the room with a sickly sweet, metallic odor. Shan knew from the excavation of previous hives that there was a chamber somewhere above this one, filled with hundreds of enthralled victims hooked up to tubes that drained their blood into this fountain. The pantry, Drogons called it. Shan would like nothing more than to locate the pantry and free its prisoners, but those lives were secondary to the mission. The only thing that mattered was finding and slaughtering Malvern. If they didn't succeed in that, many more people would find themselves enthralled and feeding their lifeblood into Drogon fountains.

Shan scanned the room for threats, but found none. The chamber was empty, the only movement the splashing blood. Apart from the main tunnel they had come down, three other wide tunnels led off from the enormous fountain room. Which one led to the Blood Lord, Shan didn't know. Every hive they'd destroyed thus far boasted a similar large chamber with its burbling blood fountain, always located at the end of the main tunnel and always attached to the tunnels that led to the Drogon's sleeping quarters, but those were the only commonalities. The chambers belonging to the Blood Lord and his chosen females were usually close together and separated from the chambers that housed his elite Drogon warriors and the rest of his court. But which rooms were where was anyone's guess.

Shan knew from taking down previous Blood Lords that killing Malvern first was a priority. Without him, the communications network that linked the rest of the hive would collapse and stay broken until a new Blood Lord assumed command and subsumed the survivors.

With Malvern out of the picture, eradicating the rest of the hive would become exponentially easier, but searching the tunnels one at a time posed too great a risk. By Shan's estimation, the Great Sun was nearing its zenith. Five or six more bells, and the torpor that seized all Drogons during the day would begin to fade. Younger Drogons would rouse first. They'd be weaker and slower while the sun was in the sky, but once it set, even the most ancient would rise at full strength. If Shan didn't find and kill Malvern before then, every Fey in the hive was as good as dead.

Shan called his commanders to his side. "We're going to have to split up. Sandar, you take three hundred Fey and search the left tunnel. Andaxis, you take another three hundred and search the right. Everyone else, with go with me up the center. With all the *sel'dor* in this place, it's imperative you establish a communication relay as you go so you can call for help if you need it." The last thing he wanted was for one group to locate the Blood Lord but be unable to summon assistance before engaging him in battle. Shan didn't trust the torpor to keep Malvern helpless, and the Blood Lord had already proved himself wily enough to have put all manner of defenses in place in anticipation of a daytime attack on his hive. "If you find Malvern, raise the alarm but do not engage until backup arrives. Stay alert, Fey, and look carefully for traps."

"Aiyah, Shan," Sandar and Andaxis said.

"Foolish Fey." As the two commanders began assembling their troops, a deep, icy voice boomed from the darkness. It came from every direction at once, echoing off the stone walls, so that tracking the voice back to its source was impossible. "To invade a Blood Lord's hive is to ask for death. Or did you think the risen sun would save you?"

Hold, Fey! Shan stepped toward the center of the room. "Only a coward hides and shouts threats from the dark," he challenged in a loud, clear voice. "You want to kill us? Then show yourself, Malvern." He pulled two red Fey'cha from their sheaths. Fire danced up the steel, glowing red vines twining around the gleaming blades like the arms of a lover. "Come, Blood Lord. Dance with the tairen if you dare!"

"Blood Lords don't dance with their food, meat."

"And Fey don't cower in the dark, hiding from their enemies, Drogon."

"Is an ant my enemy? You think too much of yourself, Fey. Or should I call you Lord Death?" A sneering laugh rang out as he spoke the name by which Shan was known among his enemies. "I will make of you a true Lord Death, Shannisorran vel Celay, First General of the Fading Lands. After my court and I dine on your delicious Fey blood, the drained corpses of you and the rest of your warriors will replace the Bloodreapers you destroyed. And then, with the greatest delight, I will send you into your camps to slaughter your allies."

He is stalling, Shan, Sandar murmured on the Warrior's Path.

Aiyah. I know it. I just haven't yet figured out why. Where was Malvern? Down one of these three tunnels? Or had he tricked them all and secreted himself in one of the offshoots they'd already sealed?

Shan raised a hand, about to issue the command to begin searching the tunnels, when his ears detected a faint susurration like the whisper of fabric rubbing against itself. The sound grew closer, louder.

Not fabric. Wings. Thousands of wings.

Fey! Five-fold weaves! Quickly. He muttered his return word and flung out now-empty hands, magic spinning from his fingertips in great, glowing ropes just as a black swarm of flying creatures burst out of the center tunnel and dove toward the Fey.

Dragats. Small, flying vermin, with bodies no bigger than Shan's hand and long thin wings edged with tiny black claws. Like birds but furred instead of feathered, and instead of a beak, they possessed mouths full of sharp white fangs. Shan got a good look at those fangs as the creatures dove, shrieking and spewing green acid flame, into his weaves. The impact shuddered down the threads of his magic, while the sonic disruption of their piercing shrieks and the acid fire of their flame ate away at the densely woven Fey shield.

Many of the dragats burst into flame upon contact with the Fire threads in the five-fold weaves. The injured and broken ones dropped to the stone floor. The ones still capable of flight rolled to the side and flew away, leaving the path clear for the rest of the column, which arrowed full speed into precisely the same spot, again and again in a formation Shan recognized.

"Tairen's scorching fire," he swore. Wall of Steel. The *jaffing* things were attacking with the same Wall of Steel formation Shan and his Fey had used against the Reapers. And the attack was working. Shan shored up the weakened spot in the dome, but as he did so, a second column of dragats slammed into another section of the dome. Then a third column, then a fourth and a fifth. The massive fountain chamber was now filled with a whirlwind of diving, shrieking dragats, all converging in a carefully coordinated pattern of concentrated attacks.

The first of the dragats broke through, shrieking and spewing poison. Shan heard the grunts and the gasps of pain as the acid flame scored Fey skin and the shrieks burst unprotected ear drums. Shan sent a Fire-wrapped Fey'cha into one dragat's tiny chest. The foul thing burst into flame and dropped to the floor. Shan stomped it with his boot.

The small hole the dragats had bored through the shield grew wider. More dragats rushed in and began attacking the Fey.

Shan turned to block a shrieking dragat diving at him from the right and felt a sting of razor-sharp claws score his left cheek. Three more wildly flapping vermin slammed into his chest, gripping his leathers with their taloned feet and ripping at the skin of his neck with fangs and clawed wings. He snatched them off, flinging the tiny, furred bodies away from him, flaming them as he did, but as quickly as he flung them away, others took their place, biting, scratching, clawing at him. Within moments, he was swarmed, hundreds of the creatures raking him with their claws and teeth. Blood was running freely now from his face, hands, and neck, anywhere his skin was not covered by protective black leather.

"Fire weaves, Fey!" Sandar shouted beside him. "Set the whole *jaffing* room on fire! Aben, Cato, Dariel! Ti'Chatokkai! Ti'Shan!" To the General! To Shan! "Get those things off him!" Sandar rushed to Shan's aid, slapping and stabbing and scorching the dragats that had zeroed in on Shan with a single-mindedness that couldn't possibly be random. The four of them spun a whirling vortex of red Fire and white Air around Shan, the rapid spinning of their weave impervious to the dragats' diving attacks. Behind them, the rest of the Fey Fire masters sent a cloud of superheated flame roaring through the chamber and held it until it was clear the attack was over.

This time when Shan ordered the Fey to tend their dead and wounded, and commanders to give their casualty counts, the news was grim. The dragats hadn't only targeted Shan. They'd gone after Shan's most powerful Fire masters. Two of them were dead. Hundreds more had been blinded, rendered deaf or had major arteries ripped open by fierce claws and teeth—the latter wounds great enough to take them out of the fight. The Reapers had tested the Fey to find out which of them packed the strongest punch. The Dragats had targeted those Fey and thinned their numbers.

"Cleanse your wounds, and seal them, Fey," Shan commanded. "Walking through a Drogon's hive with blood on you is asking for trouble. Those of you with cuts deep enough to need a shei'dalin's care, head out now. If you can get healed and back here within a bell or two, then come back; otherwise, you're out of this fight."

"They were targeting you deliberately," Sandar muttered as Shan spun his own weaves of Earth and Water to seal his numerous cuts and wash away every drop of blood.

"So I noticed."

"What for, do you think? Surely Malvern didn't think a horde of flying rats had a hope of killing Lord Death." Shan possessed such a mastery of elemental magics that few in the Fading Lands could best him in any branch. His talent in Spirit was just a shade shy of a master's level, too. With all that power combined, there were Tairen Souls who couldn't best Shan in a fight without going furry.

"I'd like to think he underestimated me that badly, but, nei, I don't think he did." Shan's shoulder-length black hair had been torn from its bindings by the dragat attack. He pulled it back out of his face and fastened it at his nape with a leather tie, then regarded the Earth-fused cuts that scored the backs of his hands. "They cut me. Spilled my blood. I'm fairly certain that was no accident."

Sandar's expression went stony. "You think Malvern's planning to do something with your blood?"

"He is a Blood Lord. We know he gains power over his victims by drinking their blood."

"Aiyah, but you're talking about victims he personally bites."

"I don't know that it makes a difference. For all our sakes, I have assume that if he set all those dragats on me, he did it to gain a tactical advantage greater than just keeping me occupied in this fight." Shan grimaced at the rips and tears in his leathers and spun a quick Earth weave to mend them. "I was going to have you lead one of the groups down that left tunnel, but now I think I'd better keep you by my side. You know me better than any of the others. That makes you the best candidate to keep an eye on me." Sandar was a thousand years younger than Shan, but they'd known each other— and fought side-by-side—for the better part of the last fifteen hundred years. He was Shan's oldest unmated friend still living. "If you see me acting strangely—if I do anything at all that gives you cause for concern—you take me down. No matter how you have to do it, don't let me endanger the mission or our blade brothers."

"Shan—"

"Promise me, Fey. Give me your oath."

Sandar glared at Shan, the muscles in his jaw working, but then he swore. "So be it. I swear to you Shan, I won't let you harm our brothers or our mission, no matter what it takes."

Beylah vo, kem'maresk. Thank you, my friend. Shan knew what he was asking. He had come here to die, but not at a Fey's hands— not at Sandar's hands especially. If Sandar had to kill him, he'd become *dahl'reisen*, one of the lost souls who walked the Shadowed Path, exiled forever from the Fading Lands. That was the last thing Shan wanted for this friend who had become as beloved as a brother to him. But if Malvern could use Shan's blood to turn him into some sort of puppet or weapon to use against the Fey, then as *Chatokkai* of the Fading Lands, it was his duty to makes sure that couldn't— wouldn't—happen.

Shan squared his shoulders. **Change of plans, Fey. Andaxis, take twenty-five quintets and clear out the right tunnel. Vendarion, you take another twenty-five quintets and clear out the left. The rest of you, with me. Time to put an end to this Blood Lord once and for all! Miora felah, kem'jetos! Joyful life to us all, my brothers!**

The Fey gave a triumphant roar and raced into the tunnels.

Chapter Three

Several bells and countless traps, delays, and ferocious battles later, Shan and his men reached a large, ornate door that opened to a Drogon sleeping chamber. He recognized the chamber's purpose from the other hives they'd destroyed in the war. Here, instead of solid rock, the floor was covered with loose, freshly tilled soil, rich and loamy and several feet deep. Malvern had tried to blind the Fey to what lay beneath by mixing copious amount of *sel'dor* dust into the soil and scattering another layer of *sel'dor* dust over the surface, but despite those measures, Shan could make out the glowing webs of magic generated by the dozen supine figures sleeping in the soil. Slender, curvy figures, each one lying on what appeared to be cushioned slabs of *sel'dor* ore.

They had found Malvern's females.

On the opposite side of the chamber stood another door even larger and more ornate that this one. The door to Malvern's private lair.

You mean to tell me that rultshart Malvern uses his sleeping women as a shield? Sandar exclaimed in outrage. **The jaffing coward. He so deserves to die.**

And so he will. Shan shared Sandar's outrage. Any Fey worth his steel would condemn his own soul before putting even one of their females in danger to save himself. Using twelve, vulnerable, sleeping females—mates, no less—as a shield against attack would be unthinkable. If Shan had a mate, he would let an enemy eviscerate him, pound his bones to dust, visit the torments of the damned upon him for a thousand years, rather than risk her safety in the smallest way.

Sandar eyed the loamy soil. **Do you think we can reach Malvern's chamber and dispatch him without waking the females? I know they're Drogon, but still...** Fey didn't hurt women—not even evil ones, if they could help it.

Maybe, but we can't risk letting them rise. Shan didn't want to harm the sleeping females any more than Sandar did. If they attacked, he'd slaughter them all—striking each killing blow himself if his Fey hesitated—but so long as they made no move against him, he would leave them be. The mortals and Elves could decide their fate. A mistake, quite possibly—Drogon females were dangerous creatures—but such was the Fey way. "Let's get five quintets in here to spin a twenty-five-fold weave. That should hold the females. The rest of us will go for Malvern as soon as the others arrive." Upon finding this chamber, Shan had immediately sent word to Andaxis and Vendarion, both of whom had already cleared their tunnels and were already heading back to join the main group.

Five quintets spread around the concubine's sleeping chamber and begin spinning dense weaves of magic across the room. If Malvern's females woke, they'd have trouble breaching the twenty-five-fold weave that was now taking shape over their resting place. Shan propelled himself across the room on a cushion of Air, careful to avoid disturbing the soil or the weaves being spun. He landed lightly on the other side of the room. Sandar followed a few moments later.

Shan. Sandar's voice sounded wary. He lifted a hand to the Fey'cha belts crisscrossing his chest. ****Your face is bleeding.****

Shan touched the side of his face and brought away fingertips smeared in blood. The dragat wounds, which should have healed by now, had broken open. He must have been idly scratching at them. Shan never did anything idly. Due to the nature of who and what he was and how close he was to slipping down the Shadowed Path, he'd been carefully controlling his every thought, word, and action for centuries.

He spun a weave to cleanse and reseal the cuts. ****Stay close, Sandar. And you'd better keep a full quintet nearby, too. Just in case.**** If Malvern could influence Shan to unwittingly open up his wounds in the heart of a Drogon hive, there was no telling what else he could make Shan do.

While they waited for Andaxis and Vendarion, Shan tried to scan Malvern's sleeping chamber, but the Drogon had prepared every part of this hive for a Fey invasion. The walls and wooden doors were lined with thick *sel'dor* plate, the chamber an impenetrable box to Fey vision. There was no telling what would be waiting for them on the other side, but every one of Shan's instincts was screaming, "Danger! Danger!"

He had learned, over the millennia, to listen to his instincts.

The sun would be setting soon. The younger Drogons had already begun rising. Shan and his Fey had already battled through several groups of them, taking heavy losses as they did. Malvern and the most ancient of his hive shouldn't be able to rise until nightfall, but this deep in the earth, maybe the timing was different.

Prepare to go in fighting, Fey. Air masters, go up. Fire masters, you take the lead. Spin fivefold Fire weaves, minimum. They've secured this hive with sel'dor, and that room's not going to be any different. Ready? Let's go!

He flung the door open and rushed inside, magic swirling around him and the red Fey'cha he held his fists.

He didn't know what to expect. What he found was large, empty stone room inhabited by a trio of beautiful Fey *shei'dalins*, dark-haired and glossy-eyed, standing on the steps of what looked like a stone tomb. "Help us," they said. "You must help us. They're coming!"

Shan stopped, confused. "What are you doing here, *kem'fallas*?"

"The Blood Lord. He took us from the healing tents on the coast. Oh, please, you must protect us."

Shan stayed where he was, shaking his head against the fog that seemed to be slowing his ability to process. It didn't make sense that the *shei'dalins* would be here. None were missing from camp, and Malvern couldn't have come out in broad daylight to steal them away.

A fourth *shei'dalin* emerged from the shadows. This one had hair the color of honey and eyes that gleamed like sapphires. She held out a slender hand. "Shei'tan," she said. Truemate. Beloved.

He walked toward her in a stunned daze, his heart swelling with wonder, but before he could reach her, her gaze fixed on a point beyond his shoulder, and she flinched back. "They're here!" she cried. "They'll kill us all! Protect us, *shei'tan*! Don't let them kill us!"

He spun around. An army of Drogons had somehow entered the room and engaged the Fey in combat. Drogons threatening the *shei'dalins*. Threatening his truemate! One of them was practically on his heels. He roared, unsheathing a *mei'cha* scimitar with his right hand, pulling a red Fey'cha with his left, and attacked!

The Drogon fought back, dodging his blows and blocking them, but strangely not striking back. "*Pares!*" the Drogon cried in Feyan. Stop!

There was something about his voice. Something familiar. Shan hesitated.

"Save me, *shei'tan!*" His truemate was behind him, frightened. In danger. He had to save her. He leapt on the Drogon. The enemy warrior managed to knock Shan's red Fey'cha aside, but he couldn't escape the thrust of Shan's sword.

The Drogon screamed, but instead of falling back, he lunged forward, driving Shan's sword through his own body. He grabbed Shan's left wrist and drove a black Fey'cha into Shan's right shoulder. Shan stared at the black hilt of the dagger in confusion. Black Fey'cha weren't poisoned with tairen venom. Only the red ones were. Even Drogons knew that. So why would a Drogon warrior grab a black Fey'cha to stab Shan with when the red ones were just as easy to reach?

"Shan! Wake up, scorch you!" the Drogon impaled on Shan's sword snarled. "I don't want either of us to die a jaffing *dahl'reisen!*" As Shan stared at him stupidly, the Drogon drew back a fist and punched Shan in the side of the head.

The blow snapped Shan's head around and made his ears ring. He shook his head, trying to clear it. As he did, the beautiful truemate at his side wavered like a reflection rippling in a puddle. One moment she was standing there, blond-haired, blue-eyed, everything beautiful, then next moment, there was red-eyed Drogon female in her place, digging her claws in his arm and shrieking, "Kill him! Kill him now!"

And instead of a Drogon impaled on his sword, it was Sandar. Pale, bleeding badly, mortally wounded by Shan's own hand. Gripping Shan's mail, impaled on Shan's sword, twisting the black Fey'cha in Shan's shoulder and shouting, "Shan! It's me! Snap out of it, Fey! It's a spell! Malvern's got your blood! Wake up, damn you!"

Then Sandar morphed into the enemy again. A growling Drogon, roaring and gnashing his fangs.

Shan's shei'tani clung to his arm. "You must kill him, beloved. Quickly! It's the only way to protect me!"

Of course, he had to protect her. He'd finally found her. He couldn't let anyone harm her.

Shan pulled a red Fey'cha from his belts and put it to the Drogon's throat. He frowned. The blade at the Drogon's throat was shining. Shan hadn't spun Fire around it yet, but there was a definite glow along the blade. Not the red glow of Fire magic, not Air either, even though the glow was distinctively silvery in appearance.

"Shan. Don't do it, *kem'maresk*." My friend. The Drogon was speaking Feyan again. His voice was weak. Blood bubbled from the corner of his mouth. "Don't let Malvern win. Fight him. Fight his spell. You are Shannisorran vel Celay, the greatest warrior in the Fading Lands. Don't let Malvern make you *dahl'reisen*. That female isn't your shei'tani, Shan. Think about it! Would your real shei'tani scream for you to spill blood? To kill? There is a truemate waiting for you, Shan. I know there is. If not in this life, then the next. Fight for her. Fight for her the way you have done for three thousand years. You are Fey. The most honorable one I've ever known. With a Light so bright not even three-thousand years of war could dim it. Use that Light now to break Malvern's spell!"

Something in the words broke through the confused fog that had gripped Shan's brain. The red Fey'cha at the Drogon's throat was still glowing silver, but suddenly Shan recognized the source of the glow. Not magic. At least not woven magic. It was the silvery luminescence that shone from Fey skin.

Shan gripped his red Fey'cha in a white-knuckled fist and focused on the bright, fierce Light that shone within Sandar, as it did within every Fey, a light so bright that it manifested in the physical world as a silvery luminescence glowing from their flesh—visible for all to behold. Because they were born to stand against the Darkness, to fight it with their dying breath.

No! An enraged voice—Malvern's voice—howled in Shan's mind. Pressure slammed into him, directives that fought to control him. *You will kill him! You will kill him now!**

Agony tore through Shan's veins as he threw off Malvern's illusions and fought his vile commands. Roaring defiance, he plunged his Fey'cha into the right eye of the Drogon female clinging to his arm. As she shrieked and fell back, a howling Drogon warrior rushed him. Shan shoved Sandar out of the way of the oncoming attack, blocked the Drogon's *sel'dor* blade with his sword, then stabbed a red, Fire-wrapped Fey'cha into the Drogon's heart, sending more Fire roaring down the blade and into the monster's chest. The Drogon screamed and burst into flame.

Malvern's illusions had dropped completely now. The Fey were battling all around. Drogons were pouring out of the ground in the concubine's sleeping chamber. Malvern had used the Fey's unwillingness to harm women to his advantage, hiding his men in an underground chamber beneath the sleeping females until it was time to spring the trap.

Leaving the Fey to deal with them, Shan spun and rushed up the steps toward the Blood Lord's tomb. Half a dozen enemy warriors dropped down from the ceiling to join the three females blocking the way to the tomb. Shan fought his way through them, shouting the Fey Warrior's Creed as he went.

"I am the steel no enemy can shatter!" His Fey'cha flew left and right, finding one Drogon's heart, piercing another's eye, burying deep in the throat of a third. "I am the magic no dark power can defeat!" He flung up a five-fold shield to deflect a swarm of dragats, then wrapped the weave around the swarm, cut all threads but Air and Fire, then drew the weave tight to incinerate the creatures trapped within. "I am the rock upon which evil breaks like waves." Three of the remaining females rushed him, claws out, fangs sharp, shrieking their rage and bloodlust. He cleaved them in two with Fire-wrapped *mei'cha* scimitars, and immolated them with jets of concentrated Fire.

He had reached Malvern's tomb and shoved the heavy stone lid aside with a thrust of powerful magic. Within the tomb, surrounded by loamy soil, lay the Drogon Blood Lord Malvern. His skin was milky white, his long hair white as well. He wore sel'dor-plated armor, polished to a gleaming black shine that flashed and glittered with the reflected glow of magic from the battle raging below.

Shan drew his seyani longsword, spinning a dense weave of Fire down the blade as he positioned it over Malvern's heart.

Malvern's eyes popped open, blood red and blazing with fury. **Stop!** The force of his gaze slammed into Shan. Pain exploded across every nerve ending as Shan's blood boiled and his muscles seized. The terrible force of Malvern's will encased Shan's body in fiery torment, immobilizing him.

Think what you're doing, Lord Death. I am ancient. I have slain millions in my lifetime. Kill me, and Darkness will consume you. You will become dahl'reisen. There will be no truemate for you. Not in this life, not in the next. Every word that Malvern spoke was true. Shan had danced the razor's edge of Shadow for a long time now. Taking a life as old and as evil as Malvern's would surely push Shan past the tipping point. Once that happened, not even *sheisan'dahlein,* the honor death, could cleanse the stain upon his soul.

Shan shoved the despairing thought away. He was a warrior of the Fey. He'd been born to fight the enemies of Light, no matter the cost to himself. And if his last act in this life was to sacrifice any hope of happiness in the next, so be it.

He drew a harsh breath, wrested control of his body back from the Drogon, and said, "Then I will die *dahl'reisen,* but I will send you to the Seven Hells before I go." And he drove his sword into the heart of the Blood Lord, blasting a master's weave of sun-hot Fire down the blade.

Malvern's body arched. His mouth opened, emitting a shriek that shattered stone and brought rocks and sand showering down from above. Shan's Fire burst from the Blood Lord's mouth, his eyes, his fingertips. His body writhed and convulsed wildly as the Fire consumed him from the inside out, turning flesh and bone to ash, melting *sel'dor* armor into puddles of red-hot metal, scorching the soil in which he lay.

The blackness of Malvern's dying soul crashed over Shan like a great wave, driving him to his knees and tearing a raw scream of anguish from his throat. Gods… dear Gods… what had he done? Shan had slain monsters many times before but never one that felt like this. The brutal, horrific, agony of it was all-consuming, pushing Shan not just into Shadow but toward total Darkness.

Nei. A voice sounded in his mind. **You will not fall. I will not let you.**

Somehow that voice, filled with such fierce determination, stopped his spiraling descent.

You are the greatest warrior in the Fading Lands. You are a Champion of Light. Fight for that Light now.

The abyss yawned below him. He was clinging to a sheer stone cliff by the merest fraction of his fingernails. A ferocious wind was howling, whipping by him, trying its best to drag him down. And this voice was ordering him to not just to hold on, but to battle his way back to the top of the cliff.

And somehow—driven by the fierce command and unyielding conviction in that voice—he did. Chanting the Fey Warrior's Creed, he forced himself to fight. Fraction by agonizing fraction. Then finger-length by agonizing finger-length. Then arm-length by agonizing arm-length, he clawed his way back from the very jaws of Darkness to embrace the weak flicker of Light inside him that refused to be extinguished.

"I am Fey," he whispered as he reached the top of the cliff and the despairing howl of Darkness fell blessedly silent. The pain that still writhed in him defied description, but pain meant he could still feel. And feeling meant that for the moment, at least, he was still Fey. "I am Fey," he repeated, his voice hoarse but stronger this time. "Warrior of Honor. Champion of Light."

He opened his eyes to see Sandar staring fixedly at him. Sandar was lying on his side at the foot of the stairs, clutching a hand to the gaping hole in his chest that Shan's sword had made. His lips were moving, chanting the words of the same Warrior's Creed that had helped bring Shan back from the brink.

Shan took quick stock of the room. The Drogons were ash, their attack shattered by the abrupt termination of their hive bonds, making them much less formidable in the face of Fey might.

Commanding Andaxis to oversee all remaining cleanup, Shan crawled to his feet, muttered the word that brought all his blades back to their sheaths, then snatched up Sandar's body and raced for the exit.

Somehow Sandar had saved him. How, Shan wasn't entirely certain. He'd been so close to falling to complete Darkness. So close, that before the sun rose again tomorrow, Shan would seek the sweet kiss of his red Fey'cha. But first, before Shan surrendered himself to the Fey honor death, he would see his beloved friend safely healed.

*

Outside, the sky was dusky, stars beginning to sparkle in the east as the Great Sun sank below the horizon in the west. Alerted by the call Shan had broadcast as he ran, Anaris Feyreisen was already there, great brown wings spread wide as he wheeled down from the sky to snatch up Shan and Sandar in his massive claws and speed them across the forest to the allied encampment. When they reached the camp, Shan didn't wait for Anaris to land, he simply slid down a raft of Air and hit the ground running.

"Shei'dalins!" he cried as he ran, "I need a healer here!"

Four *shei'dalins* in flowing red gowns came rushing out to inspect Sandar's wounds and direct Shan into the tents. "Set him down here," one of the red-garbed Fey healers ordered him in a tone of command. She was already inspecting Sandar's wounds as he did so. "Elfeya!" she called over her shoulder. "Come quickly. I may need your help with this one."

"Of course." A lush, feminine voice, that stirred memories of moonlight dancing on magical Elvian waters, made Shan look up sharply. His whole body started to tremble. Releasing Sandar, he circled round the healing cot to stand on unsteady legs before the red-haired *shei'dalin* who had just joined them.

Elfeya. The Elf-kin *shei'dalin* from Tehlas.

Light save him, she was the brightest, most beautiful thing he'd ever beheld. Her great, golden eyes reminded him of the Great Sun, shining with such Light that Shan knew even the Dark God Seledorn himself could never hope to dim it. She'd pulled her gleaming auburn hair back in some sort of plaited knot at the back of her head, but strands had escaped to curl around her face in soft, unruly waves. He drank her in, already loving everything about her: the curve of her full mouth, the pulse fluttering in her slender neck, the deep breath she drew as every part of her beautiful, already-beloved soul reached out to his in recognition and communion. In that instant, he could feel the promise of their union as the dark places inside him grew lighter and the torment of centuries of aloneness and growing despair began to ease. No illusion this time. This was real. She was real.

She had come at last.

"Ver reisa ku'chae. Kem surah, shei'tani," Shannisorran vel Celay told the truemate he had awaited for three thousand years. Your soul calls out. Mine answers, beloved.

Everyone in the tent froze, looking toward Shan and Elfeya with naked surprise. Fey warriors were famous for their stony, impenetrable visages. Elfeya's—though far less stony—gave just as little away. Her eyes, great and golden, had that same unsettling, piercing quality possessed by so many Elves—as if she could see a person right through to the deepest, darkest secrets of his soul. Shan stood beneath that gaze, feeling stripped bare and vulnerable in a way he'd never known before.

Sandar gave a groan, pulling Elfeya's attention from Shan to him. "Las, Fey." Peace. "I am here." She knelt by Sandar's side, the golden healing magic known as *shei'dalin's* love already spinning in dazzling threads from her fingertips. "You will be fine. I won't let you die."

The fierce note in her voice—the relentless conviction—stunned Shan anew. "It was you," he breathed. "It was you who held me to the Light."

Her shoulders stiffened slightly. "We can talk later," she said, neither confirming nor denying the truth. "Go now, so I can work on your friend. I will save him for you, but it will take all my attention." A swift glance flicked back toward him, shining gold beneath a veil of dark red lashes. In a soft voice, she added, "Shei'tan."

Truemate, she called him. Beloved. *Hers.*

Shan forced his trembling muscles to obey. He walked out of the healing tents into the night and stared up at Eloran's two full moons shining bright in the evening sky. Light in the darkness. Shan closed his eyes and let the cool night air caress his skin.

He'd been wrong this morning, thinking this was a good day to die.

Today was most definitely the best and most wonderful day to *live.*

Feyan Dictionary

Aiyah – yes

Beylah vo - thank you

Dahl'reisen - a lost soul, a Fey who has fallen down the Shadowed Path. He has lost his ability to feel remorse for his kills and no longer adheres to the laws of Fey honor. Dahl'reisen are banished from the Fading Lands.

Fey'cha - Fey throwing dagger

Jaff / Jaffed / Jaffing - To jaff something is to have intercourse with it. Screwed / Fucked.

Maresk / Kem'maresk - Friend / my friend

Mei'cha - Fey scimitar

Nei - no

Shei'dalin - Truthspeaker. A greatly empathic Fey woman who is both a powerful healer and capable of detecting truth from lies.

Sheisan'dahlein - the Fey honor death. Fey warriors close to becoming dahl'reisen usually choose sheisan'dahlein, so they die with their soul unstained by Darkness, thus making it more likely they will find their truemate in the next life.

Shei'tan / Shei'tani - Beloved, Truemate. The most powerful and complete Fey matebond. When completed, the Fey truemate bond combines two separate, equally powerful souls into one, never to be unjoined. Due to the power of this bond, truemates will never fall to Shadow.

Sel'dor - Black metal that disrupts Fey magic and burns like acid on Fey skin.

Seyani - Fey longsword.

Ver reisa ku'chae. Kem surah, shei'tani - Your soul calls out. Mine answers, beloved. The declaration a Fey warrior makes when finding and claiming his truemate

13Thirty Books

Exciting Thrillers, Heart-warming Romance,
Mind-bending Horror, Sci-Fantasy
and
Educational Non-Fiction

Bad Attitude & Diamond In The Rough – Doris Parmett

Bad Attitude
Meet bad boy, undercover state trooper Reid Cameron.
Meet Polly Sweet, the woman who is about to be his downfall.
In order to catch a jewel thief, Cameron wants to use Polly's house, and he comes up with a plan, whereby they play at being lovers. But when the first play-acted kiss happens, neither one is ready for the feelings that kiss ignites or for the consequences that ensue. Has this bad boy finally met his match? How Bad is Too Bad?

Diamond In The Rough
Detective Dan Murdock is on a dangerous stakeout, when advice columnist, Millie Gordon unwittingly shows up on the scene, putting them both in danger. To save her from possibly being shot when the mobsters arrive, Murdock jumps into Millie's car and throws himself over her to protect her, little realizing that the real danger starts when their bodies come together.Both of them try to deny their undeniable desire for one another, but when Millie decides Murdock would make a great "unsung hero" for her upcoming book, she maneuvers him into letting her ride along with him as his partner. How long will they be able to resist the obvious smoldering sexual attraction between them?

Romantic Times: Vegas - Anthology

The Excelsior Hotel and Casino. Built in Las Vegas in 1960 by mobster Louis "The Lip" LaFica. For decades the towering hotel has been the subject of incredible stories and rumors that have kept it in the public eye the world around. Why have so many lovers been mysteriously, magically, magnetically drawn to this magnificent edifice? And why now have so many bestselling authors at last come together to reveal the adventures of these lovers who have stayed at the glorious Excelsior?

The Third Hour – Richard Devin

The Third Hour is an original spin on the religious-thriller genre, incorporating elements of science fiction along with the religious angle. Its strength lies in this originality, combined with an interesting take on real historical figures, who are made a part of the experiment at the heart of the novel, and the fast pace that builds.

Ripper – A Love Story – Lance Taubold & Richard Devin

"Queen Victoria would not be amused--but you will be by this beguiling combination of romance and murder. Is the Crown Prince of England really Jack the Ripper? His wife would certainly like to know... and so will you." - Diana Gabaldon, New York Times Best Selling Author

Heather Graham's Haunted Treasures – Heather Graham

Presented together for the first time, New York Times Bestselling Author, Heather Graham brings back three tales of paranormal love and adventure.

Heather Graham's Christmas Treasures – Heather Graham

New York Times Bestselling Author, Heather Graham brings back three out-of-print Christmas classics that are sure to inspire, amaze, and warm your heart.

Zodiac Lovers Series – Lance Taubold

Zodiac Lovers is a series of romantic, gay, paranormal novelettes. In each story, one of the lovers has all the traits of his respective zodiacal sign.

Never Fear Series – Horror Anthology
For those who like their stories on the darker side ...

Never Fear
Shh... Something's Coming

Tales of Horror by Ten Masters of Suspense Leave the lights on with this limited time collection of short stories about fear and how far folks will go to survive in a terrifying world. The Barrens by F. Paul Wilson. New York Times Bestselling Author. A cosmic horror tale in the New Jersey Pine Barrens. Genuine pinelands lore painted with a Lovecraftian palette. Creighton reenters his old girlfriend's life, saying he's researching the myth of the Jersey Devil. But he has a much darker agenda. Control+Alt+Delete by Rachel Aukes. Amazon Bestselling Author. In the near-future where we are monitored every minute of every day, a law is passed that grants an Artificial Intelligence system the power to instantly "reform" anyone deemed a threat to society. The Agent by Michael Koogler. Up-and-Coming Author. What would you give to have it all? What would you offer up for fame and fortune? Would you give up your very soul? Would you give up even more? Andre Rossell is an aspiring horror writer with a problem. He hasn't published anything. His life is a waste. He's going nowhere. Until his agent calls... The Girl Next Door by E. McCarthy. New York Times Bestselling Author. In the old yellow fever wing of a female dorm in New Orleans, an empty sealed room holds nothing but a chair. Or does it? Student Sadie is determined to find out, at the risk of her own sanity... and her boyfriend's life. Taps by Patrick Freivald. Bram Stoker Award-Nominated Author. A series of mysterious tapping sounds leads Molly into a darkness from which she may never emerge. Forward Base Fourteen by Patrick Freivald. Bram Stoker Award-Nominated Author. One of the last survivors of an outpost on the alien world of New Phoenix, Sarah DeSouza fights on against the Takers, who kill, reanimate and control their victims. Funeral March of a Marionette by Lance Taubold. Award-Winning Author. Fourteen-year-old Corey has always been picked on ... and worse by other kids and his stepfather. Through the magic of music Corey's nutcracker doll collection comes to life to do his bidding and to enact his revenge. Gris Gris by Kathy Love. USA Today Bestselling Author. Elizabeth visits Madame Lucrece Dumas, New

Orleans' most powerful Voodoo priestess, certain the Creole voodooiene can conjure a spell to protect her from a terrifying curse. But Elizabeth soon discovers there is something stronger than Voodoo magic. Revenge. Where Billy Monasco Lay by Paul Mannering. Award-Winning Author. A band of outlaws making a run for Mexico wait by the Penasco River for the rest of their gang. Plagued by guilt after the horrific deaths of a bank full of innocent townsfolk, they meet God's justice in the form of a dead boy. Alabaster Nights by Elle J. Rossi. Up-and-Coming Author. A Vampire with a soul. A Huntress with a knife. In Nashville, Blood equals Power. Will one taste of Josie Hawk cost Keller everything? Snapped! by Richard Devin. Up-and-Coming Debut Author. No one knew where or when or how... it just happened. They Snapped. That's what people said. They Snapped. There wasn't any single sign, like you might expect there to be. No twitching or dying or convulsing. No outbreak of flu or some wide-spread contagious disease. Snap. They were human... and then... they were not.

Never Fear – Phobias
Everyone Fears Something

19 Stories of phobia from New York Times bestselling master suspense authors F. Paul Wilson and Heather Graham with a "krewe" of dynamic award-winning storytellers.

Never Fear – Christmas Terrors
He sees you when you're sleeping …

Twenty-Two Tales of Christmas Terror ranging from ancient Iceland to modern-day Iraq by New York Times Bestselling and award-winning authors, including: a new ghost story by Heather Graham, a Repairman Jack Christmas adventure by F. Paul Wilson, a spine tingling tale by master of horror Thomas F. Monteleone, and a special tale of Christmas wonder by Jon Land.

In a unique experience—a story within a story—you will follow along when the MacDonald family discovers an unidentified present under their Christmas tree. Who gave it to them? Where did it come from? No one seems to know. And when they open the mysterious gift, it sets them on a course to a Christmas of terror they could never have expected

Authored by Heather Graham, F. Paul Wilson, Lance Taubold, Aidan Russell, Thomas F. Monteleone, Lisa Harris, E. McCarthy, Richard Devin, Lee Lawless, Kristi Ahlers, Don Bruns, Ed DeAngelis, Lisa Manetti, Elle J Rossi, Deborah Grahl, Liah Penn, Crystal Perkins, Greg Linden, Connie Corcoran Wilson, Jeff DePew, Mathew Kaufman

Never Fear – The Tarot
Do you really want to know?

13Thirty Books has gathered twenty-six award-winning and New York Times bestselling authors to write these dark tales based on the Tarot.

The twist: the Tarot card would choose the author.

We took a deck of tarot cards and the list of the twenty-six authors. We read each author's name out loud, then shuffled the deck and drew a card. That card was removed. The deck was reshuffled and the next name was chosen.

The card, its traits, and the author's imagination were the inspiration for these twenty-six tales of the paranormal and the supernatural.

More Than Magick – Rick Taubold
Why me? Recent college grad Scott Madison, has been recruited (for reasons that he will eventually understand) by the wizard Arion and secretly groomed by his ostensible friend and mentor, Jake Kesten. But his training hasn't readied him to face Vraasz, a being who has become powerful enough to destroy the universe and whose first objective is the obliteration of Arion's home world. Scott doesn't understand why he was the chosen one or why he is traveling the universe with a ragtag group of individuals also chosen by Arion. With time running out, Scott discovers that he has a power that can defeat Vraasz. If only he can figure out how to use it.

Stop Saying Yes – Negotiate! – Richard Devin

Stop Saying Yes - Negotiate! is the perfect "on the go" guide for all negotiations. This easy-to-read, practical guide will enable you to quickly identify the other side's tactics and strategies allowing you to defend yourself ensuring a better negotiation for your side and theirs.

Treasures & Pleasures: A Collection of Romantic Novellas – Bobbi Smith

Eden's Gate

Kacie Cameron fell in love with Eden's Gate Plantation when she read of its history. Drawn by a tremendous longing to learn more, she made a trip to Eden's Gate. When Kacie saw the portrait of the original owner's son, Bradford Hampton for the first time, the power of the feelings that swept through her almost frightened her. She told herself it was crazy to react that way to the portrait of a dead man…of a man who'd died in a steamboat explosion so long ago. The gut-wrenching emotions churning within her as she'd stared up at the dark-haired, handsome Brad's compelling features did not disappear, though, and when she is miraculously swept back in time, she knows she must find a way to save him from that terrible fate.

Something Blue

Stationed in Arizona, Cavalry Captain Philip Long returns to Boston for the reading of his wealthy father's will and to settle the estate. Philip is deeply troubled when he learns his father added a clause to the will that dictates he must marry within six months and stay married for a year or he will lose every cent of his inheritance. Unless he chooses to walk away from his fortune, Philip knows he's trapped. But when he rescues young saloon girl Mattie Jackson from an attack by some vicious drunks on his trip back to Fort McDowell, he believes he's found the answer to his problem. He'll propose a "marriage in name only" to Mattie to save her from the life she's been forced to lead, and once their year together is over, he'll pay her a substantial amount so they can part ways…Or will they? Love might just interfere.

Lottery of Love

Elise Matthews has worked hard to make her catering service a success in order to support herself and her younger brother, Rod, after their parents died, and she buys lottery tickets every week just to keep up the tradition her father had. When she lands a contract with the rich owner of the local football team, she's ecstatic. She rushes to the auto body shop where Rod works to tell him and their friend, Zach Thomas, who owns the shop, the news. Zach is happy for Elise. He secretly loves her and has always wanted the best for her, but now that she'll be dealing with the rich folks on a regular basis, he fears she won't have much use for a regular working guy like him anymore. Elise has always longed to be rich, and when the team owner proposes to her, she finds herself torn between the surprising love she's finally realized she feels for Zach and the prospect of marrying a very wealthy man. Will true love win out? Will Zach win "The Lottery of Love?"

Time Stolen Love

For an investigative report on serial killers, television reporter Roni Mitchell is in London walking the streets of Whitechapel where Jack the Ripper once roamed. In an antique store she finds a gold pocket watch that was found at the scene of one of the Ripper's murders. As she is heading back to her hotel, she hears the muted sound of a chime. Puzzled, she opens the box to discover the watch is working. Suddenly, seemingly out of nowhere, a dark, threatening figure attacks her. Roni manages to escape, but as she flees she realizes she's traveled back to the time of the Ripper, and that she can now research her story firsthand...

13Thirtybooks.com
facebook.com/13thirty

www.ingramcontent.com/pod-product-compliance
Lightning Source LLC
Chambersburg PA
CBHW061031030726
47504CB00002B/325